A Soul's Warfare:

Book 2: The Cave Chamber
by Rosemary B. Althoff

ISBN: 978-1-956654-45-5

CHAPTER 1
LEWIS AND THE HORNED EDGE RING

Lewis Brahmindura swallowed his medicine. Lord Charon, the ruler of Tor, had sent his own personal physician to prescribe it. Dressing for a day of work in Lord Charon's laboratory, Lewis sang to himself a phrase from the musical *Oklahoma*, *"'O what a beautiful mornin', O what a beautiful day!'"*

Lewis knew that his manic mood was irrational. However, it felt so good that he didn't want to figure out *why*. Formerly a physicist from Earth, he reflected on his transference to the world named Lanthra with his younger brother and sister, Patrick and Gracie, and his best friend, Fred. At first, they had settled in a country called Bardia, where he and Fred had worked under the High Magus, Daniel. He and they had been shocked to know that they could not return home, but the pain had eased when he had fallen in love with beautiful Deirdre, the High Magus's daughter. Then … a complete turn-around … he was working for Daniel's bitter enemy, Lord Charon of Tor.

I am so happy now! he thought.

However, a tiny voice inside reminded him: *Fred betrayed me; Patrick and I were kidnapped, and Lord Charon's right hand man Barth threatened to harm my brother and sister if I didn't cooperate.*

Lewis shoved those memories away. He squashed the hollow, haunted feelings that had eaten away his soul when he deliberately switched sides to join demon-worshipping Torish magi. He congratulated himself, *Switching sides has paid off. I am now a respected scientist in Lord Charon's hierarchy.* And today – Lewis's smile could have lit an entire planet – for the first time, he would be permitted to enter the chamber that housed the portal to the stars. He began singing again.

An odd thought passed through his mind, *Hey, Lewis, aren't you a little manic?* Static tickled in his brain, but he brushed it away while he combed his dark hair. It was getting long and wavy … and maybe a little coarse because he kept forgetting to eat. His skin and eyes were a warm brown. *I look a lot like Lord Charon. How wonderful!*

His apartment had been designed and decorated for royalty, and it was near Lord Charon's own palace residence. There were no windows – *How long has it been since you even stepped outside to look at the sunshine?* interjected the annoying inner voice.

My apartment is fantastic, he countered. There was plenty of light from tall lamps. His room had a high ceiling curved like a canopy, with a beautiful carved marble lotus at each corner, and white marble walls. An ebony black lattice hid his bed, which was neatly made and covered with slate-gray silk brocade.

Lewis sat at his desk. Humming, he held up his right hand and admired the new ring on his third finger. It was gold with a black diamond – a high status symbol.

Yo, Lewis, didn't you notice what finger that Horned Edge ring is on?

Quickly, Lewis covered his hand. After a moment, feeling stubborn, he opened it to display his ring again. In fact, he was proud of it. *I like it here. I like this room, this desk, and this ring.*

An answer came that he didn't expect. *Lewis, didn't you sit at such a desk at your Earth home for journaling, when you wrote that God is nonexistent and irrelevant? Who has protected you to this day? And are you on the side of the people who love you, or the people who mistreat you?*

"No one is mistreating me! I am now a magus!" he exclaimed aloud. "I am about to become the lead scientist here! I am on Lord Charon's side because, not only will he protect my little brother and sister, he and I will help save the worlds!"

Yes, he was pleased with Lord Charon. His master, the ruler of all Tor, was on the path to become the next High Magus of all Lanthra – and Earth. The man was brilliant and powerful … *I'm like him. We connect.*

His soul flying with joy, Lewis chanted in his thoughts: *I am brilliant. I am powerful. I have indomitable perseverance. Today, after I talk with Lord Charon. I know exactly what to do. With me in charge, the locating system will work.*

You cannot sustain this mood, the voice in his heart whispered.

Lewis paused. His head drooped; he heaved a deep breath. However, ambitious resolve gathering, he raised his head. He declared to the inimical voice, "With my talents, I can prevent war on Lanthra, and even on Earth! And I can rescue Patrick and Gracie and get them back home!"

The voice in his head queried, *What exactly is in that medicine to make you so chirpy?*

"I've never felt better in my life!" Lewis insisted. "Just think – I can bring everything back to the way it was before ...." He refused to think about the "before." Humming as he inspected himself in the mirror, he repeated, I have everything under control. Soon, I'll have my little brother Patrick and little sister Gracie with me ..."

Look around you, a powerful entity inside of him commanded. The voice roared; it was a huge golden dragon coiled in his soul. Lewis sensed that the dragon was not evil, that it was the self that he felt when he was moving toward his true purpose. *You've gotten proud,* the dragon said. *That won't do. I want to give you the desire of your heart, but you will not find that here. And especially not with that ring!*

"Yes, I will!" Lewis told it. The imprisoned beast wriggled in his soul. "I don't believe in you," he told it.

To distract himself, Lewis circled his head in appreciative awe of the austere, almost holy whiteness of his palace quarters. The dragon interfered again, *Don't you really prefer richer, warmer colors – like the carpets of your Indian heritage? Who is controlling you that you cannot be yourself?*

Impelled by a sudden rage, Lewis smashed his hand onto his desk. The Horned Edge ring cut into his finger, which left a few drops of red blood on the dark wood. "My room is just the way I like it!"

The voice inside him whispered before he clamped it down

and threw it out of his head, *No it isn't. The spirit here is strange. And so are you!*

CHAPTER 2
IN CHARGE

When he reached Lord Tahei Charon's office area, Lewis rang a small bronze gong. Charon's personal servant, a tall, gaunt man in a white robe and also wearing a Horned Edge ring, appeared, and bowed the required twenty degrees to acknowledge Lewis's status.

The man led Lewis to a large, circular pillared vestibule. At that point, the servant bowed again, and Lewis stood outside Lord Charon's door, waiting for permission to enter. While he waited, he glanced around. The cold, dry, stony odor reminded him of a monastery.

Or a tomb, the dragon whispered.

"My Lord," Lewis called to announce his presence.

"You may enter."

When he entered, he felt pierced by the room's white marble that was relieved by no tapestries or ornaments, only a long narrow slit of a window high to Lewis's right. A blood-red shaft of sunlight poured through the window, and Lewis thought with surprise, *How can it be sunset already? I just got up!*

Quickly, as evening approached, the room darkened. Dim light from a crystal lamp graced his lord's solemn face, his silky black hair, and long-fingered hands.

Lord Charon sat at a desk on a straight-backed chair. Lewis saw no clutter of paperwork, no dust or ink or pens. He saw the crystal lamp, an alabaster vase of fresh coral red lilies, and a slim upright blade of smoky quartz. He knew that the blade was Charon's personal computer.

Lewis knelt before him, but Charon gestured for him to rise. "Sit down," the ruler said and gestured him onto the plush, zebra-skin settee that faced the desk. "You're looking well," he added, examining Lewis with eyes that were as black as his glossy hair, deep as a depthless pool, with a warmth of genuine liking.

"I feel wonderful, with almost a new identity," Lewis said, only partly joking.

"Yes. You were very sick when you came here," Charon reminded in a gentle deep voice. "You've made quite an improvement since you left Bardia."

"Yes, my lord, thank you."

The voice inside whispered, *You were kidnapped and manipulated into coming here. You were mistreated; that's why you were ill.*

Lewis did not want to remember anything about being a prisoner. He shut down the memory and repeated, "I'm fine now, thank you, Master. Whatever your doctor prescribes gives me a lot of energy."

Charon smiled. "Good," he said.

Lewis waited for his lord to speak again.

With another smile, Lord Charon declared, "I have good news for you. Your brother Patrick will soon join you here. Not only that, but your sister Gracie, also."

Lewis felt all his insides explode into joyful confetti. "When shall I see them?"

"In two weeks. They should arrive during the Council of the Magi."

Feeling hot tears gathering, wetting his cheeks, Lewis could say nothing.

Charon leaned forward, his eyes bright. "Will you finish your work in time for the Council? You have become familiar with the laboratory with the sonic computer. And today you will be admitted into the locating chamber. I trust you will thoroughly examine it and find the weakness that keeps us from making the connection to Earth."

"Let me think," Lewis said, to give himself time to control his emotions. *I'm about to get my life back. I'll get my family back ... It'll be so good to see my brother and sister – and, after I repair Lord Charon's system – my parents! My love Deirdre! Such a sweet thought!*

Finally, he had enough self-control to answer, "Before the Council, I think everything may be ready, but –"

Lord Charon spat, "Do not hedge with me, *Fean* Brahmindura!"

Intimidated, confused, Lewis felt his skin quiver and his stomach do flip-flops, but he made himself speak with calm authority, explaining, "I've become very familiar with your sonic computer system. It draws power from your singularity to enable the nexus between Earth and your … our … world Lanthra. At last I have a good idea why the total connection is not working. The problem is in the tuner, that is, the interface between –"

"Spare me the details." Charon snapped.

Lewis ducked his head, ashamed.

Then Lord Charon's approach changed. The ruler smiled and spoke with a warm voice full of approval, "*Fean* Lewis, you came to me for a reason. What do you want to say to me?"

Lewis raised his head, and he was amazed at his bold courage. "Master, please give me your seal of authority. Let me have me authority over everyone in your laboratory, both your scientists and your staff. Today I will gain first admittance to the location chamber. I need unlimited and unsupervised access to every part and every place of this project so that it will be done on time, or even ahead of time."

Lord Charon's eyes sparkled with liquid light. *Is he pleased?* the little sarcastic voice in Lewis's head said. *Or is he high – like you are?*

Quelling the conflict inside, Lewis pressed, "I need to do whatever I want, whenever I want, and without questions in the laboratory. Yes, I will get you a fully working system – one that flawlessly connects to Earth – before the Council meets."

A strange nudge inside added, *And you will also copy all the system's records, acquire all the technology, and tell no one.*

Charon searched him for a long time with deep, black eyes. His lips moved, as if he were consulting with someone that Lewis could not see. "Aye," he replied at last. "You may have unlimited and unsupervised access."

He fingered the blade of smoky quartz and made several small motions with his fingers. "Create a personal password. All you have to do is think it. The system will analogue your entire persona into a secure key."

Lewis smiled and thought, *Hot marble.* He remembered the marble only too well: It was the navigation device that connected gravitational entities in the universe. Patrick and Gracie had found it in a field on Earth, after one of Lord Charon's disgruntled magi had hurled it through the nexus. The nexus, before it burned out, had opened the way for Patrick, Gracie, him, and Fred to come to Lanthra. Now it was locked away in Lord Charon's location chamber, and Lewis yearned to get his skillful hands on it.

The ruler returned the blade to its position on the desk. "Remember, *Fean* Lewis, you have two weeks." He sat back with an air of finality.

Lewis knelt, received a blessing and the seal of his authority, and withdrew from Lord Charon's office.

*   *   *

From there, Lewis glided to a certain door that led to the laboratory. "*Golanoya,*" he said, "Open," and the laboratory door dissolved. The giant room was domed, containing the sonic-based system that gathered and amplified the horizon energy from Lanthra's singularity. There were also more than a dozen obelisk-like computers, and the scientists to use them. Lewis cleared his throat. He held up his hand with Lord Charon's seal, a black rod with a blood-red ruby tip. In a loud voice, he minced no words. "I have Lord Charon's seal of authority. Beginning now, I will direct all of you in the repair of the *thoyo-on.*"

Everyone in the laboratory stopped working. They stared at Lewis and the seal as if he had usurped the Torish throne. A gasp susurrated through the air. After the shockwave passed, Lewis strode from workstation to workstation, asking different variations of the same question: "Are different methods of testing the system yielding similar results?"

The scientists and staff bowed low as he approached. Time after time, the answer was, "*Alor.* There is no evidence of corruption, yet it will not connect."

Last of all, Lewis went to the two laboratory managers, whose authority he now covered. "Jeffrey, Mildred," Lewis ordered, "Bring the resonance sensors and come with me down to the locating chamber."

Slowly, a pale man with a patchy beard and a tall, intimidating, stocky woman broke off from their stations. They frowned, bowed quite short of the requisite twenty degrees, and Lewis got a strong slam of hostility while they selected tools that looked like silver wands.

"Back up your data now," Lewis said to the others. "After that, repeat the tests to get a baseline, while Jeffrey, Mildred, and I examine a new part of the system."

He swept into a special room off the laboratory, followed by Jeffrey and Mildred. The small room had black polished floor and walls. Ornate gold inlaid patterns depicted scenes from history that Lewis knew dated before the Great Rebellion. To his right, in a freestanding case of spotlessly clear glass, Lewis saw hundreds of jeweled *noretha* – marbles – labelled with Lanthran mathematical script, ready to direct connections locations in the universe.

Lewis methodically examined the noretha and read their labels. While Jeffrey and Mildred shuffled their feet impatiently, Lewis took his time. Finally, he found it: An amber noretha in the middle of the third row – the very "hot marble" that had forced the connection that caught him, Gracie and Patrick, and their friend Fred to Lanthra from Earth. He reached his hand toward the glass case, but then he withdrew it. *Later,* he told himself. *When I can come here alone, I'll get you, hot marble.*

Near the case of noretha stood an ancient door, made of dull metal like platinum, carved with subtle patterns. It had no knob or handle.

"How will *you* get in?" Jeffrey whined, but with a touch of malice. "Did Lord Charon give you our special password?"

"Your special password will no longer work for you," Lewis stated. "You have to have my permission to enter. He drew a deep breath and merely thought, *Hot marble.*

The metal door disappeared. Unlike the location entrance in Bardia where Lewis had worked, before he had been kidnapped, this one was smaller and darker. Golden light glanced onto a bronze stairway that curved downward. Jeffrey sniffed and blinked, his eyes as pale as a goblet full of spit. Mildred snapped, "What do you want us to do that we haven't done already?"

Lewis had no time for power games with subordinates.

"Follow me," he ordered and descended the stairs ahead of them. He was about to enter the most important room in the universe.

CHAPTER 3
RUMORS OF WAR

The sun set over the city of Nutman in Bardia in a big pink splash. Summer moons, little azure Bibo and big copper Wega, appeared against a net of diamond stars. Daniel, the High Magus, watched, but he was not happy. His two daughters and Lewis's sister Gracie had left for Smythe and should be safe, but – he pulled on his white-blond hair – he was still not happy. In Daniel's small, fine hands were several intelligence reports. Each bore bad news.

Somewhere out there is Earth. The Planet of the Curse is sending us its best presents, invited by my enemy, Lord Tahei Charon, Daniel thought. Feeling nauseated, he stood in his darkening office, staring out his bay window, his back against the closed door.

He re-read the first report. It was a nasty surprise: Cholera had struck his province. Dozens had died already, and Daniel knew there would be many more deaths. Charon's ally from Earth, the Shields weapons company that included a *Saoma*-worshipping sect, had dumped feces in the area's reservoirs. "Germ warfare, terrorist style!" Daniel crunched up the intelligence report and hurled it across the room.

A second intelligence report noted a massive buildup of Lord Charon's Eagle forces at his border with Tor. It was not certain when they would invade. If Lord Charon succeeded in connecting to Earth again, not only would he open the door to *Saoma's* demons, but he would cement his alliance with the Shields. They would bring over their weapons: missiles, guns, tanks, bombs … Daniel closed his eyes as if that would make the problem go away and crushed that report also; the wad rolled over the carpet. *You will be overrun,* he remembered the Master telling him.

And last, he held the very worst news, a letter from his friend Sir Edwin Forschwynn, viceroy of the neighboring province. In strong, bold cursive, Edwin had written:

> Here is a copy of the message that Baron Arthur Trager sent me. He has kidnapped my son Thomas and his servant Fred. The ransom note is definitely written in Thomas's handwriting; it is no fake. The baron's messenger brought it to me with my son's lute and his companion's ring. Trager has demanded a huge ransom; I cannot possibly pay it without selling my entire province and all I have.
>
> It may be that Trager will kill Thomas, the direct descendant of the Bard of Bardia with that bard's talents. Destroying the bard could set Bardia – and indeed our world Lanthra – back for centuries.
>
> Our nation's 500th Celebration has already begun its gathering in my province. However, any news of Thomas's kidnapping would destroy the morale of all Bardia. I have not made my son's kidnapping public, and I exhort you to keep it quiet as well.
>
> As I said, Baron Trager sent Thomas's lute and his servant's ring to confirm his message. If you are able to rescue my son – that is, if he still lives – please send the lute to him. You of all people, my canny friend, have the skills and contacts to get it done. However, the servant's ring must be hidden because of a certain inscription inside from *that* world; I'm sure you understand. Do come to the Celebration soon. Your presence will encourage all of us.

* * *

Daniel placed the letter on his desk. "Oh, my friend Edwin, I am so sorry!" At Daniel's feet lay a lumpy bag with the neck of a lute – the Lute – sticking out. The famous instrument looked sad, even dead without its bard.

He stood feeling numb as mists gathered in the Loudmouth riverbed below. Suddenly his self-control snapped. Daniel yelled and punched the wall. "Why should Lord Charon set himself against me! Why must he worship evil Saoma and want to rule both worlds? Why must we lose the Bard of Bardia? Why, why, why? Why, God, my Master?"

His office door opened behind him, and Daniel stumbled. "What is it?" he snapped.

"Your Excellency," his secretary said in his characteristic mild tone. "Your agent Hermann has returned from Tor with a report. "Will you see him now?"

"In a moment, James." Daniel closed the door in his secretary's face. *I must compose myself!* To the Master, he growled, "All right, you warned me. My plans to protect the province aren't working. In fact, everything I've set in place is falling apart!"

The Master replied, *Are you willing to trust me?*

"Yes – but not very well," Daniel seethed. "You said that my province will be overrun. You told me that I will be captured and taken to Moorway."

Trust me, e bibat. *A little faith is enough.*

Sighing, feeling calmer, Daniel said to God, "Well, at least my daughters Deirdre and Myra and Lewis's young sister Gracie are safe in Smythe." He reopened the door and apologized. "I'm sorry, James, that I lost my temper."

"I understand. You are anxious, Your Excellency," his secretary said. Daniel felt the air clear between them. "Admit my agent Hermann here. Also, James – will you be in for a while tomorrow morning to close out the office?"

His secretary shook his head. "I would prefer not, Your Excellency. My family and I are leaving for the Celebration before dawn." He hesitated.

Daniel answered the unspoken question. "Yes, you may go with my blessing. May your journey be safe and short. I will take care of myself. I must arrange help for the cholera epidemic, and then I will depart to join the Celebration. Now, James, usher in my spy."

Hermann came in. The man, with buckteeth, prominent nose and ears, and beady eyes under a flamboyant hat, bowed low. "Your Excellency, I'm sorry to disturb you so late, but I have news. Aye, indeed," Hermann said, and his voice was cheerful, "you can ignore the ransom note."

"What?"

"Sir Thomas and his slave are safe. They were indeed kidnapped and held for ransom, but they escaped and are safe in Gapstand. The locals there are quite impressed with the young bard, and they have no sympathy at all for any of the barons. In fact, they will help our cause against Saoma."

Daniel felt his entire body blaze with a fierce relief. "Good!"

Hermann's voice lowered. His face darkened. "Your Excellency, I tried to persuade young Sir Thomas to come back to Bardia, but the boy insisted on continuing his concert in Tor to rouse the Patriots. His worthless slave Fred, from that horrible planet, did nothing to stop him!"

Daniel began to respond, but Hermann held up a hand to still Daniel's next words. "Sir Thomas learned that weavers sold a great load of brown cloth to the Saoma-worshipping Torish military. Their troops may intend to masquerade as Bardian soldiers and try to invade your city by trickery."

Daniel considered. "Our city is well guarded. It is surrounded by a camp of soldiers, walled, and entered only by one gate. Nutman is not easy to invade."

Hermann was silent, but the thought came to Daniel, *Do not assume your physical safety, only the safety of your soul.* His optimism cracked. Daniel thought hard, trying to find any positive side to the news:

One: Most of my people are already evacuated to the well-defended Forschwynn province. There, the people should be safe. I will be there too, in a few days.

Two: Lord Charon's hunger to invade my province and destroy me has diverted his attention from the Patriots. Their revolt is scheduled, and it may succeed.

Three: My daughters are in neutral Smythe at Deirdre's estate. Lord Charon's forces cannot reach them there. Even if the Torish succeed in invading Nutman, they will be safe.

Daniel asked Hermann, "How are preparations going for the Patriots' revolt in Tor, especially in Charon's capitol, Moorway?"

With a toothy grin, Hermann slapped his hat on his thigh. "The Patriots have everything organized. The date of their revolt is set. They have yet some time to prepare, and plenty of morale." The spy paused, and he flapped his cloak, reminding Daniel of a bat. "I only wish Sir Thomas was not going to endanger himself in Moorway! I would like to rid him of that bungling *subua* Fred who travels with him! He could yet betray –"

Daniel cut off further discussion. "Stop! I don't want to hear any antagonism about Fred. True, the demons of Earth infected him. True, he betrayed Lewis and caused him and Patrick to be kidnapped. However, his spirit has changed. Little Gracie has forgiven him, and Sir Thomas gave up his entire inheritance to save Fred from hanging. Now, have you heard anything else?"

Hermann said, "Yes, I have reports from my sources concerning Patrick in Tor. The boy broke his ankle trying to escape after he and *Fean* Lewis were kidnapped. He was very sick indeed. Howe'er, the Patriots found a way to get him out of the hospital and into the care of one of their contacts."

"Thank *Radyah!* And … how is Lewis, his brother?"

Hermann let out a deep breath and rubbed the floor with a booted foot. "'Tis said he willingly joined Lord Charon and the worshippers of Saoma. With his help, Charon may well repair his locating system and bring over the weapons from … from the forbidden planet."

"Ah." Daniel felt as if he had been socked in the stomach. Lewis … a servant of Saoma. Lewis had been an open atheist. Then, when he and Deirdre fell in love, he had softened to becoming an agnostic. Now, however, Lewis was working with the enemy. His soul was in extreme danger. Demons from Earth would eat him up soon!

Hermann stated, "Your Excellency, I am ready to return to your mission in Tor. Do you have any additional orders for me?"

"Oh, yes: Go to Moorway immediately! See that Sir Thomas receives the lute. Help the Patriots coordinate the revolt. Do everything you can! You will have to improvise a great deal, but you are my best agent."

"Thank you, Your Excellency, for your trust in me!" Hermann bowed, sweeping the floor with his hat, and swung the lute over his shoulder. He glided out of the door, leaving a faint musty smell behind, like the odor of caves.

CHAPTER 4
INVASION

Daniel slept through breakfast, which was unusual. He awoke with a tension headache but forced himself to pack for his journey to the Celebration. All the house servants had been sent away, so he made his own lunch. In the mild evening, with dew collecting on the tea-rose garden and cooling the air, Daniel walked about the yard, followed discretely by his remaining guards. *I miss my daughters Deirdre and Myra, and Lewis's sweet little sister Gracie. I miss you so much, my dear wife Ielen! I know I will not see you again until the Master comes with the angels to heal the universe.*

He felt that Ielen was close. Tonight, she was feisty. She argued, in his thoughts, *You stayed in Nutman too long. You should have left weeks ago!*

"I needed to stay, and that's that," Daniel replied in his imaginary conversation. "My plans are made, my traps are set, and now I must wait for the Charon's forces to bite the bait."

Go to Smythe, now! This minute! The heck with the Celebration now. Join Deirdre, Myra, and Gracie in their safe haven! Ielen ordered with all the stubbornness of a woman used to command.

"No, dear." Daniel could be stubborn, too. "Trust me! I must keep the enemy focused on my province and this city of Nutman – and not on the Patriots – for as long as possible! My army still enough troops about these walls to defend the city. All they have to do is hold it for a few weeks, and then ..."

Can't you see the error in your plans? They're not the Master's plans; they're your plans!

With a little pepper in his speech, Daniel answered, "Ielen, you're dead. After the Glad-Day – and no sooner, I'm going to the Celebration to encourage my people."

No, go to Smythe! You can't accomplish much at the Celebration. Everybody knows that our fool of a king believes the liars who say that you intend to supplant him! King Norhe will try to sabotage you.

"He might," Daniel admitted. "Old Norhe may indeed believe the lies."

I think your plan stinks! Ielen retorted.

The inner conversation faded. Daniel walked a while more, trying to enjoy the well-kept garden. However, the roses' sweet colors turned to gray as evening descended. Feeling gray and tired himself, he left the garden and went back into the house.

*   *   *

He had the bedroom lamp on and a book in his hand when someone pounded on the door. *Who could that be?* Adrenaline surged, and Daniel reached for his sword – *Myra hasn't made off with it this time* – but then he relaxed. *That's what I have guards for. It's probably just another last-minute report.*

Daniel looked down at himself, tousled in striped cotton pajamas. "Too bad," he said to himself, "Forget the protocol. They can see me just the way I am." He wrapped himself in an old dressing gown.

When Daniel opened his front door, his heart jumped. His breath caught, and he held onto the doorjamb for support. "Myra! Deirdre! Gracie!" he cried, flinging the book aside. "What are you doing here? You are supposed to be safe in Smythe!"

He ran out barefoot and in his dressing gown.

Behind the girls on his doorstep stood an entire *harbath* of soldiers with Bardian uniforms, and he took them for part of the city garrison. "Why are you all here? What has happened?"

Myra began crying. Her sobs tore his heart, and he folded her into his arms. "Dear Myra, what …?

Lamplight light fell on the company surrounding him. In addition to his daughters and Gracie, he saw his close friends: His protégé and magus Mark Gregory, his carpenter brother Allen, and their mother Sadie. They were the family of his army's leader, Captain Gregory. Daniel noticed other people who should have been evacuated. "What are you doing here?" Daniel cried. "Has something terrible happened?"

A man in a lieutenant's uniform ordered, "Bind him. Take him with the others to the chapel." He told Daniel, "If you give no trouble, you'll get none."

Stunned, Daniel let the men secure his hands with a length of cord. They marched him down Garden Lane in his bare feet and dressing gown.

CHAPTER 5
CHAINS IN THE CHAMBER

Beautiful!" Lewis exclaimed when the last golden spiral ended in the locating chamber. Amethyst crystals encrusted the ceiling and walls and glittered softly in ambient white light from lamps set into the ceiling like pearls. "This room is a huge geode!"

The chamber smelled cool and mineral, like a glass of ice water in a crystal goblet – except for a faint odor of decay under the chains on the walls. Lewis could not help staring at the chains. "What are these doing here?" he demanded.

"Lord Charon ordered them to be installed," came Jeffrey's weak reply. "He granted the request of the Horned Edge magi." With a smug smile, he flashed his special ring.

Lewis flashed his own ring. "Why? Get those out of this chamber!"

"No." Mildred shook her head and puffed out her chest. "Lord Charon's grandfather ordered sacrifices to Saoma to be done here. The practice will not be changed. We have that right so that we will keep our Horned Edge magi free from traitors' control.

Huh? Lewis thought. *Those horrible sacrifices make no sense.*

"Besides, we only sacrifice non-sentient aliens," Mildred emphasized, but her eyes slid sideways. "Those Blue People are not human. They are not *homo azure,* as the Daniel's magi sentimentally call them. The Blue People are slaves, unable to speak or think. The sacrifices serve to control the population and are sweet to god."

Disgusted, Lewis turned away from the chains. His stomach churned, but he knew he could not win that battle by himself.

Another time, when he could persuade Lord Charon …

Surveying the rest of the chamber, Lewis stated, "The polished, black stone table in the center is not an altar, but the window to view the stars. It can also be a door, and that is our task, to make the window into a door so that people can pass through from this world to others."

Jeffrey shrugged. Mildred was sour. "Yes, we know that," she snapped. "I used to be in charge of the whole system."

"After Remi died, that is," Jeffrey whispered softly but cruelly, as if to put Mildred in her place. Then he added, with a sidelong glance at Lewis, "Bad things can happen to lead scientists who let the systems break down." He jerked his chin towards the chains bolted into the walls.

"What are you trying to tell me?" Lewis stabbed with his voice.

Jeffrey's face looked pained, even a little afraid. He shrugged.

Lewis felt his face go stony. "We will have no sacrifices, to Saoma or anybody else while I am in authority." He circled the large obsidian-black, oval table, which was the centerpiece of the chamber. Breathing deeply to calm himself, he examined the floor. It was covered with a gorgeous carpet woven in sapphire blue and garnet red. *The floor is covered* ... A good guess came to mind, the reason why the locating system could no longer connect. "Pull up the carpet," he ordered.

"What are you talking about?" Mildred put her hands on her large hips. "Do you think we are carpet layers?"

Lewis did not deign to reply.

* * *

Under the carpet, the chamber floor was made of polished black quartz. Inlaid on its surface Lewis saw shining metal concentric rings with patterns like Arabic script. He let out a deep sigh of satisfaction. His theory was correct. "These rings and patterns are resonance tuning and amplification structures. When the hot marble, that is, the *noretha,* was thrown though the nexus, the entire locating system strained hard to maintain the connection to Earth. The weakest parts, those rings, burned out when the system overloaded."

Jeffrey and Mildred sniffed and worked slowly, but they finished clearing the floor. Lewis copied the patterns onto a sensitive silver-plated tablet like an old photographic plate. When they were done, he ordered, "Record the tablet's pattern into the sonic computer. Back it up and do it again. After that, activate the system to find and map the dead spots – and then we'll have to repair them."

* * *

For the next several days, Jeffrey, Mildred, and Lewis descended into the cave chamber and worked long, hard hours. Carefully, they held their wands to the intricate rings, saying such things as, "This *linath* has resonance, but the next three bilinath do not." Working with very little sleep, they found the sections that had burned out and replaced those sections with new material.

Lewis threw himself into the technical work. His mind jumped and crackled, like the welding arcs used to repair the rings. His senses felt white hot, amplified. And he was delighted to be in control here, Number One, over these magi.

What you are feeling is not normal! the inner voice insisted.

Lewis tried to ignore it. However, there came an inner command. It was so strong and urgent that it cut through all the noise in his head. *Hurry! Copy all the resonance map data along with the rest of the system!*

And he did.

* * *

At last Lewis was satisfied that they had repaired the locating system. He ordered a staff party with loads of hors d'oervres and unlimited drinks, and he said to his team, "You've done well. Go and rest." Cheering, Lord Charon's scientists emptied the laboratory. So did Lewis – but he came back.

Speeding to the special room that stored the noretha, and checking to see that he was alone, he thought his password plus the symbols of the mathematical scripts in front of the marbles he wanted. As he thought, the glass pane in front of each choice vanished. Lewis took out three marbles. One was useless, burned out like an old bowling ball with a chunk missing; the second marble, he knew, connected to the coppery moon Wega; and the third was his ticket to Earth. Then he played "musical marbles." Wega's noretha went into Earth's place; the useless marble he laid in Wega's place; and the third place he left empty. He could explain, if anyone asked, that he had thrown out a defective noretha.

As he hid it in his robe, he fingered the marble that had led him and his brother and sister to Lanthra, and he whispered, "We meet again, friend."

CHAPTER 6
HOSTAGES

H ostages!" Mark Gregory said in disgust.

He plopped down on the floor of the Nutman chapel, put Gracie in his lap as if she were a very small child, and leaned against a pew. "They caught me coming home after my night shift." He was wearing the black gown of a magus, but it was badly torn, and he had bruises on his face. "What about you?"

"They rounded up Mom and me at her house, before supper," his brother Allen snapped. He wore his work clothes, including a woodworker's apron, but no shoes. "We were packing to leave tomorrow for the Celebration." He turned to Deirdre. "O Wise Noblewoman of Smythe, why did you step back in harm's way and let yourself get captured?"

Deirdre swung her thick golden braid. "Allen, shut up! We were kidnapped yesterday, right from my own property! If the queen finds out that Torish soldiers illegally crossed her border, she'll forget that Smythe is supposed to be neutral –

"Shhh," Sadie warned. "They're going around and searching everybody."

In a few minutes, Torish soldiers came to them, removed several potentially useful objects from Mark and Allen, and then went on. All around them was a low buzz of unhappy conversation, and a few people weeping. "This is dismal," Allen said.

"Where is Daniel?" Sadie asked Deirdre.

"The soldiers took him to the Torish commander. They deliberately humiliated him. They treated him like a criminal." Deirdre's eyes flashed and her right hand made a deadly sword stab gesture.

"What are they going to do with us?" her little sister Myra asked in a small voice.

"They won't kill us. We're hostages. They'll take us to Tor, I think," Mark answered.

An idea came to Gracie. She stirred with excitement, and Mark asked, "What is it, Gracie?"

She said, "Maybe, if we go to Tor, we can find Lewis and Patrick."

The group fell silent.

"Well, I hope so," Mark said. His voice had a forced heartiness to it.

The idea that she might see her brothers again was very comforting. The sticky fear eased away. Gracie snuggled against Mark's chest; he felt warm, like a Teddy Bear. He stroked her curls, the same way her dad back on Earth did when she was little.

Myra had tears running down her cheeks. "I hope they bring Dad back soon."

Allen said, "Your Dad's a genius, Myra. He may be able to talk his way out of trouble."

"Maybe so," Deirdre said. "Maybe he can negotiate to get us all a nice place to sleep tonight."

"With a hot bath in the morning," said Mark.

"And hotcakes and sausage for breakfast," Allen added.

Everybody laughed.

All at once, the tension drained out of Gracie's body. She felt very sleepy. "I've never slept in a church before."

The others giggled. "Never slept in church? How unusual!" Mark said.

Gracie didn't get the joke and didn't want to take the trouble to figure it out. She relaxed and closed her eyes. Soon she was asleep.

*　*　*

Several hours later, Gracie awoke. Inside the chapel, the light was dim. Most of the people slept or at least rested, although there was a line of people waiting their turn to use the small and now very stinky bathrooms.

Away down the aisle, she saw the front door open. Someone familiar was ushered in. Daniel! Both her eyes opened, and she sat up.

He made his way toward them through the crowd of people sitting or sleeping in the pews and on the floor. Gracie saw that he still wore his pajamas and bathrobe, and his curly blond hair was tousled, but he was no longer tied up. She sprang up from Mark's lap. Running down the aisle, skipping and jumping over legs and blankets, Gracie threw herself at him and hugged him tightly around the waist.

Daniel's face was a troubled gray, but he smiled at her and hugged her in return.

Many people left their pews or floor territories to shake bow low or shake his hand. "Here, Your Excellency. Take my place. Have my water. I can give you a little food."

Daniel greeted everyone that he could and made his way toward his family. He collapsed onto the pew.

"What's happening?" asked Mark.

"Dad, you look so tired!" Deirdre put her hand on her father's arm, and he patted it.

Daniel rubbed his eyes. "Well, the Torish now control the whole city. Everyone, including the city garrison, thought they were Bardian reinforcements – until it was too late. Someone had made a list of names and addresses so the Torish could round up hostages, who, fortunately, surrendered. No lives were lost. Of course, Captain Gregory's troops in the mountains have not surrendered, but they have retreated into hiding."

His growing audience digested this information. "Thank God, John is still safe," Sadie said softly.

"Maybe Captain Gregory can rescue the city," a youthful magus nearby said hopefully. Like Mark, he looked well roughed-up.

"Maybe he can, but what about us?" said one of the women.

Mark told them calmly, because Daniel looked as if he had talked enough for the day, "We are in no immediate danger. Their main goal was to seize the College and this city, and that they have done."

The people dispersed and went back to their places.

Mark stretched and groaned. "These others may be left alone, I think. But we'll be carted off to Moorway. Hostages."

Unexpectedly, Daniel chuckled, startling them all. "We're

very fortunate, dear family. Yes, they do intend to take you and me to Tor. However, Lord Charon chose a very good man for the seizure of the city. General Patterson is a good man, an honorable man. We won't be abused." He tried to curl up in the pew, failed, and rolled again to his back, grunting, "… and to think I voted against cushions for these pews!"

CHAPTER 7
SEIZURE

After some time, multicolored sunlight filtered through the chapel windows. However, although people were stirring, a gloomy silence lay thick inside the church. Gracie felt stretched tight like a rubber band about to snap. She had been unable to go back to sleep after Daniel had arrived. *Was it my fault that we all got captured? Is it because I'm from Earth? Suppose I'm tortured? What's going to happen to us?*

Daniel awoke. He got in the long line for the restroom. The people in line waved him on and tried to give him the first place, but Gracie was proud to see that he refused. When he came back, he began to counsel the Gregorys, his family, and Gracie. "General Patterson said he would allow us to go to my house for an hour or two. We can refresh ourselves and gather some clothes for our journey. Especially me," he joked, looking down at his pajamas.

Despite her fear and guilt, Gracie giggled.

Some of the merriment was back in the Daniel's eyes as he whispered, "But that isn't all. Because the commander is so kind, I will have a good opportunity to arrange your escape."

Their gloom changed to amazement. "Excuse my doubt," murmured Allen. "But even your cunning mind has limits."

Sadie picked up on one obvious detail, and said softly, "What about *your* escape?"

Daniel was not listening. His eyes danced, glowing in the morning light coming through the chapel's stained-glass windows. He whispered, "Part of my cellar connects into the ancient foundations of the city. There are tunnels under the entire university circle, and at least one of them leads to the playing field near the outside wall."

Myra's eyes were wide. "Daddy, I never knew that!"

Deirdre admitted, "I did. When I was ten, I found the entrance and explored the tunnels. Mom was furious, not just because I was filthy, but because she was so afraid that I would get hurt or lost. She put a lock on the door, and I never went down again."

"We'll only have a short time, but we can fit a lot into it," Daniel said. "We can take turns bathing, and I will get some clothes, of course. Also, we can eat some breakfast."

*　　*　　*

About noon, when Gracie was so hungry that she could hardly think about anything else, a dozen Torish regulars came to take them to Daniel's mansion. The lieutenant was not nice. He rudely made them march in a little parade from the chapel and up the hill and through the university gate. Instead of student magi at the gatehouse, there were now Torish soldiers. When they arrived, the lieutenant looked at a gold watch. *That's Lewis' Rolex! Dad gave that to him!* Gracie thought. Anger flooded her chest. *The Torish took after they killed the man who helped us when we crossed over from Earth!*

The lieutenant stated, "You have fifty-five minutes to prepare yourselves. Guards, follow them from room to room, even the bathroom.

"Are we to have no privacy?" Daniel exclaimed.

"I've orders," the lieutenant told him in a cold, intimidating voice.

"My daughter and I will prepare some lunch here. However, your men will not accompany of us into the bathroom," Daniel stated with all his authority. "General Patterson has given no such orders. And you will not watch the ladies dress!"

The lieutenant's eyes flicked sideways, and Gracie noticed. *What a creep!*

"Women get the larger bathroom; men the smaller," Daniel ordered.

Mrs. Gregory stayed with Gracie and Myra as they bathed and dressed, which helped Gracie feel safer. Gracie had just stepped into the tub for her turn when someone rapped on the door. Sadie opened it a crack. "What is it?" she snapped.

"I believe you'll need this." Daniel held out a towel.

"We already have – never mind. Thank you." Sadie accepted the towel. When she had closed the bathroom door, she unfolded the towel. Out dropped an old key. This she tucked into an inner pocket of her sari, and she continued to assist Gracie with her bath.

When Sadie handed Gracie some of Myra's nice clothes, Gracie was surprised. "Here you go," Sadie said. "Now you look like your 'sister' Myra. You both have auburn hair and the eyes to match."

What does that mean? Gracie wondered.

Gracie draped Myra's travelling cloak around her shoulders, brushed her curly hair, which was getting long, and reviewed herself in a mirror. Her freckled face was pale, her red hair was still damp, making her look like a damp kitten. Myra leaned in next to Gracie and the two girls made faces. "We're like twins," Myra observed, and even in such an anxious moment, she and Gracie laughed.

When Gracie and Myra were done, they ran to the kitchen. Deirdre had set out bread and ham from the pantry. "Eat fast," Deirdre ordered.

Gorgeous as ever in her beautiful sari, her long hair braided smoothly, Sadie smiled at them, her face serene as the moon on a clear night. She ate her bread – but no ham – as delicately as a queen. Deirdre wore her blue riding suit and looked regal, too. Myra picked at her food. She wore a maroon riding outfit similar to Gracie's.

Gracie devoured all her food and felt her growling stomach grow warmer and fuller. She was amazed how the meal picked up her spirits.

Daniel, who sat at the table, announced, "I'm so hungry!"

"What, didn't you eat anything?" asked the lieutenant coldly. "You've sat here long enough!"

"Not yet. I wanted to make sure everyone got enough to eat. Maybe there's more food here." Daniel rose and rooted through the pantry. "Ah! There's some headcheese in a jar. Would anyone like a slice of headcheese for your bread?"

All of them shook their heads emphatically. Myra wrinkled her nose. "Dad has some weird tastes," she whispered to Gracie.

Daniel ate a sandwich. After he finished, he sniffed at the last remnant of headcheese and exclaimed, "I thought this tasted a bit off! He tossed the gelatinous meat into the slop pail.

The lieutenant examined his watch, looking cross. "Seventeen minutes," he said.

Gracie did not like the way the lieutenant followed Deirdre with his eyes. He looked at her, well, with bad thoughts.

Allen and Mark came in. The atmosphere seemed to Gracie tense as a high wire. Mark ate a little bread, but Allen sat up straight with his arms crossed.

"What will they do to us if we're late?" Myra asked her father.

"It's all right, *bibath*; we'll be fine."

I hope so! Gracie thought. She began to get scared, and her hands felt sweaty.

"Nine minutes," the lieutenant intoned.

It was finally Daniel's turn to wash up. "If he's still in there when the time's up, fetch him out of the bathroom," sneered the lieutenant. "Clothes or no clothes."

"I won't be long," Daniel told the Torish lieutenant brightly, and went down the hall accompanied by guards.

Allen started to pace. Sadie lost her patience at last. "Allen, sit down! You are driving me crazy!"

Allen lowered his eyebrows. "I don't want –"

She hissed, "I said, Allen, sit down! Have lunch! Everybody's eaten but you!"

Obediently but glaring, Allen sat and began to stuff food into his mouth. "Three minutes," said the lieutenant.

The three minutes passed. Deirdre looked gorgeous, her golden hair brushed glossy and plaited into a thick braid, and the lieutenant alternated between staring at her and looking at his/Lewis's watch. The distracted man let a few extra minutes pass.

The High Magus Daniel, however, did not come out of the bathroom.

Vexed, the lieutenant muttered something and left the kitchen. Gracie heard him beating on the bathroom door, shouting, "'Tis time! Come out!"

There was no answer, and Gracie heard a sharp bang as the lieutenant shouldered the door open. There was a pause; then the man shouted, "Willis! Gabriel! Quickly! The man's having a fit!"

The Torish soldiers and Gracie, Allen, Mark, Sadie, Myra, and Deirdre all ran toward the bathroom.

Gracie had one peek through the door. The bathroom was a mess. Daniel, only half clothed, writhed on the floor holding his stomach. There was vomit on the floor. The room stank ferociously. The lieutenant and the guards shouted at each other. Myra screamed.

"Food poisoning!" Deirdre exclaimed. "It must have been the headcheese!"

"Hold him while I stuff his mouth, lest he puke some more," the lieutenant demanded, totally disgusted.

"Don't! He might choke!" Sadie shouted.

Gracie felt like her world was coming to pieces. *Am I going to lose him? He's not related to me the way my brothers and Mom and Dad are, but to me he's like a dad.* She whispered to Sadie, her voice all weak and trembly, "Is he going to die?"

To her surprise, there was a triumphant glow in Sadie's eyes. She gave Gracie's arm a reassuring squeeze.

The guards tried to control Daniel's spasms while the lieutenant pried his fingers into his mouth, trying to insert a rag. However, Daniel chomped hard with his teeth. "Ow!" the lieutenant shrieked.

From the front of the house, five more guards ran to help. The hallway in front of the bathroom was packed with frantic people, so two guards forced Gracie and the others to retreat to the kitchen. From the bathroom, the lieutenant was still yelling, "Pry his jaws! He will'na release my fingers! Blast you, Willis, hold him down!"

Now Gracie and her companions bunched in the kitchen, including the two guards. Without warning, Sadie grabbed a frying pan from the wall and slugged one of the guards with it. He dropped. Allen leaped on the other guard. "Deirdre!" Sadie cried, "Where's that cellar door?"

Deirdre ran toward the back of the kitchen. Her fingers played the wall in scherzo time. "It looks like part of the wall, except for a small keyhole. I used it such a long time ago ... Here it is! But ... does anyone have a key?"

Sadie pulled out the key from her inner pocket. She stuck it into the keyhole, but it would not turn.

"Hurry up!" Allen yelled.

"Here, Mom, let me …" Mark grabbed the key and turned it with all his strength. The key bent, but the lock did not turn. Mark tried to pick the lock by inserting a table knife, but the blade broke, cutting his hand. Blood spattered everywhere.

Allen cried, wrestling the guard, "Get going! I can't hold this guy much longer!"

Gracie and Myra huddled together. Still bleeding, Mark pointed to the fireplace and ordered, "Deirdre, get me that thing!" He stuck the kitchen poker into the keyhole, splintering wood, until the entire lock mechanism burst out of the door and left a hole. With the claw of the poker, he pulled, straining, until, with a hideous squeal and flakes of old paint, the door began to open outward.

Gracie cringed. The dark opening into the cellar resembled the maw of a hungry animal. There was a cloud of spider webs across the opening.

Sadie grabbed Myra and ducked into the cellar without hesitation, leaving behind shreds of waving, dusty spider webs. Next, Deirdre put her arm around Gracie, "Let's go, girl!" But Gracie panicked, her stomach squirming and her chest exploding. That black opening – it looked so spooky … There were spiders, and maybe mice or even monsters …

Just then, the soldier that Allen was fighting wriggled free. The Torish man bent his foot around Allen's leg, slipped an arm under his shoulder, and jerked. Allen was forced over, with the guard's foot on top of him. "Help me, Mark!" Allen cried. Mark took the guard down with a fluid toss, kicked his weapons away, and broke a chair over the man's shoulders.

Holding Gracie's hands softly, Deirdre drew her up to the cellar door. "Come on, sweetie; we'll be okay."

However, the other guard that Sadie had hit with the frying pan shook and rolled to his feet. Quickly, he snatched Gracie and pulled her to his chest.

Gracie screamed, a sharp yelp like a car-struck puppy. All her adrenaline rushed to her hands and feet, but she couldn't move because both the man's arms wrapped so tightly around her that she could hardly breathe.

"Surrender, or I'll break her neck," the guard ordered in Lanthran. Deirdre put up her hands. Allen and Mark stopped short.

The man called loudly for reinforcements, *"Marador, marador!"*

Panting, Mark stepped next to Deirdre. His hand dripped blood where the knife blade had slit the skin, and unaware of the bleeding, he wiped his forehead, leaving a long trail of red, then he, too raised his hands.

Allen, however, grabbed the poker and menaced the guard who held Gracie. "Imagine what I can do with this, man! Let the girl go!" The guard shook his head and gripped her throat tightly, and they heard the pounding of many feet. Allen bawled to Mark and Deirdre, "He won't kill her; it's a bluff. Make sure you get out safely!"

Deirdre cried, "I can't leave her!"

"You can't help her!" Allen yelled. He punch-kicked Deirdre through the cellar door, shoved Myra after her, slammed Mark through it with a fist, overturned a cabinet to block the opening, and crouched in front of it.

CHAPTER 8
SUDDEN ANGER

Lewis was eager to see his lord's face when he told him that, probably within one more day, they could positively and certainly connect to Earth. *Lord Charon will reward me! He'll let me go to Earth, he'll reunite me with my family!*

When Lewis approached Lord Charon's throne room in Whitehall, he heard the servant announce, "My Lord, your servant Barth Layhew from Torgard has arrived."

What?

Very quickly, Lewis rounded a nearby pillar to keep from being seen. A hated clear tenor voice resonated through the vestibule, "Greetings, Master." Footsteps and shuffling told Lewis that Barth had entered and kneeled.

Behind the pillar, his heart pounding, Lewis closed his eyes and let out a deep breath. He had hoped that he would never again see or hear the man who had kidnapped him. Forever without Barth was not long enough. Also, *What is my lord doing, seeing that brute?*

Charon's office door closed, but apparently Barth had shut it carelessly because the door eased partially open again. Sounds of the conversation carried well across the marble floor and Lewis's ears were very good.

A heavy thud told Lewis that Barth had plopped onto Charon's zebra-skin covered settee. "Ugh," Barth complained. "It's hot and steamy as a smithy in your city, as usual. Give me my home Torgard any day. The mountains are never as humid as here on the plain."

Lord Charon's pleasant deep voice said, "Have you been

given refreshment? I'll call for some ice water."

"Ice water?" Barth snorted. "No thanks. I'll get a real drink later."

He got to his point. "So, Tahei, you got Louie Brahmindura to repair your locating system? How did you manage that? A little session downstairs with the thumbscrews?" He snickered.

Anger drenched Lewis with a hot hose. He wanted to run into Charon's office and punch Barth's teeth out. However, although he clenched his fists, he stayed behind the pillar, listening.

Charon's reply sounded light and smiling. "Nay, nothing like that is necessary. The man is more than willing, as well as very able."

"My Lord Charon, be careful. He cannot be trusted. Put me in authority on this project."

"No," Charon said. "He's brilliant, more than you, Barth. Besides, a daily dose of a powerful solanaceous alkaloid and constant gentle allosuggestion keep him pliable."

Lewis stiffened all over. If he had not heard the words from Charon's own mouth, he could not have believed it. His stomach began to feel very sick. *Is that all I am to the Master? A tool, a dupe?*

Lord Charon said, "*Fean* Lewis manages the project. However, you are loyal, and I want you by my side."

"Well," Barth drawled. "I'm relieved you won Louie over so easily. It's just as well that he decided to collaborate with you, since we lost the one real lever we had on him."

"You mean his brother? Or his sister? Or both?"

Lewis stiffened. His hands trembled and he clasped them tightly.

Charon's voice sounded dark and angry. "What are you telling me –"

"Patriots," Barth spat disgustedly. "Torgard Patriots. Patrick had been injured – it was Lewis's fault! The blasted Patriots grabbed the boy from the hospital before he even woke up from his surgery. My dear brother Nark rounded up most of the traitors from his city. That was sweet – I got to be there when he gave them to Saoma. One of the nurses at the hospital died by Nark's favorite torture – it was most entertaining. However, no amount of questioning could reveal who took the boy."

Lewis felt a sudden surge of nausea. He put his hand to his mouth to keep from vomiting.

"I need the brother," Charon said stiffly. "Lewis is waiting for him and his sister to join him here in Moorway. You promised –"

Barth replied, his voice defensive, "I searched every brick in Torgard. The boy's description was sent to every garrison in Tor, but the results have been zilch. The Patriots are too well organized in this."

A silence fell. Lewis leaned his head back against the pillar. *Patrick has escaped!* However, he had no room for joy. He imagined what Nark and Barth must have done to the poor nurse. The euphoria, all the pleasant lift in his soul, hardened into hate. He thought, *Barth, I swear I will get revenge for what you did to me and those other people.*

Barth began mouthing excuses over losing his main leverage over Lewis. As he hid behind the pillar, Lewis thought, *He's screwed up badly, and Charon will tan his hide. Perhaps literally.* He could always hope.

However, Barth ended his long defense with a line that froze Lewis to the marrow: "If you need to hook Lewis, besides the drugs and the mind control, there's always his sister. I can make a special trip to fetch her."

No! Lewis silently screamed. *Not Gracie! I wanted her and Patrick to join me here, but not, not, not as prisoners!*

Charon stated, "I have sent for her along with the other hostages from Nutman. However, Barth Layhew, you have stumbled badly."

Another silence settled over the vestibule. Barth began babbling, "Master, forgive me, please forgive me. I will bring the girl and … Patrick."

Charon's voice was sharp, as if puzzled by a new thought. "You came to like the lad, didn't you?" he asked.

Barth made a sudden odd noise, as if he had been drinking beer and had backwashed. He coughed and choked and finally said, "No! I love you with all my heart, with all my life! You alone are my brother and my father!"

Lewis clamped a hand to his own mouth to stifle an exclamation of disgust. *Barth likes Patrick? After tying up my brother and threatening to slit his throat?*

Lord Charon replied softly but cruelly, "Aye, I believe you. By the way, speaking of brothers, you've brought me one in *Fean* Lewis. I've come to love the lad."

Lewis fled. He'd heard enough. Now he needed to think. He needed to plan.

CHAPTER 9
FROM BOY TO GIRL

At first, Patrick thought he was at home, Earth home, in his own bedroom. Drowsily, he lay contented for a while, happily noting the quiet blue color of the walls, the clean white curtains that stirred in a fresh spring breeze, and he listened to the soft sound of rain outside.

Then: *Where am I?* He tried to lift his feet, but his right ankle was bound in bandages and a heavy splint and propped up on a roll of cloth.

Immediately, everything came back to him. All the wretched details of his kidnapping swarmed into his head. He remembered the hay-smelling cart where he was tied up, the sharp knife ready to slice his throat, his older brother's terrified face, the tangle of rhododendrons where he broke his ankle, and the awful jostling wagon to this place. To what place?

He had a fuzzy painful memory of a plain, cold hospital with medicine smells, but how did he get *here?* He tensed all over and his heart did flip-flops in his chest. Suppose the guy with the knife came in? He couldn't run away!

"Lewis!" he called. "I'm awake now. Where are you?"

A lady came into the room, saying, *"Dee, dee, pipasa."* Patrick sank obediently back onto the pillow. The lady's face came into focus. She was very pretty. She had violet blue eyes, rosy cheeks, and dark hair. "You must not get up yet. Tomorrow, you can get up for a little while, but we've a journey to make soon, you and I and my girls, and we'll help you get strong for it, but today you must rest."

He wished he could die of embarrassment when she brought

him a bedpan, but he did not fight her when she helped him use it. She felt his leg and his forehead for fever. "Good, all cool."

Patrick was full of questions. "Where's Lewis? What journey are you talking about?" He suddenly felt fear seize his middle and make him cold all over. *Is Barth Layhew going to stride into this nice blue room and take me away?*

The pretty woman was still talking, laughing, and her eyes were twinkling. His heart calmed a little. *I have no idea where I am, but this lady seems all right,* he thought.

When she had checked him all over and given him a sponge bath, she sat down on the edge of the bed. He looked up at her beautiful eyes. They looked like eyes he could trust. She said softly and seriously, "I'm not one o' them, the worshippers of Saoma," she said. "There are still many of us in Tor who have'na been deceived. Ne'er again will we be servants of demons." She smiled at him and gently touched his cheek. "I've a daughter, Bessie, a little older than you. About ten years old, aren't you? She's twelve. You'll meet her soon, and also Katie and June."

"Unsa gan eaya?" Patrick asked, feeling a little glow of pride that he knew how to speak Lanthran.

She answered in Lanthran, and he Anglicized her name in his head, "Mrs. Jane Tuttle." She said, "This is no hospital, it's my home. I'm no nurse, but I'll care for you so long as needs be. You had the surgery on your ankle and medicine at the hospital, and we Patriots slipped you away afterward. Ah, there was such a fuss when the Wolf Riders found you were missing! They will be looking for you, and I'll hide you as well as I can. But as soon as possible we'll be leaving for Moorway to live with my brother Curly, a cook in Lord Charon's kitchen, for my widow's stipend is'na enough for us to live here in Torgard."

Words burst out of Patrick before he could hold them back. "What about my brother Lewis? Isn't he rescued too?"

The smile vanished from Mrs. Tuttle's face. She slowly shook her head. "He was here in Torgard with Baron Nargoleh Layhew, and from there to Lord Charon in Moorway. We canna' reach him right now. But we shall see what can be done."

Sinking back on the pillow, Patrick tried to organize all the new information. He had been rescued out of the wolf's jaws, but Lewis had not. It wasn't fair. After all, he was the one who had made all the mistakes. He had found that crazy marble and thought it was such a great thing, but he had dropped it in front of all those awful Shields of the People at the picnic. The SOPs had chased them, and they had found themselves in this crazy world, and right away he had twisted his ankle. If only he could rewind time and do things right! He declared, to himself as much as to Mrs. Tuttle, "When we get to Moorway, I'll have to find a way to rescue my brother Lewis."

The lady suppressed a smile. "We will try to find a way to rescue your brother. We Patriots have plenty of friends here and in Moorway." She rose and went to the door. "I'll bring you some breakfast, Pat."

Patrick responded, "*Gan eaya* Patrick. My friends call me Patrick."

Mrs. Tuttle smiled. "Well, Patrick, I'll send your breakfast in with my Bessie, when 'tis ready." The sound of her light, firm footsteps receded downstairs.

*   *   *

Later, Patrick awoke from a deep sleep. There was a big noise downstairs; somebody was thumping on the front door. He heard a girl's voice exclaim, "*Ma! Fordetasa e'oya!*" A crack of breaking ceramics, probably a dropped baking bowl, made him wince. The thumping at the door threatened to break it down.

In a room near his, a baby started wailing. Patrick heard Mrs. Tuttle's voice saying, "Katie, take care of baby June! Quick, Bessie!"

The girl's light footsteps clattered quickly upstairs, and Mrs. Tuttle's oldest daughter Bessie burst into the room. In her arms was a large bundle. She tossed an untidy assortment of feminine clothes and toys around the room. Then, she produced a wig of long, black hair. "Wear this!" she ordered.

"No way!" Patrick responded.

She stamped her foot. "Do it!"

"No!" he insisted.

The girl glanced back down the stairs. "You must! And I'm getting in bed with you. Move over!"

He had barely opened his mouth to protest when she jumped onto the bed, slid under the covers, and cuddled up against him.

She thrust the wig into his hands. His face flamed with

embarrassment, but he put it on.

Apparently, Mrs. Tuttle had let in the aggressive visitors, because Patrick now heard voices murmuring on the floor below. Several sets of heavy footsteps began coming up the stairs.

Heart hammering, Patrick waited. The sheets suddenly felt very hot and sticky

He heard Mrs. Tuttle protesting, "What is it that you're seeking? I've but myself and my four girls living here. The only man o' this house was killed three months past by the Bardians at the border."

Peeking out from the covers, Patrick saw a man in a gray uniform with the Wolf emblem on his sleeve. He was burly, tall, and had a large handlebar moustache. Two other Wolf Riders stood behind him. The first man growled, "Step aside, ma'am. We'll have a look about. Orders, ma'am, for the whole city." Beneath the gruff words, Patrick heard a faintly apologetic tone.

Mrs. Tuttle slipped past the man into the bedroom. Through the increasingly loud screams from baby June and the insistent "Hush!" from Katie, Mrs. Tuttle said, "Sir, I've two wee girls sleeping – not that they're still asleep with all the noise ye were making, and two in bed here sick with the –" She used a word Patrick did not know. There was an anxiety in her voice, however, and he wondered if he or Bessie had some dreadful virus.

Maybe I've got ebola, he thought, his stomach sinking.

Mrs. Tuttle said, "If any o' ye have'na had … T'would be wise not to get too close. The disease has small effect on a child, but a grown man may become … may lose his ability to beget children."

The tall burly man's face twitched. One of the men behind him said, "I've ne'er had the disease."

"Nor I," added the other.

In his mind, Patrick squeaked, *Nor I!*

"Look anyway." All three men entered the room. Bessie croaked, "My throat hurts, Ma. My cheeks feel swollen like a chipmunk's."

Patrick opened one eye. *I can't talk. My accent will give me away.* Instead, he let out a moan. Bessie whispered painfully, "Marty's sick, too." The Wolf Riders scanned them and the untidy room briefly but came in no further.

A small dark-haired girl about four years old entered the

room, holding the hand of a screaming toddler. She said, "Mama, baby June won't stop crying. Maybe she's wet."

Mrs. Tuttle patted the small girl's shoulder and scooped the toddler into her arms. "Thank you, Katie."

Little June calmed down immediately. "Daddy? Daddy?" she queried uncertainly. "Daddy come home?"

"Nay, little June bug," said Mrs. Tuttle. There was a catch in her voice. "Daddy's gone. These are soldiers, friends o' your daddy."

In unison, June and Katie slipped their thumbs in their rosebud mouths and stared solemnly at the intruders.

The Wolf Rider with the big moustache cleared his throat nervously. He shuffled his feet and looked down at the well-polished floor. "All's in order, Ma'am. We'll be leaving straight away." He turned, gathered up the other two men, and hastily led them downstairs. Patrick heard the front door bang as they left.

Patrick pulled off the wig and threw it onto the floor. "Hooray! I don't have to be a girl anymore!" He was not surprised when Bessie turned toward him angrily. He made a face at her.

She got out of bed and stamped her foot. "You're too stupid to be a girl!"

Patrick threw a pillow hard at her head, but Bessie caught it. It was funny: He liked the way her eyes sparkled when she was angry. He was hoping she would throw it back, and the little girls laughed, egging him on, but Mrs. Tuttle scolded, "Enough! Now that we've told the 'boz that you are sick in bed, you have to keep pretending to be sick in bed. Or do you want the neighbors to call the 'boz back to our home?"

Patrick immediately sobered.

"We have to work together, children, because there's danger afoot," Mrs. Tuttle continued. Patrick noticed that her eyes flashed just the same way Bessie's did. "Tomorrow, Bessie, I want you to help Patrick with his crutch. Five times daily for ten minutes a time you'll walk about the hallway, lad."

She paused as a new thought came to her. "We canna' keep calling you Patrick."

Startled, Patrick felt his jaw gape open. This was the strangest thing that had happened yet in a whole six months of strange events. "What? What's wrong with my name?"

The lady was silent for a moment. At last, she said, "You've been called 'Marty' already for short. Your new name is Martha. You will call me 'Mama.' Now I have four daughters, Bessie, Martha, Katie, and June."

A surge of hot rebellion filled Patrick's insides. He wanted to yell, but Mrs. Tuttle ordered, "You must drop your pride, Martha. It has no place in these times. We – all of us – have a job to do. Let my girls talk with you. Listen to them with both your ears and learn our speech well. You must talk as we talk, or not at all. And when the time comes for us to move to Moorway, as in a week it will, you'll wear the wig, and, aye, a dress, too."

Patrick felt his mouth open and close soundlessly, like a fish in air.

CHAPTER 10
THE HOSTAGES LEAVE NUTMAN

Daniel felt horrible, yet triumphant at the same time. Allen was restrained, and Gracie looked terrified but unharmed. He was dirty and smelly, but all the other dear ones had escaped.

Report of the escape brought General Patterson himself to Daniel's house. He looked ready to murder the lieutenant when he heard the story and saw the blood and vomit, the lieutenant bandaging a ravaged finger, and two very injured soldiers.

General Patterson said to the lieutenant, his voice stabbing, "A *rida* of soldiers defeated by one short, middle-aged viceroy, his little daughter, and an unarmed, barefoot Bardian? Where are the other prisoners?"

Flushing scarlet, the lieutenant saluted. He waved his uninjured hand toward the battered cellar door, now open, and surrounded by crashed kitchen furniture. "Sir, the prisoners went that way. They got through this door, and, though my men followed them, they somehow sealed off the passage and we have'na been able to get through."

"Get through," General Patterson ordered. "And find the end of it." The general wheeled around to glare at Daniel. Daniel was certain, however, that there was also a measure of admiration in his eyes.

* * *

Not long later, Daniel took a deep breath and said good-bye to his home. It was amazing how a beautiful day could be so unhappy.

As he left, he cherished the fragrant roses, pink, yellow,

scarlet, that bloomed in the garden and on trellises. A hummingbird zoomed past, headed for the honeysuckle. In the strong mid-morning sunlight, with blue sky and stately clouds floating past, he probably looked his part, the High Magus the Viceroy of Rockeerie, clean now and dressed in fine travelling clothes. However, he felt gray inside, like dirty dishwater.

With one arm, he held Gracie gently. The girl was shaking. "I love you," he whispered.

The Torish had brought up a carriage pulled by a sturdy pair of Clydesdales, and Daniel and Gracie climbed inside while the soldiers loaded their small luggage. The carriage rolled away, with a large company of cavalry accompanying them. For a long time, neither he nor Gracie talked, which made the creaking of the leather seats sound loud. However, as they and their convoy clopped under Nutman's shady gate, he hugged the little girl to his side and looked down to her beautiful face. Her hazel eyes stared at him; she seemed stunned, but attentive. "I think you had better call me 'Baba' or 'Daddy,'" he told Gracie. "Also, speak to me always in Lanthran."

"Why?" Gracie asked. Correcting herself, she said, "*Vina?*" Her wide eyes met his.

"They think you're my daughter, Myra," Daniel whispered. He was warmed when in reply she took his hand and held it to her cheek. Then tears welled in her eyes, her mouth quivered, and she began to sob. Daniel gave her his handkerchief and stroked her hair. She shook and cried as they rode, until she wore herself out.

After a while, the carriage felt extremely hot and stuffy inside. The windows were dusty. Daniel felt uncomfortable, and he knew Gracie did, too. But there was nothing to do about it except endure.

*   *   *

When, hours later, in the forested hills, they came to the end of the paved road. Here, the carriage stopped. A Torish soldier opened its door, gave Gracie a hand down the long step, and Daniel followed. Three *harbath* of mounted soldiers – about two hundred men – waited to escort them on the next phase of the journey to Tor. Daniel was ushered to a small blond mare that danced impatiently as he climbed into the saddle. Gracie was put on a rangy, dependable black plodder.

All along the way, through forest with its many ferns and shy shade flowers, Daniel felt such turmoil that he could hardly think two connected thoughts. *I thought my family was safe in Smythe! I thought the city could ward off the invasion through the summer!*

To add to the irony of the situation, pink ladies' slippers were in bloom, with flowers more beautiful than queens' dresses. They reminded him of Ielen, and that made him think of Deirdre and Myra. He found himself worrying crazily about them in addition to Gracie and himself. Plotting, planning, scheming, analyzing yielded no solution. He and Gracie were prisoners.

The Master said, *Rest.*

But I'm the High Magus, Daniel replied, and there was more than a little whine in his thoughts. *I should draw from your Spirit to rescue us all! I know your power! With one breath you could scatter the enemy and –*

The Master commanded, irritated, *Stop it! Rest!*

But –

The Master did not waste time arguing. Daniel inwardly grumbled for a while, until he got tired of it, and then saw himself from the Master's perspective and laughed out loud.

"What is it?" asked Gracie.

"A funny thought. I'll tell you about it later." The cavalcade continued, under the huge shady mountain trees.

Once his mind was quiet, Daniel felt a ripple like the softest breath of a summer wind across still water. The Master said, *You need to create a delay.*

The mare felt the change in his hands and legs. She skittered sideways. With a gentle nudge, Daniel brought her back in line.

"Why, Master?" he asked, not caring if anybody heard.

I am sending someone to meet you, the Master told him plainly, *and he needs time to catch up.* Then Daniel's high-strung mare jumped again, this time at a whirling leaf, and he realized what he must do when the right time came. Stroking the mare's neck, he hummed, and she quieted.

When they climbed the last ridge, Daniel looked down through the trees and saw the Winerush River roiling far below. His gut wrenched with anger and more than a little fear.

Despite all the Bardian efforts to prevent it, the Torish had built a bridge, the first successful bridge over the Winerush between the Sapphire Lake in Smythe and the Forschwynn

Province. Towers had been brought in sections and assembled at each side of the river. Steel cables spanned the rushing water. The cables supported a broad road. The whole apparatus must have taken many years to design so that it could be built quickly. *It shows how much Tahei hates you, how much he wants the power you have guarded,* the Master told him.

Daniel looked back at Gracie. Although she looked exhausted and her face was very pale, he saw a determination in her posture that pleased him. *When I create the delay, Master, please protect her.*

The Master affirmed, *I will.*

As they descended a rough road down the river gorge toward the bridge, Daniel chose his opportunity. He kicked the mare hard but simultaneously yanked back on the reins. Very confused, the horse startled violently. Already struggling down the steep descending path, the animal slipped sideways. She rolled to the ground, and Daniel flew off. His head hit a rock and exploded in pain. The mare shimmied back and forth, trying to get up, and Daniel felt a hoof strike his hip. Soldiers yelled, "Get him away from the horse! It's going to kill him!" He heard Gracie shriek. Both he and the mare slid, propelled with dirt and loose stones, toward the river cliff. Rolling over and over, Daniel knew that he was sliding to the brink of the gorge, a hundred *wisto* drop to the raging river.

Every second stretched out in slow motion. In a weirdly calm corner of his mind, he said, *It's all right, Master. I'm ready to die and be with you and Ielen. Just take care of my girls and Gracie.*

Daniel scrambled for a way to stop sliding, but he was out of control. The mare screamed as, kicking wildly, she reached the cliff and dropped over.

Bam! Daniel hit a tree root at the edge of the cliff. His fall stopped. Gasping, his heart hammering, he tried to pull himself to a kneeling position, but began to slip again, so he lay in place. He shook his head from side to side to clear it. That did not help; his ears rang, he saw deep red with flashing white stars, and he could hardly breathe. Meanwhile, in a detached part of his brain, he heard the Master telling him, *You will not die. You will go to Moorway. Tahei Charon will gloat over you as his prisoner, but I will be with you.*

CHAPTER 11
BLUE PEOPLE

Once the Tuttles and Patrick left Torgard's mountains, the weather turned from cool and damp to hot and steamy. Mrs. Tuttle drove a cart with a horse, and the older girls and Patrick took turns with her on the buckboard or else in the back of the cart with June. For meals, they passed around a basket with summer sausage, homemade biscuits, dried apples and peaches, pickles, and a little maple sugar candy from the Skye country above the Winerush. They all slept in the cart as well, waking up stiff, hungry, and cranky. All the time, Patrick submitted to wearing a black-haired wig, a red-checked dress, and he let the Tuttles call him "Martha" without losing his temper except once or twice. This went on for six days, because they took the longer road to avoid the steep mountain slopes – and the Wolf Riders.

Finally, on a morning that dawned still, warm, and muggy, Mrs. Tuttle awakened the sleeping children. "We're near Moorway. Look closely – the Blue People live in villages here!"

Patrick scanned the area. All around them was a flat swampy plain. Near at hand, as far as he could see, sprawled a tangle of tall reeds and cattails. A big bowl of blue sky arched above. However, away in the north, he saw snow-covered peaks. Patrick thought they looked like floating clouds over the horizon.

The girls all started talking at once. Patrick, complained, "I'm hot! My foot itches like mad, and I can't get to the itch because of the cast!"

Bessie leaned from the buckboard seat and plucked a stiff reed. "Here, Pat – I mean, Martha. See if this helps."

Patrick felt both grateful and annoyed at the same time. The reed did not quite reach the spot, but it helped.

In a few minutes, as the morning sun rose and the horizon became hazy gold with the moist heat, Patrick's neck dripped with sweat. Under the black wig, his head sweltered. Also, his crotch felt itchy. He would have traded the whole world for a chance to scratch his privates, but he would not receive the whole universe to let these girls see him do it. He panted with heat and thirst. Then he felt an irritating presence near his sweaty head. "Arck! Gnats!"

Tiny flying bugs and large whining mosquitoes buzzed all around him. A big, fat fly tried to land on his forehead. "Get lost!" Patrick yelled and waved it away. It buzzed off. "Ouch!" A sharp itching on his shoulder told him that the fly had come back. "It keeps biting me!" He wanted to howl with frustration.

"Look! There!" Bessie exclaimed.

A flock of big pink birds with long spoonbills and crimson wing-pits flew overhead. They flapped and landed in a lily-pad area of the marsh.

Patrick forgot his itch for a moment. "Wow. There must be a thousand of those big birds!"

The road crossed a causeway over a canal. On the other side, they could see some boats floating in the canal that looked like kayaks woven of reeds. "*Ta Rethappath!* Blue People! Look!" Bessie and Mrs. Tuttle said together.

A half-dozen blue children stood in a semicircle near round huts. Their body hair was blue-gray, and their heads were purest white. Most of the children hung back, but one of the bigger boys jumped forward. Keeping pace with the Tuttle's horse, he made signs with his hands and waggled his long red tongue. Patrick recognized the sign from his encounters with Blue People in Nutman. The boy's graceful motions asked, *What's up?*

Jane Tuttle signed a reply. With her pinkie finger, she traced a circle, ending with a flourish of the whole hand. Katie, sitting next to Patrick in the back with June, said, "That means 'Going home.'"

An hour passed, and they crossed canals at least a dozen times. Frogs cheeped, crickets buzzed, plus they heard croaks, whirring, and booms from some hidden swamp creatures. After a while, the ground began to rise. Once they began to pass houses, the horse snorted and quickened its pace.

"Now, we're coming into the city," Mrs. Tuttle said. "I don't want to draw unnecessary attention. Pretend you are asleep. It's unlikely that anyone will ask us questions, but just in case …"

Long, low buildings made of brick blocks lay on both sides of the road. "Ma, what do they make in those factories?" Bessie asked.

"They make soap," Mrs. Tuttle explained. "The Blue People harvest marsh plants whose seed produces a fine oil, and, in the factories, they blend it with an herb called 'passion ruby' for its wonderful perfume. Moorway soap is the finest in Lanthra."

Patrick, lying down on luggage with little girls, did not care a drip about Moorway soap. He began to imagine himself as a hero. *I would meet with a secret society to overthrow people like Barth Layhew who worship the Satan demon, Saoma, and I would find Lewis.* He imagined himself, bold and strong, slipping through the cisterns under a dark and menacing fortress. He'd fight giant rats with his sword. Once he got into the dungeons, he'd find his brother chained to the wall. With a mighty sweep of his sword, he'd sever the chains and lead his Lewis to safety.

Patrick smirked. *The guards will find only the severed chains, and they won't have a clue as to where Lewis went. Meanwhile, we'll steal horses and ride back to Nutman. Gracie and the Gregorys will be so excited! Lewis will put his arm over my shoulders and tell the story of the remarkable rescue. And then …*

The cart hit a bump. Patrick's ankle banged against a box. "Ow!" he yelled. Nearby on the road, three Blue People walking together carrying big baskets on their heads and two human merchants behind them stared at them curiously. Mrs. Tuttle glanced back at him, then pulled the cart to a halt at the side of the road.

Her cheeks were red with heat and alarm, and her eyes darted to the left and right to see who was looking at them. However, the passersby paid them minimal attention, and she sighed with relief. "Children," she said, "It's verra' important that we are not questioned. I feel a great weight, because my purpose in Moorway is a secret. Please be patient and quiet. I'll get us to our new home as soon as possible. Later, we'll have a meeting and I'll tell you more.

The children nodded. Patrick resolved to keep his mouth shut, but inside he tickled with curiosity. *What is the secret? Can I have a part in it?* His thoughts clicked in his head. *Jane Tuttle is one of the Patriots, and they are planning to overthrow rotten people like that awful Barth Layhew! Ho! I'm caught up in an adventure!*

The factories gave way to rows of narrow, crowded houses. When the horse finally pulled up in front of a tall, narrow brownstone house on a side street, they were all stiff, hungry, and cranky.

Mrs. Tuttle announced, "We're here!" June woke up and began to cry.

Patrick yawned and stretched while Bessie and Mrs. Tuttle opened the back of the cart to let them out. "Where's here?" In the quiet, deserted street, his voice came out as a bellow.

Mrs. Tuttle winced. "Shhh! Quietly now, Martha!"

She gathered June into her arms, but the two-year-old June began to yowl. Katie, who was five years old, wailed, "Ma, June kicked me!"

The rows of houses seemed to frown, lowering over them as the stood around the cart on the brick street. Mrs. Tuttle tried to quiet the girls. "Hush, little June bug; hush, Katie."

Patrick volunteered, to his own surprise, "Let them go in with me. I'll play with Katie and June until you and Bessie can unload the cart." He let himself down from the wagon to the street and hobbled on his crutches to the little girls. His wig was on crooked, and his skirt was bulky because he insisted on wearing pants underneath, but he wanted to do his best to cooperate with the family who had befriended him.

"Here, June, take my hand. Katie, hold on to my sleeve."

The little girls quieted and held on tightly to Patrick as he followed Mrs. Tuttle. She walked up a narrow lane that led to the back of the brownstone houses, where there was a large common courtyard. At the third house on the right, she pulled a key from her pocket. "My brother Curly is'na home yet. But I'll let us in."

It took a long time to unload the wagon and stable the horse. Finally, Patrick and the other children sat at a large, sturdy wooden table in the kitchen. There was complaining and crying until Mrs. Tuttle laid out a small meal and heated water for tea.

When the tea was ready, Mrs. Tuttle sat down with the girls

and Patrick at the table. Her face was drawn, dark smudges were under her eyes. "'Tis a fine day."

Patrick knew better, but he bit his lip because her voice sounded as cranky as "Mom" ever got. She went on, "Your uncle Curly should be home later. He's a baker in Lord Charon's kitchens at Whitehall. He'll take care of us. We have a nice house to live in, the good company o' my brother, and enough of everything that we need."

Patrick burst out, "Do I have to wear this wig and skirt inside all the time and hide? Why can't I just be myself? Nobody here in Moorway knows or cares who I am!"

Mrs. Tuttle snapped, "Mind your speech!"

Patrick shut his mouth.

She replied, "I canna' let you go about proclaiming that you're a foreigner. The Eagle Guard of Moorway will be as happy to grab you as the Wolf Riders of Torgard, and it's my family that'll suffer the punishment if they find you! As for going out, aye, you can exercise – in the back yard and side lane. And you'll be wearing your wig and the dress!"

Patrick expelled air in a big sigh to conceal his rising anger. He stared darkly out of the window. If only he weren't wanted by stupid people who worshipped the devil! If only he weren't dragging a broken ankle around! He missed Lewis and Gracie. Plus, deep inside, he missed his mother and father so much that he felt he could break down and wail.

I wish that I hadn't found that stupid hot marble! Patrick picked at a bit of thread on his stupid dress. He looked down so the girls wouldn't see the tears starting in his eyes, and he knew without a doubt that this was going to be the worst summer of his entire life.

Chapter 12
PRISONERS AT THE TORISH CAMP

The first morning after they had crossed the bridge into Tor, Gracie awoke early. She was in a tent, and, despite a decent cot with a mattress, her back was stiff. Her eyes felt shriveled up because she'd cried so much. A mosquito had bitten her cheek, which now had an itchy bump. There were others buzzing around her head, too. She rolled over and sat up. The mosquitoes were like bad memories. Gracie had faced long, long, scary, horrible, no-good days. Her friends and family were gone. Daniel had hurt his head – and he was the only one she had left.

Pulling aside a thin screen, Gracie went to Daniel. He lay very still on his bed under a quilt, breathing softly, but his hands were warm. The Torish doctors had worried over him most of the night because of his concussion. Finally, they had let him (and her) go to sleep. Daniel and she had a nice tent, almost luxurious – not a plasticky green thing, but a big blue silky cloth one that let in some light and didn't smell. The soldiers had brought in an antique-looking table, a laver with a pitcher, a mirror, and other furnishings. *Okay, God,* she thought. *Thank you for the good things.*

She had to relieve herself. Her tent was beside headquarters and there was a screened-off latrine for the officers, relatively clean, with enough privacy to accommodate a little girl. However, the latrine was a long walk across the trampled grass past a dozen tents. Gracie had used it last night, but it was less embarrassing then, because of the darkness. This morning, however, a hundred soldiers could see her walking to the latrine. She put off her need a little longer to "get presentable," as Mom always put it.

They had let her bring a small bag of "necessities," as Mom called them. Thinking of Mom helped her feel more grown up; Gracie could imagine Mom saying, *Here is the washcloth. Did you bring the pearly-handled comb that Myra gave you? What a nice outfit, Gracie; it goes with your hair and eyes.*

Looking at herself through her mother's eyes and feeling like a lady, she washed and dressed in one of Myra's outfits, a smoky gray blouse and dark gray riding pants.

What to do now? She couldn't wait any longer. It was time to mosey out and head for the latrine.

Afterward, feeling much better and on the way back to the tent, Gracie took time to sightsee a little. Far away, a turtledove hooted. Across the Winerush River, on the Bardian side, she could see the bridge spanning the gorge and the mountain forests ascending steeply beyond. On this side of the river around the camp, the highland was flatter and grassy; she could see the dewy grass sparkle with ripples of gold from the rising sun. Her heart rippled in response, with a tiny current of hope. Blue sky brightened over the treetops. Beauty pierced through the numbness in her mind, and she remembered the Sunday School song:

> *Jesus loves me, this I know,*
> *For the Bible tells me so.*
> *Little ones to him belong;*
> *They are weak but he is strong.*

Just as Gracie reached the tent, she heard a very familiar voice. "Reporting for duty, Colonel Ruse, sir! I am Lieutenant Mark Holdman, on special assignment to you from General Patterson! Here are my orders."

Mark Gregory! Her hand went to her mouth. She ducked behind the tent flap. *He's pretending to be somebody else!*

The thin, crinkly-haired young man stood at attention before the officer who had taken Daniel and her to the camp. Mark wore a gray Torish uniform with a special red armband that Gracie didn't recognize. Colonel Ruse, a tall man with dark hair and a craggy face, read the orders, then Mark saluted boldly, saying, "General Patterson ordered me to report to you and to accompany the prisoners to Moorway because I know them personally."

Gracie startled and almost fell backward.

"So the orders say," Colonel Ruse said. He looked hard at Mark, up and down. "What does that armband mean?"

"I am in Special Intelligence, a magus, and an agent for Lord Charon. I infiltrated the College and helped with the invasion."

You did not! thought Gracie. *What a crock!* She felt very uneasy. *What if Mark has been lying to us all the time?*

"Debrief at HQ, Lieutenant Holdman. Afterward, report again to me here."

Mark saluted, "Yes, sir!"

*   *   *

The morning dragged on. A woman brought breakfast, warm rolls with butter and scrambled eggs with sausage, which tasted pretty good.

Sitting in a fold-up chair by the tent flap, which had become "her" place, Gracie listened to the noises of the camp: clinking, clanking, bumping, footsteps ambling or marching in unison, the clop and thud of hooves, chatting of general soldiers, and the sharp commands of officers. Closer, she could also hear Daniel's soft breathing. He was still bundled in a quilt, whereas she was beginning to feel hot. Shyly, she approached him and put her hand on his forehead. It was cool and clammy. He did not wake up. A knot of fear gripped her. *Is he going to die? Will I be left all alone?*

Soon she heard the colonel's voice approaching the tent and scooted to stand behind her chair to be as invisible as possible. Four men ducked into the tent, Colonel Ruse, a white-haired man that Gracie recognized from last night as the Torish doctor, and two guards. The colonel said briskly, "Dr. Mainstay, he's still sleeping. I'm worried. Last night he complained that he felt nauseated and cold. He did vomit several times."

Dr. Mainstay shook Daniel awake. "Sit up, if you can," he said.

With a groan, Daniel opened his eyes and rubbed his forehead. "I'll try." One of the guards brought forward a chair, and they carefully lifted the High Magus into it. When Daniel saw Gracie, his smile was sunshine. "Hello, *bimi*."

"Good morning, *Baba*."

With the ease of long practice, the doctor peered into Daniel's eyes and tested his reflexes. He hummed a little tune as he went through his routine. Gracie watched him deftly clean gashes on the viceroy's scalp and hip. He remarked, "You're verra' fortunate, you should know, for one who's received wallops to the head."

"Fortunate?" Daniel said weakly. "Thank you, Radyah." He winced when the doctor touched a particularly tender spot.

"Do you remember what happened?" asked the doctor.

"I don't remember," Daniel stated.

"Can you remember what day this is?"

"Ah – I think it's … No."

Gracie did. She remembered absolutely everything that had happened since the beginning of her terror. Her insides were still screaming.

"You're fortunate indeed that your skull is'na cracked. At least, I have no reason to believe it is, and you've no blood in your ear canals. Ne'ertheless, your pupils are dilated just a wee bit unequally, and you've certainly suffered a concussion."

Daniel closed his eyes. "Yes, I have a headache. It feels as if my head were crushed."

"It very nearly was." As Dr. Mainstay sewed and dressed Daniel's scalp lacerations and other injuries, he smiled at Gracie. "Is this your daughter, this pretty lass? What's your name? You remind me of someone, *bimibath*."

Gracie couldn't force words to come out.

The doctor gave her a long, curious look. "'Tis a certain look about you. You remind me of a young laddie with a fractured ankle, oh, three fortnights ago, right here in this camp. And his older brother …"

Gracie felt a hot explosion in her middle. "Pat – !" she began, then covered her mouth with her hand.

Dr. Mainstay and Colonel Ruse both shot a searching look at her, but at that moment, Daniel slumped over in a faint. His face was very white.

"Quick," called the doctor. "Help me lay him back down on the bed. Get his feet up!"

The two Torish soldiers rushed over to help. From her corner of the tent, Gracie shuddered, and her heart pounded, but its racing engine mixed fuels of fear and hope. *Patrick and Lewis were here. They're alive!*

CHAPTER 13
GRACIE PLAYS CHESS WITH THE ENEMY

Several long, boring, days passed. Gracie's quivering insides got more relaxed as Daniel got better. Often, in the tent or outside walking, enjoying the sunshine, Daniel and she talked softly. Mostly they told jokes and stories. Gracie confided, "I've been writing a book. I lost my journal when we …" She took a deep breath and went on, "… when we found the hot marble. But I still have the story in my head."

"Don't lose it. Keep going with your story," Daniel told her solemnly.

Gracie enjoyed talking with Daniel. She heard about how the High Magus and the Viceroy of Rockeerie had risen to power. He had been a commoner, the son of a goat farmer. His father had helped him enroll in the College of the Magi, and after graduating with honors, Daniel started as a low official in the Rockeerie government. In a short time, however, he rose like a rocket in the Bardian hierarchy because of mentors all over Lanthra, and (he blushed), some talent for diplomacy.

Daniel described his family. "I married beautiful, kind Ielen, a noblewoman of Smythe. Deirdre was born, later Myra was born, and our family had years of happiness. However…, he paused, "My wife was killed when her horse fell on her."

Daniel's voice got thick. He wiped his cheeks, and Gracie thought, *Oh, my goodness, Daniel is crying!*

Abruptly changing the subject, Daniel began, "Remember the marble, which stores the gravitational resonance coordinates from Lanthra to Earth? This marble, the *noretha,* is a tool used with a *thoyo-on,* the system that powers the connection between points far removed in space ..."

Gracie didn't understand a thing about gravitational resonance. However, she was glad to be with Daniel, no matter how boring he got.

*   *   *

One evening, Dr. Mainstay ducked into the tent. This time, Colonel Ruse was not with him, nor any guards. Examining Daniel thoroughly, he said, "Your pupils are dilated equally. Ears are fine, heart and lungs are fine, your reflexes are fine, you are well oriented, you've regained your memory, and you seem physically much stronger. I'm going tell Colonel Ruse that he can send you on your way."

"Yes, I know he must." Daniel smiled sideways. "Not that I have any choice but to go with him."

Dr. Mainstay looked around carefully, then leaned close to Daniel's ear. Gracie heard him say, "I'm recommending that you be sent by way of Torgard for further medical observation. I've friends there. We could get you out."

Daniel, in the barest whisper, answered, "I cannot go to Torgard. I must go to Moorway for the midsummer Council of the Magi, whether I am a prisoner or free. However, ... do you know anyone in Moorway who can help my little girl?"

Dr. Mainstay considered. "Maybe. One of our people will get in contact with one of your people."

"Look for Hermann," Daniel said. "He's the best agent that I have."

The doctor nodded, "Aye. We know the man." He closed his bag and left.

Gracie suddenly discovered a terrible flaw in Daniel's plan. Tears filled her eyes; they dripped down her cheeks. "But who's going to help *you?*" she asked.

A brief smile crossed his lips. "I'll be safe. It's you and the others I'm worried about. Otherwise, everything's going the way I planned."

She didn't agree, but she didn't know how to argue with him, the High Magus and the Viceroy of Rockeerie.

Up to this time, Gracie had not told Daniel what she had seen and heard between Colonel Ruse and Mark Gregory. The idea that Mark might be a traitor was so terrible that she could hardly endure to think about it. However, now that Daniel was getting well and they were going on to Moorway, she felt she had to say something. She began, "*Baba,* I saw —"

Just then the tent flap opened with a slapping noise. A cloud of night bugs headed for the lamp. Several soldiers hauled in a desperate-looking young man in a very dirty and loose Bardian uniform. His hands were tied behind his back. They threw him down onto the floor.

Colonel Ruse entered. He stood over the prisoner.

Gracie barely remembered to keep quiet. Her stomach sank. *What is going on? I thought Mark was a Torish agent? Is he ...? Is he someone we can trust?*

Daniel winced as he turned his head. Gracie saw quick amazement flash in his eyes when he recognized Mark Gregory, replaced by a bland poker face.

"Your Excellency," the colonel demanded, "who is this man? We caught him lurking about the camp. He claims to know you."

"Yes!" Gracie blurted. "He's —"

"*Bimi,*" Daniel put his hand on her arm. "Let me talk."

"But —"

"Let me talk," Daniel emphasized. He turned away from her to Colonel Ruse. "Let me think ... He does look very familiar ..."

Mark's face was screwed tight with fear. "Your Excellency, *Hegofean,* he thinks I'm a spy, but I'm not. Don't let them kill me!"

Colonel Ruse drew his sword. He put the point of it at Mark's throat. Swelling to his full height, towering over Daniel, Gracie, and Mark, he roared, "Unless I know more, he will be destroyed immediately. Your Excellency, tell me, who is this man?"

Mark cried, "Don't you remember me, *Hegofean?* I'm Mark Holdman, a student magus at the College! I was one of the hostages! Didn't you see me with the others in the chapel? Please —"

Daniel interrupted, his voice fierce, "Colonel Ruse, I'm appalled that you dragged your captive here to this tent where my daughter and I are being housed. Do you actually plan to kill him here, in front of my little girl?"

Colonel Ruse said, unrepentant, "He may a spy. If so, yes, I will kill him."

Gracie shouted, "Sir! No! He's not –"

"Wait!" Mark writhed on the floor, a dent in his throat where Ruse's blade pressed. "I can prove I'm not a spy. I'm a magus; I was one of the hostages. The little girl can explain –"

Immediately, the colonel walked over to Gracie and pulled her chin up. "So, explain!"

"What?" Daniel sounded totally shocked. "Colonel Ruse, are you making my little daughter responsible for deciding whether you will kill a man?"

Gracie's throat went dry. All the Lanthran language she knew ran out of her mind like a dog bounding through an open door. There seemed to be a boulder in her chest, keeping her from breathing.

The colonel tilted her chin higher until Gracie's neck hurt. He demanded in a low, dangerous voice, "Little girl, what do you know about this man?"

"Stop it!" Daniel shouted. The colonel ignored him.

Gracie's legs trembled and she couldn't make them stop. She held onto the chair to keep from falling. Yet, at that moment, when all eyes were fixed on her and darkness began to fill her head, she saw Daniel Higgins wink fractionally. He made a hand motion that the Blue People used in Nutman. It meant, *It's all right.*

She took a deep breath; her mind cleared. Daniel knew what he was doing. And Mark – he was pretending to be someone else to fool the colonel. Gracie thought, *How would Lewis handle this situation?* She knew. Lewis would play chess with the colonel. *He taught me to play chess and I was pretty good. I even beat him five times. Very well, I can play chess with this awful man.*

Gracie found she had control over her mouth again. *Start with my knight, follow with a pawn.* Every word from here on was a feint, her own contribution to this weird game. In a barely audible voice, in Lanthran, she moved her knight. "Mark always said 'Hi' to me when I went to visit *Baba* at the College. He always had a smile for me."

She made her face and eyes look innocent. She made herself meet Colonel Ruse's cold black eyes. "*Baba* told Mark to take care of himself." Her knees began to shake. "Please don't hurt Mark, sir," she pleaded. "He was only trying to help us."

Colonel Ruse released her chin. Gracie was sure there was

going to be a bruise on it from his hand. He threw a searching gaze at Mark and Daniel. Something about the set of his jaw told Gracie that he was satisfied with what he saw. He growled, "*Fean* Mark, you may stay with your master. We will question you quite thoroughly indeed in Moorway. Then, should you prove to be not a would-be rescuer but a spy, you'll be given the appropriate penalty."

Ruse described in gory detail what that penalty would be. Gracie felt all the blood drain from her face. Mark and Daniel, too, looked stunned.

"The magi have outlawed such punishments," Daniel stated.

"Saoma rules now, and he has his own laws." Ruse sneered. "We of the Horned Edge worship him. He is God, not your weak Radyah. We're not controlled by the Bardian-dominated magi." He gathered his two soldiers and swept out of the tent.

*   *   *

After the Torish soldiers left, Daniel moved to Mark. "Sorry, *fean*. Thank you for trying to help us." Laying his hand on Mark's head, he blessed him.

"It is my honor, Hegofean Daniel, to serve you and glorify Radyah."

Daniel had no knife, so untying Mark took a long time. The lamp flickered and smoked and drew more bugs. After Mark was finally freed, a servant brought them a pot of stringy stew, cold bread, and sliced turnips. Daniel thanked the Master for the meal in the traditional Lanthran chant, but otherwise they ate in strained silence.

*   *   *

After the meal, Daniel began to relax somewhat. He watched Gracie slap at mosquitoes in the warm tent air and scratch at bumps where the insects had bitten her. He was impressed that she could handle such stress so well. Meanwhile, his heart ached – and so did his head.

After Gracie had fallen asleep and the only sounds were the frogs of the forest, Mark and Daniel began to talk. They spoke, not in Lanthran, nor in English, but in the secret language of the ancient magi.

Mark said, "After we escaped through the tunnels, we came to the exit in the gorge behind Nutman hill. No one saw us. We divided up. Sadie took Myra to Smythe."

"Good!"

Mark continued, "Deirdre has headed southeast to Kingsport. She thinks she can persuade the king to help the patriots fight in Moorway."

Daniel's heart rose. "If anyone can do that, Deirdre can. Old King Norhe's wife, Margaret, loves Deirdre, and you know who the real power is behind the throne." Daniel chuckled, remembering Ielen.

Mark told his story. "After we escaped through that tunnel, I acquired a Torish uniform rather violently." Mark's whisper was the faintest breath in Daniel's ear. "I followed your escort over the bridge. While you were unconscious, I presented myself to Colonel Ruse as a double agent. Gracie did an admirable job of keeping my secret, although I know it shook her confidence in me."

Mark continued, "I'm supposed to gain your trust and milk you of any information that I can before the Council of the Magi. Ruse and I planned how to get me in your tent, and we came up with the 'poor, scared, newly captured prisoner' routine. I'll be kept with you as far as Moorway. After that, look out – they will interrogate me! But I can endure."

Daniel touched Mark's arm. The effort to control himself gave him the hiccoughs. "May Radyah preserve you from the enemy!" he gasped, "And they call me devious! Hic! Oh, my head!"

Time passed. Frogs cheeped in the wet places and in the trees around the camp. A nightingale sang in the forest. It had been hot in the tent, but as the dew fell, the air felt cold. There was much shifting and rolling before they all felt comfortable enough to try to sleep. Finally, while Mark snored on the floor and, behind her curtain, Gracie breathed softly on her bed, Daniel talked to the Master, friend to friend, *I know that we are in mortal danger. But the worst situation is not here; it's with a little hot marble and a young man from Earth named Lewis in Moorway!*

The Master replied, *Oh, yes, you've got that right!*

Chapter 14
STARS

In the privacy of the cave chamber, Lewis inserted Earth's noretha into a slot on the obsidian table. A swirling field of stars appeared on the tabletop. "The system works. We're almost done." His hands fumbled over the controls. He zoomed out, zoomed in, wandered around in the Milky Way around Earth.

Despite his galaxy sightseeing, his mind fought for control. *Patrick is alive. Gracie is alive.* He took several deep breaths. Again, Lewis repeated aloud, "My brother and sister are alive. I will find them."

But how? And, if I do find them, how could I keep them safe?

Overhearing Barth and Charon had tilted his entire universe. It was as if he had reached for a glittering ring in a corner but found his hand in fresh feces.

Slowly, painfully, Lewis admitted the truth. Charon only wanted to connect to Earth to get power. There was no altruism involved. And Lewis, Lord Charon's prime helper, was not a hero, not even a prisoner, but just a fool. He had willingly collaborated with a bad plan and bad people and had thought he could stay above it all. He had only dirtied his soul and helped innocent people die. Now, by finding a way to repair the thoyo-on, he had created a mess, a big mess.

Perhaps his eyes were watering, but it seemed to him that the stars on the monitor were dancing.

"Impossible," he murmured. His insides writhed like a bag full of worms. He wanted to run far, far away, but there was no place to go, so he peered at Earth's galaxy and touched a groove to augment the nexus.

Glory! Millions upon millions of stars! Lewis bent over the table. For a moment, he was transported to a vast auditorium, surrounded by a myriad of rejoicing beings. It was like being in the center of a living diadem, twinkling pinpoint gleams reflecting from many jewels.

An odd thought came to him. He was in the presence of pure joy. How could that be? How could he be evil and yet perceive good?

With Lewis were persons that he could not see, but he could feel them. The spaces between the stars were alive, and they were singing! He slowly extended a hand, hoping to touch someone, an angel perhaps, but he only felt the surface of the table.

The table's cold smoothness broke his concentration. His breath drew in sharply, and he cut the nexus. Collapsing, his knees weak, he sat on the cold floor next to the table and put his head in his hands.

God. People had all kinds of notions about God. Lewis had lost his god and he did not want to review his reasons again, especially not now, when his heart ached. But he had to deal with the glory of the stars. It was not just in his perceptions. If he went to sleep or died, the joy would still be there. That meant there must be another Person perceiving the diadem of glory that was the universe and rejoicing over it.

The stars reminded Lewis of an old phrase: "… with angels and archangels and all the company of heaven …" Where had he heard that phrase before? In church.

Perhaps all that Christian stuff was true, that the morning stars sang together …

Standing up again in the amethyst-encrusted chamber, Lewis tried to grasp hold of himself, but fragments of a song from youth camp played in his head:

> *I danced in the morning when the world was begun;*
> *I danced in the stars and the moon and the sun,*
> *I came down from heaven and danced on the earth,*
> *At Bethlehem –*

Something stung his back like a wasp, and Lewis yelped. *Ridiculous!* he heard. *You are merely shocked out of your mind because of what you overheard between Charon and Barth.*

Throwing away godly thoughts, Lewis straightened up and

wiped his sweaty hands on his black robe. "All right," he said aloud. "I've seen stars before. Now look at the Earth."

His fingers gently manipulated the nexus toward his home planet. There it was, the blue beauty that the astronauts saw from space. Some mastermind in Lanthra's past had engineered the system so that he could zoom down easily and smoothly.

He dived closer to North America, to Alabama, to his parent's home. There was the house in its suburban neighborhood. A few more houses had been built since he, Patrick, Gracie, and Fred had disappeared. Lewis wandered into the Brahmindura kitchen, the living room, all the bedrooms, even the basement. No one was home. "Rats!" he protested. The familiar rooms looked so close, so real. His hand felt the hard obsidian monitor in the chamber, but he did not try to pass through the nexus. The hideous truth: He had joined Saoma. He was part of the people who sacrificed humans to their god. He was a dirty, soul-stinking wretch, and he did not deserve to ever go home.

Lewis began to weep. *Home! I want to go home! But how can they accept me, now that I've become ...*

As he stared through the impassable chasm that separated him from his family and his past, he sensed tumult. He could hear a noise with the ears of his soul. It sounded like baying dogs chasing prey in the forest. Suddenly, Lewis felt like the desperate fox. He should hide in the thorniest thicket he could reach before the wild dogs caught him and tore him apart.

Cut the nexus and run! an inner voice warned him. *Those are bezubs. Get out of here now!*

His hands shook but Lewis could not remove them from the table. Something in him wanted the hunters to destroy him. He was a rotting soul, and he deserved to die. The noise got loud, approaching swiftly. If those were bezubs, would the incomplete nexus hold them back? Probably not. They were spirits, noncorporeal; they had identified him. His mouth opened wide, his body pressed hard against the table, both palms flat on it. He was a traitor, a piece of turd.

A drenching cold splash of thought hit him like chills after fever. There might be devils and Satan. There might be a hell. If the bezubs took him, he would be trapped with them in hell. And hell would be watching Patrick's terrified face, a knife blade cutting into his throat, except the horror would be eternal. He would never get out.

In his mind, he saw razor-teethed gremlins rushing toward him, while his hands surrendered on the table. Bezubs, coinhabitors of his own world, were taking back their own.

"No," he groaned. "There is no god. There is no devil. That jargon isn't true; it's just myths and folk tales."

But Earth's spiritual flies buzzed in a whirling mass, entering him as if through a broken kitchen screen to smelly garbage.

"No!" Lewis screamed. He tried to pull away, but an inexorable force bent him forward, and a frightened whimper escaped from his lips. A jolt like electricity from a live wire stabbed through his hands into his body. The bezubs had seized him. He was conquered. He had lost himself.

A powerful blow yanked him away from the table. Lewis stood shaking and staring. Somehow the nexus had shifted. In the black void, bezubs pressed futilely against the surface of the table, but they were unable to get through to him. He could still feel the inner tickling of fly feet in his soul and a strong buzzing noise, but he was still alive. He was not yet in hell.

Except for his breathing, the cave chamber was silent. Time moved again. Dimly, Lewis realized that his appointment with Lord Charon had long passed. Soon, Charon would send someone to look for him. Lewis knew that his soul was very weak. Even if Charon threatened to hurt Patrick or Gracie, he could not refuse to continue being a traitor. He would enable Charon to go on with his plans to conquer two worlds – and the bezubs would reign on both.

There were only two choices. He could kill himself, the so-called expert. Or, he could destroy the table and kill Charon.

Before Lewis could second-guess himself, he ran to a red-lacquered cabinet. Yanking open a drawer, he found a tool, a chisel. For one long, long moment, he held the chisel over his wrist. Then he began to cut, and blood welled onto his skin.

Chapter 15
LORD TAHEI CHARON

That's Whitehall," Viceroy Daniel Higgins explained to Gracie in a hushed voice. After their long trip, they had arrived.

She looked upward at a glimmering white marble dome that towered above them and shivered, although the breezy night air was warm. Daniel continued, "We're going to meet the ruler of Tor, Lord Tahei Charon."

Gracie felt terror shake her soul. *Lord Charon could take me away from Daniel and Mark. He could hurt me.*

After some formalities where their captain reported to the Horned Edge's commanding officer, several of the new guards with eagle insignia rode up to the prisoners. Their first act was to separate Mark from Daniel and Gracie. "This one goes to the compound," the Eagle commander ordered. The lamps shone on him, a squatty figure with a broad face. "I'll see him later for the questioning. The viceroy and his daughter will go to South Gate. Lord Charon wants to see him as soon as he arrives."

Questioning? Gracie gasped with an awful thought. *Does that mean they're going to torture Mark?* She felt every muscle go taut like a piano string. When Mark rode away into the dark with the group, her self-control snapped. She broke into sobs, holding onto the horse's mane with one hand and muffling her face with another. She hated crying like a baby, but she couldn't stop.

Daniel lifted her from her horse and put Gracie with him on the mare. Strong, comforting hands embraced her. As they rode with their new guards, he whispered, "It's all right, dear little one. We're both scared."

At first, park trees obscured Whitehall's dome, but then they broke out into a wide, well-lighted paved boulevard that ran straight up to the palace. The viceroy's horse danced nervously. "She just wants food and rest, like we do," Daniel commented cheerfully. He hummed at it, and the restive animal quieted. So did Gracie's fear, a little bit.

The Horned Edge guards and their prisoners entered a large gate. Their horses clopped through an archway then turned aside into a tunnel. When they came to a large chamber with many arches, the company stopped.

"This is it," Daniel whispered. He lowered Gracie and dismounted beside her.

"Up these stairs," the commander ordered.

Daniel nodded and followed, holding Gracie's hand.

Flanked by guards ahead and behind, Gracie and Daniel climbed many marble steps. The white marble looked rich and cold in the glow of pearl-like spheres mounted on the walls to either side. Gracie was breathing fast by the time she reached the top of all those stairs. At last, before them arched a grand door. A tall, heavy guard with a handlebar moustache waited at the door. He looked like an enormous preening pigeon in his gray and white uniform, and there was a heavy gold and black ring on his right hand – a Horned Edge ring.

"Lord Charon is ready for the prisoners," he informed them pompously.

The commander opened the grand door. Gracie found herself in a huge round, pillared foyer. She felt very small and very scared, as if she were on trial in a courthouse. Their guards led them to the entrance. "They are here, Master," the commander called.

"Bring them inside, Commander Gort," a deep voice said.

They entered. "Bow before the Magus of Moorway, High Lord of Tor, Tahei Charon," Gort ordered. His voice sounded mean, and Gracie found himself shaking. Not far away she saw a tall black-robed man. *Lord Charon!* Soft, straight black hair fell past his shoulders. Strength showed in his finely chiseled face and power in his long-fingered hands.

Daniel sank to one knee and lowered his head. Gracie tried frantically to remember what a viceroy's daughter should do. At least the riding clothes that she wore looked classy, if rumpled after days on the road. Gracie managed an old-fashioned curtsey, bowing her head, then kneeling. She was proud to be thought of as Daniel's daughter, even if it was only make-believe.

The guards behind them and even Commander Gort also kneeled.

For a long, humiliating minute, everyone waited for the Lord of Tor to release them. Silence drew out painfully. Finally, Charon said, "You may stand."

Daniel raised himself, gently brought Gracie up by the hand, and greeted his captor. "Good evening, Tahei."

In a deep, precise voice, the Lord of Tor answered, but not kindly, "Greetings, Daniel ... my old friend." He put a sarcastic twist on the word, "friend."

Gracie could not help comparing the two men. Her "father" Daniel was six inches shorter than Lord Charon, but he projected a large personality, full of confidence and poise. Charon looked more majestic but there was something wrong about him. Gracie could not sense his soul behind the shield of command.

"Quite a motley lot," drawled a new voice.

Startled, behind Lord Charon, Gracie noticed a man that she recognized. He sat on a zebra-covered bench with his arms and legs sprawled out. He was huge, not fat but muscular, with dark blond hair and a new, curly beard. He had full red lips and his icy blue eyes speared them.

Who is this? Why didn't he have to kneel like we did? she wondered.

Suddenly Gracie remembered when she had seen the big man. She'd been at supper with her adopted family, the Gregorys. Patrick, Lewis, Myra, and Deirdre were with them, too. Fred and some of his friends had barged in. *This guy had been with Fred! What was his name? Barth Layhew!* She glared at Barth and clung to Daniel's arm.

Meanwhile, ignoring Gracie, the blond man looked insolently back and forth from the Torish lord to the Bardian viceroy. "Tahei? Daniel?" Barth stroked his moustache with a finger. "Are you two really old friends?"

Lord Charon answered, a note of bitterness in his voice, "We were friends." He turned to Daniel. "After thirty years you look verily the same, the blithe lad I remembered."

"Thank you, Tahei," Daniel replied lightly, but Gracie could feel tension through his arm. "However, after thirty years, you look somewhat more ... formidable."

Barth Layhew laughed outright.

Charon's smooth cheeks creased with a reluctant smile. "Aye," he replied, "from your perspective, I suppose I do."

With a wave of his hand, the Lord of Tor dismissed all the guards except for Commander Gort. Despite his bulk, Gort had unhealthy gray hollows in his cheeks and small, unfriendly eyes. Gracie had felt safer with the guards around her than she did now, with only Charon, Barth, and that pig Gort facing Daniel and her. She held on tighter to her "father's" arm.

Without prelude, Charon got to the point. "Daniel, I require your help to finish a matter we started long ago. At that time, you and I were merely graduate students from the College of the Magi. However, you and I had made a binding pact. We wrote a formal plan together that exhorted the Council to turn away from their complete suppression of electronic technology. I still have a copy."

Daniel stirred, but Charon continued forcefully, "At least for now, you are the High Magus. You could have led the Magi to enact our mutual plan and free the world. Instead, you have reduced the magi to being mere advisers. It is time for us to change that. When the regular Council meets at Whitehall in a few days, you must advocate our position so that any who are undecided will vote with our supporters."

Charon added, and this time there was now a softer note of persuasion in his voice, "Everyone knows you are a powerful man, and all are wondering why you allowed your province to be taken. Perhaps you deliberately opened up Rockeerie Province to my control so that you could join me?

Gracie's stomach flopped when she felt Daniel shudder.

"I will produce my copy of our plan to the Council. Also, the rumor that we are now allies will be proved true." Charon's voice dropped to a conspiratorial whisper. "Changing your Bardia-controlled position will only enhance your power in the Council."

Daniel snorted. "So you say, Tahei. However, that document is no more binding than the love notes I wrote to my childhood sweetheart – whom I did not marry, I might add." He lifted his chin and smiled at the Torish ruler, but he was showing his teeth.

Charon's eyes narrowed, but he still sounded persuasive. "It is time for us to lead the College of the Magi to a new future as we planned to do. This is the opportunity for us to complete our pact."

"So that you can legally obtain the technology to conquer Lanthra?" Daniel retorted.

"Daniel," Charon replied in a soothing tone, "I need your help to finish the matter you and I started long ago. We contested this before, as I recall, but now I believe you'll come to my viewpoint."

"Oh?" Daniel said amiably, raising an eyebrow. Silence filled the chamber. Gracie held her breath. She didn't understand much, except that Lord Charon was inviting Viceroy Daniel to join him and rule the world.

Abruptly, Daniel changed the subject. He waved his hand, saying, "I've stayed in Whitehall before as an honored friend. Do you remember? I came up from Rockeerie to meet you here, and then we left together to search the northern mountains for the palace of your ancient ancestor, Amen Charon. We were friends. We had beautiful plans. Together, we could have done just about anything."

Daniel's face suddenly seemed younger. So did Charon's. Gracie could imagine the two men happy, full of energy, exploring forests, lakes, and mountains.

Daniel looked at Charon in the eyes. "What adventures we had! We could begin again, start a new adventure together."

The Lord of Tor's face softened. Gracie wondered if Daniel had agreed to work with Charon's plans. The idea turned her stomach. *Would Daniel really try to conquer Lanthra? I trusted him! I was sure he was good!* However, she was surprised when Charon's eyes looked down and his mouth twisted as if he suddenly saw something unpleasant that he had overlooked for a long time.

Barth broke in. "Wasn't that the time you two argued over who got what technology? Daniel Higgins, O Goat Lord, you ran off so that you could send a special force to the Snowy Mountains to raid Amen's cache."

Charon's face hardened and he stepped forward angrily toward Daniel. The room seemed to darken as he snarled, "You *cilathoon!* Do you hope to woo me with fond memories? You worm! You could ever tickle a man's will to consort with your own, save –"

"Save yours?" Daniel interrupted, lifting an eyebrow. "Think, Tahei! Those good memories were real! Another chance, a new future – a wholesome future – is a real possibility!"

Charon continued to approach, radiating such cold hatred that Gracie involuntarily gasped and stepped backward. In a bitter, steady voice, the lord said, "Always you've gotten your way, climbed up men like stairs to become the highest of all, the High Magus, and deceived them all with your winsome manners. Aye, you bend every man's will. But you will no longer."

Charon leaned over the Bardian viceroy intimidatingly. However, then he turned toward Gracie. Her stomach twisted with alarm, and she wanted to run, but she couldn't. The ruler raised his long, ivory hand, and she flinched, expecting a slap. Instead, the Lord of Tor ran a finger gently down her cheek. She huddled against Daniel, and he swept his arms around her protectively, but Charon reached and took hold of her right ear. Gracie gasped.

"You see, Daniel, old friend, I know what you are afraid of."

Daniel tried to put Gracie behind him, but the Commander Gort blocked them. Barth leaned forward eagerly on his zebra-covered bench as Charon put his face so close to Gracie's that she could feel his breath. It smelled cold and minty, with a sour, bitter under-tang like cleaning solution. "You've a pretty daughter, Daniel," Charon said. "I know you want to take good care of her." His voice carried a suggestion of threat.

In his plush chair, Barth stirred with a sudden intensity. "What's your name, girl?" he asked sharply. His eyes scanned her up and down, as if he were trying to match her with someone in his memory.

Gracie opened her mouth, but nothing would come out.

Daniel knocked Charon's hand away from her chin. "Stop frightening her! Her name is Myra." He held Gracie tightly against his warm chest.

Charon straightened to his full imposing height. "Aye, she's much like you, Daniel, with these curls and a vixen face. You're a fool to have let her be taken with you. There's only one deed that will protect her now, and you'll perform that at the Council."

Gracie hid her face in Daniel's cloak.

Daniel's voice was unsteady for the first time as he replied, "As ... as you wish, Tahei. You have that power over me. However, consider this! I might have come to share your viewpoint freely ..." Daniel paused, then finished firmly, "if you would listen to me when I tell you the truth!"

Gracie peeked out to see Charon's reaction. The Lord of Tor blinked, taken back for a moment. He replied at last, "Truth from you would be only for my undoing."

"Tahei," Daniel's hands went up together in a pleading gesture, "try to remember the way we began, a long time ago, before finding the old technology, before the drugs, before the war, before the bizeor divided us. I know that you think you cannot go back, that you've gone too far into their dominion. But I'm not lying – you can be free of them!"

For a long series of heartbeats, Charon stood with spasms of emotion passing over his face. Gracie saw uncertainty, then a kind of gentle softening, almost a beginning of hope.

Barth squeaked his boots loudly as he stood up. "His Excellency is playing mind games, Lord Charon. If I had to bet on who was going to control whom, after this performance I'd have to put my money on the Goat-Lord."

Instantly, Charon went rigid. His eyes sparkled with tears of rage, or possibly regret. "Isn't that your way, Daniel?" he hissed. "Soft words, sweet friendship, and a knife thrust in the belly when the wooing's all over?"

Daniel's stepped forward, still holding Gracie. She jumped and almost fell when he shouted, "Would you but believe me! I have never lied to you, not ever!" His temper ebbed suddenly. Gracie felt him tremble, which frightened her more than his sudden shout.

Echoes rang futilely against the hard, white marble walls. Charon's face was closed and set. He produced some keys from his robe and handed them to the commander. In a cool, formal tone, he asked Daniel, "Is that all you have to tell me tonight, Viceroy?"

"Yes," Daniel said humbly. "Please have the commander take

me and my little girl to our quarters now. We are very tired."

Commander Gort clapped a hand on Daniel's shoulder to signal him to kneel and he complied. Everyone kneeled, waiting for Charon's dismissal.

Charon turned his back on them all. Gracie felt a cold presence fill the room. Slowly, Daniel and she rose to their feet. With a curious glance at Gracie and one eyebrow raised, Barth stayed with Charon as they left the ruler's chamber, leaving her and Daniel alone with the commander.

"Come with me," Commander Gort ordered. He produced handcuffs.

"You won't need those," Daniel said calmly.

"Yes, I will." Gracie noted with disgust that Gort almost drooled with his power. He cuffed Daniel's hands behind his back and pushed him forward as the guards followed them.

Chapter 16
CAVE CHAMBER TRAP

Blood welled down Lewis's wrist. However, his deadly trance broke. Raising the chisel slightly, he thought, *Suicide is final. How then will I save Patrick and Gracie?*

An idea came to him. Furious, feeling like Jack the Ripper with a victim, he stabbed the obsidian table over and over, hacking apart its control panel, chipping the hot marble still in its slot.

The table became black and very cold.

"There!" Lewis panted. "You'll never get through now!" A sob escaped him, and he threw the chisel to the floor. "No one will, ever again!"

    *   *   *

Lewis sped up the winding bronze stairway that led out of the cave chamber. Feeling goaded, as if an impatient rider were kicking him with spurs, he murmured the words that shouted inside his head. "Hurry! Kill Charon! Do it now, before you lose your nerve."

He imagined stabbing Charon. Behind him lay the chisel he'd used to vandalize the obsidian monitor, the chisel that had almost sliced his wrists for suicide. Tensing, he started to run down the stairway and get it. But – his whole body cringed – it gave him the creeps to even think about going back to the cave chamber … yet. No, he couldn't make himself return there.

What, then?

Do it now, do it now, do it now! urged voices in his head in a tragic antiphon.

He beat his fist against a case and all the noretha rattled

violently. He mentally screamed, *I hate you, Hot Marble!*

It was time to make himself go out into the lab. However – he caught sight of his reflection in the glass cases – he looked like a wild-eyed lunatic. Using his handkerchief, he mopped his face. He smoothed his robes and ran his fingers through his hair.

"Hot Marble," Lewis snarled. The metal door evaporated. He passed quickly into the laboratory, leaving the glittering noretha behind.

Mildred and Jeffrey were not there. *Thank goodness!*

"What happened to you, Lewis?" asked one of the laboratory workers, named Labeth, a small woman who had batted her eyes at him more than once. "You're all sweaty. You look like you have a fever or something. Then she stared. "There's blood all over your hand!"

"I'm fine."

"Can I help you?" Labeth asked.

"Not right now," Lewis declined. However, she hovered next to his elbow, peering over his shoulder. He could feel her warm hand on his arm, even through his sleeve.

Annoyed, he glanced at her. She smiled up at him. Labeth had applied kohl to outline her almond eyes and a shimmering coral lipstick to her mouth. She also smelled of perfume, a flowery scent that reminded him of a tropical garden. Her glossy black hair hung loose, spilling over her shoulders and down her back. Her small hand squeezed his arm gently.

The touch abruptly reminded him of the woman he loved, Deirdre. She was the real beauty in his life. And here he was, planning a murder. His heart twanged and vibrated uncomfortably, another big emotion on top of all the others. His insides were a veritable spumoni of emotions: gladness, despair, rage, love, guilt ... *I wish I were back in Nutman with Deirdre,* he thought longingly. *I wish none of this insanity had ever happened.*

But it had happened.

Lewis shook off Labeth's hand. She pouted at him, but that was too bad.

"Thank you," he said with a nod, all boss and no boyfriend. He headed for the door that led into the palace. *Do it, do it, hurry up and do it,* the voices told him.

As he strode down the elegant, arched corridor, Lewis's mind flipped through ideas at lightning speed. His breathing became ragged. Very soon, he would kill the Horned Edge ruler and the whole universe would be much better off.

In the central area of Whitehall, about halfway to his room, Lewis heard voices. One of them was Charon's. *Oh crap!*

The voices came from above him. People were descending the marble stairway from that spiraled to the main level of Whitehall. Lewis froze. *Where can I hide?* He had stopped near the base of the stairway. Around him spread a large dome-roofed gallery. Around the curving walls, doors led to corridors and conference rooms for visiting dignitaries.

He ducked into the nearest conference room. It was beautifully furnished and – bad luck for him – it was also brightly lit. The voices got closer and now he was trapped.

A small alcove to one side of the conference room led to a restroom. Lewis preferred not to hide in the loo. He stayed in the alcove and flattened his back against the wall.

From his hiding place, he could see part of the well-appointed conference room. If anyone walked toward him, would he stick out like a sore thumb?

Lewis analyzed the possibilities of being seen and caught. Good – the conference room walls were paneled with a dark wood like walnut. The ceiling was covered with bronzed metal sheets that had been patterned in a sea theme. The room contained sea green couches and chairs and a large woven rug the pale beige of sea oats. There were also paintings of the Lanthran ocean and large ornate mirrors on the walls. *Fine – there is lots to look at, besides me.*

He eased deeper into the alcove until he could no longer see the couches and chairs. If he couldn't see the people who sat on them, then they probably wouldn't see him, either.

CHAPTER 17
PLANNING MURDER

By the echo of footsteps, several people had entered the conference room, perhaps as many as four or five. Lewis pressed into the shadows. His heart pounded. If *they spot me,* he decided, *I will pretend that I was just using the restroom and was embarrassed to pop out among them.*

He heard the thud of heavy butts hitting the couch and chairs.

"There's no time to wait until the regular High Council of the Magi," Lord Charon's serene baritone voice said. "I have called a special emergency meeting, and you must preside over it. By two-thirds majority, the emergency council can change the rules of the Order. Its decisions will be binding on the High Council and by this meeting our course for the future will be set."

"What need is there to call an emergency meeting?" asked a pleasant but rather strained tenor voice.

Lewis thought, an electric jolt jumping through his body, *I recognize that voice! It's Daniel, High Magus, and Viceroy of Rockeerie! What in God's name is he doing here?*

Daniel continued, "The Council meets here in just two weeks! What exactly is the emergency? If you would wait –"

"Nay," Lord Charon interjected. "Too many of the High Council rattle in the pockets of your robes. I must present my proposal before an unbiased assembly."

"Unbiased!" the viceroy's voice sputtered. "You mean unbiased toward you and your control!"

Charon did not reply.

Daniel asserted, "Tahei, when you changed the Council's meeting time without adequate notice, I felt like I'd tripped over a rake in the grass. Now you've changed it again! As High Magus, I object to your decision. You do not have valid grounds to call an emergency meeting. Most of the High Council will be unprepared for the schedule change. Only the people you no doubt carefully selected will have enough notice to get here and vote! You are deliberately blind-sighting the rest of the Magi!"

In his alcove, Lewis quickly understood what he was hearing. He gritted his teeth. *Can anyone stop Charon? Can I kill him in time?*

Charon answered, "I have sent notice to all of the magi."

"When?" Daniel shouted. "Yesterday? Or – to your cronies – last month?"

Charon stated coldly, "There is no need to lose your temper. I repeat, all the magi have been notified. The emergency Council will meet tomorrow morning. You will make an opening address. During that address, you will support me as a collaborator."

Charon's voice did not leave any room for any negotiation.

Daniel responded, and the steam in his voice could have run a turbine, "Collaborate with what? I cannot support overriding the One Law and beginning traffic with Earth. Through your allies, those so-called Shields, the bizeor will rule all Lanthra again. We will endure a level of oppression and destruction greater than Lanthra – or Earth – has ever experienced."

While the High Magus argued, Lewis noticed a nasty cold writhing in his stomach. It felt like guilt. A mocking voice in his head sang, *You abandoned your friends and family. You switched sides to join the devil. You're a fool. No, worse, you're a traitor.*

Desperately choking down bile, he tried to justify himself, *I only cooperated to save my family. Now I've hacked up Charon's precious locating table. I will kill Charon. I will make up for my weakness.*

With an effort, he tuned out the mocking chorus and dragged himself back to the present situation. In the discussion, Daniel seemed to have won some ground. Charon was listening and not interrupting.

"On the one hand, I cannot open the door to the forbidden world. On the other hand," Daniel reasoned, "I can agree with your policy of restoring the old technology. Technology is not harmful; humans and their twisted values are harmful. I'm sure the regular High Council would approve that part of your proposal if I support it. Please wait the two weeks, Tahei, for the rest of the Council to arrive."

Lewis warmed a little, perhaps a degree above freezing. *If only Charon will change his mind! Then I won't have to go through with the murder.*

Daniel continued. "I will stand on the foundation that I've promoted for the past thirty years! Imagine, Tahei – even if I did change my position on the One Law, who would believe it? Everyone would know that I have been forced to comply with you."

"They will not." The Lord of Tor sounded adamant. "They will know that you and I have finally settled our differences. We have allied to restore the Old Order."

"We have allied to restore the old technology. That's it. I will not go any further."

There was a silence. Lewis realized that he was wringing his hands. He made himself stop.

In a grunting, full-bellied piggy tone, another man spoke up. Lewis knew that voice, also. The new speaker was Commander Gort, the leader of Charon's armies. Once, Lewis had encountered Gort waddling toward Charon's office. The commander was short, with a large stomach, heavy jowls, scraggly beard, and tiny, mean eyes. Although his phalanx of Eagle soldiers had bowed low, very low to Lewis, knowing him to be a Horned Magus high in Lord Charon's favor, Gort had brushed past without even looking at him.

Now, Gort was saying, "Listen to me, Your Excellency. You have publicly defected to the Horned Edge. You gave them full control over your province and turned it over to your successor, Tahei Charon, who will be voted the next High Magus. With your following and prestige, you will challenge the Bardian throne. And you will succeed! Then you will retire and hand control of the new College to the new Hegofean."

There was puff of expelled breath from Daniel, as if someone had punched him in the stomach. "You illegitimate upstarts!" he said through clenched teeth.

Lewis had trouble breathing properly. He now understood why Daniel was at Whitehall. *His province has been invaded and he's a prisoner. Charon wants his support to lend credence to his actions. Daniel and I are both his puppets. Charon will lie, steal, ruin reputations, use people, manipulate, blackmail, even murder to get whatever he wants.*

Lewis's chest felt completely hollow. Lord Charon had loved him and treated him like a son. His Lord had promised a new life, with prestige, exciting work, and – most importantly – that he would get his family back together.

If Charon gets his way, there will be no future, even if I survive to see it. Yes, murder was the only way to stop that man from ruining the world.

His mind jerked back to the present when he heard an unfamiliar voice. This one was silky and cultivated. *Who is that?* he wondered.

"As Commander Gort says, Viceroy," the aristocrat stated, "you belong to us now."

"Go on, Baron Trager," Commander Gort said, not suppressing a belch.

The silky voice began a meandering trail of commentary, disguising threat under an amiable expression. To Lewis, although the voice was new, something about the man's inflection sounded vaguely familiar. Searching his memory, he caught a resemblance to the way Tom Forschwynn talked. *Fred's magic ear would know if they're related.* Suddenly, with all the other grit in his head, Lewis missed Fred. *Stop it, Lewis – he hates you now!*

Baron Trager concluded his speech with, "Your Excellency, Rockeerie is under our control. Also, our forces have now captured the Forschwynn Province. We will punish them for supporting you, and, moreover, King Norhe of Bardia will not stir even one draftee to help them! He believes the rumors that you have ambitions to rule Bardia. Very likely, he will try you for treason in absentia, so that you will have your excuse to seize his throne … for us. You are quite an important asset, Your Excellency, to all of the Horned Edge."

Daniel snarled, "I will not help you infect my own people with Earth's demons!"

"Professor Higgins!" said a new voice, a voice so familiar that Lewis almost jumped out of the alcove. Mark Gregory! Can my friend really be here in Whitehall? Can Mark help us?

Mark sounded respectful but patronizing, a young protégé correcting an older man who has made a large mistake. "I know what you're up to, sir."

"And what is that?" Daniel snapped.

"I believe that the pressures of your great position have damaged your reason. You want so badly to fix the universe that you believe that you should rule it."

Lewis could not believe that Mark was saying these things. *What is happening here? Everything is standing on its head!*

Mark continued, speaking firmly, intervening for his erring master, "Daniel, I know you, better than you realize. I know that you could lead us all; you are a brilliant man, extraordinary, experienced, and with your talents you could be the ruler of Earth! With Lanthra's communication technology and Earth's war technology, you could conquer the universe! But you are sick. You have even had a breakdown! That is why we had to bring you to Whitehall, you and your little girl."

In the alcove, Lewis stifled a gasp. *What? Is Daniel really a madman who wants to rule the world?*

For a moment he doubted everything. *Logic, Lewis. You're a scientist. Use logic.*

The null hypothesis was that no one spoke the truth. He already knew that Lord Charon was a liar – no need to review that again. According to the null hypothesis, Daniel was a liar, too. His mind sped, gathering data; the effort calmed him.

In a quick mental analysis, Lewis reviewed the data. When he was first transported to Lanthra, Daniel had sent Captain Gregory to rescue him, Patrick, Gracie, and Fred from dangers. In Nutman, Daniel had helped them find jobs, friends, and shelter. Deirdre, his beloved, was Daniel's daughter. Every encounter with the man had been straightforward and positive. Therefore, analysis of the data disproved the null hypothesis: Daniel was telling the truth. As a corollary, the others were lying.

"Mark Holdman," Daniel snarled, "I have trained you for years – I thought that I could trust you!"

In his unnoticed corner, Lewis took in a sharp breath. *Whoa! Mark Gregory's here, not Mark Holdman. Then, why did Daniel call him that? He and Mark must be playing at some sort of game.*

Mark continued, his voice dripping with condescension, "I am your disciple! But not the way you think. Stop destroying yourself! Come to your senses, dear Hegofean Daniel! We've deflated your secret rebellion. Commander Gort has the list of the Patriot rebels' names and descriptions. The only choice open to you – if you want to keep your sanity – is to let go of your plan and adopt ours."

Lewis heard a scuffling and guessed that Daniel had thrown himself at Mark. There were grunts and blows and the scrapes of furniture. Lewis felt sick to his stomach, but his doubt was gone. He trusted Daniel and he loved Daniel's daughter. However, Lord Charon threatened them all. He would murder Charon. Then everything would be all right.

Apparently, someone had restrained Daniel, because quiet took over as everyone sat down again. Suddenly, all the men's voices began talking at once.

"Quiet, quiet," Commander Gort squealed to still the furor.

Lord Charon, in a voice like dark velvet, summarized, "As for the rebel uprising, I'm sure Commander Gort will make the arrests promptly. Daniel, Hegofean, the current High Magus, your role is this: Beginning tomorrow night, you will preside over the emergency Council of the Magi. You will declare yourself my ally. You will demand that the Magi of the Horned Edge shall eliminate the renegade College of the Magi in Nutman until this unrest is over. As High Magus, you will do this so that your supporters in Rockeerie may not face retribution. Please stop your warmongering so that your people may not be punished and so that we can return to a peaceful, united era." Charon paused. Then he added softly, "And so that you may keep your little daughter close to you."

Lewis felt a flame of anger twisting in his chest. *That snake! Charon threatens to kill Daniel's people, even his daughter Myra, if he doesn't do what he wants. But whatever Daniel does, he will look like a traitor.* He wanted to burst out into the chamber and murder Charon right then and there. Maybe he should forget the subtle murder and squeeze Charon's throat until it crackled like bubble wrap.

"Your arguments are slightly compelling," Daniel said sarcastically. However, his voice shook. "Let go of me. I have to think." His footsteps came toward the alcove where Lewis was listening. By a quirk of light in a mirror, the two men saw each other at the same time. Daniel took in a quick breath; Lewis covered his mouth to muffle his exclamation.

Their eyes met. Daniel's face looked pale but resolute. He spoke clearly, looking Lewis in the eye, "Many people will be endangered, no matter what I decide. Therefore, by the *Grace* that is here with me, I'll do what I must do. May the Master help me."

Grace? He's talking about Gracie! Lewis's numb self-control shattered, with pain and fear and hope bursting out all at the same time. *Oh God,* he pleaded, *Don't let them hurt Gracie!*

This was too much. Lord Charon was creating a terrible double bind for them all. Daniel had to betray his principles and his people to save the life of a little girl – not Myra, but Lewis's own sister, Gracie. Lewis had to commit murder to prevent more murder.

CHAPTER 18
THE CHISEL

Lewis ventured to peek around the corner as High Magus Daniel walked back to the others. Lord Charon, Commander Gort, Baron Trager, and magus Mark all stood up. Mark bowed low; the others did not even incline their heads.

Daniel declared harshly, "Assemble your renegade meeting! Oh, I'll preside. I'll smile and bow at your bidding. And I'll be damned if your foolish plot succeeds!"

Gort grabbed Daniel's arm. He marched him out of the chamber and the others followed.

Once the room was clear, Lewis came out of the alcove. The paneled walls seemed to spin. He felt weak and he sank onto a couch. Cupping his aching head in his hands, Lewis forced himself to decide what to do next.

He knew what to do. He knew every detail. First, he would send Charon an urgent message, "Come to the cave chamber before the Council, so I can demonstrate our amazing success." The news was a wonderful, potent, irresistible bait to draw Charon into the trap. It promised that Charon's weapons and allies from Earth would arrive on time, or even a little early.

Decisively, Lewis rose. There was pen, paper, and ink in a drawer in the conference room. He wrote a short note in his neat, angular strokes, taking care not to allow any stray inkblots.

Next, striding to the grand vestibule, that central area that led to so many strategic Whitehall rooms, he looked for the messenger he wanted: the white-haired old man who presided over the waiters at palace meals – Lewis dimly remembered his name as Myron. Soon, among many servants preparing for their lords' dinner, came Myron, properly officious in a gray and white Whitehall uniform. The old man carried an order list on a beautifully polished silver tray.

"Take this to Lord Charon," Lewis said authoritatively, handing his note to Myron.

"Dinner is about to begin, sir," the old gentleman protested. "I'm taking the guests' orders to the kitchen."

"Finish your business first," Lewis reassured him, and the chief waiter's face warmed toward him. Lewis stood up straight and spoke with all his authority, "After that, deliver the note. Lord Charon will be very pleased to get this news."

"Yes Fean," said Myron, looking relieved. His expression softened and he looked at Lewis with concern. He pressed his lips together as if holding back words, took a deep breath, and then blurted out, "What about yourself, sir? You don't look well. The master steward has been worried about you. You work too hard. You should eat something to keep up your strength. Aren't you coming to dinner? Or can I send something to your room?"

Lewis winced. Of course, he didn't look well – he was about to commit a murder. Images came to his mind of plunging that chisel into Charon's chest, the gushing blood, the surprise and pain on his mentor's dying face. He was a lost soul, but he must cut out a malignant cancer before Charon could take over Tor – and Earth, before Charon could destroy his family!

Myron waited for Lewis's reply.

Lewis ground his teeth. Was the entire Whitehall staff talking about him? What did it matter to them whether he ate? Tonight, of all nights, he could not force himself to eat. In fact, he did not feel hungry although he hadn't eaten anything except a half a roll and a cup of soup since ... when? Yesterday?

He lied. "Thank you for your offer, Myron," he said, sincerity and gratitude filling his voice. "I'll take supper in my room later. Now, this is of the utmost importance: Give Lord Charon the note. Tell him that I am waiting for him in the laboratory."

"Yes, sir." Myron nodded. Tucking the Lewis's note in his breast pocket, the chief waiter headed toward the kitchen.

Lewis hurried back to the laboratory, sweeping past servants and guards who glanced at him, a little surprised but asking no questions. While he walked, Lewis played out his deadly storyboard, image by image, in his mind.

Charon comes down to the cave chamber. I bow. I gesture toward the obsidian table triumphantly and proclaim, "My lord, we are ready to complete a nexus. Please observe while I – Oh no!" Suddenly, apparently noticing the vandalism for the first time, I look horrified. Amazed, I pick up the offending chisel. "What's this?" I exclaim. Holding the chisel firmly in my hand, I stare wide-eyed at the vandalized control panel. Charon, shocked and angry, bends down to look. Then I kill him.

His mind's storyboard ended just as Lewis came to the end of the hallway. "Golanoya!" he ordered grimly, and the door opened.

As he swept through the laboratory door, however, Lewis literally ran into Lord Charon. The lord staggered. Lewis was hurled against the wall.

"Master!" Lewis gasped, scrambling back to his feet. *Adapt your storyboard to this surprise opening,* he admonished himself. *Recover and get on with it.* Then he saw that Lord Charon was not alone. There was a very large man with him, the man who had kidnapped him and Patrick – Barth Layhew.

His stomach clenched, the laboratory dimmed in a dull brown fog, and Lewis sagged down the wall until his body lay in a tangled heap on the floor. He tried to look up at Charon and Barth and drive on with his plan, but when he opened his mouth, only a croak came out.

Their faces astounded, Charon and Barth stared down at him. Laboratory workers crowded in a circle and murmured in shocked tones. A woman's brassy voice, Mildred's, said loudly, "He's been pushing himself and us to death. No wonder he's passed out."

Lewis slowly pulled himself onto his knees. From there, he managed a floppy bow. Charon gestured, and Lewis staggered to his feet, asserting to himself, *I am not afraid. I will get control of myself.* It was hard to stay balanced. He clutched a nearby table.

Get on with it, do it, kill Charon! inner voices yelled.

I will, he promised.

Still driving forward with his plan, Lewis said, "My lord, the locating system … We can –"

"I know," Lord Charon said gently. The ruler nodded to one of the lab workers, who steadied Lewis, holding onto his arm. Charon asked, dark eyes soft with compassion, "Why did you miss your afternoon appointment with me? What happened? Are you ill?"

"No. Yes. I – I didn't feel well." That much was true. "I was working, and I forgot the time." Also true. "However, I now understand both the problem and the solution. We can complete a nexus tonight!"

"Show me," Charon stated, his eyes glinting with excitement and approval, his voice eager.

Although the room seemed to spin, Lewis shook off the lab worker's supporting arm. He said, emphatically, "Now, come with me to the locating chamber." He glanced at Barth and then away. "Just the two of us, Lord Charon," he added.

Barth snorted, "You won't get rid of me that easily, Louie boy. Did you hope that I'd vanished from your life forever? After all, next to you, I'm the greatest authority in Tor on Charon's locating system. I'm coming down with you and my Master."

In their circle of curiosity, the lab workers continued to press close and chatter to each other. Lewis snapped, "All of you, clear out! Get to work!"

Abruptly, the workers scattered back to their stations. Lewis frowned at Barth. "If my Master gives permission, you may come down with us."

Barth raised himself to his full height and pushed his face closer to Lewis's. "Who are you to –"

Lord Charon interrupted smoothly, "We will go down. Now. The three of us."

Barth shut his mouth. Lewis turned his back on the huge man.

They went through the special room that housed the noretha and came to the ornate metal door that led to the cave chamber. Lewis did not bother to speak; he grimly thought, *Hot Marble.* The door opened, and they started down the spiral of the bronze stairway. Lewis had to grip the rail hard, but he did not stumble. His heart pounded, the world still spun around his head, but his brain felt cold and calm as an arctic lake.

At last, Lewis had Charon where he wanted him. He'd kill Charon, and then Barth would destroy him. *Too bad.* With his own death so near, the amethyst crystals on the chamber walls had never glinted so lovely, the solid black obsidian table had never shone with such mysterious beauty.

"The last barrier to Earth was the resonance tuning," Lewis lectured, his voice cool. "Now, as you can see, I've removed the carpet that surrounded the locating table. See the augmentation rings around the base of the table? Many were burned out, but now they are repaired. The system is ready. Master, you may connect from world to world."

While Lewis talked, he bent down, caressed the gleaming polished gold rings, and grasped the chisel. Then he let his eyes turn toward the control panel on the side of the table as if it were a ship's wheel and he the captain. He let his jaw drop, his eyes bulge, and dramatically gasped. "What's this!" he exploded.

As Lewis had planned, Charon quickly bent down to look at the control panel. Barth crouched down, also. "Aw, crap!" Barth exclaimed. "Somebody's hacked at the solid-state structure. The whole thing's ruined!"

Calm and detached as a man playing chess, Lewis saw that Charon was in position. *It is time. Now I must strike.*

But he hesitated. A voice rippled in his heart, faint as water flowing over smooth stone, *What about your family? Suppose Patrick and Gracie get hurt because of your action? Suppose they get hurt despite your action! What will your parents think if they hear about it? Their son – a murderer!*

Charon straightened. The strategic moment was almost lost. It was now or never. Lewis took a step toward the ruler. He drew back the chisel and swung it hard toward Charon's chest.

His aim was awful. He missed, swiping only air.

And then Barth grabbed his arm.

The strength of boiling anger surged into Lewis's chest. He ripped his arm away from Barth's grip and stabbed at Charon again. The ruler, his face stricken and sad and angry at the same time, like a man who has been bitten by his beloved dog, jumped back but stumbled against the edge of the obsidian table.

Lewis leaped at Charon. He grabbed the Lord of Tor around the neck and pressed the chisel hard against the man's jaw under his ear. "Remember this, Barth?" he snarled. "Remember your stinking son of a bezub's butt holding a knife to my brother's throat? Beginning to cut so that the blood trickled down?"

He pressed even harder so that the chisel cut into Charon's skin. However, the man's smell of clean soap and rich cloth reminded Lewis of his father. Compassion and respect fought with the fury that controlled him.

Barth crouched, ready to spring. His face was red, and his accusing eyes fixed themselves on Lewis's.

"What have you done?" Charon gasped. "What possessed you to destroy months of your own hard work?"

Lewis felt a sting like a reprimanded child, but he held on to his chisel and Charon's neck. "Nothing," he said in a voice of steel, "possessed me."

Barth's red lips snarled, his eyebrows drew together, and his hands drew into claws. "If you hurt my lord, Louie boy, I'll kill you," he promised. "Slowly."

Clutching Charon even tighter and digging in the chisel so hard that blood indeed began to run down Charon's neck, Lewis replied, his voice steady, "Bartie, do you think I care? No. I utterly reject you and your Master, and your stupid Saoma. Charon must die. If I die also, so be it. The locating system will never be repaired. You are cut off from Earth forever!"

Close to his ear, Charon spoke, "You ken not what you're saying, Fean Lewis." His long, calm hand rose and stroked Lewis's deadly hand, and suddenly, overcome by total shame, Lewis drew the chisel an inch from Charon's throat.

Barth pounced. He yanked Charon away from Lewis. The Torish ruler sprang out of range; the lord was breathing hard, blood seeped into his gray robe from the wound on his neck, and his face was pale. Charon's dark eyes, so warm and intelligent, caressed Lewis's. They were wet with tears, but he blocked the stairway with his body to keep Lewis from escaping.

Chisel firmly seated in his hand, Lewis edged around the table, keeping it between him and Barth. Inexorably, he moved closer to Charon.

Barth, however, said, "Fred told me all about, you, Louie. You arrogant butt brain, he hates you! You have no friends anymore because they've all become sick of you. Nobody can trust you. For instance, you're lying about the table. My guess is that you're exaggerating the damage. It could be repaired easily enough if you put your mind to it. The schematics are stored in the computer files. You and I can cast a new control panel." To Charon, he added, with a nasty sneer on his red lips, "With a little leverage, your prize scientist will come around again. Consider some physical persuasion. Torture perhaps. He scares easily."

Still a few feet away, Charon replied, his voice cool but trembling slightly, "Think you so?"

"Yes," Barth stated.

Lewis watched Barth's eyes, which were cold and mean and purposeful. He saw the tiny spark that signified the attack, and when Barth lunged forward Lewis dodged easily. He felt entirely calm. Power surged in his mind and his heart. He had no doubt that he could kill the larger man.

From behind, Charon slammed into Lewis. He grabbed Lewis's right wrist and squeezed, trying to force him to release the chisel. Silently, relentlessly, Lewis fought back. He used Charon's grip to swivel around and began to win the tug-of-war until he pressed the chisel inexorably closer toward Charon's neck once more.

"Stop, Lewis!" Charon yelled. "I've done nothing to hurt you!"

While Charon struggled to hold Lewis away, Barth crept forward. Striking quickly, he kicked Lewis's feet out from under him and threw his heavy body on top of him. Lewis stabbed at Barth, but the big man clutched his wrist and held on, the sharp metal tip quivering inches from Barth's eye.

"Master! He's insane! Go get help!" Barth gasped. Charon sped up the stairs.

Breathing hard but unbroken in his determination, Lewis forced the chisel closer and closer to Barth. The big man stank of heat, sweat, and fear. Strength coursed steadily through Lewis's body, and he knew he would be victorious. Barth's face began to look terrified. "Help me!" he screamed.

Sounds of feet pounded down the stairway. Charon returned with gray-uniformed guards and several lab workers. Two strong men seized both of Lewis's hands. The one on the right twisted his wrist so that the chisel fell to the floor. With Barth's help, they flipped him face down on the floor and pinned his arms behind his back.

Even now, Lewis felt preternaturally calm inside. It occurred to him that he was only in the eye of a hurricane and that more terror was to come; however, his mind seemed completely detached as handcuffs clamped around his wrists. He did not struggle when the two guards hefted him to his feet but stood quietly, dangerously ready to attack again if he got the chance.

Barth, his chest heaving, sweat pouring down his face, stepped back as if Lewis might still overpower him. His hand went to his eye as if to see if it was still intact and he spat a Lanthran word that Lewis had never heard before.

Lord Charon, keeping a safe distance, shook his head sadly. "You have so much promise and I trusted you. However, I can trust you no longer." He gestured toward the distal end of the cave chamber, farthest from the stairway. "*Epah!*" he ordered.

Where there had been amethyst encrusted wall, an ironbound archway now appeared. "*Pyo te!*" The guards moved Lewis toward the archway.

Barth dropped to his knees before Charon, breathing hard and sweating dark stains on his shirt. "Give him to me, Master. I'll make him fix the damage he's done."

Charon looked at Lewis. "Perhaps that will bring him back to me. Very well, Barth. Have your way with him – but keep him alive."

Barth rose. He waved toward the archway and Lewis saw a dark rock passage beyond. "Take him to the dungeon," Barth ordered the guards. "Cell number thirty-four."

They swiveled their prisoner around and began to march Lewis off into the passage.

"Bye, bye, Louie," Barth called sarcastically. "I'll see you later."

CHAPTER 19
MEETINGS IN MOORWAY

To the flaming pit with Baron Trager, and cheers for muddy Moorway," said Tom Forschwynn with a satisfied smile. "And here's to the Canal Street Tavern, a great place to work before my concert at Whitehall." He raised his cheese pastry from the bakery next door in a mock toast and took a huge bite, an expression of near ecstasy on his face.

"Cheers," Fred seconded, toasting the Tavern with his heavily buttered, partly chewed sourdough roll. He turned his face upward to soak up rays from the summer sun. He added lightly but with double entendre, "And here's to our 'adventure.' It ends here in Moorway … 'and they all live happily ever after.' I hope."

Fred and Tom lounged against the back door of the tavern's two-story brick building, taking a mid-morning break. They had come up from Gapstand and found a job here before the planned Moorway concert. Morning sunlight poured down over the industrial cityscape like warm honey. So far, the day was pleasantly warm, not stinking hot like it would be in the afternoon.

Tom took a long, deep breath. "Ah, the Moorway air! It smells of road debris, horse manure, wet mud, piles of garbage, factory effluvium, and – thank Radyah – the glorious aroma of baking bread."

"Sure, it's wonderful. Don't forget the canal perfume." Fred could see a faint chartreuse haze gathering over the canal that bordered the tavern on the left. It gave off a questionable odor, like water seeping through a septic field. "Where are all the mosquitoes this morning? Where do all the bugs go when they're not bugging people?" he wondered aloud.

The back door banged opened and their employer, Mister Swa, the Canal Street Tavern owner emerged. He was a short, plump, and middle-aged man with a shiny balding head, a large push-broom moustache, dark skin, bright eyes, and more than his share of energy. His Lanthran name was long and unpronounceable, so Fred called him "Mister Swa."

Mister Swa bustled out into the pleasant air and light on the back stoop, holding a steaming mug. Fred smelled hot coffee, a strong-tasting import from the Laestes Isles.

Tom inhaled appreciatively. "Ah. A wonderful aroma."

"There's a fresh pot in the kitchen," Mister Swa said.

"I'll get some." Tom moved to go back inside the tavern. However, Mister Swa held up a hand to stop him.

"Wait a second," the tavern owner said. "You, my star performer," he beamed at Tom, "have your concert opportunity at Whitehall. In front of Lord Charon himself!" Pulling a fat envelope out of his pocket, "You've done well for me since you came up from Gapstand, and I'm very happy with you. Now, take a look at this."

Tom took the envelope. "It has the official seal of Whitehall! But it's addressed to you, Mister Swa, not to us."

"Well, open it and find out what it says!" Mister Swa demanded cheerfully.

Tom handed the envelope to Fred. "You open it."

Okay, okay, let the subua handle the hot potato. Fred noticed that the classy envelope was neatly addressed to the tavern owner in swirly, loopy calligraphy. The wax seal was firmly attached, so Fred pulled out his large switchblade which he had recently bought at a Moorway shop. *No airport gate on Earth would tolerate it, hehe. However, after Trager I've got to carry a good weapon.* Delicately, he pried the seal loose, slit the envelope, and pulled out a folded sheet of fine linen paper.

"Looks scary, Mister Swa!" Fred put the knife discretely away in its ankle sheath.

"Read it!" Mister Swa urged. "It's from our high ruler!"

"Do you already know what it says?" Tom asked.

Mister Swa smiled, his face smug. "More or less."

Fred held up the document and read it aloud. Then he looked

up, both eyebrows rising into his hair, which needed a cut. "O boy, this is like getting an invitation to the White House. Hey – it is getting an invitation to the White House!" He laughed.

Tom grabbed the letter and read it to himself while Mister Swa waited, rocking on his toes and heels. "I can't believe it!" Tom exclaimed. "Despite our twisty route to get here, that concert is going to happen." However, to Fred's great amazement, Tom dropped his hand and his face fell.

"What's the matter?" Fred asked. "We wanted to get into –"

"You'll do fine," reassured Mister Swa, misreading Tom's anxiety, and patting him on the back. "Just do what you've been doing in my Tavern, and all of Tor will pack themselves into Rose Hall to see you."

Tom smiled, but it looked forced. "Thank you, Mister Swa."

Fred echoed, "Thank you for the opportunity!" His heart beat faster; his chest seemed to have gotten bigger as he tried to imagine Tom and him in Lord Charon's palace.

"There's more, Tom. A man came by last night. He gave his name as 'Hermann' and brought me a large package. He just said it was for 'the Forschwynn lad.'" Mister Swa winked. "Forschwynn? The Bard of Bardia – I could guess what he brought. Never mind – I put the package in the cupboard behind the bar and I planned to surprise you with it today. What better time than now, when you have the go-ahead letter for the concert!"

Tom asked, "So – you know what's in the package?"

Laughing, Mister Swa bounced up and down with excitement. "Let's just say it has beautiful curves and vibrates when you caress it! Now, if it were a woman ..."

Tom's jaw dropped. "The lute! Let me see it!" He jumped into the tavern like a setter leaping to retrieve a pheasant.

"Hermann –" Fred began excitedly, but just as Mister Swa began to answer, Tom came back in triumph, carrying his precious lute.

Beaming, the bard said, "I had no idea I'd ever see this again! I can't believe –"

"Play it for me!" Mister Swa insisted. "Let's go into the public room."

Fred held the door so that Tom with his glorious lute and Mister Swa could file into the tavern's common room. The interior was still cool, rather dark because only a wall lantern was lit, but all the doors were opened to let in fresh morning air.

The three men sat at a round table. Fred set the contract, the pen, and the concert invitation down on the tabletop, carefully avoiding the coffee ring by wiping it with his t-shirt. Mister Swa leaned his chair back, tapping his foot in anticipation, and Tom cradled the lute in his arms, fondling the wood and tuning the strings.

Tom began to play. Suddenly Fred sensed that the tavern's large common room felt enchanted. Every trouble and every happiness he had ever experienced gathered to rest at this single instant in time. It was as if the magical pinpoint of the primordial universe was in his heart, ready for the creation moment.

Immediately the clatter back in the kitchen ceased. Even people walking on Canal Street outside paused near the double doors to listen.

Tom sang a children's song that had a pretty andante tune:

> *Joy, I give you joy!*
> *No summer morning dawns so bright,*
> *Nor little children sing*
> *Expectant of such good as might*
> *Those here now listening.*

When the sound at last died away, even the strong sunlight seemed to fade. Street noises again drifted through the open door and the cooks resumed their clatter in the kitchen.

A rosy-cheeked woman had stopped near the boardwalk near the door to listen to Tom's music. Fred noticed with approval her heart-shaped face, dark eyebrows like wings of a soaring bird, and smiling lips like the petals of a pink rose. She wore a blue gingham dress with white lace and her thick hair was coiled about her head in a braid.

What a beautiful woman, Fred thought. His heart melted inside him.

As she came closer, Fred saw an energetic brood of four dark-haired girls in her wake. *Cute mom, cute daughters,* Fred thought. He wished he could give them all an armful of daisies and sunshine. The smallest was a toddler holding her mother's hand. The next smallest jumped happily up and down in time with Tom's music. The next largest, a pretty preteen with glossy black hair tied back in a ponytail, had her sapphire eyes fixed on Tom's face. Tallest was a husky girl with braided hair who leaned on a crutch, favoring her right cast-enclosed foot.

Because he felt sorry that the attractive lady's daughter was very lame, Fred looked at the girl more closely. She had a rather round face, thick eyebrows curving over intelligent brown eyes, a straight nose, and full lips. *Who does that girl remind me of?* he wondered.

He began to mentally tick off names from his past: *Amanda, the pretty Lebanese girl down the street when he was in junior high school? Percale, from Spain? No, no, no!* The lame girl looked so familiar, but he couldn't pin down who –

At that moment, the lame girl looked away from the bard and his lute, and her brown eyes met Fred's. A current like a strong electric shock jolted Fred from his head to his feet. His jaw dropped open. "My God, Tom," he exclaimed, "look over there!"

Tuned into his own music, Tom did not pay attention.

"For the love of Pete," Fred yelled, "there's Patrick!" He leapt to his feet. "Patrick! Patrick! It's me – Fred!" He whistled, jumped up and down, and waved his hands. In the process, he knocked over his big mug of milk. "Oops! Sorry, Tom!"

The milk ran swiftly across the table. It poured onto Tom's lap, soaked his crotch and, worse, leaked into the lute.

"*Bilitye as!*" Tom swore, scooting backward.

The girls giggled at the potent Lanthran expression. The lady quickly turned and shooed her children away from the tavern. The girl who was apparently Patrick looked back, gave them a mischievous wave, but obediently followed the lady across the street.

"Wait, Ma'am, wait!" Fred called. He ran out of the tavern into the street, almost getting run over by a carriage. He sideswiped two horses, dodged an old lady with a cane at the side of the road, knocked over three Blue People carrying a load of lumber, and pursued the lady.

In front of a small grocery shop, the young woman stopped. She got between Fred and her children, facing him. Her very blue eyes glittered hot sparks and, although she was petite, she straightened boldly to her full height. "What do you want?"

Behind her, the girls' faces were all wide-eyed and

apprehensive, except for the lame one. The brown eyes that had met his blinked in surprise, but they were also filled with recognition, and the full lips broke into a beaming smile. She – he – was definitely Patrick, despite the long braid and red-checked dress.

Suddenly Fred realized that he must look like a large, sweaty sleaze ball with a stubbly face who had rushed out of a tavern. *Ack,* he thought, *I've got to change my approach.*

He held his hands out, palms toward the lady. "Please, ma'am. I'm not drunk and I'm not trying to be rude. But I really need to talk to you." He lowered his voice, "I know Patrick Brahmindura and he knows me. I'm his brother's friend. We came from the same place. Do you understand?"

Her voice was firm when she said, "No." However, she glanced at the girl that Fred had recognized as Patrick.

Fred followed her gaze pointedly to show her that he absolutely knew he was right. "She" was a more mature version of the roly-poly preteen who had found the hot marble. He had grown several inches taller, gotten slimmer, but his expression was the same: lively, curious, and imaginative.

Patrick pressed past the girls. "I know this guy. He's okay." His voice had deepened. It broke on the last word, and Fred almost laughed.

The lady measured Fred very critically. "What do you call yourself?"

"Uh," Fred suddenly felt very stupid. *The prettiest woman I've ever seen on two worlds is talking to me, and here I stand, looking like a fool.* He remembered the Lanthran equivalent of his name and winced. His last name sounded ridiculous in Lanthran. He hoped it didn't mean anything obscene. "Fred Jontz."

"I'm Jane Tuttle." The lady relented a little from her defensive stance.

"Where do you live? When can I visit?" Fred asked.

Jane Tuttle considered, then made up her mind. "You can meet us tomorrow night. Wait at the fourth hour at the corner of Canal Street and Bowser Lane. There's a streetlamp there, a household goods shop, and a bridge over the canal. My brother and some friends will find you. We'll hear what you have to say."

She swept her children and Patrick away. Fred watched,

feeling both elated and stunned, until they turned a corner out of sight.

Chapter 20
CAPTURED ON CANAL STREET

At dusk – about ten o'clock in the evening, Earth time, he figured, Fred walked purposefully south up Canal Street. He tried to act casual. *Let's see,* he thought, *I'm looking for a corner where there's a streetlamp, a shop and a bridge over the canal. There must be a hundred of corners like that on Canal Street. One of them is Bowser Lane.*

Several mosquitoes buzzed around his face. Fred swatted one that had landed on his arm, leaving a mess of blood and smashed bug. "Gotcha!" He swatted another. Even in the evening it was so hot and steamy that he wore a sleeveless tee shirt, which exposed plenty of meat for the predators.

Canal Street ran due north, straight as an arrow. Away in the distance, the Snowy Mountains seemed to float above houses, shops, and a mass of squatty brick factories to mock low, hot, humid Moorway. Whitehall, Lord Charon's citadel, towered to the northeast.

Fred wasn't yet sure where Bowser Lane was, so he stopped and swatted at another mosquito. Before he finished his downswing, however, a strong grip stopped his forearm. "What – " he began, but another grip tightened on his other arm. Despite the heat, his body froze with alarm.

Two men with shaven heads and biceps like steelworkers held his arms with comradely "affection" but more than brotherly strength. Fred struggled to break loose and swing at them, but, behind them, a familiar bass voice growled in Lanthran, "Don't."

They steered him around a corner into a dusky alley. There was no street sign, but Fred hoped, he really hoped that they were taking him down Bowser Lane and not to a dead-end where he would get Dead.

CHAPTER 21
YOU STINK!

Patrick fidgeted with his crutch, stumping around the Tuttle's kitchen impatiently. "Why do we have to go to bed early?" he complained, for the tenth time.

"Yes, why?" his "sisters" Bessie, Katie, and June chorused.

"We're having a meeting," Mama Jane replied. Uncle Curly tipped his chair back with a "Do not argue" expression on his face.

Mama Jane pushed back a stray lock of dark hair from her forehead because the kettle on the stove was adding steam to the already muggy air. "Besides, it will be all talk and no play."

Before she had kissed them all goodnight, Mama Jane lifted a jar full of molasses cookies. "Now, take a cookie, get a kiss, and upstairs with all of you!"

Patrick grabbed the biggest cookie he could find and stomped out after the girls. Bessie carried the candle lamp. However, before he started up the stairs, Uncle Curly's voice called, "Patrick, come back. I want you to stay downstairs with us for a while."

Patrick almost choked on his bite of cookie. Coughing and hacking, he clumped back to the kitchen. When his throat cleared, he gasped, "Uncle Curly, you … you didn't call me 'Martha!'"

Uncle Curly sat at the table, back to the wall, empty chairs to each side. As usual, his face looked cheerful, but his eyes seemed serious. Mama Jane, lips pressed together and tension around her eyes, perched on a stool by the wrought iron stove.

"I don't want Patrick down here when your friends come," Jane stated.

"I don't agree," Curly said. "He needs to identify this 'Fred' person tonight. It would be like the Horned Edge to trick us with an imposter."

His heart leaping for joy, Patrick jumped so quickly that his crutch got tangled in his feet and he almost toppled over. "Fred? Here tonight?"

"I understand why you want the boy here," Mama Jane retorted, giving Patrick a steadying hand, "but I'm afraid. If he should know too much about our plans, he'll be in great danger."

When he heard that, Patrick spurted out, "Learn what?"

Uncle Curly responded to Mamma Jane, "You don't want the lad to get hurt. Neither do I. But we must risk it. We might be fooled about Fred, but Patrick won't. Do not forget, Jane, the boy's from Earth, as is this person Fred."

Jane winced. "Do not speak of the forbidden world!"

Curly pointed out bluntly, "'Tis absolutely necessary. People from Earth bring our doom – they also bring our salvation."

"He's only a child!" Jane exploded. She looked angrier than Patrick had ever seen her before. Her form darkened and she towered over her brother and Patrick. The kitchen's atmosphere crackled with emotion.

"Aye," Curly responded, and his voice was soft. "I know. Howe'er, Jane, we need him tonight. Let him stay."

Closing her eyes, sighing deeply, Jane began to relax. Patrick could still feel electricity in the air, but when she opened her eyes, Jane looked calm again.

So full of excitement that he could hardly contain himself, Patrick propped his crutch against the wall. He gathered the obnoxious skirts in one hand and hefted himself onto a stool next to Jane. Once he got settled, he took a more careful bite of his cookie, and then asked, "When is Fred supposed to arrive?"

"Soon," Curly said. His eyes ran over Patrick and took in his wig and dress.

"Can I take off the wig?" Patrick asked.

"No. Yes." Jane and Curly spoke simultaneously.

Patrick snatched off the braided wig and instantly felt pleasantly cooler. *Fred's coming; oh boy, that's great!* Perched on his stool, a grin splitting his face in two, he felt happier than he had for ages. Of course, it was a typical summer night in Moorway, which meant breathless heat and sticky humidity. Of course, his skin was sweaty, and his privates itched under the skirts, but he didn't care. *Fred's coming!*

Uncle Curly and Mama Jane talked to each other, grownup talk that didn't sound interesting, so Patrick turned his attention to seeing Fred tonight. *My buddy, Fred!* He remembered Fred's jokes, his hugs, and the way he could play computer games so well but still let you feel like an expert, too.

If Fred had been with us, he thought, *Lewis and I wouldn't have been kidnapped. Fred's big and strong; he and my brother would have fought Barth off.*

At that moment, a deep ache lodged in his right ankle. *What'd I do? Maybe it's the crutch.* Patrick shook his leg, but movement did no good. *Maybe it's just a pinched nerve.* He tried to forget it and think about Fred.

Thinking about Fred didn't help. The ache grew more intense. Like an internal snake, pain like a red-hot poker stabbed the inside of his anklebone, the one that had been broken.

Patrick's mouth opened to yell, but he stuffed his fist in it. Meanwhile, Mama Jane said, "Many of Moorway's physicians are Patriots. Could they rescue the boy from Moorway the same way they rescued him from Torgard?"

Curly looked hard at Patrick, apparently deciding whether to discuss secrets in front of the boy. "Nay. The Horned Edge is suspicious of medical people since the day you and the children left Torgard. The doctor and a nurse were arrested. Even under torture, they wouldn't tell where he was, and they died."

Horrified, his stomach twisting, Patrick looked at his new family in the cozy kitchen. *If I complain about my ankle, Jane and Curly will take me to a doctor. Then the police might find out and ...*

Torture. He looked at Mama Jane, who was getting out coffee cups from a cupboard and his mouth went dry. He looked at Uncle Curly, who was easy-going, gentle with him and his "sisters." His stomach felt sick at what he imagined.

Carefully not wincing, Patrick shifted his weight on the stool. The ankle hurt like crazy. *Maybe it will quit hurting by the time Fred gets –*

A rap sounded at the kitchen door. Curly stood up. "It's Nat and Harwath."

Patrick forced his attention to the two men coming in. One

was a short but very broad-shouldered man. "Nat!" Curly smiled and shook hands with him. "I'm glad you could get away from your stables. Sit here and have some coffee!"

Nat kissed Jane and said, "Aye, Janie, coffee would be great. Even better if you have a nip of whiskey to put in it!" He had a small bullet head on a thick neck, slick black hair tied back in a braid, and a large gold nose ring. He laughed, gestured freely, and showed all his teeth when he smiled. Patrick had seen him before at the Tuttle's midnight conferences.

In contrast to Nat, Harwath was long, thin, bald, had an aristocratic face with a long nose, and looked perpetually sleepy. By what he had overheard during his nights of sneaking down from bed, Patrick knew that Harwath had an important position at Whitehall and he wasn't sure what it was, but he knew for sure one thing: *Uncle Curly, Mama Jane, and these guys are Patriot leaders. They're organizing the revolt.*

Patrick forgot his ankle when he heard an insistent scratching noise outside. It sounded like a dog wanted to come in, but the Tuttles had no dog. Curly, Jane and their fellow conspirators suddenly became silent. "That's Hermann and the others. I'll get the door," Jane said. She jumped up from her stool, but Nat rose and blocked the way.

"No, Jane. I will do it," Nat stated. A short metal rod appeared in his hand, the lamplight reflecting in a long red line across its length. Patrick thought, his mouth dropping open, *Is that a gun? Having lethal electronic technology is completely ... He could get a death sentence if he's caught!* He held his breath as Nat slowly withdrew the bolt from the door.

Another scratch sounded at the door and Nat jerked it open. Patrick's heart pumped hard as a man who looked like a black vampire slid through the door. Two other large men crowded into the small, dim kitchen, arms gripping another man, apparently a prisoner. Patrick could smell their rank sweat mixing with the scent of coffee from the stove. It was scary, but somehow exciting, as if he were in an adventure movie.

The prisoner was ... "Fred!" Patrick yelled. The next instant – he didn't even remember jumping up and running – he had both arms around Fred's neck.

"Patrick! I can't believe it!" Fred exclaimed, hugging Patrick.

"I can't believe it!" He drew back and held Patrick by the shoulders, looking at him as if to rememorize his appearance. "I thought you and Lewis were dead! But here you are –"

"And I thought –"

"And I was, but everything's changed!" Fred beamed at him. His curly blond hair had grown longer, he'd lost most of his gut, but he still had the same twinkling blue eyes that Patrick remembered from months ago.

Patrick leaped and danced, even though his bum ankle screamed.

"Uh," Fred began, his voice a little tight like he had to make a confession, "Patrick, I … need to tell you …"

Trying to reassure everyone, Patrick painted the happy picture he had kept in his memory, "Fred's cool. He's my brother's best friend. He came with us when we found that hot marble and he helped –"

Curly said softly, "I very much doubt, *bibat,* that he's still your brother's friend." Nat's face was very hard, too. So was Harwath's. They looked like they could rip Fred apart.

Hermann, looking more than ever like Dracula, bared his teeth and said, "Fred Jontz – this *dittiean,* this empty bag – tried to fill his aching, jealous belly by sucking up praise from Torish spies."

"Huh?"

"Don't you remember Barth Layhew?"

Patrick remembered only too well.

"Fred – this *ath bilat asde* – helped Barth kidnap you. The *sebizeorath* used you as a hostage to force your brother to open a special door – do you remember that, too?"

Cold horror prickled every vein in Patrick's body.

"This *nobbo* Fred intended to go with Barth to serve Saoma in Tor, but Barth wisely left him behind. Lewis and you … kidnapped and abused! Nine – no, ten innocent magi … slaughtered!"

"No!" Patrick cried. "That's not true!" When he saw Fred's face, however, he wasn't so sure. Fred hung his head and looked at the floor.

Hermann continued, "Now this piece of filth has come to Moorway. Laddie, I think that he plans to betray us again. Some friend!"

Patrick felt a blow to his stomach like a horse had kicked him. He imagined the terror of the magi in Bardia when Barth and his accomplices had murdered them. Then he pictured the kind nurse and doctor who had helped him, followed by a horrible image of them being skinned alive. His arms began to shake with anger. In that instant, Fred's blue eyes looked deceptive instead of friendly.

He pulled away from Fred as far as he could get without falling off his stool. "You stink!" he yelled.

CHAPTER 22
THE SOUL'S JEWEL

After Curly helped Patrick get upstairs to bed, he came back to the kitchen and said to the Patriots, "All right, are ye satisfied that this man is truly Fred Jontz?

Hermann said through his teeth, "Yes. Kill him."

Fred, his heart pounding, broke in, "What you said about me was true, but it isn't anymore; I've changed! I belong to Sir Forschwynn now. He redeemed me!"

Contradicting Hermann, Jane asserted, "Truly, we can trust the Bard of Bardia. Do not kill his subua."

Taking a deep, deep breath, Fred hoped he could live … for many more years.

Harwath pursed his lips. "We have little time. Therefore, we must bring Sir Thomas here as soon as possible."

Curly nodded toward Fred and addressed Hermann. "You know the bard. Go, find Sir Thomas. If he confirms what this … Fred person … has told us, then we might include him in our plans. If not —"

His eyes flashed meaningfully at Nat's weapon. Fred imagined his bloated body floating in a Moorway canal, a black laser hole in his eye, and his stomach lurched.

Hermann left, the Patriots conversed, ignoring Fred, except for keeping their weapons at hand and guarding the door.

"There's another way to look at things," Nat said in his broad Moorway street accent. "'Tis terrible that Rockeerie fell to invasion and that Viceroy Daniel is taken prisoner. Howe'er there's something to be gained by it. King Norhe must rescue his viceroy, and very shortly he'll send an army. The entire Horned

Edge oppression will be destroyed!"

"I thought that King Norhe believed the rumors about Daniel," Curly replied, raising his eyebrows.

"The old goat did." Harwath snorted with disrespect. "But Daniel's daughter, Deirdre, made such a strong case and impressed so many in the royal court – especially Queen Margaret – that he had no choice but to respond with the help she asked for."

Fred choked and coughed. Deirdre! He pictured Deirdre the way he'd last seen her, peachy, creamy, powerful and soft at the same time, but her eyes on Lewis. Instantly, he smelled something like burning rubber while the old jealousy stabbed his heart. *I could put a kink in the Patriots' plan! Once they trust me, I could jinx their revolt, and nobody would realize it was me. Suppose Lewis gets killed – then Deirdre will look at me the way she used to look at him!*

However, even as the jealous fury in him got stronger, an inner advisor with a sense of humor, said, *Fred, give yourself a Time Out. If you don't settle down, I'll make you go to the basement until you can be nice!*

Fred's mood changed instantly. The image tickled him, and he snickered.

"What was that about?" Curly asked suspiciously, pressing the gun to Fred's forehead.

"Oh," Fred replied, afraid again but about to laugh hysterically, "I remember Deirdre very well. If anybody can stir up the whole Bardian army, she can."

*   *   *

Fred slumped at the table for another weary hour or two, while the Patriots talked and drank coffee and kept their eyes on him. Finally, Hermann scratched at the door; he and Tom came inside. Everyone stood, including Fred, and bowed.

Soon, after they were all seated and had yet more hot coffee, Curly asked the Big Question: "Sir Thomas, can we trust Fred not to betray us?"

Tom looked at Fred, silent, while Fred's stomach did loops. Tom finally answered, "I want to help you, Fred; that's why I came here with Hermann. However, I have a few questions to ask before I can give my word to these people that they can trust you."

Fred let out a deep breath, trying not to faint.

"If you betray us, we will lose you." Tom said. "You may not be killed by us, but you will certainly die." His voice sounded cold. "Do you think, after buying your life, that I want to lose you? Or, have you decided that you are not important?"

"No. That is, all right – Sure, I am important."

Hermann snorted, but the rest of the Patriots curiously watched Tom and Fred.

"That answer is not good enough," Tom said. "Your life's story is part of a terrible war. The war is not only about Bardia and Tor, even Earth and Lanthra, but with you and the powers in the heavenly realms. People will be devastated if Saoma – yes, he is real – gets his way. Tell me again, are you integrally important in this war?"

Fred thought, *Me? Important? Har!* He realized that he was grinding his teeth, but he thought he should bluster and say what they wanted to hear. Fear pressed hard as he stared at Nat's high-tech, deadly weapon. However, a subtle nudging in the back of his mind made him sweat even more. He knew what he should say now, but he didn't want to admit the truth.

I can't do that, he told the nudging presence.

You must, an inaudible voice said.

Fred shivered, even though it was stiflingly hot. *They'll kill me if I tell what I'm really thinking,* he whined to the voice. *It's just not good enough.*

You'll have to risk that, the voice replied.

Fred felt sweat ooze down his forehead, the salt burning his eyes. The one thing he did not want to do was what he had to do. *Okay, all right, I'll do it. I'll tell them the truth.*

Feeling like he weighed a million pounds, Fred forced his head up to look at everyone. He raised a hot, damp hand "Ever see a Moorway cockroach, folks?" He coughed because his throat had knotted up. "That's what my inner space is like. I betrayed Lewis because I'm a stinking vermin. I thought, when I became Tom's subua, that maybe I could fix that; I wanted to somehow atone for what I've done. But even just now I was thinking about betraying you to get in good with Charon's crowd, see an end to Lewis, and have Lewis's girlfriend, Deirdre."

Curly looked totally bewildered. He turned to the bard. "Sir Thomas, I thought you said we can trust your subua! Can we, or can we not?"

Tom glared at Fred and exploded, "Don't you understand anything, Fred? Are you so blind? Can't you see who you really are? Why did I pay the ransom to keep you from the death penalty?"

Fred retorted, "Because you are an idiot!"

"Well, at last!" Hermann laughed. "You finally tell the truth!"

"Tom," Fred continued, "you are just an altruistic teenager. You are gullible enough to pity me, rich enough to throw money away on me, stupid enough to go out on a quest with me as your sidekick. Why should I matter? I'm not the greatest or the best at anything. I don't have any amazing talent like you or any secret formula to make people want me. I'm not even –"

He coughed on some burning liquid in his throat and could not continue.

"Finally, the truth," sneered Hermann.

Tom said an Anglo-Saxon word that Fred had not heard for a very long time. "No, Hermann. He admits one truth – but not the other." Pounding the table, the young man yelled, "Keep talking! Who are you, Fred?"

Immediately a long-hidden insight gushed out from Fred's deep places. He struggled to push it back, but words and sobs broke through, "I'm a small red ruby. Not the biggest jewel nor the brightest, but still one of the adornments that beautify God."

He felt completely spent, as though he had run a hundred miles a day for a hundred days carrying a huge rock but had just set it down.

Curly said to the others, "It seems that we can trust the man."

Chapter 23
MIGRAINE

Where were you, Daniel? Why weren't you at breakfast?" asked Roger Whitehaven of Smythe, running to catch up with Daniel. His red-blond eyebrows crooked like hawk wings over narrow-set eyes.

Daniel barely glanced at him. His mind was busy replaying this morning's stupid drama with the Commander of Charon's armies. Gort had taken him down from the tower and had read him the riot act in a side chamber on the main floor. Gort's piggy face sweated and menaced as he told Daniel that he must do nothing to change Charon's script for the Council — or else.

Daniel strode forward. Roger and dozens of other magi in formal robes followed him through Whitehall's great central vestibule. The opening reception and sumptuous breakfast buffet — which Daniel had missed — had energized the magi and they were talkative, but his own stomach churned. The oatmeal he had eaten with Gracie in their tower prison lay in it like an indigestible lump.

Roger snared his attention by putting a firm hand on his arm. "Daniel! Did you hear me?"

"I had my breakfast, ahem, upstairs," Daniel replied with a meaningful cough.

He glanced casually back toward the military officers that followed him, and Roger's eyes followed. Tall, broad, and very impressive in their gray and white dress uniforms complete with swords and sheathed daggers, Charon's men kept a few paces behind Daniel. Each wore a gold ring with a black stone on his right hand.

Roger's hazel eyes flicked and returned to Daniel's face as the two men matched each other stride for stride. The hawk-wing eyebrows rose again in surprise. *Where are the usual ceremonial attendants from the College of the Magi?* his nonverbal signals asked.

As you can see, they have been replaced, Daniel signaled in return.

Roger's lean face showed a working muscle in the jaw that contradicted the usual smooth, friendly expression. The tufty eyebrows drew close together. He asked Daniel loudly and bluntly, "Why is the Council of the Magi having an emergency meeting before the regular meeting? What exactly is the nature of the emergency?"

"Have you not asked Charon?" murmured Daniel.

"Of course, Fean," Roger emphasized, using the common address for a magus with an undertone of asperity. "But I wanted to hear what you had to say."

"As you might guess, I have much to say but little freedom to say it." Daniel and Roger started up the marble stairs near the front of the mob of magi. He asked Roger a polite question that had an urgent undertone, "Are you prepared for the coming proposals?"

"You know how much I want to end the abominable cruelty to the unborn Blue People." Roger's keen eyes shot him a predatory glance. "However, I suppose that the issue cannot be addressed properly in this Council. Otherwise, yes, I have been briefed very well by the Thamaon, her Majesty of Smythe." One eyelid fluttered in a wink. The signal brought a small ease to Daniel's troubled stomach.

As they climbed the spiral of marble steps together, Roger probed, testing his boundaries, "I never believed that you had allied with Charon and the Horned Edge. However, present appearances vie with my previous perceptions."

"Appearances can be deceiving," Daniel replied meaningfully.

Roger glanced casually over one shoulder at the Horned Edge guards and then his eyes met Daniel's. Pursuing his questions further, he began, "What —"

Daniel gnashed his teeth. If he allowed Roger to go on asking questions, his friend and ally might end up stuffed in a closet with a knife in his heart.

* * *

They reached the top of the stairway to the great meeting room. Hot light shone around them from the tall, broad windows. They were open, but Daniel saw a sheen of sweat on Roger's face. The magus from Smythe shook the gold-lined sleeves of his robe to let in more air.

"We're going to suffer today, Radhegoya," Roger said in a humorous tone, but Daniel heard the double meaning. Roger had used the full title of the High Magus with the overtone of the Suffering Servant.

Daniel shook his head. "Hegofean is enough for me." He refrained from wiping his face on his gorgeous ceremonial robe. "This is where I leave you to head the procession."

The magi began organizing themselves. To a deep, dramatic beat on tympani, Daniel in his stately gold robe walked in front. All the fean entered the great hall and filed to their places. Followed by his (unfortunately, Horned Edge) ceremonial guards and the rest of the High Council, Daniel ascended to the crown of the hall where rose the High Seat, which was made of fine Laestes Island mahogany and tooled with pure gold.

He and the rest of the High Council remained standing until the last magus had found her station, but Charon was quite conspicuously absent, like a front tooth missing in a smile. Raising his hands, Daniel pronounced the ancient blessing, *"Ba te Aya te Fama Woto, de osa foroya dileh. Totbao-on, luradoya, lugoye to."*

Silence fell over the assembly like golden dew. He sat. Everyone followed suit. An orchestra, choir, and soloists began the introductory anthem of the magi – the Bard's song.

From his elevated seat, Daniel viewed the sea of men and women in their dark gray robes. The colors of the other magi's sleeve linings indicated the countries that they represented. Only one black-lined robe from Bardia was in evidence, and that was Walt from Kingsport – who was older than he, resentful of Daniel's rapid rise to power, and known to jealously covet Daniel's position. Roger, of course, was there with the gold-lined sleeves of Smythe. At least two dozen sleeves showed the bright white of Tor, which was clear evidence that this meeting was stacked by the Horned Edge. In addition, Daniel noted the expected mandarin orange for Eleaemana, flame red for Siphe, royal blue for Raphe, wheat yellow for Poiemana – and an unusually large number of robes lined with brilliant indigo from Swetha in the Southern Continent.

Daniel almost had to laugh. He knew for a fact that there were more indigo-robed people here than there were true magi in Horned Edge-allied Swetha.

Throughout the beautiful musical performance, Daniel wondered, *Where is Tahei?* He shifted his legs on the High Seat while Walt gave a long rambling speech, welcoming them all to Moorway and then giving a not-very-brief account of the last 500 years' history.

Very bored, Daniel looked aimlessly around the room. Above the gathering, sparkling chandeliers gave plenty of light and ambience. The floor below was carpeted in a warm gray and scarlet, woven by skilled Poiemanan artists. To his near left – he could touch them if he leaned far enough – tall open windows with low sills let in bright sunlight, a little fresh air, and a dramatic view. Far below, he could see the deep river gorge that circled the east side of Whitehall like a natural moat. The gorge was filled with shadows, like his heart.

Despair welled up inside. *I've failed everyone. I don't deserve to live. Master, help me!*

The river gorge seemed to say, *Your whole life has been dedicated to a useless dead idea. The Master is nothing, only an illusion.*

At that moment, Charon arrived. The Lord of Tor walked in solitary procession to the dais, tall, straight, and splendid, his glossy dark hair flowing to his shoulders and eyes sparkling like bright black diamonds. His robe was dark gray with Torish white sleeve lining, but he also wore a new stole over his shoulders embroidered with silvery platinum threads. A hush fell throughout the hall. Daniel realized, *He's acting as if he, not I, commanded the College of the Magi.*

Lord Charon strode toward his traditional seat, which was on Daniel's right. After Charon sat, the others also took their seats, leaving him, Daniel the High Magus, to formally begin the meeting as custom demanded.

Daniel took a deep shuddering breath. Thinking of Gracie and all his loved ones, he called up from memory the long-rehearsed spiel which Charon and Gort had concocted for him. Without looking at anyone, especially Charon, Daniel intoned, "Let the Council begin."

* * *

After the morning meeting, which was mostly establishing protocols for the rest of the sessions, Daniel led the High Council out in pomp and splendor and, inside, total shame. Once all the fean had recessed, formality broke into disorder. Hungry magi swarmed through the double doors into the dining hall. Many went to find comfort facilities, and more than a few aimed themselves toward Daniel with loud questions.

"Stand back," Daniel's Horned Edge escort ordered curtly, which was fine because he could not bear to speak to anyone right now.

Daniel turned to his guards. "I need to piss," he snarled. He shot them a cold glance, daring them to interfere, and strode to a side chamber – the very one where he had conferred with Charon, Gort, Trager, and Mark Gregory yesterday. He marched inside, went through the alcove into the restroom, found himself a stall, and locked himself inside.

At last, privacy! He could live without lunch, even though hunger pangs were making him feel ill. For several minutes he leaned against the marble wall, the cold stone soothing his sweating forehead. Also, his temples throbbed with every heartbeat …

"Lewis must repair the sabotage." Lord Charon said suddenly nearby. The magus quickly entered the stall next to him, grunted, and made plopping noises. Daniel tried not to breathe.

"Did Daniel behave?" Barth's voice asked. Prolonged tinkling sounded by the urinals.

"Aye," Charon laughed.

Charon and Barth were done. The splashing sound of hand washing reverberated through the restroom.

As he and Lord Charon left, Barth muttered something Daniel couldn't catch, but then the man exclaimed, "We need to make Lewis hurry up! How about I take that little girl down tonight while the ex-Viceroy of Rockeerie runs the Council?" The restroom door swung shut.

A freezing shiver of terror sped down Daniel's spine. *No! Would Barth and Charon hurt Gracie? Even if they think she is my daughter Myra?*

He did not doubt that they would.

Frantically summoning every genius of thought and intuition he could imagine, Daniel realized that he could do … nothing. He groaned aloud, from habit rather than faith, "Master, help me!"

Immediately, as soon as he exited into the side chamber, his head exploded with the worst pain he had ever felt in his life. Collapsing, he screamed, and his Horned Edge guards sped inside. They dragged him to an armchair, where he lay back, panting with pain.

"I feel sick," he gasped, and it was completely true. His tortured eyes saw a glowing lattice pattern. Even the soft white light from the chamber's globe lamps turned red and smote his eyes, and intense nausea made him bead with sweat.

"Is he giving you trouble?" asked a young man's voice. It was Mark Gregory.

Despite his distorted vision, Daniel saw Mark's proud young mesomorphic shape in a gray robe. A familiar taller man in Torish dress uniform stood beside him: Captain Ruse, Daniel's captor and conductor to Tor.

"What's wrong?" Ruse asked the guards coldly.

"We don't –" began a Horned Edge guard.

"Migraine headache," Mark interjected. The young magus sounded detached, clinical, and cool. He did not approach Daniel or greet him. "The High Magus is stressed out. I've seen him this way before. He'll collapse if he doesn't rest, so you'd better take care of him if you want him to preside over the Council. In fact – I warn you – you ought to have him skip the afternoon session and keep him quiet until the evening program."

The Horned Edge guards bunched closer together to express solidarity. Their spokesman, a large man with a square jaw and a heavy moustache, stated, "We've orders to take him to the Green Room. He'll have his lunch there, away from the others."

Daniel gagged at the thought of being forced to eat.

"Take off his robe before he throws up on it," Mark suggested.

Daniel felt like a helpless child as two Horned Edge guards took his arms and pulled the gold robe over his head. Pain hammered so violently in his brain that he was afraid that he was having a stroke.

Ruse ordered, "I'll relay to Charon to excuse him from the afternoon session. Fean Holdman, the High Magus is yours. Do whatever it takes to get him well enough to run the Council tonight." He quickly strode away. The sound of his boots were crashing cymbals on the stone floor.

Mark ordered the guards, "Have the kitchen send up hot towels for the headache – a very large pile of them! Use the largest covered platter that you can find to keep them hot. The Lord of Tor requires the High Magus's service tonight and he must feel well enough to preside over the assembly."

"Yes, fean." A guard saluted and left.

Mark and a Horned Edge guard firmly took Daniel's elbows on each side. Feeling humiliated but too weak to resist, he stumbled up the stairs between them. About halfway up to the tower, a surge of sickness overcame him, and he vomited. They carried him the rest of the way up to the tower.

When he arrived in his tower prison, Daniel dimly heard Gracie exclaim, "Mark! What's wrong? What happened to him?"

Mark did not answer. He and the Horned Edge guard pushed Daniel past her to one of the room's two narrow cots, laid him down, turned away, and locked the door behind them.

He was promptly sick again.

CHAPTER 24
HERE WITH ME

After cleaning up Daniel and the floor beside his cot with cloth napkins from her lunch tray, Gracie had zero appetite. A soup tureen under the tray lid contained chunks of mystery fish swimming in a pink sauce that had gray bits of who-knows-what in it. *Yuck! Double yuck!* To her nose, the whole room reeked with all the appeal of a Moorway slime-filled canal simmering under a noon sun. Gagging, she threw the tureen, soup, and soiled napkins out of the tower window.

Good – maybe it hit a Horned Edge magus on the head. She could hope, anyhow.

Despite her defiance, a thrill of fear made her heart beat fast. *Suppose Daniel dies – what will happen to me?*

"Hey," she told herself, "there's nothing I can do about that." She imagined the fear as small as an ant. She stepped on it.

Just then, a guard opened the door. A short, grizzle-faced man in kitchen uniform who looked hot and anxious, carried a huge tray inside. He left quickly without conversation.

Her stomach complaining now with hunger, Gracie slowly approached the new tray. It was as big around as a pregnant mare's belly. At least it didn't smell bad. "What in the heck have they brought us this time?" she exclaimed.

Daniel squinted at the tray with one bloodshot eye. "They've brought up hot towels for my headache." His voice sounded feeble.

Gracie shook her head. "Hot towels on what must be the hottest day of the summer! Why didn't they bring up something sensible, like aspirin?"

"Bimi," Daniel said, "That's the only treatment that ever helps me. Please wrap them on my head."

The rest of Gracie's afternoon was spent tending Daniel. She didn't mind. He wasn't her Dad, but he was like her Dad. She could hardly remember her own real father. He was just a shadowy tall figure at the dinner table in a place called Earth. Wait – she could remember his big brown eyes, beautiful like Lewis's. She could remember him speaking tenderly to her, coming home from work and playing ball in the evenings.

Fatherly love – that's what Dads were all about. Her Dad had shown fatherly love. So had Daniel on the long journey from Nutman to Tor while she pretended to be his daughter.

Father Love, she thought, looking at Daniel's face, which was scrunched up with pain. *My Dads watch out for me. I've got three Dads, a God Dad, a Daniel Dad, and my Dad Dad.*

Gracie wished with a deep pang that she could see Dad and Mom now. Then this mess would all be over, and she would be safe. But – speaking of reality, she was not at home, she was here locked up in a tower in Tor with a man named Daniel who looked half-dead.

She'd rather be active than sit like a blob and wait for the world to turn around. As the afternoon hours passed, Gracie alternated between applying hot towels to Daniel's head, bringing him cool drinks from the big stone jar in the corner, and stretching her arms and legs in short walks around the room. The light swung around. The air seemed cooler as a breeze drifted through the window.

Towards evening, Daniel got up.

"Do you feel better now, Baba?" she asked, shoving the towels and tray in a corner.

"Oh yes, I do," he said and smiled. She was unconvinced. His face was gray.

"One good thing about this place is that you can still see out the window when you sit down on the floor," Gracie said. "I'll put pillows down. Come and sit with me."

Daniel joined Gracie. She leaned affectionately against his shoulder, looking out over the Torish landscape.

"Why aren't there bars in the window?" she asked. "There's no screen or glass, either." She turned in surprise when she felt his muscles flinch.

"I suppose it's too far to climb down, even with a rope," Daniel answered. His voice sounded heavy. His eyes were fixed toward the northwest, where a river, red in the westering sunlight, snaked through its deep gorge.

Military camps sprawled below all around the Whitehall area, and Torish soldiers marched in gray columns up and down roads. "I hope the mosquitoes drive them crazy," Gracie declared. She was glad to see Daniel give a ghost of a smile.

"Look," Daniel said, pointing with a small tired gesture. "Can you see the Snowy Mountains?"

At the far northern edge of the horizon floated a line of blue clouds with white peaks. Feeling comfortable and almost drowsy, Gracie nodded.

Daniel said, "Once long ago, I travelled to the Snowy Mountains with Tahei Charon. We were friends then and both of us were graduate students at the College of the Magi."

Gracie sensed that he needed to tell his tale. She was sure she would understand about as much of it as she did Lewis's lectures. "All right, tell me," she said, steeling herself.

"It's a long story," he warned with a brief chuckle.

She settled back against his arm to listen.

He talked for a long, long time about two young men, full of fun, exploring the mountains. "Tahei Charon found the lost summer palace of Tahei's great-grandfather, Amen Charon," Daniel said, with a look of remembered wonder in his eyes, "It contained millennia of knowledge and invention that had been hidden since the Great Rebellion."

Although she tried to listen, Gracie felt drowsy and snuggly, and her mind wandered while he described places and events that were beyond her experience. A flock of white egrets wheeled over the distant marshes. They looked so peaceful.

Daniel began another part of his story, and Gracie tried hard to listen. "When I caught Tahei using the thoyo-on to travel back and forth to Earth and when I confronted him about playing dangerously with the bizeor, he tried to kill me. My best friend tried to kill me!"

Gracie immediately thought of Fred betraying her brothers, and her stomach knotted up. She was now paying deep attention to Daniel.

He said, "But I was faster, and I had help from the *foroya,* so I got away. I struggled over the rough country back to the College in Nutman. I told the High Magus, Heysel, the whole story. He didn't believe me at first. Finally, he sent magi to investigate Amen's palace, but Charon had already cleaned it out. Tahei had brought his grandfather's thoyo-on to Moorway and set it up at the old seat in Whitehall. That wasn't bad in itself – after all, it was his inheritance – but Tahei began to use it to worship Saoma."

"Okay," said Gracie. She knew that what Daniel had said was important, but she did not understand it all.

Daniel talked some more. Finally, he ended, "Tahei would like to hurt me because I remind him that he's still doing wrong. He might try to hurt you, too."

That she could understand. She was in danger. To her amazement, it didn't bother her. Why worry? There was nothing she could do about it.

Daniel drew back and twisted around to look in her eyes. "Why aren't you afraid?"

Gracie thought. "I don't know," she confessed. "Maybe those mountains make me feel safe."

"I don't understand," Daniel said. He sounded frustrated and angry.

She realized that he really did want to know the answer. It felt weird to have a grownup man who was famous and important ask for her opinion about mountains. Her stomach squirmed and she felt her face get hot. She wanted to weasel out of talking, but Daniel had gotten very intense and his eyes were expecting an answer.

Staring out of the window and wrapping her arms around her knees, Gracie tried to think. She didn't know what to say. Her mind had gone blank. After a minute of tense silence, she gave up thinking and just opened her mouth to say whatever came out.

"When I see the mountains, I think about God. Now, I know the mountains can't help me. They're just big hunks of rock. They're way out there, and I'm in here. But they're huge like God and beautiful like Jesus and *they* are in here with me."

There. That was it. That was why she wasn't afraid.

Daniel closed his eyes and heaved a deep sigh. Gracie waited for a comment, but none came. His eyes opened. Their gray-blue depths looked clear and brave as if a stopped-up pipe had opened and was now flowing with clean, cold water. "Thank you, bimi," he said.

Chapter 25
GLOP FOR SUPPER

Daniel got up abruptly, almost knocking Gracie flat on the floor. Pillows strewed everywhere. "Where's my jacket?"

"Under the cot," she answered, getting up and dusting off her rear end. "It's been way too hot to wear a jacket." She pointed to a box stored under their crude beds.

Daniel riffled through the box. He patted down the jacket until he found a little brown glass bottle. "Ah!" he said with a note of satisfaction. "This will do the job." Just then, the door swung open with a banging noise.

"Your supper is ready," proclaimed a deep bass voice.

Quickly, Daniel put his hand behind his back. The manservant, a small man with a great black beard, laid their supper tray down on the small table by their cots. Gesturing toward the huge tray full of towels, he asked, "Shall I take these away now?"

"Not yet," Daniel said, and the servant left without comment.

"Dear Gracie," Daniel said. "I thank you so much for your words to me."

"What words?" Gracie replied, confused. "About the mountains?"

"You strengthened my heart," he told her. Taking her hand, he led her to the supper tray. "What happens in the next few minutes will affect everything – absolutely everything."

"Okay," said Gracie uncertainly. "What does that mean?"

"It means that all of us may be rescued. You will be safe, first."

Gracie knew that Daniel meant to get her out of the tower, even though she had no idea how. It was a hard, scary thought that she might soon go to yet another strange place alone, leaving her Baba Daniel. She knew that it should feel good to be rescued but she was not happy. "What about you?" she said, her heart beating fast.

Daniel smiled confidently. "I have work to do, bimi. I'll be all right."

Saying a blessing over the meal – like Dad, Daniel lifted the lid from the tray and a nice curl of steam came out. Even though her stomach ached with hunger, Gracie hid her eyes in case it was another nasty fish dish.

"Come on, Gracie," Daniel said, laughing. "We have a nice cornmeal porridge, creamed tripe, and stewed prunes for dessert. It's wonderful!"

"Wonderful," Gracie echoed sarcastically.

Actually, the smell wasn't too bad. Her mouth watered. She dreaded what she might see but made herself look anyway. The porridge looked like white glop. The creamed tripe looked like brown glop. The prunes looked disgusting as bloated cockroaches.

"Oh, that looks delicious," Daniel exclaimed in a hearty voice. He scooped a large helping of tripe, porridge, and prunes into bowls that had come with the tray. To her surprise, he also produced his brown bottle, pulled off the stopper, and poured a little clear liquid into her prune bowl.

Gracie frowned at him. "What are you doing?"

Daniel gushed on, "Bimi, you'll have to eat enough to keep up your strength." He handed her the doctored bowls.

She felt suspicious. "What did you put on my food?" she growled.

"Just some medicine the doctor gave me when we crossed the Winerush. It will make you stronger."

"What about you?" Gracie asked. This looked suspiciously like a set-up. Daniel's explanation did not explain. "What about you keeping up your own strength?"

"I really don't think my system can handle food yet," he complained. "I have to be, er, strong enough for the evening session of the Council." Daniel emphasized, "Trust me. It's very important that you eat this."

She caught Daniel's meaning. *This is it. This is the rescue.* She didn't understand how Daniel and the Patriots were going to get her out of here, but all she had do was be obedient and eat her glop.

With a deep sigh, Gracie turned to her food. She dipped her spoon into the stuff and began to eat. The prune syrup was as thick and heavy as cough syrup. The cornmeal porridge tasted like unsalted grits. The tripe wasn't bad … She ate it all.

In a few minutes, Gracie began to feel extremely drowsy. "Baba," she yawned, "I feel so tired, I could go to bed already."

Gently, Daniel took away her bowl before she fell sideways onto her cot. "G'night," she said, her voice slurred. The last thing she saw before her eyes closed was Daniel's face. He looked loving, hopeful, triumphant, sad, and scared all at once.

* * *

The tower room was nearly dark, and Daniel had just lit a candle when he heard the door open. He turned around to look. The guard at the door let in several visitors. The first man was dressed in an apron like one of the Whitehall kitchen staff. The newcomer had big ears, prominent front teeth, small beady eyes, and a fluffy, thin moustache. He looked remarkably like a human rodent.

Daniel recognized him immediately. *Hermann!* His face must have lit up, because Hermann pressed a finger warningly against his lips.

The second man was a Horned Edge guard. He was young, hard-faced, and well-armed. He looked like he was trying hard to be a tough guy but hadn't quite mastered the role.

The last visitor, a man with a short beard, wore ordinary citizen's clothes, dark baggy pants, and white summer shirt. Daniel knew that the red close-fitting cap and the black leather bag the man carried showed him to be a physician.

"The evening session starts in a half-hour," the Horned Edge guard told Daniel. "Get your things. Charon is waiting for –"

"I'm supposed to examine the High Magus first," the physician interrupted. "I'll need ten minutes."

Daniel felt tense as a stretched wire. If the Horned Edge guard stayed in the room, there would be no rescue. He would have to go down to the Council and, as soon as he was out of the way, Barth's boys would take Gracie.

The physician did not wait for the guard to object. He gave

him a stern look and said, "I want to examine the High Magus privately." Rolling his eyes, the Horned Edge guard nodded and stepped outside.

"Well, I've gotta clean up these trays before anybody does anything," Hermann drawled.

Immediately, Daniel pointed to the great tray and the untidy pile of towels in the corner. Hermann nodded. He went directly to Gracie, who lay limp on the cot. Folding her arms and legs close to her body, he then cocooned her in towels. The doctor and Hermann shifted Gracie onto the great tray, closed the lid loosely, leaving ends of towels sticking out, and Hermann heaved the tray onto his shoulders. Immediately, he left the tower room.

Meanwhile, the doctor performed a cursory exam. "You're fine for the Council tonight."

Daniel heaved a sigh. His heart soared. "Thank you!" he told the physician fervently while he stuffed towels and clothes to make Gracie's cot look like the little girl was still lying there.

"*Lurada luradyah, lutaya,*" the doctor said poetically.

Daniel knew then that he was a worshipper of Radyah. He made the fervent reply, "*Alor, lurad eyah!*"

Straightening his appearance, he called the guards. "I'm ready. Open the door"

The door opened. Daniel turned toward the cot. "Good night, little one," he said tenderly. "I'll see you in the morning."

CHAPTER 26
DUNGEONS OF WHITEHALL

Lewis crouched in his cell in the dungeon caves below Whitehall. Cold bands secured each wrist to a ring in the wall, his boots had been removed and heavy shackles fastened on his ankles, and a grate over the cell opening was fastened in place by a heavy padlock. Like icy brine, his blood ran cold – but with murder, not with fear. His captor Barth Layhew stood outside the cell, his huge body backlit with lamplight.

"Louie, your brother and sister are here in Moorway. You want to see them again, don't you, after you fix the damage you did to Charon's locating system?" said Barth in a falsely nice voice.

"I do want to see them, but I know you are a liar." *I'll fix your system all right – to destroy itself!* Lewis inwardly added.

He bent over coughing, spat, and raised his head. "Fix it yourself." Running through his head was a constant theme, *I'm in the perfect position; I can stop them from completing their plans. I can save Patrick and Gracie. But I mustn't give in too easily, or they'll suspect.*

He had been given very little food or water for two days. However, although his tongue was swollen with thirst and he had developed a painful cough, fear did not seem to reach him. His emotions were remote as the stars.

Barth growled with anger, "I can torture you –"

"You have no choice but to kill me," Lewis sneered. However, he didn't plan to be killed; he planned to be destructive. He felt a gentle warning tug inside, as if a skilled trainer was pulling him back and saying, *Don't try this by yourself,* but he was too angry to obey. "You are Lord Charon's pet. Go fix the system yourself."

Barth slammed his hand onto the grating with a noise so loud that the cave corridors rang with echoes. "Damn you, damn you," he railed. "My brother was a fool to send you here. You've been nothing but a sneaking, murdering, treacherous piece of –"

"And you're a son of *Bizeboborya,*" Lewis snarled, using an extreme Lanthran insult.

Only the locked grate protected him from being beaten to death on the spot. Barth shouted curses until his voice got hoarse. He battered the grate and kicked it. Finally, the big man stopped shouting. He hissed through the grate, "I'll be back. And you'll be sorry." Barth left. With him went the lamp.

The dungeon was completely dark. Lewis could not see his own hand before his face, but he savored his defiance so much that it didn't matter. He sank with a satisfied sigh back into the awkward position that the chains and the confines of the cell afforded him.

After a while, dim spots and lights floated in front of his eyes. His retinae were firing off signals from his own blood circulation. He coughed and spat. Meanwhile, he thought swiftly and deliberately, working out his situation as he did any problem in practical science, *One way or another, Barth and Charon may eventually repair their system. However, right now, they believe that they need me to do it. I must let Barth force me to give in ... But I mustn't give in too easily or quickly; I will have to let them —*

A remote inner voice warned him, *It is not necessary to let them torture you.*

Lewis shook himself to clear his mind. He went back to his calculations. After he wrecked their system –

It is not up to you to destroy their plans, the inner adviser said.

Dismissing the advice, he insisted, *Yes, it is up to me. I'm in the strategic position. I'm the only one here who can do it!*

The reply came, *Who said that I wanted it destroyed?*

Lewis's stomach swooped like a screaming roller coaster. "Who are you?" The dungeon corridors echoed.

At that moment, Lewis saw light again. In a mad dance, shadows and light flung themselves around the walls and floor and ceiling, approaching his cell. Although he was prepared and his mind felt detached, a little involuntary fear squeezed his stomach. He took a deep breath. His time – his opportunity had come. He had to be strong to manage what must happen next.

Soon a turnkey with a lantern and three Horned Edge guards came to the grate of his cell. Lewis squinted and blinked to adjust his eyes to the light while the turnkey opened the grate. One of the guards came and unlocked Lewis's chains. Lewis stumbled forward out of the cell. "Come on, get going," the Horned Edge guard prodded him. Without comment, the guard led him to a part of the dungeon he had not yet seen.

They passed through a natural cave chamber. Here, the turnkey's lantern light gleamed on white stalactites that thrust down from the ceiling. One wall was a smooth rippling golden agate; this curved into a sheet of smoky quartz that glittered with gold flecks. The air smelled frosty, and Lewis felt dampness settling into his clothes. On his left, he heard a watery roar. He guessed that a subterranean waterfall poured into an unknown depth, and he thought, *Fred would be ecstatic to see this. I wish that ...*

He wished that he could see Fred and be friends again and explore caves like this, laughing and joking together. But that time was over, never to come again.

On Lewis's right side, a side chamber had been carved into the natural cave wall. Light from a glowing globe spilled out onto the floor by his feet, which made the side chamber seem dark.

"Go in," a Horned Edge guard ordered.

This is it. Lewis's insides froze to absolute zero. He could not feel anything, even his own body. It was as if he were a detached brain floating over the cavern floor.

When they began to walk through the door into the side chamber, one of the Horned Edge guards croaked, "What –?" The guard slipped sideways, staggered, and fell. "Who hit me behind the knee!"

The surprise brought Lewis out of his self-hypnosis for a moment. A few feet away squatted a black smooth onyx globe six feet in diameter, crowned by soft gray bat dung. Lewis saw a ragged human shape scamper behind the onyx sphere, and he heard a mischievous laugh echo down a hidden tunnel.

"Blasted old woman!" cursed the fallen guard.

"Crazy Lady is slinking around again," said another. "I bet she's stolen a set of keys and has been blithely taking off the prisoners' chains. If I see her, I'll throttle her!"

"Nay, leave her alone," said the turnkey, helping the guard stand back up again. "She saves us the job o' cleaning the prisoners' muck, else t'would be choking foul down here and 'tis foul enough already. So what if she unlocks a chain or two? They canna' get out, and neither can she!"

They pushed him into a well-lit chamber. Blinking, Lewis looked around. A structure that looked suspiciously like a rack loomed in the back corner. Over it dangled pulleys and weights that Lewis felt sure were not meant for exercise.

You made your choice, someone taunted him from within, *so look at what you are going to face.* The thought knocked away his detachment. *They will take away your clothes. They will twist you until you are screaming, and they will not release you until you break. You are strong. It will take them a long time. When you finally give in –*

Lewis cut them off. Detachment returned.

On a wooden chair by the rack sat Barth Layhew. He looked comfortable, legs crossed. The tall boots, leather pants, and black leather jacket accentuated the huge, muscular body. A Horned Edge ring adorned his well-groomed hands. However, on Barth's face was a snarl that showed his incisors. An inflamed scab ran down his cheek, the wound from Lewis's chisel.

Lewis was ready. He shook off the guards' hands. He had to provoke Barth. That might hurt him, but he would win in the end. "Sorry about my appearance," he bantered, dramatically shaking out his rumpled black robe. "But you look great. Nice black jacket. Nice red scar on your face."

"What happens next is up to you," Barth drawled, anger pushing out the words, "If you agree to repair your vandalism, then you can just walk out of here and get to work. If not ..." He let his words trail off.

Lewis opened his mouth to say something scathing, he but could not speak. Conflicting messages almost tore him apart. One bold voice said, *Make Barth do it to you. He'll be sorry in the end!* However, another voice full of out-of-place humor reminded him of Bobbie the talkative teddy-bear back in his apartment a long age ago: *You are the most stubborn human being alive. For once, soften your granite determination!*

The first voice argued softly, sweetly, *Lewis it's up to you to save everyone. You will suffer, but you will eventually get your way!*

The second voice insisted, *Do not go through with this!*

He made his decision. His eyes went to the rack.

Barth turned to the Horned Edge guards holding Lewis. "Very well, lads, give him a little treatment."

The guards stripped away Lewis's black robe and threw it onto the floor. Cold cave air made his skin bumpy. They hustled Lewis to the hard bench and strapped him firmly face down, except for his left arm. This they attached to a pulley that hung overhead.

Lewis swallowed hard but did not struggle or cry out. The annoying inner advisor returned to say: *If you can quit being so stubborn for a minute, then do this: Speak to Barth now. Maybe he will change his mind. He might even help you!*

Okay, it's worth a try. Lewis turned his face toward Barth, who still sat on the chair.

"Barth," Lewis said, and he was surprised that his voice sounded strong, "Your world Lanthra is in trouble. Right now, it's still beautiful and full of happiness. But imagine what will happen if you let Charon connect to Earth! He thinks he's in charge, but he's only a puppet. Demons will rule Lanthra. Your people will become gluttons, greedy, murderers, thieves, complainers, and liars. They will mow down your forests, fill your streams with poison, and ruin the air with smoke. They will dope fathers and mothers with drugs so that they are too depressed to take care of their children. Come, Barth," he pleaded, amazed at the caring that surged out of him, "work with Radyah! It's not too late to turn this around!"

Amazed at himself, Lewis thought, *Radyah? I don't believe in God – why did I say his name?* Silence filled the room.

For a moment Barth shifted uneasily. His eyes almost crossed with conflicting thoughts and Lewis saw yearning on Barth's face. The big man softened a little; tears sprang to his eyes and his big hand rubbed them away. Lewis held his breath. Maybe he had succeeded ... maybe Barth would think and change his mind ...

maybe this whole sick scene would change to a healthy, triumphant one …

Then Barth lifted one sardonic eyebrow. "Louie, you never quit trying, do you?" He laughed until the cave rang. Turning to the Horned Edge guards, he said, "Get on with it."

Lewis shut his eyes tightly. With a stretching noise, the pulleys lifted his arm unnaturally backward.

The pain began.

With practiced ease, the torturers tugged the rope. Lewis's left arm slowly stretched back and upward. When the joint reached its normal limit, it was forced further. He heard himself screaming, and they kept pulling. Something went *pop!* in his rotator cuff, but they kept on pulling, letting things strain and tear.

"I'll help you, just stop!" he cried.

The pain continued, on and on.

He wept and shouted, "I swear, I'll help you. Just stop, stop!"

CHAPTER 27
DEPARTING FROM THE SCRIPT

It was the evening session, and Daniel stood before the Council of the Magi. This time, the grand windows framed deep dusk blue sky and twinkling stars. The windows stood open to let in the cool evening breeze.

Daniel waved a hand, and vivid three-dimensional holograms in Lanthran script appeared. He said, using a sonic baton to "point" as needed. "Some of these proposals were discussed at our last Council and some of the proposals are new, but all of them are essential to resolve the present conflict. We will address each in turn."

He continued, "First: It was suggested that the College of the Magi in Bardia be decentralized. At this meeting, the Council can vote on a modified form: The proposal adds new branches of the College in each of the twenty-four countries of the Lanthran world. The Bardian site at Nutman will remain but will use its resources to generate the new independent branches."

Many of the magi gasped. This proposal, proclaimed from own Daniel's lips, was confirmation of the rumors that he had defected to the Horned Edge.

Do I have to go keep acting like a fool? he asked the Master. Cannot I speak a word and expose Charon's plot?

You could command everyone in Whitehall to turn pink, and they would do so. However, please control yourself.

Repressing a surge of rebellion, Daniel made himself go on with Charon's script, for, at the right time, he would gather his strength, and … Master help me! He would turn this Council away from Charon. A demonic image of the tortures he might suffer brushed his mind. He trembled under his gold robe and felt cold sweat on the back of his neck.

To illustrate the first proposal, a hologram showed the planet Lanthra. The College of the Magi at Nutman appeared as a bright star. It divided, with small stars coming out from it and settling in the proposed twenty-four branch sites, and each site was designated to have its own thoyo-on, eventually … once the magi could figure out to build them.

If this proposal becomes law, there will be chaos among the nations. Tor has already invaded the Bardian province of Rockeerie. Who would invade whom next with a working thoyo-on?

Daniel ground his teeth, but then he relaxed his jaw and added, "The second and third proposals before this Council are these: Lanthra will reverse its ban on electronic technology and the One Law. After the proposals have been voted upon in this Council, the implementation of the new arrangements will be made immediately."

Sounds of indrawn breath rose from all the magi. Excited and pleased comments rose from the Torish and Swethan representatives. However, other magi muttered with grave displeasure. Roger sat below at the second table from the front, looking stunned, his jaw dropped. Walther of Bardia shook his head and rolled his eyes as if to say, "I told you so; the High Magus is a traitor."

Daniel continued, "As long as the locating systems in the twenty-four nations are monitored by the magi, as long as weapons are distributed to the nations to protect Lanthra, every electronic use is possible and even desirable."

Daniel braced himself to add a portion not in his script; "The Horned Edge proposed – er, I propose the plan. I pray that Lanthran – and Earth's – electronic technology will be used for peaceful purposes."

Beside him, Charon made a slight movement of his right hand which said, Keep to the script – or else. A Horned Edge guard coughed with threatening meaning.

Daniel deliberately stammered, "Ch-changes in the script – I mean, in the p-proposal …"

Some of the magi caught on. He paused to let the few amused

chuckles die down, and then he said, his voice very strong, jabbing the hologram with his sonic baton as if cutting holes in it, "We emphasize: The new proposal calls for full and immediate reversal of the ban on electronic technology. It also calls for immediate and full reversal of the One Law. Lanthra will be under the domination and regulation of the College of the Magi in a new controlling order, widely called The Horned Edge, allied with Earth's weapon's manufacturers, the Shields –"

A rustle like leaves in a storm drowned out his next words. The response went on so long that Lord Charon rose and stilled the noise with a gesture. Charon's deep resonant voice rang out, "My friend Daniel and I long thought that full use of Lanthran's ancient technology should be restored. At one time, the ban was useful; howe'er, new times have come. Each of the twenty-four nations of Lanthra will have, not only its own College of the Magi, but also a seat of location and training in the technology to use it to study and begin ecumenical discussions with other inhabited worlds."

Charon took his seat with a gracious smile. The chamber filled with a deluge of voices.

Daniel's heart felt heavy as a stone. How many of them realize what will happen? The new centers led by the Horned Edge will become predators and in turn become food for bigger predators – the bizeor, the demons of Earth.

Another hour swept by in discussion of the bombshell proposals. The Horned Edge and Swethan Magi interrupted the proceedings many times with arguments and blame at being "held back" for so long by the Bardian overlords. A dyad from Siphe, magi with ornate headdresses and much jewelry, kept asking trivial questions that required elaborate answers. It was clear to Daniel that Charon had choreographed this. His supporters were intentionally tiring out the assembly.

Therefore, Daniel prepared to begin his personal assault.

Not yet, not yet, the Master told him.

He waited, still sitting. While the others carried on, he quietly held out his hands, palms up. Taking a deep breath, he mentally piled on them his many cares. I give you my fear for Gracie. I give you my longing to see my dear daughters Myra and Deirdre again. I give you my anguish over what has happened to my province. I give you my flaming rage over what Charon is doing at this Council.

Slowly, he let his hands drop and the burdens fell off. Like a sharp blast of cold wind in his mind, the Master ordered, Stand up. Raise your hands again and receive gifts.

He stood. At that moment, the meeting hall became dead quiet. He opened his eyes. Everyone stared at him.

The assembly quickly stood, also, with much rustling and scraping. Absolutely everyone stood, including, looking surprised, Lord Charon to honor the High Magus.

"Thank you, Radyah," Daniel said in a ringing voice for all the assembly to hear. "I hear your mercy and I trust you. You show me the way to go, and I love you." He raised his hands in worship.

Total silence froze the moment. All the assembly, the High Council, even the Horned Edge magi, stood still as stones.

Daniel dropped his hands.

"Be seated," he said quietly.

Robes swished as the magi sat.

"Soon," Daniel told them, "if the One Law devolves, many Lanthran magi will visit Earth – as the Horned Edge already have without lawful authorization. You think that you can control Earth; however, Earth's bizeor will control you – indeed, they do already."

Charon stiffened. Horned Edge magi glared.

Daniel continued, addressing the assembly, "Yes, in the confusion that these proposals could create, the bizeor will rule – can't you hear the invisible vermin laughing? However, if you have already given yourself to the Curse of Earth, there is hope for you. The Curse is broken because of Radyah. We can say to the bizeor, 'Radyah has invaded your house. He will bind you and destroy you, Saoma sebizorath!'"

Shocks burned Daniel's back as if he had been whipped by an Eleaemanan jellyfish. What the – -? Daniel suddenly realized what kind of instrument had hurt him. A bilatesath was a marvelous sonic medical device used to stimulate the motor function of muscles that had become flaccid after strokes or paralysis. However, who had the idea of converting a Lanthran tool for healing into a tool for torture? He cried out; his knees trembled so that he sank down into his chair.

Charon quickly got the crowd's attention. All eyes were on his strong features as he said, "To ensure peace, the High Magus and I have joined forces."

That was an outright lie.

Charon went on, "We share a common goal, which is to improve the life of our people. We ask you today, join us. Make the decisions that will lead us to a better way, one that will make this Council remembered as the greatest in our history."

Charon rose and bowed to great applause. Some magi got to their feet, as if Charon had suddenly assumed the right of the High Magus, but when they saw that Daniel was still seated, their feet shuffled, and they looked embarrassed. Most of them sank to their seats.

"Who's leading this Council?" a magus from Polunking in her pink-lined robe dared to call out.

Her neighbor cried, "This council is like a tennis match: back and forth, back and forth."

In a few minutes, when it was obvious that he did not have a majority following, Charon slowly sat down again. The council room hushed.

Daniel got up. He said, "It is too late this evening for any further business. I, the Hegofean, announce the conclusion of this session." Sudden talking and applause filled the great room. Gratefully, the tired magi waited for the conclusion of the day's business.

It's time, the Master said gently. Don't mince words.

Daniel nodded. Master, when they kill me, take care of my family.

"Here are my closing words, fean of the Council," he said. The assembly applauded for a long time; however, the Horned Edge magi crossed their arms and looked grim.

"Do not forget," Daniel said smoothly and clearly, "that while we deliberate the foundations of world peace in Whitehall, outside these borders there is still war. Have you heard that the province of Rockeerie has been 'restored to its former independence?' That is incorrect. My province of Rockeerie, which is subject to Bardia, has been invaded and captured. In all our talk of restoration and new beginnings – in a Council that was called too suddenly so that many magi could not attend, do not be so blinded that you allow yourselves to be deceived by intentional lies."

As Daniel raised his hands for the formal blessing, deafening noise erupted from the assembly. Charon's face went white and his hands clenched. Red-faced, the Horned Edge guards roared, "Quiet! Quiet!"

"Well, look at him," the magus from Polunking told her associate, "He won the match."

CHAPTER 28
CRAZY LADY

Lewis awoke with a start when something whiskery nudged his leg. "What the –" he shouted, and a cat-sized animal scurried off. His cell was very dark, his whole body flamed with pain, and chains rattled on his wrists.

"Aaaawww," he groaned, swaying on his feet. The pain was unbelievable. His left shoulder was on fire. He remembered too well the torture, and he knew that his shoulder's inner structures had been ripped apart.

At that moment, a sound like sharp toenails scrabbled toward him. Little forearms gripped his ankle; sharp little teeth gouged a bite out of his flesh, and all his self-control fled. "No!" Lewis screamed at the top of his voice. He kicked hard, but slipping and twisting, he fell hard onto his butt on a wet, stinking floor. The animal fled. However, too soon, scratching noises approached again. Dozens of squirming bodies swarmed onto his feet.

Lewis panicked. A cramped space, the chains, a torn shoulder – he couldn't defend himself. The vermin climbed up his robes and dozens of sharp little teeth nipped at his skin. Possessed by terror, convulsing into a fetal position, Lewis screamed, "I'll do anything you want! Just make them go away!"

An old woman's voice ordered sharply, *"Yoswa he!"*

Instantly, the horrible little animals scuttled away.

Lewis slowly struggled up. He whispered, "Who's there?" Loud, slow breathing sounded outside his grate, coming through a nose that rattled with snot.

The woman said, "They call me Crazy Lady, but I have a name. Howe'er, you must tell me yours, first."

"My name is Lewis Brahmindura. The last name means 'Justice of God.' Now it's your turn."

Cautiously, she said, "I am Mary. That's all I'll say now. I am one o' the Torish, but I married a Bardian man." Lewis heard more rattling breathing, and then she went on, "We're in the dark, but I hear your accent, laddie. 'Tis strange, though …"

"You – you're the person who kicked that guard behind the knee, before … before …" *Before the torture.*

She said slowly, "Your speech tells me that you're *ta cilavitboz* … those nasty people that the Magician Lord brought over from … from Earth." With a disgusted snort, she began to back away.

"No! I mean, yes!" Lewis suddenly remembered what the guard had said about the Crazy Lady who stole keys and unlocked a chain or two for the prisoners. He desperately wanted her to stay. "I'm from Earth, but I'm not one of them – oh, hell, yes, I am, but I don't want to be. How can I explain this? Arggh …"

She spat.

"No – please, please don't go! I'm in these chains because I began to fight back. I hacked up the system! Then I tried to kill Charon."

He heard a sarcastic grunt in the darkness. "Too bad," she said. "You failed."

Lewis heard shuffling further down the corridor. "Wait!" he shouted. "I can make their whole system collapse into dust. Believe me – that's the truth!"

"The truth!" the woman echoed with a sardonic cackle. "The truth is, You are trapped down here in the dark. Feel the cold rock! Feel the chains on your wrists and ankles! Smell the stench from standing in your own urine!"

Lewis wanted to plead, but he coughed instead. He coughed so much that he doubled over, and the chains rattled wildly. The tortured shoulder screamed.

He begged, his voice stammering, "P … please, ma'am, don't go away! Listen! Bardia was my adopted country after I came over from Earth. I … I lived in Nutman; I worked at the College of the Magi for the Hegofean Daniel, the High Magus –

Now suddenly closer, the woman asked eagerly, "You worked for the Hegofean? He knows me!" Silence. Then: "Do you know my Johnny? He watches the Nutman gate."

Lewis could hardly think, much less remember someone named Johnny in Nutman. "I – I'm not sure …" But a white-bearded face with twinkling blue eyes came to mind, a Santa Claus face. Despite the pain, his memory clicked. "The Nutman gatekeeper is your husband? Did you know that he knowingly let B … Barth Layhew cart my b … brother and me out of the city?" Anger swept through him, seething through his teeth in a hiss. "We were tied up and destined for death! And your husband knew it!"

She imitated his hiss. "Yesss, he opened the gate! And he opened it more times than once! Oh, poor Johnny, they took me away, so he'd open the gate!"

Lewis's river of rage backed up, leaving him completely confused. "He is a traitor!" But then he began to cry. Hot tears rolled down his cheeks, and he rubbed them off with his dirty hand. "And so am I."

Mary's hand reached through the grate. It was knobbly as if it was either arthritic or had been broken, but it was warm. Sobbing like a little child, Lewis snuggled up close. Her hand caressed his cheek. "So… you're from Bardia and you're from Earth. What happened, laddie?" Her voice demanded an answer, and she removed her comforting hand.

Lewis took a deep, shuddering breath, which made him cough and cough.

"On Earth, before we, uh, crossed over, my brother, my sister and I found a noretha. It looked like a toy, a marble. After studying it, though, I found it was dangerous, not from Earth, and I was going to turn in it to my boss, but before I could, some Shields –"

He coughed, hard. Images of Patrick and Gracie and Fred came brilliantly to his mind, and the coughs became more sobs.

The Crazy Lady – Mary – continued his story. "Go on. The noretha brought you to Lanthra."

"Yes. After that, well, … I met Hegofean Daniel … I met his daughter …"

With a dagger's stab of grief, Lewis thought of Deirdre. He saw her lovely face in the park's lamplight with the spring trees and flowers around them … "Mary, the music in your voice sounds a lot like her."

"I, too, am a daughter of the faetha."

"I am so sorry they put you in this horrible place."

Mary cursed, "Damned chains! Rats will eat you if you're chained; they know you canna' fight back. Here, laddie, I won't let them hurt you."

Once again, he felt her warm hand touch him, and he snuggled to her shamelessly. Strong fingers gripped Lewis's right wrist through the grate. He could feel the cold metal of a key sliding over his skin until it found the shackle's keyhole. The woman's acrid breath on his face smelled like wormy kittens. There! His right wrist was free!

Suddenly Mary froze. She whispered, "They're coming! Radyah help you, *e bibat taboon*." Abruptly she slipped away from him into the dark.

Pliers of fear squeezed Lewis's heart. He flung up his free right hand to protect his eyes as three dungeon guards and the turnkey came up to his cell with a lantern.

The turnkey peered in at Lewis. When he saw his prisoner's freed wrist he spat sideways onto the floor. "That blasted old woman!" He opened the grate, which made a metallic screech. "*Zitath!* Crazy Lady's been at her work again." Breathing threats, the turnkey roughly unlocked the chains, pulled Lewis out of the cell, and pushed him down the dungeon corridor.

Funny … he felt so afraid that a cool detachment overcame his pain. Physically, Lewis was stumbling in front of the guards like a tricycle with two wheels, but mentally he scrolled through the schematics of Charon's locating system.

He had made a copy of the resonance system; that was good, the only thing in his dungeon world that was good. With his right hand, Lewis explored the inner pocket of his filthy robe. His index finger touched the tiny, flimsy piece of plastic. *It's still there!* His heart thumped. He had copied the resonance patterns of the thoyo-on because … because part of him wanted to live.

But – Lewis stifled the hope of surviving. He was going to die soon. He would only live long enough to destroy …*Yes, I know the weak spot – I know what to do. I can reroute the current that wells up from Lanthra's singularity. Then, when someone – hopefully Barth – touches one particular control, it'll be like hooking jumpstart cables to the wrong battery terminals. Instead of connecting to Earth, we will all crumble into small molecules. The End!*

Lewis thought of his own death. Finis. No more anything.

Think again, said a faint voice in his mind. *Are there demons in the universe?*

While he stumbled along, Lewis answered mentally and emphatically, *Yes.*

Demons are real spirits, but Radyah's Spirit isn't real?

Lewis shut down the argument.

CHAPTER 29
DEADLY EXECUTIVE

S oon the turnkey's light shone onto the heavy door that led out of the dungeons and into the locating chamber. Once again, Lewis saw the amethyst walls of the locating chamber glittering in globe light, but the chains on one wall darkened its beauty.

Too nearby, clad in crisp Horned Edge robes of gray and white, Barth Layhew stood by the obsidian table. He was scowling, a livid wound on his face, strong arms crossed, looking like an evil genie.

"I want the system working tonight," Barth said as soon as Lewis came into the cave chamber.

"That's impossible," Lewis told him wearily.

"It is possible," Barth stated, an angry muscle throbbing on his temple.

"No," Lewis stated, knowing that he finally had power to make his own terms. "Tomorrow night."

Nostrils flaring, Barth raised a hand. "We've got a big concert tomorrow night. It's the end of the Council. Not a good time for us to … do our work."

"If you want to 'do your work' and not embarrass yourselves with a failed connection, you'll wait until tomorrow night."

Barth spat an overripe Earth obscenity but gave in.

Slowly but professionally, like a dentist exploring a tooth for cavities, Lewis examined the damage he had done to the obsidian table and its components. He had to admit to himself, *It's less hacked up than I thought. Barth is right.*

Barth said, "Charon says that you had the thing nearly

working before you went berserk." His big hands worked as if he longed to wring Lewis's neck. "While you were otherwise … occupied, we repaired some things. We still have to repair the table control panel, plus the noretha that guides the nexus to Earth, but that shouldn't be hard."

"What do you need me for?" Lewis asked scornfully. "It looks like you have everything in hand on your own."

Barth glowered, his eyes narrowed and hot like boiling beakers. Lewis could imagine himself boiling alive in them, kicking and screaming. Reluctantly, as if every word cost him a fortune, the big man seethed through his teeth, "My Master, Lord Charon, … ordered me … to appoint you … to coordinate the work. He believes that you are the only one who understands the whole system. I will not, I repeat, I will not let you embarrass me."

Lewis coughed for a minute or two, partly for sarcastic effect, but partly because his chest was a fluid-filled bagpipe which some doughty highlander was squeezing. He swayed on his feet, and the guards came up to him, but he shook them off. His mind already had the job organized.

Slowly, like a very old man, Lewis bent down to look at the hot marble, which was still stuck in the control panel. It sported a deep crack on its amber surface.

Do I truly have to repair the hot marble? Its subatomic structure maps the route through the gravitational structures from Lanthra to Earth, and I don't want Charon to connect there; no, not at all.

Immediately a very distracting buzz broke into his thoughts. It reminded him of the noise in an elementary school lunchroom with enameled hollow block walls, painted cement floor, and a hundred small children talking shrilly. *Shut up and let me think!*

Through the cacophony, a very clear, clean voice said euphonically, *Repair it all, Lewis. Repair the hot marble. Get the whole system working. And make a clean copy of everything – and I do mean everything for yourself.*

Lewis cocked his head, listening with senses that had little to do with his ears. Deep down in a place that wasn't hurting, afraid, or confused, he felt a microgram of peace. *All right,* he agreed. *If I live long enough.*

What a novel idea – he might live through this nightmare.

Hey, he *already* had a copy of the resonance tuning structure. Why not go for the Full Monty? Why not go for the entire system, including the Hot Marble? Even if he died, it would be fun to literally have the universe in his pocket.

"Before I begin," Lewis said to his guards, "I want to look a little better than this." He brushed his good hand down his robe, which was torn and dirty and had a certain pungent dungeon smell. In the process, he also palmed the flimsy copy of the resonance system.

From the cave chamber, the guards led Lewis up the stairs to his own suite. Removing the ugly sling that secured his left arm to his neck, they helped Lewis strip off his soiled robe – "Ow, ow, ow," he cried – and he threw the robe disdainfully on the floor. "Now," he ordered, "I want a bath, some nice clothes, and some food. And a doctor."

Palace servants washed Lewis, shaved him, and trimmed his hair. They cleaned his nails. They clothed him in a beautiful new gray robe with the white lining of a Torish magus. The soft, light material – probably a weave of cotton and marsh reed fiber – flowed handsomely over his skinniness.

How quickly I change from a ragman to an executive.

Outside, he looked elegant, authoritative, knife-blade thin, professionally attired. Inside, Lewis felt hard as a cold ceramic tile. He could, as Barth said, repair the system quickly. However, he intended to fulfill his purpose: To repair the locating system but rig it to destroy itself. And, contradictorily, during the repair process, he would make himself a copy of the entire system.

Lord Charon's own personal physician came to Lewis's room to wait on him. Lewis had a long coughing spell and spat into a bowl that the physician supplied. There was blood and yellow mucus in the spit. "The last time I saw you," the doctor said with fatherly concern, "you had pneumonia. Now you've got it again! You've been working yourself to death! And what happened to your left shoulder?"

"I had an accident. I fell," Lewis lied.

The doctor supported the injured left arm in a neat sling made of black linen with a handsome gold border. It supported the shoulder properly and Lewis began to feel the pain ease. He ate for the first time in several days, a small meal of summer fruit, toasted oat bread, and hot fragrant tea from Siphe. He dumped a lot of honey in it.

"Let me give you something for your cough," the doctor said, producing a small brown bottle from his pocket and tilting it toward the teacup.

Lewis held up his hand. "Wait." When he had arrived at Whitehall, so sick that he almost died, the doctor had been a great comfort. Now he knew that the palace physician was Charon's willing pawn. *You gave me drugs. Mind-controlling drugs*, he thought. "No," Lewis asserted.

"Well, then …" the doctor began, drawing out another bottle, a green one, but Lewis imperiously held up a hand.

"No."

The doctor's genial round face flashed with an ugly look. "Lord Charon expressly ordered –" he began, but Lewis cut him off.

"No. You can go now."

The physician left with a red, angry face. Young, deferential Whitehall guards escorted Lewis from his room to the laboratory. A short distance from the lab, Barth in his Horned Edge uniform met them. He took in the "new" Lewis with a tightening of his rosy mouth and jealous sparks in his eyes. "I'll take him from here," he told the guards and dismissed them.

"I know you are stalling," he hissed in Lewis's ear.

Lewis did not bother to reply. His hand did not need to tap the pocket of his new robe to know that the flimsy copy of the resonance system was safe. Now he would harvest the rest of the crop.

When Lewis entered the laboratory with Barth, the lab staff straightened up. Some stared at him, all of them bowed. Labeth's lovely eyes darkened with desire, Mildred smirked, and Jeffrey's colorless eyes glanced knowingly at the sling.

Barth announced unnecessarily with an official tone, "Fean Brahmindura has been away for a few days. He's been ill." He stepped back to put Lewis back in charge.

Lewis swayed a little, coughed, yet his mind purred smoothly forward: *Here goes!*

He began, looking at each of his staff in turn as if he or she were the most important person in the universe, "We can get the thoyo-on fully restored and operating by tomorrow afternoon. This is what we have to do …" Calmly and succinctly, Lewis summarized the steps he had organized in his mind. The staff hung eagerly on his words, excitement growing on their faces although Barth sneered resentfully with his lips curled and nostrils flared.

Lewis finished, "We will have to work through the night. Let's get started."

CHAPTER 30
THE PATRIOTS' PLAN

Once again, an intent group of conspirators crowded the Tuttle kitchen. On Fred's right, Tom tilted back in his chair, fingering his precious lute. The bard softly stroked the strings, making very little noise but apparently creating a new song in his head. Long-faced lugubrious Harwath was there, but Nat was absent, and Hermann, also, was occupied with other business.

Fred leaned on the kitchen table, enjoying how the candlelight shone on Jane Tuttle's rich dark hair. Across from him, the lovely lady sat and toyed with an empty teacup. When she looked up and saw him looking at her, she smiled.

Fred's heart melted. *I would really enjoy a future with her. Could she ever like me?*

Next to Jane sat her brother Curly, who looked energetic and wide awake, even though he had been baking at Whitehall since before dawn the previous day and would be leaving for work again in an hour. Curly diagrammed the Patriot plan on the tablecloth with one stubby but very clean baker's finger.

"My napkin represents Whitehall's main entrance, South Gate. 'Tis very well guarded. We'll leave it alone. The northeast side – put your cup there, Jane – represents the gate for military and Horned Edge magi. There's no way for us defeat them. The best we can do is to block off the gate from the inside. Nat's spoon, on the west end, is the kitchen delivery entrance. That's where the Patriots will come in. Our group will capture Whitehall from inside out; Nat's fellows will capture the city while the guards are fighting us in Whitehall."

Fred asked, "How will the Patriots get enough people in Whitehall to take over?"

Curly smiled, looking very assured. "That's all taken care of. On concert night, our lad Thomas Forschwynn will draw a very great crowd to Charon's palace. I expect more than three thousand *foaya,* including barons, wealthy citizens, and the magi attending the Council. Naturally, such a large gathering will require a large staff! And most of us are Patriots! We have arms. Also, thanks to your employer's entreaty, Whitehall will broadcast the concert to the *biaya* – the common folk – in the Moorway streets. Many of them will help Nat to take over Moorway."

Fred's eyebrows zoomed up. "And what technology could be doing that?"

"Never mind," Harwath said. "Nat set it up – but you don't want to know more than that."

"Not only the staff, but many of the rapt audience will be our Patriot friends. Therefore, Nat's people will lead from the city, and Harwath's people, stationed here and here ..." Curly's finger jabbed at several locations on the table between the teacup, napkin, and spoon, "will lead the take-over inside the palace."

Fred's stomach suddenly felt unsettled. Maybe it was just the Moorway heat, or maybe it was the fact that he might die tomorrow night ... He gulped another swig of tea. *Tea is supposed to calm a queasy stomach, right?*

"What about the military camp?" asked Nat. "They've got a mighty big anthill around that northeast gate, plus both the city and the palace are full of Eagle and Horned Edge soldiers."

Curly's face looked bland. "We've got a plan for that, too."

Jane dropped her teacup. It hit the floor and the handle cracked off.

"Apparently you're not so sure about that part of your plan," Fred commented, and Curly scowled.

"I am sure. But that part is none of your business!"

Tom gave a crooked smile and kept running his fingers over the lute. "Here's my part: I keep everybody enthralled with my magic. When I give the signal, however, the real performance shall begin." The bard strummed a dramatic chord.

Fred chugged another sip of tea, but some of it sloshed down his chin. He kept his voice even and deleted every trace of sarcasm. "Okay, it sounds like it's all very well planned. What's my part? Do you trust me to help or do you intend to lock me in the closet?"

Fred knew there was bad news when nobody would meet his eyes.

Curly said in a mollifying tone, "We can't risk it, Fred. You're from Earth. You're especially vulnerable –"

Fred broke in harshly, "To what? To betray everybody again?" Pain stabbed his heart when Jane looked down. The whole room seemed to go dark.

"Aren't you forgetting something?" a small voice said from behind. Fred jumped. Patrick had sneaked into the kitchen.

"What do you mean, *bibath*?" Curly asked gently.

Patrick said, his boyish voice edged with anger, "What about Lewis?" He limped forward. Fred saw that his usually good-natured brown eyes were dark, and his eyebrows had drawn together. "You haven't mentioned him even once. Aren't you going to rescue him like you did me?"

An odd hardness spread over Harwath's face. "He's not on our side, laddie."

"How do you know he's not?" Patrick argued. "Maybe he's just pretending to help Charon, waiting for his chance –"

"No." Both Harwath and Curly shook their heads.

"Why not?" Patrick said, his voice rising angrily. The crutch tapped the floor with a sharp *donk!*

"Yeah, why not?" Fred added.

Harwath gave Fred an intimidating look. "Keep out of it!"

However, Fred felt anger flare and his fists clench. He looked hard back at the Patriots, willing them to understand. "This boy's been separated from his entire world! So … why not?"

"I'll tell you why not," Harwath said. His tone was final. With a conscious effort, Fred clenched his hands below the table.

The Patriot's long face glowered. "I know – I am intimate with people in Whitehall – that Lewis is one of Charon's closest associates. He is allowed into Charon's secret places; he has his own private password. We cannot trust him, and there is no way for us to get to him." Harwath added dryly, "Because of your brother's skills, Charon can connect to Earth. The Horned Edge shall obtain the Shield's experts and weapons – and bizeor – and then he will begin to destroy us. Your brother is in league with evil!"

"If you can't get to Lewis, how do you k … know…" Patrick stuttered, and he began again. "How do you know he's not trying to help us?" The crutch banged on the floor. "You've got all these great plans. Can't you plan to rescue him?"

Jane bit her lip; Curly closed his eyes and sighed, but Harwath looked steadfastly at the boy and lines deepened around his mouth. "We canna' rescue him if he doesn't want to come."

In the lamplight, Fred could see tears glistening on Patrick's cheeks. Pushing past the others, he put his arm around Patrick's shoulder. "I will," Fred asserted, "I will have a part in our revolt. My part will be to find Lewis and get him out of there, whether he wants to come or not! Now, who can go with me? I need somebody that knows his way around Whitehall."

Harwath began, "No one –"

Jane interrupted, "Hermann. Fred can go with Hermann to rescue his friend."

CHAPTER 31
PATRICK'S MISTAKE

Before dawn on the Big Day, Patrick made a decision. For once he was awake before anyone else, except Curly who had already gone to work around 3:00 a.m. or the *nin brot,* as the Lanthrans called time. He was sure that he could move around the house without being noticed.

Patrick waited, lying on his narrow bed in the dim bedroom, pillow and sheets dumped onto the floor because it was too hot to cover up, even at night. In the distance hooted a turtledove. The house was quiet, except for Bessie, his pretend sister, who slept on the bed next to his, emitting little snorts. He figured he could get past her well enough.

This was his opportunity to help the Patriots – by getting out of their way.

His ankle still hurt. In fact, his ankle felt as if a miniature strong man from the circus had gotten in there and was pounding away with a sledgehammer. It was going to be harder and harder to conceal the pain. Words circled through his head over and over like a dour poem:

> *If I stay here, Jane will see that I'm hurting and take me to the doctor.*
>
> *The doctor may tell the bad guys about me.*
>
> *If the bad guys find out about me, Jane and her family will get hurt.*
>
> *Therefore, I've got to disappear until after the revolt.*

Now there was enough gray light to see. Patrick swung himself to a sitting position. His "Martha" costume, the dreaded red-checkered dress, draped the chair. On the dresser looking like a furry dead animal was the wig of long dark hair. Should he wear them?

No. It's too hot. Besides, I hate, I hate looking like a girl. I want to be me!

Leaning against the wall by his bed was the crutch. Should he use it? *No. The crutch will call attention to me. Pain or no pain, my ankle will hold me up for another day or two.*

He would walk out of the house with boy's clothes on and try to look as normal as possible. There had to be lots of kids like him in Moorway. He didn't have to hide forever, just long enough for the Patriots to do their stuff.

Moving quietly to keep Bessie from waking up, Patrick fumbled for a pen and paper. Tongue in teeth, he scrawled a note to Jane in Lanthran:

Gone for a walk. Be back soon. Love, Marty.

After he inspected his note, he thought, *Good grief, my handwriting is awful. Maybe I should become a doctor.* The thought pleased him. For a moment, he imagined himself: cool, authoritative, famous, and elegant in a white coat with a stethoscope. His latest patient, Bessie, sat on the examining table, wincing and moaning. "The x-rays show a greenstick fracture of the right ulna," he diagnosed. "It will have to be set in surgery under anesthesia." She looked up at him with admiring, grateful eyes. Patrick added, "I'll get prepped …"

The real Bessie snorted, and he instantly turned off the fantasy. *Uh, oh. Is she waking up?*

However, Bessie rolled over, and the soft sounds of her breathing continued rhythmically. Slowly and quietly, Patrick put the note on the dresser by the wig. Careful not to let the bed creak, he stood up. *Ow!* Could he stand to walk on that foot?

I can and I will.

First, he had to find pants and a shirt. The Tuttles weren't rich. All "Martha" had to wear was the red-checked dress for every day and a green shift for laundry day. There was no Glad Day in Moorway. All "Patrick" had to wear was a blue t-shirt and his (thank goodness!) male-style underwear.

Carrying his shoes, he took a few tentative steps. *Ow,* step, *ow,* step, and *ow* again. *I can do this. Keep going.* Patrick tiptoed past Bessie, into the hall, and into Curly's bedroom. The whole room smelled like warm bread, as if the aroma of Curly's job at Whitehall had come home with him. The wonderful smell made his mouth water. Could he put off his escape until after breakfast?

No. He had to be tough. He might not get to eat all day, if that was what it took to stay out of sight until the Patriots had done their thing.

Mostly by feel rather than sight, Patrick got a pair of Curly's pants out of the wardrobe and tried them on. They fit rather badly. For a baker, Curly was tiny. The waist was too tight, and the legs were too long. However, if Patrick sucked in his stomach and rolled the legs into cuffs, the pants would do. If he didn't tuck his shirt in, he could forget to button up the last button on the pants and give himself a little belly room.

After getting dressed, Patrick firmly pushed his glasses up onto his nose and stared at Curly's mirror to see how he looked. A little light sifted through the window, but only a Patrick-sized form could be seen in the gloom. He decided, *I'll blend in the crowd.*

Holding his shoes, he quietly moved barefoot down the stairs, through the kitchen, and outside into the back alley. *Ow. Ow!* The huge tree made the back alley cool and very dark. He leaned on the tree and listened to the early birds chirping sleepily overhead.

When the pain eased, Patrick rounded the block of row houses, followed several lanes, and reached a brick-paved main street. So far as he could see, he was the only person outside. Which way to go? When he looked around, he saw monotonous dark rows of narrow, three-story houses. However, the rosy-fingered dawn gleamed on a white mountain – Whitehall. That way!

When Patrick neared the river, he turned into a tree-lined boulevard of large patrician houses. Between the houses, the perspectives showed that he was very close to the river. Dodging hedges and walls to shortcut toward the bridge, Patrick laughed out loud at one very small dog doing its business on manicured grass. "I bet you're on your neighbor's yard!" The dog guiltily wiped its feet and then walked – as Patrick had guessed – back onto its own yard. When Patrick passed, the dog barked furiously. "Hush!"

No more houses. He had come to a low wall at the end of a

cul-de-sac.

Wow – look at that!

Patrick stood on his toes to see over the wall. Down, down, down below, a river sparkled with diamonds in a deep, purple-shadowed gorge. He raised his head and looked up. Across the gorge soared white stone palisades, and behind them – Whitehall's gleaming dome.

Wow, double wow! That's where Lewis is. Maybe I can help rescue him. But, how can I get over there?

Patrick looked for a bridge. There it was to the left, peachy white with blue shadows in the early morning light. *Perfect. I'll cross the bridge and find a place to stay. And then I'll rescue my bro'.*

Patrick took his time crossing because his ankle was screaming. By now, it was Moorway rush hour. People-pulled carts full of ice, meat, and milk, or brushes, brooms, scissors, and tools …

A ripe-smelling honey-wagon trundled by going the other way. *Ugh!* He held his nose until the stench passed.

As Patrick neared the end of the bridge, he stopped to hang over the bridge rail. *Ahhh, there's a breeze!* Very close now rose the tall peak of the Whitehall dome. *My brother is in there, a captive of the Dark Lord.*

Patrick pictured himself sneaking into Whitehall via a hidden door. His clothes were black, and he wore a mask over his face. He was invisible and stealthy as a ninja. He'd listen in the shadows until he learned where Lewis was. *He's probably locked up in a tower.* Then, as silent as smoke, he'd creep up hundreds of winding stairs. At the top would be a locked door.

How would he get in?

Pausing on the bridge, Patrick felt in the pocket of Curly's pants. There was a funky coil of metal in it, an interesting piece of trash that he'd picked up several neighborhoods ago. He could use it to pick the lock on the tower door.

Back to the rescue: As soon as he opened the tower door, he'd see Lewis. Poor Lewis lay on a ratty old blanket. His hands were tied, and his mouth was gagged. When he saw Patrick's ninja mask, his eyes got huge. He shrank back. But, when Patrick peeled off the black cloth that veiled his face and said, "Hey, bro', it's

Patrick! Come on, let's get out of here!" Lewis's face lit up with joy. With swift, sure movements, Patrick removed Lewis's gag and cut his bonds. He helped his brother stand up.

Lewis hugged him tightly. Glowing with grateful pride, Lewis held Patrick at arms' length and looked up and down at his disguised form. "Patrick! I can't believe how completely awesome you are! I knew you would come for me!"

The imaginary adventure collapsed like a dynamited high rise when a bolt of pain shocked Patrick's ankle. "Owww!" he cried out. The daylight seemed to turn red. He couldn't take another step. Sweat rolled off his forehead. "O Lordy, that hurts!"

A wicked spear pierced his ankle again. He slid to the pavement.

Immediately, several coaches and carts stopped. People rushed toward him, a disorganized crowd; there were hands and feet all around him. One guy, a great big man with rich clothes and a fancy hat, put his arms around Patrick and lifted him.

"Thanks," Patrick croaked. The red haze in his head dimmed to twilight. He let himself be carried like a baby to a coach. The big rich man laid him gently inside on the leather upholstery, got in with him, spoke urgently to the driver, and Patrick felt the coach lurch slowly forward, starting and stopping because it was stuck in traffic.

The inside of the coach was much cooler than the bridge pavement. It smelled like the expensive area of a men's store, like leather, shaving scent, and a hint of oiled metal. Once the pain eased, Patrick's eyes came back into focus.

"Hey," he began, "thank you for …" Blinking to clear his vision, he turned to look at the man's face.

"B … Barth!" he sputtered. His stomach sank a million miles.

"Yep, it's me."

"How did you know –?"

"What other eleven-year-boy would limp and then collapse on Whitehall Bridge?" Barth answered sarcastically. He firmly clasped a huge hand over Patrick's wrist. There was no use struggling, even if his ankle were okay, which it wasn't.

"Where –?"

"Calm down! You'll have enough talking to do when we reach Whitehall."

Patrick shrank back, just as he had imagined Lewis doing, but he rallied and tried persuasion. "Can't you just let me go? I'm just a kid; I won't hurt anybody."

Barth did not answer. His full-moon face darkened, his light blue eyes narrowed, his nostrils flared, and the too-red lips pressed tightly together.

Eventually the coached escaped the traffic jam and headed toward Whitehall. Barth's hand squeezed Patrick's wrist; It hurt, it hurt. Vividly, Patrick replayed that evil night in the Rockeerie mountains; he remembered the ropes on his wrists and the knife against his throat. Once again, he heard Lewis begging Barth to save him. *No! Please, no! Don't kill the boy! Please don't hurt my little brother!*

But Lewis wasn't here this time.

To his shame, Patrick began to shake. His knees knocked and his whole body spasmed. Barth glanced at him briefly. His hold on Patrick loosened slightly.

Patrick mentally snarled at the enemy, *I hate you! I hate you! If you torture me, I won't talk!*

However, the truth stared in his face, saying, *If they torture you, you will talk. You'll give away the Patriots' plans and they'll get slaughtered.*

*   *   *

Lewis did not know what time of day it was, nor did he care. He went to his suite for fresh clothes and another meal – it might have been breakfast. Afterward, the doctor visited and tried again to give him medicine.

"Your chest is full of fluid," the doctor said. "You have a fever, and your heart rate –"

"Never mind." No more drugs.

The doctor left. His valets washed him, shaved him, trimmed his nails, and brushed his wavy hair. Lewis cried out a few times when his shoulder moved, but he made it through the grooming process without too much embarrassment. They brought him a change of clothes: a mahogany brown robe with a silk oyster white lining. Clad and complete with sling, Lewis checked his appearance … he looked very good indeed for an angel of death.

A dim memory of the old Lewis came to mind as he looked in the mirror. Since that Hot Marble of Doom had entered his life, he had evolved from the standard nerd wearing a white shirt and dark pants to a Bardian apprentice magus in a simple black robe. Now he, in this fatal moment, wore robes fit for a rajah.

Not two, but five Horned Edge guards waited in the hallway to escort him back to the laboratory. This amused Lewis, because he had no desire at all to escape. He chuckled to himself, *Charon's plans will crumble. While everyone is entertained tonight at the concert, Barth and Charon and I will open the connection to Earth. Some weapons may come through, but not many, and soon we will turn to dust.* His graveyard humor was interrupted by a bout of coughing. Before he went out, he spat phlegm, blood, and yellow pus into a spittoon held by one young valet, who looked totally grossed out.

Lewis surveyed what had been his apartment in Whitehall for the past months. Suddenly the suite looked beautiful, warm, inviting. *Don't leave,* said the glittering gold-flecked walls. *Come back to us,* said the canopied bed, his desk and chair, the sofa, the gorgeous, jeweled lamps.

Sorry. He turned his head away and stepped into the hallway, Horned Edge guards flanking him before and behind. For the rest of the day and the night, he expected to be in the bowels of Whitehall, in the cave chamber. But after that he'd be … maybe nowhere.

However, a brief thought flitted across his mind like an erratic butterfly: *Life isn't over yet!* It made him pause.

The thought reminded him of Deirdre. She was soft, sumptuous, with a mind keen as a polished knife and a touch as cool and sweet as a highland stream. *Maybe, maybe there is a resurrection. If so, I'll get to see her again.* He laughed out loud all the way to the laboratory until the hallway rang and the Horned Edge guards looked at him as if he was crazy.

CHAPTER 32
WHERE'S HERE?

Gracie gradually awoke from a refreshing sleep. Every atom in her body felt perfect and her mind flowed as easily as the breeze on her face. Outside, a whole flock of birds sang a morning concert – but she dimly remembered that there was only one tree, a huge tree in the back courtyard.

"Hey, Tree, the birds really like you," she murmured.

Her eyes opened wide. *Could I be back home? Are the birds singing in my climbing tree, and could I go out and find my notebook? What a story I have to write! Mom and Dad will –*

But she wasn't in her bedroom back home.

Gracie pushed away the ugly sadness that suddenly brought tears to her eyes. *I don't want to think about home. Where am I now?*

She slid out of bed to look out the window. Heat shimmered on stone or pavement, the breeze through the window reminded her of sitting with Daniel in the tower. He and she were prisoners. Daniel had a plan to rescue her. *Oh yes, I remember now. I ate glop, went to sleep, and somebody brought me here.* However, the memory did not answer the question: *Where's here?*

Immediately, the bedroom door swung open and a very pretty woman in a blue dress came in. She smiled welcomingly but Gracie caught the worry and fear haunting her eyes. There were only the usual morning sounds outside and a small hubbub inside of some kids downstairs eating breakfast, so why was this lady so upset? "What's going on?"

The woman said quickly, "Hello, Gracie. We need to –"

"How do you know my name?" Gracie asked cautiously. She

was pretty sure that she was in a safe place, but it didn't hurt to check. "Where am I? What's going on?"

"There's no time for questions, *bimi,*" the lovely lady said. "Call me 'Mama' and put on these clothes and the wig." She pointed to a red-checked dress and a wig of long dark-brown hair that had been laid carefully on a bureau. "After that, come on downstairs and meet my girls, Bessie, Katie, and June. We're a family and now you're part of it. By the way, your Uncle Curly works at Whitehall as a baker."

"But why –?"

"I don't have time to tell you more right now."

CHAPTER 33
READY FOR THE CONCERT

At Mister Swa's tavern entrance, a huge black and gold carriage drew up and parked. "Rented it for the occasion," Mr. Swa said with a rich contented sigh.

Fred stared at the four matching bay horses in harness while Mr. Swa made last-minute arrangements with the driver. His belly did flops. "You look great, Tom," he commented, just for something to say to break the tension. The bard wore a matte black suit, boots, and cape that set off his long legs and black hair. His waist was girded by a black leather belt with a silver buckle and a dramatic but fake sword with a silver cloisonné handle. "You could pass as Zorro."

"Who's Zorro?" Tom looked anxiously down at his performance clothes.

"Never mind. Do I look okay?" Fred strutted like a ruffled grouse to show off his clothes. *I'm acting like a child.* But he was so wound up that he couldn't stop it. His outfit was mostly brown, but subtly patterned with gold highlights. He, too, wore boots, a cape, and a fake sword with a handsome gold pommel.

"Ready?" asked Mr. Swa, bouncing on his booted feet and grinning happily.

"Ready," Tom replied glumly, clutching his lute with intense affection, as a mama might hug her baby before going to the hospital for major surgery.

"Ready," Fred echoed. He imagined the "ready" word bouncing off a thousand walls until it reached Whitehall. *Ready indeed. Ready to support the Patriots. Ready to rescue Lewis. Ready to undo all the harm I've done.*

And he was ready. He had the mandolin for tonight's opener, his hidden knife, and the copied hot marble – which at present was not hot. *But it will be.*

Fred fingered the inches-thick velvet stage curtain and opened it a few inches to examine Rose Hall from backstage. *I'm not scared, not scared at all that in an hour or two I'm headed to the dungeons to rescue Lewis – with Hermann the Bat-Face, no less.*

Too jittery to stay still, he began to babble in the semi-darkness behind the great curtain, his stomach twisting like a tangled kite string, "This place is really impressive; even you and I look fancy. You're as black as a Black Rider from Mordor – the Horned Edge crowd ought to love you. The light will make me look like Golden Boy."

"*Subua! Dit!*" Tom interrupted. He jerked his chin toward several Horned Edge military magi conversing in a dark corner near them.

"Okay, okay, I'll be quiet," Fred whispered.

Fred checked his watch – he didn't have a watch. He guessed that it was an hour before the curtain was to go up. His skin felt an electric charge and cool breath of air as before a thunderstorm, while various techies wandered back and forth to examine props, tools, ropes, wires, lighting, and other backstage necessities.

He went back to peek through the curtain. This time he analyzed Rose Hall's acoustics. *These pink marble walls – enormously expensive – will reflect the sound so that every overtone of voice or instrument can be heard. To prevent confusing echoes, they put up baffles – looks like some kind of wood inlaid with gold, very pretty. And the what-cha-call-it ...bishop's pulpit roof ... projects the sound as well as a microphone ...*

Tom took Fred's place and pulled aside the curtain an inch.

Fred was so pumped up that he became ridiculously optimistic. *I may be rich and famous if we live through this ... and maybe the Patriots will succeed after all ... and maybe Hermann (bleh) and I'll rescue Lewis and Pat and get them back home ... and maybe I'll get married and have a family of my own –*

"*He fup!*" Tom swore, his voice a cherry bomb in Fred's ear.

Fred jumped, his heart pounding. "What the –!"

"My evil uncle is in the audience – *szttitsa!* And I have only a rubber sword." The kid's knuckles were white, clutched on the useless sword pommel.

Fred felt his own stomach drop to the cold floor. "Oh no, not Baron Trager again!" He looked out over the sea of faces, fine clothes, and glittering jewels that filled Rose Hall. "Where is he? There must be a thousand people in here already. How could you possibly see him?"

"He's the bearded gentleman in front of the third pillar on the left," Tom said grimly, and Fred followed his eyes.

"Augh!" Fred peered around Tom's head. "Ah, yes. I see him … smug aristocratic face, pointy beard, gold cane. And his guys in the nasty plum-purple uniforms. Great Scot, they're all armed, too – why in the heck did Whitehall security allow that?"

He and Tom looked at each other, thinking the same thing: *Charon may know about our plans. All his people are armed and ready. But it's too late to pull back now.*

CHAPTER 34
NOT EVEN ONE SYLLABLE

Before the concert, Daniel, splendid in the gold-lined robe of his office, ascended the marble stairway to the Council Chamber to give the final address. Every word of it was completely scripted. He remembered the severe warning to stick to it.

"If you depart from even one syllable," Commander Gort of the Horned Edge had privately assured him in the dressing room a half hour ago, "Your little girl will suffer."

"All right," he had told Gort submissively, "Not even one syllable." *Ha! he thought. Gracie is gone, safely away from this ghoulish dome.*

Followed by a grand train of Council members, officials, staff, and scowling Horned Edge security guards, Daniel took his majestic time, step by step in his soft leather boots. He knew that the slow procession would impress the assembly and also irritate Charon's people into emotional hives.

Charon thinks his plans are set – well, mine are, too.

Before the Council officially began, when the magi were finding their seats, Roger, the representative magus of Smythe, pushed through the crowd to Daniel and bowed low. "Hegofean, High Magus Daniel," he asked, his face calm but his hawk-gold eyes shining with urgency, "May I talk with you later, during the feast?"

"We –" Daniel began, but Commander Gort grabbed his elbow from behind.

Daniel turned, gritting his teeth at the impertinence, but Gort shook his fat head. "The places at the Hegofean's table have already been assigned."

Roger persisted despite Gort's evil glare. "After the concert, then?"

"Hegofean Higgins will not be attending tonight's concert." Gort's small eyes, deep in their folds of fat, were as red and mean as a wild boar's. "He has other business."

The Horned Edge phalanx pushed Daniel away from Roger toward the balcony steps. However, Roger kept up with them along the gorgeously frescoed hallway, determined to get an answer. "Surely," Roger said, "tonight, we –"

Daniel again felt the crushing grip on his elbow. He restrained himself from screaming in a tantrum. *Gort, you biz-bag, I'm still the High Magus. Do you want me to fry you into greasy bacon with a curse?*

Yes, he could do that. He served the Master. He was the Hegofean, for goodness' sake!

Do not curse him, Daniel.

What should I do, then? Daniel argued.

I'm the Lord of Rest. You shall rest.

He sighed, submitted to both Gort and the Master, and demurred stiffly to Roger, "Sorry, Fean of Smythe. We cannot talk tonight; I'll be detained." Daniel raised one eyebrow, just a small intentional twitch, and Roger returned a fractional, understanding, but frustrated nod.

Daniel, Commander Gort, and their Horned Edge entourage swept past the representative from Smythe, but Roger did not give up. "The Thamaon greets you! She says that her friends will visit you soon after the Council!" He spoke some more words in a Malay dialect, an Earth language known well in Eleaemana but seldom studied by the magi in Tor.

Without turning around, Daniel flicked his right hand to show that he had understood.

Roger headed for his seat because the Council was about to begin. Despite the Horned Edge guards and Commander Gort's humiliating directives, Daniel's soul joyously leaped. *Charon's foray to kidnap my daughter Deirdre made the Thamaon of Smythe furious. She is sending help to support the Patriot's Revolt! Thank you, Roger!*

He was last to enter the High Council balcony that overlooked the assembly. Lord Charon, looking calm and inscrutable, had already taken the seat at Daniel's right hand. However, the magi below swayed and stirred and murmured at higher decibels than usual, for tonight they were to vote whether to restore the ancient technology. They were also faced with a deeply emotional choice: Could they uphold the One Law if that technology were restored?

If they restored the ancient technology, Lanthra could bloom with creativity. Daniel supported this. If they voted to uphold the One Law, however, any physical connection to Earth would be forbidden. Perhaps then the magi could stop Charon's plans to conquer Lanthra. If this Council did not support the One Law ... Daniel shuddered to imagine the war that would ensue. The Shields could conquer Earth, the Horned Edge magi could conquer Lanthra, and ... Eventually, the two would be pitted against each other for control of both worlds.

The very room shivered with tension. Below, Daniel saw Mark Gregory dressed in the gray and white robe of the Horned Edge military magi. They made eye contact, briefly.

When Daniel reached his seat, he faced the assembly, standing, his hands raised in blessing. Everyone stood, even Charon. The chamber, filled with August evening sunlight, became completely silent. Sunbeams with shining motes brushed his left sleeve. He still sensed a vile malice nearby, one among the spirits that haunted Whitehall.

To Radyah ta foroya te bizeor yovinovit ... He laughed inside at the pun in the English translation: *Big biz-ness is about to collapse.*

He began to speak. As promised, he stayed with the script. And, afterward, the magi voted.

CHAPTER 35
TRUST

You mean Patrick was here? And now I'm pretending to be him pretending to be your daughter?" Gracie couldn't believe it. So much was happening that her brain had frozen like a locked-up computer application. Her hands moved automatically, detached from her brain as she put on the wig that "Mama" Tuttle provided.

"Yes, bimi, your brother was here." Mama Jane's pretty oval face looked pale, even in the bright late afternoon sunlight.

"Where is he now?"

"I … I can't tell you that."

Although sweat already trickled in her hair under the wig, Gracie felt cold inside. Before, in her Earth life, even in her Lanthran life with the Gregorys, she would have been quiet and accepted the non-answer, but too much had happened since then. She had nothing to lose anymore – except her brothers. She'd almost despaired when she thought they were dead, she'd quaked inside when she found out they were captives, and now she burned like a forest fire.

Patrick wore these clothes. He slept in this bed and stood where I'm standing. I'm only an inch of time away from him, and I won't give up until I can see him and touch him again.

"Mama," she said fiercely, in a voice that would have made the schoolteachers back on Earth jump out of their shoes, "Tell me what happened to Patrick!"

"There will be a house-to-house search. Soon. I'm afraid –"

"Mama, if you won't tell me more, I'm going to scream until somebody comes running to find out what's going on!"

For a moment, the muscles in Jane's neck tensed like cords. However, then Gracie saw the pretty lady relax. A pleasant blush came back to her face; her hands released their fists, and she took a deep breath. "Good, bimi, you know your power." She looked proud of Gracie, not offended. "Come on down to the kitchen. It's cooler there. Get to know Bessie, Katie, and June while I serve iced melon."

"And you'll tell me everything?"

Jane smiled, a lovely smile but very sad. "I don't know. This information is dangerous – to us as well as to you. All our plans and hopes may collapse if … Howe'er, you've a right to the truth. Come downstairs for supper. My girls look forward to meeting you and we can talk together about … everything." She left Gracie to complete the more intimate routines of getting dressed.

Bewigged and dressed, Gracie bounded downstairs. However, a full mirror caught the light near the house's front door, so she stopped to look at herself. She hadn't been near a mirror for months.

In addition to being dressed like Patrick, like "Martha," she saw that she had gotten long-legged from growing, pale from being cooped up, and thin – almost skinny – from prisoner food. The dark wig did not become her. She didn't like the way she looked and felt, even though (at last!) she had nice, clean underwear. A brief unpleasant memory darkened her mind, a picture of herself washing out her panties in full view of leering Torish soldiers.

Gracie took the memory and twisted until it broke its neck. In its place, she substituted another memory. She replayed the proud look that the High Magus often gave her, as if she were lovely and precious. Now, when Gracie looked at herself again in the mirror, her jaw was set and her eyebrows straight with determination. *No one can scare me anymore.*

While she stared at her reflection in the mirror, she felt a hand lightly touch her shoulder. She turned, but no one was there. Jane and the girls were away in the kitchen. Gracie turned back to the mirror and gasped.

"Jesus!"

A young man stood behind her, his hand on her shoulder. He looked a little like Lewis, except not as tall or skinny, and red highlights glinted in his rich dark hair. Although he wore jeans and a plain blue work shirt, lovely white sparkles escaped from him when he moved.

Gracie leaned into his embrace. "I'm so tired," she said. "And there's nothing I can do to help anybody. From the beginning until now, I've been useless."

Jesus said, "*Tabitha,* you are the most important person in this story. Without you, all the others will die, eaten by the bezubs."

"But how –?"

"Because you are the one who trusts me."

"I do?"

However, the young man had gone.

CHAPTER 36
SABOTAGE

Lewis leaned straight and proud against the laboratory's conference table. Soon Lord Charon would call for him and the proceedings start to connect with Earth. As promised, Lewis and his staff had repaired the thoyo-on before the evening concert. Lewis also had secretly copied everything, absolutely everything about the system, and had the little flimsy spiral of silicon-laced plastic safely in his pocket – in case he lived.

A rough voice cut through his thoughts, *How the hell are you going to live? You're dying already!*

Chills shook Lewis's body as if he had fallen into a winter pond. Surreptitiously he coughed. Only a little bloody phlegm came up, so he discretely wiped his mouth on his fine mahogany brown robe.

For the moment, no one was looking at him. His left arm in the sling blocked a view of his right side so, with his right hand, Lewis drew out the bit of plastic that he had hidden in his robe. It was stronger than it looked: A mere gossamer curly ribbon, but stronger than steel, made of carbon fiber. A rainbow spectrum of light flowed across its surface before he pocketed it again. It reminded him of a Bible image …

I remember! The captive prophet Ezekiel wrote about a rainbow, a sapphire throne, wheels, wings, cherubim … Images of a strangely beautiful God turned in his mind like a kaleidoscope. He remembered the time, back on Earth, when he had recorded his thoughts in a journal. Thinking about God – even though he didn't believe in God – ignoring God as if he were inconsequential and boring. *My atheism is quite useless here. God cannot be dismissed. Not when a demon that Lanthran people call Saoma and Earth people call Satan goes after your loved ones. But I will die before I see Patrick and Gracie again.*

You are not going to die. The assertion was a mere tickle in a corner of his brain.

Oh, yes, I will. I've jinxed the system. Everyone in the cave chamber will evaporate. Just the certain touch on the controls ...

No.

Lewis sighed. *Whoever you are, leave me alone. I'm so tired.* For a second, he felt a nudge inside, as if his old dragon was stirring from long torpidity. *Stupid fantasy,* Lewis scolded himself. *There are no dragons.*

At that instant, something in his soul sneaked up, grabbed him, and captured him. It pricked his heart, and emotions exploded: Rage, fear, and grief. They gushed out like the pus from a lanced boil. Lewis bent over trying not to retch.

While Lewis's soul poured out horrible emotions, the red-gold dragon sprang from its cage in his subconscious. It clutched him with sinewy wings and terrible gleaming claws and turned him toward the rainbow. Out of the rainbow came a voice: *Lewis Brahmindura! What are you doing?*

Lewis wanted to black out or just turn into ashes on the spot. The dragon forced his trembling hand upward so that he must see the curl of plastic, the copy of that sonic computer. *After Barth kidnapped Patrick and me, I helped steal! And innocent people were murdered at the Bardian lab because I was too cowardly to defend them!*

Yes, that happened. Now, here you are, ready to murder people again. And I told you to make the copy and keep it when you return from Lanthra to Earth. How will you do that if you are dead?

A coughing fit seized Lewis's chest and the poor lab intern ran in to get the spittoon. Lewis pocketed the plastic film, and in an instant the dragon seized him so tightly that no one, not even himself – especially not himself – could pry him away from his vision.

"Go away!" He groaned. His attendant stared at him with confusion.

"Get out!" Lewis wasn't looking at the attendant, but the

intern rose and ran off, leaving the spittoon.

His dragon said in a voice like a storm, *You have a dream. The man on the rainbow commands you to remember it.*

"What stupid dream?" he said out loud.

A few laboratory people noticed, but they shrugged and turned away.

You know what your dream is. The dragon roared, clutching him so hard that he felt steel talons crack his ribs. *The one you had before this story began, the one you have carried in your soul since you were a boy.*

Lewis grunted out loud as pain shredded his heart. He remembered. *Time travel. I wanted to explore time travel and make it a reality.*

With a cry as raucous as a thousand crowing ravens, the dragon laughed. Its golden-red scales shone; strong nails dug into his Lewis's flesh. *It is not only your dream – It is His!*

Funny – Lewis still leaned against the table, but at the same time the dragon snatched him away into a gleaming rainbow. He was kidnapped by a dream. Lewis smiled.

At that moment, Barth barged into the conference room. "Are we ready? Look at you; you're absolutely spiffy!" Lewis blinked, trying to come back to the present, his soul flaming in the dragon's grip. How odd … the room was full of colors. Blue, gold, crystal, silver, copper … Barth's strange lips were so red they looked like he had applied lipstick.

Lewis straightened up. "If Lord Charon is ready," he replied, "so am I."

"Hurry up. My Lord is waiting for you in the locating chamber."

Lewis walked stately as a prince behind Barth through the laboratory toward the anteroom where the beautiful noretha were kept. However, on the stairs, he stumbled, and some of the laboratory assistants rushed to help him. He waved a hand. "I'm all right."

"Get away from us, you lab rats! None of you are allowed into the cave chamber!" Barth ordered in a grating voice.

The laboratory staff, however, at least a dozen scientists and technicians, looked to Lewis for direction. Mildred's face was so white around her mouth and eyes that he guessed that she was actually depending on him for this success. Even Jeffrey's pale eyes glowed with hopeful anticipation. Labeth shook her shimmering long black hair, mooned at him with her seductive eyes, and sighed deeply.

Barth noticed their admiration and his face blackened.

Lewis ordered, "I want all of you to leave this laboratory. Immediately! Leave! Go to your homes and take two days' leave of absence. You have worked day and night. It's time to rest." *And there's no reason why you should be killed when the thoyo-on destroys itself.*

The staff gave him curious looks, their faces fell, but adamantly, Lewis forced them all to leave. Then he walked behind Barth's broad back toward the ancient door.

Automatically, to fight the fear, Lewis detached his mind just like he had during the torture. His consciousness rose a few feet above his body like a floating balloon with eyes. *No, you are not going to block out fear,* his dragon said inside. When he reached the cave chamber he tried to drink in the beauty of the amethyst-encased cave walls. It was no good. Lewis looked at the chains and smelled the faintly fetid air, and he was afraid, down to his aching bones and his dislocated shoulder.

CHAPTER 37
STEPS OF DESTRUCTION

It was time to connect to Earth. Lord Charon stood by the restored obsidian table in the center of the cave chamber.

"The Council is over, and the concert will begin soon, fean," Lord Charon said. "We have to act now, before the Patriots start their rebellion." His black eyes met Lewis's for a moment with their old warmth, but the look faded into sadness.

"I'm ready." Lewis solemnly knelt before him as he had before ... before murder had filled his heart. Then he stood, reached out his right hand and started the destruct sequence.

Step One. It was that easy.

Barth knelt also, deliberately bowing even lower than Lewis. "I am your servant, Master, ready for your command." He turned his face upward to receive Lord Charon's blessing.

Lord Charon, however, frowned at Barth.

"What have I done?" Barth protested.

Charon began to turn away.

"Master!" Barth cried, "How have I offended you?"

"I do not love you anymore. *Fean* Lewis has repaired and managed my *thoyo-on* well. You have done nothing."

The big man's nostrils flared, and he shot Lewis a look of pure hate. As if by accident, his elbow knocked Lewis to the floor.

Lewis's injured shoulder hit hard stone. Searing pain pierced through his shoulder. "Ow!" he yelled and rocked on the floor to keep from screaming. *I mustn't let my body hurt because my heart hurts too much ...*

No, you will feel hurt, his dragon whispered.

Barth hissed in his ear while apparently helping him up – by the injured arm, "You worthless brownnoser!"

Lewis could not answer because of the pain.

"Look around, Louie. It's getting exciting in here," Barth remarked in a creepy false camaraderie. "We've got six guards and five magi – I see they're wearing their Council robes. And the knives are polished, ready for the sacrifice. I wonder who will be the honored one?"

Lewis thought, *Probably me.* He touched another control, very gently.

Step Two. Edges of sacrificial knives glinted with violet light, but instead of feeling terror, the tortured pain in his left shoulder, or the tight heaviness in his chest, he suppressed all his physical feelings and touched the controls.

Step Three.

Barth again jogged Lewis's injured arm and whispered in his ear with a drizzle of hot spit, "You thought that you could serve Lord Charon and win points to take my place – even take his place someday. For that you are going to die, and your precious pride will melt away when you begin screaming your guts out."

"Be quiet, Barth," Charon said coolly. "You're behaving like a child."

Then Lewis saw Barth's facial muscles literally writhe with anguish. A tri-tone dissonance vibrated in the room and Lewis smelled a strange sourness, something between sweat and skunk. Barth drew back out of reach. *He's afraid,* Lewis realized. *Saoma is tormenting him.*

Lord Charon turned his back to Barth.

"Master!" Barth cried, sweat dripping down his face and neck. He stepped closer to Lord Charon and looked pleadingly at him, but his Master drew away and talked privately with his other Horned Edge attendants.

"Let us begin the sacrifice," Charon announced. "Our part is ready."

Okay, even if I'm the human sacrifice to the bezubs, Lewis realized, *That won't prevent this system and us from evaporating. It'll be quick. It may even explode before they're done with me.* He gestured toward the control panel.

Step Four.

Stubbornness kept him committed to suicide; however, hot

dragon's blood surged through his veins, and a voice from above the rainbow spoke like the ringing of a glass: *Yes, you will feel pain when you live. However, I am taking you away from death to your dream.*

Lewis thought, *No, my dream is impossible.*

Step Five.

Lewis's finger moved just slightly to finish the deadly sequence. Meanwhile, he heard, "The Lord is ready," in English. "Saoma is ready to receive us unto Himself, to fill our hearts with His power and might. We offer Him the first fruits of our labor, the sacrifice of our love."

Distracted, Lewis saw a covey of men entering the far end of the chamber through the dungeon door. They wore black robes with white-lined sleeves, and each proudly displayed a Shields gold ring with its star-shaped diamond. Teeth bared in fierce smiles and faces red, they opened their circle to reveal a dark-haired boy, shoulders drooping, head down.

"You snake, Charon!" Lewis swore, and it was the dragon's anger that he felt as well as his own. "You've brought a *child* to offer to the bezubs!" He flung himself at Charon, to rip his face off, to tear that glossy hair right off his scalp.

"Secure him to the wall," Lord Charon ordered quickly.

Barth grinned and grabbed Lewis by the neck. He hustled him over to the crystal-encrusted wall and held him while a Shield with strong garlic reek fastened a chain to Lewis's right wrist. Lewis shouted, "Damn you, servants of Satan!"

Barth drew back, laughing triumphantly and turning to Lord Charon for approval. However, his Master did not look at him or even nod at him.

Eyes streaming with water, chest heaving, Lewis stood up straight against the crystal-encrusted wall. The dragon inside him did not allow him to detach or get away from his pain. Every breath hurt, throbbing powerfully, his shoulder burned like fire, and he felt it all.

The sacrifice to Saoma began. Endless time went by with ceremony. Twisted Scriptures were read. Prayers were intoned, someone chanted, and the whole Shields group babbled in tongues. Lewis's skin crawled. Heart racing and testing his chain, he thought, *I will do anything to save that child.*

But the dragon that had captured him amended the thought: *No, Lewis.* You *cannot save the boy!*

Lewis's stomach wrenched as Lord Charon gracefully raised his hands in blessing. *I can't bear to feel any more, this is horrible!* But the dragon clutched him and would not allow him to go numb. Meanwhile, the Shields knelt and lowered their eyes as Charon began a chant of praise to Saoma.

The dragon forced Lewis's eyes to look at the boy huddled on the cave chamber floor. He saw brown skin, scruffy dark brown hair, and big brown eyes that even now were curious as well as afraid. For a moment Lewis wondered if Lord Charon had brought a small Lewis-look-alike to torture because, in some weird way, the vicarious sacrifice would satisfy the bizeor. He felt so disgusted that his heart surged almost into explosion.

The boy raised his head, saw Lewis, and startled. "My stars! Lewis! Wow … you've changed. I …" his voice stammered, "I … I didn't recognize you."

"Oh my God, Patrick!" Lewis cried. A sickening vertigo filled his head. He tried to say more but his mouth didn't work; he couldn't breathe, his heart jerked to a stop, and very quickly Lewis could not perceive anything at all.

CHAPTER 38
IN THE CAVES

Unnoticed during the applause and hubbub that followed one of Tom's marvelous pieces, Fred slipped away from Rose Hall via the innocuous stage door. According to plan, he met Hermann in the hallway. The Bardian spy leaned against a marble pillar, arms crossed. *He looks like a black blot on the landscape.*

Although his insides jittered, Fred insolently tipped his hat at him. "Hello, friend! Give me some info! How are we going to get into the dungeons to rescue our friends?"

To his pleasure, Hermann blanched with alarm and hissed. "Shut up, you idiot!" The spy flicked his eyes nervously at several amblers, including a clutch of pink-sleeved female magi and somber male Horned Edge companions who streamed past, headed for refreshment before the intermission crowd.

Fred stubbornly crossed his own arms and waited for an answer. *I will not be treated like a betrayer.* Although Hermann's nose flared and he jerked his chin, Fred refused to budge. Silence stretched; Hermann's end snapped first.

"A much-respected steward will meet us at the banquet hall and show us the way to –"

"Okay, let's go."

Palms so sweaty that he wiped them on his pants, Fred followed Hermann into a large, stately white-marble banquet room. It was softly lit and already set up for the concert crowd. Cream brocade linen covered the tables; the chairs were graced with a gracious lotus lily pattern in soft pinks and greens; and rich gray silk hangings softened the marble walls. Fred licked his lips. "This is scary," he whispered. "I feel like I'm visiting the emperor's court."

"You are," Hermann stated acidly.

Fred exhaled to release some tension. *Focus on the drama, O Nervous One; it's all a play and you are the jester.*

They waited. Each banquet table had been loaded with smoked trout, small quiches, sizzling chorizo in chafing dishes, breadbaskets, bowls of brown rice, vegetable entrees, fresh fruit, gorgeous pastries, pitchers of ice water and juices, and more. Servers in gray uniforms stood ready at each table with carts of more potent drinks. At once Fred's mouth watered. *All I can think of is food.* He turned to Hermann. "Okay, I see the servers all prim and proper, but where's this contact of yours?"

"We're supposed to hang around the hors d'oeuvres tables on the east wall," Hermann said. "Don't spend too much time stuffing your fat stomach."

"Thanks for the advice," Fred shot back. "And stay away from the fruit, Bat-face!"

They waited. Even in the banquet room, Fred could hear and feel Tom's music vibrating through the walls and floor. *The acoustics here are totally awesome.* The bard began a simple piece, a sweet child-like melody that gradually built into the deeply emotional credenza that he had practiced so long. For a moment even Fred, who had heard Tom's credenza over and over, stood spellbound. The music evoked a dance of emotions, sometimes joyful, sometimes fearful, but all with a promise of joy to come. *I want that,* he thought. *Deep Spring, will you, eternal living drink, refresh the dead?*

One of the servers nearby whispered, "I'd heard that the Forschwynn lad was good, but no one told me he was that good!"

"Verily," Hermann replied. The server left with the deep sigh of a moved spirit.

Then Hermann pointed, "Look at the grand old man walking toward us – he's the one we want to meet! His name is Myron." He smiled at the elegant gentleman and waggled his furry eyebrows.

Myron made eye contact and gestured for them to take some refreshment. Although the steward stood at less than medium height, slightly bent over, head crowned with wispy white hair, he radiated: "Perfect Servant." On one arm, Myron balanced a gold tray holding a bottle of white wine in a crystal ice bucket, and a gold-rimmed plate of beautiful fresh-made sushi snacks. "Would you care for some light refreshment, my lords?"

Fred opened his mouth to say, "Yes –"

"No, thank you," Hermann interrupted genteelly. "However, do you have any *wavetops?*" He put a slight emphasis on the last word.

Fred recognized the term as the Lanthran equivalent of very strong whiskey. *I sure could use a drink, but can't I have some snacks first?*

"Certainly," Myron nodded. "Our best *wegavitappa* is stored in the wine cellar. Let me take you there." He winked.

Fred gave himself a knock on the head. *Duh, now I get it! Myron's a Patriot and Hermann's just given him a password! This is it! Here we come, Lewis!*

Myron set down the tray and graciously waved Fred and Hermann toward the kitchen double doors. Fred hung back long enough to grab a roll and chewed it covertly as he followed Hermann and Myron.

The next few sequences followed quickly and easily. They entered the extremely large and clean kitchen, which brought back memories of a much less clean kitchen, the one at Baron Trager's castle, but there was no time for memories now. Busy cooks rushed everywhere. One of them was Curly. The Patriot leader looked over his shoulder and made eye contact, but that was all. Hermann said nothing and neither did Fred.

Myron directed them toward a handsome white-painted door with a cut-glass knob. He opened it easily. The "cellar" was a huge walk-in storage room, very cool inside, and frosty curls of air tickled Fred's skin. He saw shelves holding hundreds of bottles of wine, whiskey and beer, their liquids ranging from ice white to glorious crimson, mellow gold to fiery orange. When Myron pushed a panel, a whole section of shelves swung open, and Fred saw a hidden door, small, old, gray, and covered with dust. Myron coughed, Hermann blasted out a sneeze, and Fred nearly choked. *Woohoo! This looks like Jack Benny's basement!* A spooky winding stairway circled down into darkness.

Myron opened a compartment inside the door and handed them well-fueled hand lamps and very real swords with sheathes and belt clips. "Feel free to explore," he said in his stately old voice.

They lit their lamps. Hermann bowed to Myron; Fred did the same. With a polite wave and a small smile, Myron graciously closed the door behind them, and Fred dimly heard him swing the shelves back into place.

Fred followed Hermann down the winding stairs. "Be quiet," Hermann warned, "quiet as smoke. The dungeons will be guarded."

"Uh huh." Fred gobbled the rest of his snack. It tasted rather dusty.

CHAPTER 39
THE NINJA

Patrick watched Lewis's eyes roll back and his body crumple until his whole weight dangled from the chain on his wrist. *No! This is not the way my story is supposed to happen!* "Lewis!" he shouted and leapt toward his brother, but Horned Edge hands held him back.

Stately with purpose, Lord Charon rolled an amber noretha on the palm of his hand. "Please awaken Lewis," he said to Barth. "It is time for my dear son to serve me again."

Barth snarled, but he tapped one of the Horned Edge magi, who released Lewis's wrist from the chain, while another lowered him to the floor. They had him sit up, put his head between his knees for a minute, and then helped him to stand. Once Lewis straightened, Patrick felt a surge of pride. His brother looked awesome in his robe, like a prince, his eyes narrowed fiercely.

Charon said gently to Lewis, "We know that, because you are from their home world, the bizeor will not drive you mad as they do our people. I'm asking you to have the honor of accepting them."

Lewis met Patrick's eyes in a look of pure compassion, but then closed his eyes as if he were looking inward and trying to make a decision. He spoke unknown words to an invisible companion. Both of Lewis's hands clutched against his chest, looking so powerfully like steel-strong dragon claws that Patrick could almost see his brother whipping out huge wings and breathing searing flames. Through the odors of sweaty arousal, cold crystal, metallic controls, garlic breath, and body odors, Patrick smelled a fire so hot that it could burn steel. It was a video game turned real.

Patrick's tears diffused the glow of the hot marble in Lord Charon's hand as he watched his brother turn back toward Charon. "I cannot operate this system any longer," Lewis stated. "It will destroy us."

Charon said solemnly, "It will not destroy us. Lewis, *e bibat luan eaya,* my noble son. Please understand why we are connecting to Earth, your home, the place where your family lives: It is necessary to save us all."

Lewis's eyes seemed vacant for a moment, as if he were being mesmerized, then doubtful, as if he were becoming convinced. However, he startled as if a bee had stung him. "Liar! Such help, such love! My Lord – and this is the last time I shall ever call you that – How I wish you were what I thought you had been! I let myself be totally deceived. All the time that I served you, I served Saoma!" He gestured toward the dangling chains, "Do you want me to continue this service, ignoring the evidences of my senses?"

"Your senses do not see it all," Lord Charon said, laying his right hand lightly on Lewis's shoulder, "Trust me. You shine like a star, and so does your task. There is nothing to fear."

Patrick struggled against the hands that held him back and yelled, "Don't listen to him, Lewis!"

Sorrowfully, Charon added, "Do you think that Saoma is evil because of these? I tell you, he is the light in every star of every universe! From where else did the inspiration come for your world's Renaissance? Who inspires your own brilliant mind, Lewis? Listen! The evil attributed to Saoma comes from the frightened minds of ignorant people; 'tis not intrinsic to him!"

Patrick could see that Lewis was struggling because his face turned gray ,and his hands shook. The wrong kind of magic had seized him.

"Stop it! You're putting mind-control on my brother!" he yelled at Charon.

However, it was hopeless; one of the magi clamped Patrick's mouth with a firm hand, and Patrick's heart pounded. He could hardly breathe.

With courtly dignity, Lewis knelt like a prince before his emperor and raised cupped hands. Lord Charon rolled the gently glowing marble into his upturned palms. The ruler continued, placing one hand on Lewis's head in a blessing, "Fean Lewis, begin the connection. Your genius will help many, many people. You will let your brother and sister return to your parents while you accomplish great things – such as only you can do!"

Patrick's chest burned. His brother's eyes became glazed and distant. *I've got to help him.* He broke free from his captor's grip and shouted, "Look at yourself, Lewis! Stop it! You don't have to believe those lies!"

Desperately he called forth his imagination. "Lewis! Mentally, he's got you tied up! You can't move, and a tsunami wave is rushing so high that you know it's going to drown you! Nobody can stop the wave but me … Let's pretend that I'm a ninja warrior! I can cut your ropes! Then – *Mmph!*" The magus again clamped his mouth closed.

CHAPTER 40
HEADED TO RESCUE

Fred wormed after Hermann like the tail end of a Chinese dragon until they reached the bottom of the stairway. Their hand lamps now revealed stalagmites, stalactites, pillars, pits, and crevices. Most surfaces were pure white marble punctuated with large zany swoops of agate, a few pockets of tantalizing amethyst, ruby, topaz, and sapphire, and some green malachite with flecks of gold.

After a while, Hermann crept along a straight path, but too soon, Fred saw human-made doors in the cave walls. When they heard a rumbling noise at one door, Hermann snatched him into a dark crevice. "Put out your lamp!"

Squeezed uncomfortably in the crevice, Fred whispered, "What now?"

"We'll move without light for a while. I've studied the map. The plan is to go –

"Ouch!" Fred grabbed his pants pocket. "Good grief, it's that hot marble I made." He drew the marble out with his hanky and felt his stomach swoosh like the mad dive of a rollercoaster. "It's glowing! That means Charon's connecting to Earth!"

"*Dittiean cilanthoon!* Hide that noretha and shut up!" Hermann seethed.

Fred clumsily shoved the hanky-wrapped hot marble back into his pocket, where it burned uncomfortably through the cloth. Two seconds later, they heard a clear clink of the door opening. Fred and Hermann kept very still. Fred tried to quiet his breathing, but it still sounded like surf after a hurricane.

A Horned Edge guard walked past their crevice, then

unlocked another door and went in. When they could no longer hear his footsteps, Hermann relit his lamp to the tiniest flame that he could manage. "This way."

They crept out. "Ah! There!" On the left, Hermann's lamp showed a crack in the wall, tall but very narrow.

"I'm not going in there!" Fred said, imagining himself forever stuck, starving to death in the endless night.

"Oh yes, you are."

Shivering, Fred squeezed through the crack, grunting, ripping his shirt. Following Hermann, he wound, twisted, and inched his body through a long, tight canyon that delved endlessly into the bowels of Whitehall's mountain. After they wiggled past a waterfall that soaked their clothes, Fred's nose tickled, and a great sneeze exploded.

"Quiet!" Hermann hissed.

"*Aaah – choo!*" Fred exploded again. "I can't help it. The air's musty." He sniffed, wiping his nose on a sleeve. "And I smell a stench, like poop."

"Just keep going!" Hermann held his lamp higher. Just past the waterfall, a low archway broke the marble surface.

"Oh great." Fred twisted through a peculiar drill hole, like the inside of an insane screw. Huge shadows flickered around his bobbling hand lamp and … "*Yiii!*" He stumbled into a stinking chamber filled with centuries of excrement from roosting bats. Millions of bats! Flapping, climbing all over each other, hanging upside down, packed together …

A furry, bony creature dropped onto his head. "Help!" Fred screamed. "Help! Lemme out of here!" Fred's brain was a shrink-wrapped package of raw fear. Another creature wrapped around his face. Fred jumped, kicked, and screamed.

Even while he spun in circles, an authoritative thought cut through the madness: *Get yourself until control, Fred. You are subua. You are the property of Sir Forschwynn, who is my servant, and this is the work I assigned to you.*

"Lemme out of here!"

Sorry, Fred. This is your place in the story.

Fred's heart pumped so hard that he felt dizzy, but then the bats flapped one more time and flew away to join their cauldron.

Hermann snapped, "Calm down, calm down. You don't need

a heart attack."

Fred retorted, "You look just like one of them and I can put up with you … barely!"

Hermann's buckteeth bared, his beady black eyes bulged out, and his hand lamp shook. "I … I …"

Fred cringed for a punch. However, Hermann too was covered with crawling bats.

"Out of here! Fast!" Hermann shouted, and he and Fred ran past the bat chambers at Olympic speed.

*   *   *

After one more squeeze and no more bats, the path ended in a musty, cave cold room. Here, a glowing globe had been fastened to the wall, so Hermann put out his lamp. Fred saw that a big granite door blocked further progress, and even from six feet away it radiated invisible bad vibes, a palpable hostility.

Tiptoeing, Hermann approached the door. His hands brushed over its heavy lock system. "I've got a key from … well, never mind …" he tried the serendipitous key, "but it does … not … turn!" His large hairy ears twitched, and his shoulders slumped so that to Fred he looked more than ever like an ugly great bat.

"Are you a magus, Hermann?" Fred asked softly. "Can you *golanoya* this door?"

"The military magi accepted me at the College. So, yes, if Radyah wills it so." However, Hermann hesitated. "After we enter where the beasts of Saoma threaten your friends, what then? There will be too many for us. Also …" he lowered his voice to a mere breath, "Lord Charon can pin a man down with a mere spell of control."

"That's no problem, Hermann," Fred replied as cheerfully as he could. He flexed his big arms and wiggled his powerful fingers. "Didn't I hear that the Horned Edge worship Saoma, 'the Lord of Control,' but our Master is *Fao,* 'the Lord of Rest?' So, all we have to do is get through this door, find Lewis and Patrick, have a glorious fight with a whole lot of mean fanatics, escape Lord Charon's spells and a horde of bezubs to get out again, and rest during the process."

Hermann's face wrinkled. He snorted, his ears twitched, and incoherent sputters escaped his mouth. *Wow,* Fred thought, *He knows how to laugh!* Showing a marvelous set of teeth with sharp incisors, Hermann grinned. "Yes – you're right. *E Fao totoye.*"

Passing his lamp to Fred, Hermann kneeled in front of the door. He raised his hands. "*Maradoy, Tot-Bao-on, fo-or gola de.*"

Fred readied for the door to vanish, but nothing happened. Nothing at all. He waited, tense, smelling his own sweat in the cold cave odor. "Maybe you didn't say it right? Try again, Hermann."

"No." Hermann wrinkled his forehead, looking extremely displeased. "The Master's rest does not respond to our control."

Fred had no answer for this. *Rest – what does that have to do with this Big Problem?*

Immediately, he felt a hot pain in his pocket. "Yow!" He drew out the hot marble.

It glowed bright as a tiger's eye.

As Fred pot-holdered the hot marble with his hanky, images of the area behind the granite door reeled before his eyes. "Behind that door, Hermann, is a chamber covered with amethyst crystals. Hey, I can see Lewis! And – uh, oh – Charon and Barth and Horned Edge magi and a lot of Shields from Earth! Oh my God! They've got Patrick, too!"

His intestines kinking, Fred groaned. "I sure hope this isn't what I think it is! I see a swarm of magi chanting around the monitor, beginning some evil ceremony. Human sacrifice? Hermann, beyond this door is a portal to Hell!"

Fred stared dejectedly at the locked door, hoping it would magically open by itself. The air throbbed with a spooky breathing noise and smelled like a subterranean garage. When a scrabbling noise sounded behind them, like a cave crab the size of Hercules, Fred's heart froze. "Hermann, do you hear –"

"I hear it." Hermann drew his sword. The scratching and scrabbling noise got louder. Fred's legs turned to jelly, and he wobbled.

"Tis a wretch of a prisoner!" Hermann murmured. He walked a few steps forward, holding up the lamp, and Fred heard someone sobbing. "Ah, they've put her in a pit!"

"Her?" Fred whispered. *Oh God, not Deirdre!* Heart hammering, he cautiously drew even with Hermann.

CHAPTER 41
THE WILLING HOST

Through wet, unfocussed eyes, Patrick watched Lewis insert the hot marble into the obsidian table's control panel. He could hardly breathe with the man's big hand clamped over his mouth and he mentally pleaded to whoever might listen, *Help! Don't let this happen! If you can't rescue him, then show me a way!*

Patrick saw a dim glow spread across the table's black surface. All the magi murmured, "Aaah." Beautiful stars twinkled, and Lewis's fingers played controls like a concert pianist.

Soon Patrick saw the asphalt surface of a large parking lot. Lewis augmented the focus. Patrick now had a view of a large fleet of semi-tractor-trailer trucks, engines running, lined up as if to unload cargo. Like magic, the first truck drove forward and disappeared, followed by another, and then another.

They are sending weapons to conquer Lanthra, Patrick realized.

"Praise the great Saoma, he has brought us weapons to restore His kingdom!" sang the Horned Edge magi. Some jumped for joy, and even the magus who held Patrick quivered.

Lewis bent over the table with a concentrated, abstracted expression, as if he were trying very, very hard to figure out a new problem. As well as he could with one arm in a sling, he raised his hands. Very slowly, he lowered them to the controls one more time.

Patrick twisted away from the magus's grip and bounded around all the Horned Edge magi to his brother. "Lewis," he shouted, "You don't have to let them control you!" With strength that he had never imagined, Patrick leaped over the obsidian table toward his brother. He landed. Instantly, he heard a *snap!* A supernova of pain sliced through Patrick's anger, and he collapsed onto the floor.

All movement in the cave chamber stopped. After a long *tick, tick* of time, Lewis stepped back, jerked the glowing marble out of its slot, and flung it to the floor. The table's surface went black.

With a long, long sigh, Lewis squatted and put his good arm across Patrick's shoulders. "Hello, Sport," he said. "I don't think you have any idea how many lives you saved just now." He smiled, and even though his face looked sick and scared, he looked like the brother Patrick loved so much.

Horned Edge magi moved forward; some drew knives. Lord Charon waved them back. "Let me handle this."

Somehow through the red fireworks of pain, Patrick saw Lord Charon's sidelong glance toward Barth and the upward, sideways eye motion that meant Charon had a new idea. "Guards, carry the lad to me. Also, secure my dear son so that he cannot interfere."

Horned Edge magi seated Patrick on the opaque black table. He closed his eyes. *Ow, ow, ow ... I hope I don't cry like a baby ...*

Barth shoved the Horned Edge magi aside and held Patrick with surprising gentleness, but Lord Charon warned, "Stand away. I will reopen the connection and the deliveries will continue. However, this time I will ask Saoma to lend us his armies as well as Earth's weapons. The lad from Earth is resistant to them; he might survive the madness."

Barth moved slowly to one side. Charon positioned himself at the table beside Patrick. Once again, a Horned Edge magus forced Patrick to stay still on the table. To Patrick, every second seemed like an eon.

Lord Charon spoke, "Relax, laddie. We'll be done soon." He sounded like a cheerful dentist about to drill deep and hard into a tooth. Patrick watched a Horned Edge magus pick up the hot marble and place it into the table's control center.

As before, lovely stars and galaxies appeared on the surface where Patrick was sitting – but then the tabletop went blank. Lewis, who stood taut as a bow, suddenly relaxed; and Patrick wondered why.

Lord Charon muttered softly, "The lad is very resistant. Without some change I cannot use him, and if he remains so, his angel will continue to provoke us." Placing his cold hands on Patrick, he called to a magus, "Twist his ankle."

Barth growled, "What are you doing, my Lord?"

However, Lord Charon motioned with his chin to the Horned Edge magus. The magus grabbed Patrick's injured foot. Patrick screamed in terror and pain.

Barth walked up. He slapped Lord Charon's face so hard that the man staggered. "Stop this right now!" Barth yanked the hot marble out of its slot.

For a long minute, tall, stately Lord Charon and massive Barth faced each other. Barth scowled; Charon's eyes stabbed into his. "What do you think you're doing, Barth," Lord Charon asked in a soft voice.

"You know that you need a willing host to welcome the bizeor."

Charon scoffed, "Just as I've suspected: you've always been soft about the boy. So, if I cannot use him as the bridge, what else do you have to suggest?"

Patrick hurt. He was moaning. Yet he had enough mind left to be surprised when Barth stated, "I suggest something I should have thought about long ago. You can use me."

Silence.

"You have regained my love. Howe'er, the bizeor may destroy you," Lord Charon warned. His face was solemn. He put a hand on Barth's shoulder. "And I will need your mind to help manage my technology."

"You have spineless Lewis fastened to a chain."

Patrick felt raw pain, but he heard Barth state, "My Lord, you have me, right here, and I'm willing to be a sacrifice to them."

Lord Charon's eyes sparkled. He murmured, "Aye, that may do."

"No more arguments. Let's begin."

Lord Charon nodded. Barth accessed the controls. A Horned Edge magus carried Patrick to Lewis and dumped him onto the floor. Confused, whimpering, Patrick watched the drama. Barth was scary; Barth was weird. Yet, Barth had protected him.

Swiftly, not looking at anyone, Barth placed the hot marble

once more in its slot. He bent his neck over the table and a soft starry glow shone on his face.

CHAPTER 42
RUNNING

In Jane Tuttle's pleasant kitchen, with the back door open, the wonderful odor of fresh biscuits, birds singing outside and late afternoon light fading into evening, Gracie heard the worst news she had ever imagined.

"After your brother Patrick left the house and disappeared yesterday …" Jane Tuttle's violet eyes moistened as she leaned against the pantry, a bowl of fruit in her hands, "we learned that he's now in Horned Edge hands. And, if they tor – um, questioned Patrick, and if they've …"

The iced melon ball in Gracie's mouth suddenly felt like a frozen tennis ball. She spit it out onto her plate.

Across the kitchen table, little Katie and baby June giggled and cackled so hard they almost fell of their stools. Gracie understood. *They know their mama's sad, but they don't understand why. The only thing they know to do is laugh and hope that cheers her up.*

Next to Gracie, sat her new "sister" Bessie. The dark-haired girl put her hand onto Gracie's shoulder. Compassion flowed from her into Gracie's aching heart.

"How about Lewis?" Gracie asked Jane hopefully.

Jane hedged no words. "Your brother Lewis has become a leader in the Horned Edge, a willing participant in Charon's plans."

Gracie's mouth went dry. Lewis? An enemy? Worse – a servant of the bezubs! Staring at her slightly chewed melon ball on the white plate, she pictured Lewis as he had been at "home" home. There she knew him as handsome, so brilliant but so absent-minded, no clothes sense at all, and not too proud to frolic with her or listen to her talk. After she had been forced out of her world into another, when her new home was the Gregory's house, he was still her wonderful big brother. When Gracie had watched him drink in Deirdre's love with his big brown eyes and – *finally!* – try to dress properly, a warm candle had glowed in her heart. Now the candle of joy melted into a mess. *What awful thing has happened to Lewis? Has he totally forgotten me?*

"Mom, I can't eat anymore," Gracie said. When she stood up, her hand knocked her plate. It slid off the table and shattered into a million sharp pieces. Without looking at anyone or offering to help clean up the shards, she banged through the back door into the courtyard.

It hurt to think, and it hurt even more to feel. Gracie closed her eyes, but that didn't help. Opening her eyes, Gracie began to run around and round the huge tree. Twenty circles – and she wasn't even breathing hard. More and more big circles – she couldn't exhaust herself. Some of the neighbors sat outside on their patios and watched her, calling, "Yo, girl, when will you ever stop?" or "Go on – see how many times you can run in circles until you fall down!" Gracie did not care. She ran.

Bessie came outside. "Ready to come in and have some lunch?"

"No!" Gracie shouted over her shoulder.

"All right, I'll bring you a snack so you can keep running until you finally wear yourself out!" Bessie went back into the house, came out again. "Gotta stop, sister, if you want anything. I've brought a giant cookie and some water."

Gracie stopped when her orbit around the tree brought her back to Bessie. Her new sister's eyes twinkled. Grabbing the water and cookie, Gracie bolted it down.

"Are you ready to come in?" Bessie asked, tossing her wavy black hair in a friendly way.

Hot adrenaline pumping through her body, Gracie stood still for a second. "No. But thanks." She turned away, declining Bessie's friendliness. She found a sitting place on the knobby roots under the tree. Its trunk was so big that it must be a pillar to hold up the universe. The tree's branches rose high as the sky, but here, under the dark canopy, was a private place. It reminded her of her tree back home, where she hid her journal under its roots. She had written stories in it …

Gracie laid her arms on bent legs and rested her head on her hands. Mosquitoes whined near her face. She didn't care.

"I'm so totally angry with you, God! What did we do wrong that you're letting the bezubs eat my brothers?"

No one answered. Gracie continued fiercely, "Maybe you're not God at all. Maybe you're just a bad dream. I can't do anything to fix this, you're not doing anything, and I don't know what to do to make you do it. This story is hopeless! I feel like a big puddle of stinking vomit! I hate you!"

The door of the Tuttle's house squeaked, and somebody came out. Jane's voice called, "Gracie? How are you?"

From the darkness under the tree, Gracie answered, "I'm fine! Go away!" Jane went back inside.

CHAPTER 43
ARGUING

Fred and Hermann leaned over the edge of the pit. Hermann's lamp could not penetrate to the bottom, but Fred caught a gleam below of tangled long yellow hair.

"Help me!" a woman whispered. "Help me; oh please, help me!" Her voice sounded vibrant but cracked, as if she hadn't had water for a long time. She spoke with the delightful overtones of the Bardia-Smythe border.

"We'll get you out of here, my lady!" Fred answered. "Just wait! I'll climb down with you, and my companion will help us both up again."

Hermann pushed the lamp into Fred's stiff fingers. "Not that way, you romantic dolt! The dungeon guards will have placed a rope or a ladder nearby, I'm sure. Hold the lamp up while I look."

With the lamp held high, Fred looked deeper into the pit. The woman's face had been grotesquely battered. He caught a gleam of her eyes looking up at him, but even through the bruises they were large and lovely.

"Oh, you remind me of Deirdre!" Fred breathed. All the air in his chest rushed out. His head spun and he put his hand on it to keep it from falling off. The woman began to cry, small kitten-like mews. Diamond glistening tears dropped from her cheeks.

Hermann returned. Those big white front teeth shone, and he said triumphantly, "A rope ladder. Verily, we can get her out – no trouble!"

Wildly ratted hair appeared first; next, two determined eyes blackened with bruises. Hermann grasped her wrists to pull her over the brim and Fred saw, his stomach twisting like a towel in a wringer, that her hands had bumps and lumps as if they had been broken, and dirt rimmed her ragged fingernails. At last, she stood on firm ground, and Fred passed Hermann the lamp. He ran to her and embraced her with his strong arms.

"Thank you," she whispered and buried her face in Fred's shoulder. His insides melted with compassion.

Taking her right hand, Fred caressed the broken fingers. "It's all right now, my lady. Thank God that we found you!" It was clear that she was much older than Deirdre, but battered and stinking as she was, in his eyes she was beautiful; even her bruised limbs looked graceful sticking out from her filthy, thin cotton shift. The woman shivered in the cave cold.

"Hey, Hermann, let me have your cloak. My costume cape isn't going to be warm enough."

Hermann swept off his long black cloak and handed it to Fred, who wrapped it around the woman. "We'll take you with us," Fred promised.

"Fred, think again."

Fred looked up.

Hermann's pointy ears drew back more than usual; his upper lip drew back showing a gleam of incisor teeth, and his face twisted with an irritating mixture of duty, compassion, and irony. "Aye, the lady needs help. Can we give it to her? Nay. We still have our original task before us."

Fred hollered, "What is the matter with you! We have to take her with us!"

"Nay! You … are … so … thick-headed!" Hermann hit the cave wall with his fist and a dozen stalactites showered down on his head. Sputtering and wiping away the debris, he insisted, "No, we cannot! 'Tis not so simple as you might think. Your heart is ruling your head!"

"What? Abandon her in this stinking place?" Fred snapped. "Rescue Lewis and Patrick but leave her behind? You're crazy!"

Hermann did not retort at him. He didn't roll his eyes or make frustrated, controlling gestures; instead, he stood still and calm.

At this, Fred paused. He let his hands fall and his stomach dropped a thousand miles. Hermann was right. "What is your name?" he asked the woman, and he heard the deadening disappointment in his voice.

The lady's mouth twisted. She said "Never mind; I hardly have a name anymore. Here they call me 'Crazy Lady.'"

Hermann caught the neck of Fred's shirt. "Come on, you *as-on bibat!*" Carefully avoiding a deep crack in the floor, moving his lamp so that the cave shadows twisted horribly, Hermann turned away.

"Wait! What about this lady?"

"Come. Now that the woman's out o' the pit, she'll be fine! After the revolt is over and we take Whitehall, we'll certainly return to her. Meanwhile, we must find another way to go! 'Tis Lewis and Patrick that we're rescuing, remember?"

"No!" the woman growled. "There is no other way to the Lord Charon's cave chamber except through that door, that wicked door – where they took my Lewis!"

Fred couldn't help thinking with an evil twinge in his gut, *Oh great. Even crazy old women love Lewis.*

She snarled, "I found him, kept the rats away from him. We talked. He told me his true name: Lewis Brah ... Brahmindura. And he knows my husband, Johnny at the Nutman gate!" Surprisingly fast, she slipped past them to the crevice. There she stopped, blocking it with her thin body. Snarling, she ordered, "You must take me to Lewis! I will not be left behind."

Shadows danced adagio on the cave walls as Hermann rubbed his mousy whiskers. "Lady, stand aside!"

She said cunningly, "You've no key to unlock the door."

Hermann demanded, hand on his sword, "Lady, move away and let us pass."

The old woman stood firm. Her large, battered eyes lit with a feral gleam as she stated, "No."

Hermann seethed through his teeth, "Lady, stand aside or I'll put you back in the pit!"

Fred couldn't stand the stupid argument. Tearing at his hair, he yelled, "Stop it, Hermann! She's telling us that she has keys, for God's sake." He entreated the woman, "Lady, please! If you have keys hidden somewhere, just get us the one key so we can get to Lewis. We only want to help him because he's our friend, too!"

Still guarding the crevice, she cocked her head. "You're not quite Bardian, from your voice. And you're not the Layhew monster, although you're nearly as big. Are you from Earth like Lewis?"

Silence. Their breath fogged in the moist cave air and Fred imagined that Hermann's reaction was similar to his: *How in the world could she guess that I'm from Earth?*

The woman bargained with them, "If I find the key, will you take me with you? Not ..." her voice trembled, "back into the hole?"

Hermann looked at her warily, but, crossing his hands on his chest, Fred bowed. "My word on it, and ..." he hesitated, "my knife as a pledge." Hermann shot him a dirty look, but also gave a short, stiff bow to the lady. "Now hurry and bring the key!"

She quickly slipped away into the darkness.

"We will not take her with us!" Hermann said.

"We have to. I promised."

"You're an idiot."

Fred and Hermann returned to the dead-end chamber and stood before the door. Here, the air felt breathable as lead; the globe lights glowed weakly, and the door palpated with hate. "If the cave feels creepy here," Fred whispered, "imagine what it will feel like on the other side of that door!"

Minutes later, the woman appeared. Although she shot Hermann a fearful glance as if she expected some treachery, she produced a key from under Hermann's cloak.

Fred extended the knife to her, and Hermann received the key. "Now," she declared holding the knife expertly, "I will come with you to rescue my Lewis."

"No," Hermann said.

"Then – the hell with you!" Flinging away Hermann's cloak, she disappeared into the passageway.

"Hermann, you two-tongued snake!" Fred hissed. Again, he felt an intense spot of heat in his pants pocket. He yelled, "Dammit, the marble's hot!"

"Keep your voice down, stupid," Hermann hissed.

Fred pulled out the glowing orb with his handkerchief and stared at it. "We may already be too late, Hermann!"

At that instant, a scream vibrated through the ravaged cul-de-sac. The cave walls and floor shuddered as the scream rose and rose to a terrible strength of fear that made them cower, covering their ears.

The sound died away. The air shivered.

"We have to go in there," Hermann whispered.

They drew their swords; Hermann fit the key into the lock and turned it.

CHAPTER 44
FAILURE

Barth Layhew leaned against the obsidian table in the amethyst cave chamber, licking his bloody fingers. Blood welled from his mouth and his mottled face was hideous where veins had burst in the skin and eyes. He leaned on the tabletop, which rippled with light. "Greetings to you, *Raca,* and to you also, *Moron,*" he said insolently to Fred and Hermann. "We've been waiting for you."

Fred's body tingled with cold fear as he looked around the chamber.

Besides Barth's huge hulk, he saw Lord Charon's elegant worshipful pose, a slew of somber Horned Edge magi in their black robes, some Shields with robes and big rings, and, huddled against the wall, Patrick and Lewis. The boy cowered, his arms wrapped around Lewis. Robed like a prince but painfully thin and with one arm in a sling and the other chained to the wall, Lewis coughed and coughed, spitting out bloody yellow phlegm.

How are we going to rescue anybody? Fred thought. His throat tightened; the hairs rose on his head.

"You were too late," Barth told him calmly. He hitched his rear onto the tabletop and crossed his arms, swinging his booted feet. His purple tongue slid out of his mouth and tasted the blood around his lips; he smiled. "Your rescue, your rebellion – all have failed. You might as well surrender."

CHAPTER 45
GRACIE'S POWER

Under the humongous tree in the Tuttle's back courtyard, Gracie sat like "The Thinker" but she wasn't thinking at all, just listening. Mosquitoes whined, a few tomcats yowled, smaller animals scuttled from their hiding places to enjoy the night. A verse swam slowly through her mind:

The eyes of all wait upon Thee,
And Thou givest them their meat in due season;
Thou satisfieth the desire of every living creature.

There it was: Daddy's table prayer. *So what? God, I hate you. You've left us alone.* Gracie imagined Jesus, offended by her raw emotion, turning his back on her and flying back to heaven. Once he'd disappeared, all the roses turned into plastic, the breeze smelled like garbage, and food tasted like sawdust. She thought of home: not the Tuttle's home or the Gregory's home, but Home home.

I feel so lonely. Gracie's insides cracked into pieces like a smashed eggshell.

She tried to hold it back, but it wouldn't stay inside – a gush of hot tears flowed out from her broken heart. Sobbing, rocking back and forth in the darkness under the tree, Gracie cried and cried and even wailed until the tide of grief ebbed. When the last cry was cried and the last tear had fallen and her nose ran no more, she wiped her face on her skirt. The waters behind her broken dam stilled, not because she felt better, but because she felt exhausted. "I suppose that it's time to go inside," she said out loud in a voice that sounded a lot like Mom's. *Earth Mom's.*

After she walked off the stiffness, Gracie came back to the

Tuttle's back door. Quietly, she opened it. A lemon-smelling candle flickered in its glass holder and a cup of creamy goat's milk sat ready for her on the kitchen table. The kitchen felt warm, nicely warm, because Jane had baked bread for breakfast. Gracie inhaled deeply. It smells so good!

Slowly she began to relax. First Gracie washed her hands, then, seating herself comfortably at the table, she drank the milk. Next, she stole one of the warm loaves from its cloth wrapper, biting into its delicious crust to reach the lovely softness inside.

"Do you feel better?"

Gracie startled and turned around. Mama Jane came into the kitchen and sat on a stool. She wore a bathrobe, and her long hair was braided loosely, with lots of fluffy ends sticking out around her sweet, sleepy face.

"Uh-huh," Gracie answered, stuffing the last big piece of bread into her mouth. When she had finished chewing, she asked, "Mama Jane, do you believe in Jesus? Can he help us?" She added fiercely, "And don't give me some answer that doesn't answer!"

Mama Jane got up. Gracie stood up, too. They stepped toward each other; Gracie found herself tenderly folded in Mama Jane's arms. Jane kissed her forehead. "Beautiful Gracie," she answered. "He said that he loves us; he loves us."

And, at once, Gracie realized how a little girl can save the universe.

CHAPTER 46
BARTH

Lewis came out of his coughing fit to see the cave chamber's dungeon side door open. Two dim figures filled the opening: one bulky, glittering gold and brown, the other thinner in a flapping black cloak. He had no idea how to interpret what was happening. Patrick cried out, and Lewis knelt to comfort his brother – or maybe to be comforted by him. A familiar voice growled, "Forget fencing, Hermann. I'm playing football!"

"You do that, Fred; I'll use my sword," the smaller man snapped.

Fred! All the data came together. Lewis saw the Horned Edge magi freeze with shock, Lord Charon's serenity collapse, and Fred coming to the rescue. In a flash, Lewis also glimpsed what must be happening in the world above: A matrix of people and spiritual beings struggling for dominion.

Hermann threw his sword like a javelin. It skewered one of the Horned Edge magi, and Hermann sprang to retrieve the sword.

Fred bellowed, rushed forward, and tackled a Horned Edge magus who fell against two more magi. When these stumbled, Hermann immediately impaled them.

Lewis watched. Amazed, he saw that Lord Charon ignored the fighting. The ruler stepped to the black table and held out one hand to Barth, who got up and approached him like a fawning dog. Barth licked his master's face, leaving a large drool of bright red blood. Charon put his finger to the blood and tasted it. "*Tod!*" he ordered, raising the palm of his hand. Barth giggled but obediently backed up a step.

Next, Charon walked close to Lewis. The magus' dark eyes met Lewis's. They no longer sparkled at him; now they looked like dead pools of black oil. All of Lewis's physical senses reeled while Charon spoke softly and intensely over the roiling crowd: "*Yovinavit, Saoma, e seris eaya fean.*"

Lewis felt a heavy black blanket cover his mind. He struggled, trying to free himself from Charon's hypnotic spell.

CHAPTER 47
THE ABYSS

Huddled against Lewis's knees, Patrick heard terrible things. He shook, he wanted to faint. *What counter-spell can stop these fiends? I don't have the power!*

In a long-unused corner of Patrick's mind, he thought that asking Someone for help was better than trying to drag up magic powers.

"Please, please, God," Patrick prayed in a whisper, "send a miracle to save Lewis."

He didn't get magic or miracle, he got mad. Abruptly he shouted, "That's only mind-control, Lewis. Don't let the stinking hocus-pocus get you!" Although his voice sounded like a lamb's bleat and hot baby tears ran down his face, Patrick continued, "No matter what you do, Bro', I will not give up on you!"

* * *

Lewis enjoyed the dark cloud of hypnosis. He gloried in it because it took away his terror. *You fool,* his dragon roared with a powerful surge of its wings, shaking him. *You're so easily deceived; it's a false calm.*

Stubbornly, as through a dim, dirty window, Lewis resisted the dragon. He relished the fighting in the chamber. *Good. Let them all die. Swords and knives, shouts and screams, bodies smashing and crashing: I can't wait until they all go to hell, and I go with them!*

Lewis heard himself laugh, an ugly, evil laugh. An awful voice came out of his mouth, "It's too late! I gave myself to Saoma! Look at me, snarling with rebellion and dark witchcraft —"

The dragon's claws pierced Lewis to the heart. Its scorching breath incinerated all the hate squirming and biting inside his body; it blew the devils in his mind away. Instantly, silence enveloped Lewis. He tried to shout again, but he had gone mute.

In the soundless place, he saw a vision.

He stood on a plateau at the edge of the Abyss. Darkness and death ruled in the Abyss. Feeling dead inside, Lewis saw a plateau on the other side, far, far, miles away, illuminated in plain, hard noon sunlight. The road where he stood looked the same as the road that he could imagine across the gulf. *How can I cross the Abyss?* This side was familiar; the other side might be a dusty, dead waterless place.

God stood on the far road. He wasn't shining brightly, and he didn't have angel wings or a crown. To Lewis he looked as ordinary as a telephone pole or a streetlight. God said, not in a shout or a yodel but as a clear statement inside Lewis's head, *You cannot cross the Abyss without help, but you can refuse to cross. Let me help you.*

Lewis hesitated.

Are you afraid that you'll leap and fall?

Lewis nodded.

Are you afraid that the other side will be worse than the side you're already standing on?

Lewis nodded, shivering.

It is the better road. I will hold your hand and take you to the other side. Trust me.

Lewis whispered aloud, "I want to believe you, God. I want to believe that whole Jesus stuff, with angels and heaven." Gulping, he continued, "I've betrayed you; I've worshipped the devil. But I want you to take me back. Amen." Immediately, Lewis found himself on the other side of the Abyss.

God said, and a cool, soothing sensation like the late afternoon ocean wind brushed against Lewis's face, *Don't be afraid. Let's go for a walk.* They went side-by-side on a plain, bare desert road.

Lewis said, "I don't think I like you very much, God."

God wasn't bothered about that.

As they continued, Lewis saw dry grass and a hardy bush or two. "If I stay with you, I've got to find something to like about you." He thought for a while. "'Christ,'" he pronounced. "The word reminds me of 'clash' or 'crash.' 'Christian' – same thing. Let me find another word."

An alternate image came to him; he pictured the spring ice storm when he had glowed inside with the treasure of love that Deirdre and he shared. On the window had glittered jewels of frozen rain ... Lewis pondered, "Deirdre said that her name was really *Delanoreth*. It means 'Child of the Living Jewel.' Jewel ... Crystal ... Christian ... All right, I can tolerate being called a Christian." He and God walked on some more.

Lewis told God, "It looks like I've stepped into the whole Christian mess, with the Apostle's Creed and all that stuff."

"Yep," said God. "And don't forget that part about 'the resurrection of the body.'"

"Huh?" He was amazed at the new universe that had opened in front of him.

The silence lifted. He was out of the vision, and back in the cave chamber.

Then Lewis remembered what he had done to sabotage Charon's *thoyo-on*. He hit his head with his free right hand, sending shots of agony through his left shoulder. "Oh my God! I've set the system to explode!"

*　　*　　*

At that moment, while blows and blood and bodies rampaged throughout the amethyst chamber, Barth stirred. His red eyes, staring at Lewis, glowed like a demon's. Slowly, Barth picked up a glittering sword from the floor. Patrick screamed; Lewis shut his eyes. The possessed man lumbered forward until the blade lay against Lewis's throat. He gloated, "Thought you'd jimmied our thoyo-on, didn't you, Brahmindura the Great! I know what you did! Saoma just told me! You set up a fatal protocol, a little jinx in the sonic computer, just the wrong twaddle of a control."

"What?" Lord Charon seized Barth's arm.

"We can't operate down here any longer until we undo his jinx! So – Bye!" The table went dark. "You're nothing but trouble, Louie," Barth snarled. "I really want to kill you, you rat!"

"No!" ordered Lord Charon.

"Yes. Later. But right now, my Lord, I'm taking you to a safer place." Without a backward glance, the monster that had once been Barth Layhew turned away from Lewis and pulled Lord

Charon to the stairs. He pushed the magus upward, leaving the rest of the astonished magi behind in the fray. Swift footsteps clipped to the top of the spiral staircase: Barth's pounding; Charon's lighter and sounding forced.

I should be completely exhausted, comatose, catatonic, Lewis thought. However, for the first time in months and months he began to feel strong.

CHAPTER 48
APOLOGIES

Seeing that the tide had turned, a quick-thinking magus forced his way past Fred, followed by a herd of the remaining Horned Edge magi. They galloped up the winding staircase toward Charon's laboratory.

Only one laggard now faced Hermann, and he was too unnerved to fight any longer. "Surrender," Hermann ordered, panting and sweating.

The magus hurriedly dropped his sword. It clanged loudly on the floor. Falling to his knees, the magus – a young man with a handsome but already depraved face – put his hands behind his head. Hermann secured his prisoner's wrists to a set of chains and checked the fallen people for life. "This one's severely wounded in the neck. I'll staunch the bleeding. Maybe he'll live." Hermann didn't sound very hopeful.

"You do that," said Fred, "I'm going to see if Lewis and Patrick are okay."

"You do that," Hermann snapped.

Stepping through blood and over bodies, breathing fast as a steam engine, Fred picked his way forward. The obsidian table lay between him and Lewis, but it was more a symbol than a metaphor, because Fred's head drooped as he noted Lewis's bright smile. He could no longer quit feeling jealous of Lewis than he could undo his sullen withdrawal and hostility in Nutman. *I finally got to where I can rescue Lewis and I can't even say, "Hello, how are you."*

Filled with shame, he mumbled to Lewis from across the table, "So this is Charon's locating system … black obsidian table like the one that was at Nutman – only this one's horizontal to the floor instead of vertical … and what are these concentric rings?"

Surprised, Fred saw that one of Lewis's eyebrows crooked up, both puzzled and amused. "Fred," Lewis remarked in a parched, husky voice, "you're totally different and yet you haven't changed at all."

This apology is not going the way I had imagined, Fred thought.

"Hey, you!" Hermann shook one of the bodies. "You're faking!" He stomped the breath out of the magus's back, grabbed up the cursing man by the collar, and chained him to the wall near the other Horned Edge magus.

Glancing at Fred, who was still doing nothing and feeling guilty about it, Hermann shook a fist. "Quit admiring the furnishings and help me rescue your friends!"

Fred managed to look up as far as Lewis's chin. "Hey, Lewis, let's see what I can do to get you out of that chain."

"I'd like that," Lewis said. He laughed and then he coughed and spit a wad of bloody phlegm.

"Man, you're sick," Fred said. Slowly he raised his eyes until he fully made eye contact with Lewis. "You're all beat up, too. And skinny as a rail – haven't they been feeding you here?"

"The cafeteria food is awful. Mystery meat, stale pizza, and limp salad." Lewis smiled, and there was no wall, no bitterness in his face.

Fred leapt over the obsidian table and wrapped Lewis in a bear hug; words came out of his mouth in groans, "Lewis, I can't say or do anything to undo what I've done. I was so jealous of you, and I let myself … I'm so sorry …"

Lewis hugged him back but winced when the motion pulled his injured arm. "Fred, you idiot, I haven't been so good, either. Look at my outfit and see my fancy ring! I became a Horned Edge insider, a Saoma-serving … I had it in me all the time … the ability to become a traitor! When we were at Nutman I was such a self-righteous boil on your butt …"

Fred smiled, which hurt so much that he figured that his face was pretty battered. "Boil on my butt, were you? And what was I to you – jock itch?"

* * *

"Look after Patrick," Lewis said, and Fred bent down. He lifted the boy up, and Patrick buried his face in Fred's chest. His whole body jerked with sobs. Fred could feel the hot tears through his clothes.

"I'm so stupid!" Patrick cried. "We're going to …" he paused as if afraid to say the awful possibilities, "all because of me! I wasn't strong enough … I told Barth everything and he didn't even have to hurt me!"

Fred cradled his best friend's brother and rocked him. "It's all right, Patrick, it's all right." And, at that moment, for him, everything was all right. The tiny spot of forgiveness in his heart painted itself into a yellow sailboat on a calm lake.

CHAPTER 49
KEYS

See if you can get this fetter off my wrist," Lewis said through clenched teeth He coughed. His chest felt like a sack of wet mud and his throat stung. Wherever he might be with God, his body was still in Charon's dungeon, and it very much wanted to get out of here. "I set the system to vaporize itself if –"

Hermann jumped back. Fred's head jerked up. Patrick's tear-streaked glasses turned his way. "What?"

"I was going to set it off, but Patrick stopped me, thank God. Before he and Charon ran out, Barth said that he knows what I did and that he can stop it – but suppose he can't? The next person to try to control this system will make it explode!"

"Lewis, that was really, really stupid," Fred said through clenched teeth.

"I know."

"Let's stop it!" Patrick shouted. He squirmed to get down from Fred's arms, but Fred would not let him go. "For heaven's sake, cut the chain or yank it out of the wall!"

Hermann looked desperately around the clutter. "Is there no tool we can use?"

"There was a chisel," Lewis told him, "but I tried to kill Lord Charon with it, and he made sure the tools were taken out of here."

"There are swords all over the place!" exclaimed Fred.

Wearily, Lewis sighed. "The metal in these chains was forged by the wicked old Lanthrans. It can't be cut by swords –" He tried a joke, "A sonic screwdriver might help, though, if you can find Doctor Who."

"Who?" Hermann asked, falling into the trap.

Lewis laughed. He coughed. It hurt.

Patrick shouted, "So find the right key!"

Methodically and as quickly as possible, Hermann moved about the chamber, rifling through the pockets of the dead and the badly wounded magi, collecting keys. "These *bizbats* must have every key to every closet in Whitehall." He patted down the chained young magus, who glowered but remained silent. "*He fup*," Hermann swore, removing a huge ring of keys from the man's pockets.

Gathering the hefty pile of metal, Hermann approached Lewis and sighed. "I have to try these one by one." He jingled the rings.

"Oh well," Lewis said with mock patience, but he was trembling.

"When will the system explode?" asked Fred anxiously. "How much time –"

"I set the actual ignition on a key touch, not a timer. The actual command is a little sonic applet which is looking for a certain little physical manipulation there in the –

"How much time do we have?" Hermann screamed.

"Depends," Lewis said, "on when that little manipulation is done. We are all incredibly fortunate that it hasn't happened already! All it will take is a certain touch on the controls. As I said, I was intending to set it off myself."

"Oh, great, Lewis," groaned Fred. "You tried to be a suicide bomber!"

Lewis saw him shudder. "We won't set it off, accidentally or otherwise," he explained. "But it's only a matter of time before Charon or Barth or someone else tries to use the system. And then, if they haven't disabled the applet …," his voice became blunt, "then Whitehall and everything in it will atomize."

*   *   *

In a slow and unsuccessful routine, interrupted by Lewis's nasty coughing fits, Hermann fitted key after key into the chain's lock. Lewis closed his eyes. "Hope hurts so much." he said, "I didn't realize how much I had gotten used to despair."

"Uh," Hermann grunted, not listening.

To restrain panic while he waited, Lewis concentrated on serial math problems. He rehearsed several algorithms in locating technology. He worked a twelve-dimensional problem in the gravitational "pins" that tie the expanding universe together. His mind soon bogged down; Lewis was running out of panic-reducing options. Quietness came; the solution appeared.

"It's taking too long," he said. "Time for you all to go."

"No!" Patrick slid out of Fred's arms and stood up, but his face contorted with pain, and he crumpled.

"Whoa, Sport, let me help you," Fred told him. He lifted Patrick and handed him a long sword to use as a cane.

Lewis smiled at his brother, but he grieved for himself. He did not want to be left behind – to say the least, but it had to be done.

Tongue between his teeth, Hermann tried one more key. It fit in the lock. The man's eyebrows drew together; he smiled.

"That's it!" Patrick cried.

For Lewis, the whole cave chamber seemed to glow. Hope's saw-toothed edges suddenly felt so good, so good …

The key would not turn. "*Szttit!*" Hermann hurled it across the room. The scrap of metal ricocheted off the crystal wall and scooted along the floor until it stopped in a puddle of clotting blood. "There are no more options, Fean Lewis."

"That can't be true!" Patrick swung a fist but sliced his hand on the sword and Fred grabbed it away from him. "Find another key! No, get away from me, Fred – I'm going to free him!" He stumbled forward, howled with agony. Fred pulled him back and lifted him again. Patrick fought to get down.

Lewis could not bear to watch. He felt an unwelcome tear roll down his cheek, and he ordered, "Go!"

Suddenly, decisively, Hermann stepped away from Lewis. His whiskers twitched as he straightened his features and his small black eyes flattened with pity. "We'll have to leave you here, Fean Lewis."

CHAPTER 50
THE PLAN

The Council was long over, the Bard of Bardia's concert was almost over, and Daniel, still wearing the robe of the High Magus, waited in Lord Charon's study. He was elated by the Council's decision: A close vote but a successful outcome. Daniel assured himself, *What I have set in motion races straight to the target: Peace on Lanthra.*

He would have left the study, except that he was protected – no, constrained – by a group of military Horned Edge magi Nearly suffocated by his robes and the body heat of five sweating men in gray robes, Daniel got up to find a fan – *surely even Tahei gets hot!* A heavy hand on his shoulder tried to force him back into a chair.

Immediately Daniel spun around. "Do you dare to touch me? With a word, I could command your death."

It was not an idle threat, and even these high-ranking Saoma worshippers knew it. Although their various faces were strong, insolent, disciplined, and hardened, he smelled their fear. The Horned Edge superior officer, a medium-sized man with dark glittering eyes, backed up several yards, saying quickly, "Forgive us, Hegofean."

"Then bring me a cold drink," Daniel requested. Just as the Horned Edge magus opened the door, however, Tahei Charon swept into the study, followed by Barth Layhew. Crowded outside were many very sweaty, wild-eyed Horned Edge magi plus some red-faced stragglers from Earth's Shields sect.

Lord Charon commanded his followers with a sweep of his arm, "All of you – get out! Except for my servant Barth and the

High Magus – they will stay."

The room cleared; its door closed. Tahei went to his desk chair and sat very, very still. His face might have been a black cameo silk-screened onto white paper.

However, Daniel could not take his eyes off Barth Layhew. Gone was Barth's casual, bored pose, the rough familiarity. His face was now hideous, mottled, bloated, with burst veins, bloody lips, and red eyes. Beyond Barth's physical appearance, Daniel sensed the gods that filled him: Spirit princes, governors, and ranks and ranks of slaves. Charon's austere study had become a headquarters for a demonic empire.

"Oh, Tahei," Daniel groaned, "you connected to Earth tonight. The Council vote meant nothing to you."

"Let's begin," said Lord Charon as if he were talking friend to friend. His beautiful dark eyes brushed Daniel's face.

"Begin what?" Daniel asked. Hadn't he known what Tahei was doing? Of course. But he'd hoped that events would whirl away Charon's efforts before he could –

Barth spat, a large blood clot hit the floor, and he finished Daniel's thought, "We will now begin to take over the worlds, Danny Boy. That Patriot rebellion that you masterminded is going to fall flat on its funny little face."

Daniel asked the Master, *Is this true?*

What he saw in his thoughts contradicted Barth's assertion. He saw the concert music ending and fighting begin. Rose Hall throbbed with frightened aristocrats who huddled against its pink marble walls, using chairs as barriers against war. Meanwhile, many determined and dangerous Patriots had strategically attacked and cornered sets of Horned Edge military, inside Rose Hall and out in other areas of the palace. In the vision, Daniel saw Whitehall's great entrance doors open as more Patriots from the city swarmed in. Barth had lied. The Patriots were winning.

Daniel's heart leaped. *Thank you, Master! My plan is going well!*

Immediately he heard a rebuke in his wife Ielen's voice: *Can't you hear the illogic in what you just said?*

Beautiful Ielen, what do you mean?

Even very good plans by very brilliant men can fail. So, how shall you deal with failure?

Neglecting the warning, he smiled, remembering her cheeks bright with arousal, the small, soft hairs on her temples curling. Ielen was so gorgeous when she was angry. He tried to grasp her spirit, but it was like trying to hold perfumed air in his hand.

Nearby, Charon's lips twitched, a slight but triumphant movement, as if he had heard Daniel's thoughts. "Little friend Daniel, here is an item that you may not have considered when you made your plans: It was easy to guess that there would be an attempt to seize Moorway and my domain. Therefore, I have gathered secret reserves, north of the city. As soon as the Patriots believe they have victory, my soldiers will destroy them."

The Master showed him that it was likely, and Daniel's joy withered. "How will this happen, Tahei?" Daniel murmured.

Charon said, and his voice was as gentle as the artistry of ink brushes on rice paper, "We have Earth weapons now, thanks to my Fean Lewis. Once the palace is filled with rebels, my soldiers will seal them in and kill them. We have guns, gas, explosives …"

The hideous mouth that belonged to Barth's body said, "After that comes the fun part! When we clean up the city, we'll tie rebel families together and set them on fire. Some people we'll keep alive to sacrifice to Saoma, but we will cut off their hands and feet. Crowds of rioters will go from house to house, looting, raping, and killing. We will –"

"That's enough, *Sebizorath,*" Daniel commanded.

Barth's mouth shut with a snap.

Tahei continued, "Daniel, now that everyone knows that you are my ally …"

Daniel felt his face flush. "And just how do you come to that conclusion?"

"Hegofean, my friend, the world believes 'tis true. After all, everyone knows that t'was your province that you arranged to have invaded, your skillful scientist Fean Lewis – from Earth, no less – who studied under you and then brought us what we needed to repair our thoyo-on, and your leadership at this special Council that broke the ban on electronic technology and overturned the One Law –"

Daniel felt hot blood rush to his head. "We upheld the One Law in the Council despite all your cheating, Tahei. May Saoma rot your soul!"

"After tonight, dear friend," Charon replied, "there will no longer be anyone alive who can contradict the resolution that will be publicized tomorrow – by you – that the Lanthran magi have repealed the One Law. Earth and we are now partners."

Barth added, "And you and we are partners."

"What?" Daniel realized that he was shaking.

"Oh, Danny Boy," Barth said, "Didn't you ever think, Daniel, in all of your machinations with Patriots and bards and so on, that the Bardians who are sick of senile King Norhe might decide to make you king instead?"

Daniel wobbled inside. He had stepped too far onto a broken bridge. *What have I done? My plan – Ielen, you have tried to warn me.* "That was *never* part of my plan," he answered defensively, but then wished he could have stuffed his fist into his mouth. *My plan.*

"Yes, there is a small army from Kingsport of Bardia marching upon us to rescue you. That should not have been, Daniel. T'will invite us to invade Bardia," Tahei Charon nodded as if agreeing with an inner adviser. "And then we'll remove Norhe, put you on his throne, but keep you here, dear friend, where we can work together."

"And guess what." Barth's horrible face leered. "Your dear daughter, Lewis's girlfriend Deirdre, is only a few miles south of Moorway with the army. Just think what we'll do to her after we chop your *deus ex machina* Patriot rebellion to bitsy pieces."

Daniel felt all the blood drain out of his face.

Monster Barth stuck out his tongue, making a very suggestive, sexually charged gesture with one finger. "You will watch, Hegofean, when –"

"When what?" Daniel said coldly, although his insides withered. He reached up a very scared hand to the Master and addressed him as he would have his dear father the goat farmer, *The devil's just a great, big liar, isn't he, Pappy?*

CHAPTER 51
OUT OF THE DUNGEON

Lewis's eyes blurred with exhaustion. The amethyst crystals of Charon's cave chamber shone with a purple halo. "If only I could get free, I could open the laboratory door – we could get out so much faster! And, then I'd clear the destruct command from the computer! But since I cannot go with you –"

"We go back the way we came." Hermann answered dully. "Through the dungeons, the tunnels, from whence we came. It will be safer for us than for you, Fean Lewis."

The Bardian spy turned away in a flap of black cloak. Fred followed, while Patrick screamed, "We can't leave him!"

"Stop!" came a shout like a crack of thunder.

A filthy woman with skinny limbs sticking out of her sack of a dress blocked Hermann's progress. Lewis recognized her, partly by her stealthy but accurate movements and partly by her powerful stink: she was Mary, the woman who had helped him fight rats in his cell.

Pushing the others away, she came to Lewis. There was enough light in the cave-chamber to see her clearly, but he felt totally accepting of the ugly picture. With his free hand he took hers. It was filthy, broken, knobby, and age-spotted. He touched her cheek. Both of Mary's eyes were blackened and her lips scabbed from multiple cuts. However, although she stank like dirty crotch and suffering had nearly ruined her beauty, Mary looked – not only looked but felt – so much like Deirdre that it knocked the breath out of his chest. She had once had Deirdre's soft cheeks, the dauntingly intelligent eyes, and the bloom of her lips; he felt that she still had a soul like a bright sword blade.

"Laddie, brave but not always wise," she said, "You cannot take on the big demons. Do not fight Lord Charon any longer. Go back to Nutman. You must tell my Johnny what's happened to me!"

When he thought of all the events that had "happened" to the woman Mary, the innocent wife of the Nutman city gatekeeper, shivers tingled his spine and Lewis's insides boiled. "How can people be so evil to one another?" He began the most horrible curse he had learned during his time as a Horned Edge insider: "*He fup ta heseditla ...*" but then coughed painfully.

Rage slowly faded to reality. Pushing her gently away, he said, "No, you go with my friends. Go home to your husband. I'll stay here."

"Why?" Her eyes narrowed.

Lewis held up his chained hand, "We have no key."

Hermann nodded, moustache drooping, while Patrick bawled into Fred's sleeve. The Bardian spy shepherded them toward the door that led back into the dungeons.

Leaping with extreme speed, Mary blocked Hermann and pulled the knife that Fred had given her from her nasty dress so quickly that it hissed in the chilly air. "You will not leave my friend behind!"

"Save your knife to defend yourself. We have no other choice," Hermann said in a flat voice, putting his own hand on the hilt of his sword.

The woman's eyes gleamed with wolfish anger, but then her knife hand relaxed. "Ah, Mary," she said to herself, "you've gone soft in the head. You demand what they cannot do and all the while you alone know what they've needed." Hermann began to push past her, but she yelled "Wait!"

Quickly, Mary stepped through the gore to one corpse. "Ah – he's the one ... the key-keeper and a cruel bird he was, too!" Searching quickly, Mary brought out a small key from some hiding place in the corpse's intimate lower body. "You wouldn't have thought to look for a key here ... Now! Take Lewis and yourselves out, you black starveling bat!"

Hermann grabbed the key. Deftly, he loosened the cuff around Lewis's wrist. "Done!"

"Now," Lewis rubbed his aching shoulder, "we'll go out

through the laboratory."

"But what if someone –"

"It's faster. I sent all my staff home, so it should be empty. And I hope to – I have to – disable the code that would let the next fool that handles this black table's controls to hit the wrong button."

Hermann offered him a sword, but he decided against the weapon. "My shoulder's a useless mess. Also, …" he gulped but went on matter-of-factly, "when … when I was about to blow everyone up, but they brought out Patrick, I fainted and hung my whole weight from my right wrist. That arm is numb, too. You and Fred will have to be the warriors."

They raced out of the cave chamber via the spiral stairs that led up to the laboratory. Lewis looked back. The old woman was still in the bloody chamber, rifling among the bodies. "What about you, Mary? Come with us!"

"Nay. I have something to do yet."

The old woman quickly wrapped herself in a fallen soldier's cloak. Like a wraith or a wisp of gray smoke, she disappeared from the cave chamber through the dungeon door … and then it was time for Lewis to think the password to let them into the laboratory: *Hot Marble*.

CHAPTER 52
ON THE MASTER'S PATH

After only a few minutes in the deserted laboratory, Lewis felt much calmer. "I deleted the applet," he told the others. "The destruction command cannot work." Then coughed and spat into a towel that he had pulled from someone's workstation. "So, as far as I know, in this story, the evil mad scientist's laboratory will not explode."

"Thank the Master!" breathed Hermann, eyes lifted heavenward.

"Wow," Fred commented, looking around at the laboratory, "This place is swank. There is far more stuff here than there was in Nutman! Can we take any of it home?"

Lewis paused. Thrusting his hand into the pocket of his robe, he felt the reassuring spiral – his copy of Lord Charon's entire locating system. *Shall I tell them that I can take it all home?*

An intuition said, *No.*

Fred went on, "And to think you were in charge of all this! I'm jealous!"

Lewis felt a fuse melt, and he suddenly wanted to pound Fred's face with a large blunt object. "Don't start that jealousy thing! Look where it's led us!"

Flinching, Fred backed up a step. "I'm sorry … it was just an expression."

Hermann touched Lewis gently on the shoulder. "Fean, we cannot linger here; Lord Charon will come back with his people. Can you lead us toward the kitchens? That is where we must go out of Whitehall, and I want to look purposeful, as if we have an official errand there."

"Yes." Lewis teetered on his feet, but Hermann caught him. Although he wanted to lie down and sleep or just die, Lewis gathered energy from all the reserves he could find. "I'll do my Horned Edge best to look authoritative and murderous, and you will all be my minions. Now, my first order – let us remove this unfortunate, severely injured, pesky adolescent boy from the palace."

He looked at Patrick, hoping to get a laugh, or even a smile, but Patrick's face was pale. His hair dripped with sweat. "Patrick, I was just kidding. You are the bravest one of us."

"I'm a burden and I'm slowing everybody down."

Patrick could not walk. Lewis guessed that his ankle was nearly killing him. While Hermann held the laboratory door, Fred swept Patrick up into his arms, and they went out.

In a few seconds, they heard loud strides approaching. "To arms," whispered Hermann. Lewis's heart galloped and stumbled. Now that he had his brother and friends with him, he had begun to hope. *Hope is painful.*

But nothing happened; the footsteps clattered away "Why did those people run away from us?" Patrick asked.

"They were afraid of us," Lewis answered. "Consider our appearance ... I resemble Lord Charon if you look very fast and don't know him well. Fred could remind somebody of Barth –"

"Fred will never remind me of Barth!" exclaimed Patrick.

"Speak for yourself, laddie," Hermann said.

"And Hermann's black and ugly as a vampire bat," Fred retorted.

Lewis summarized, "Our faces should all look sinister, powerful, and mean as snakes, except for yours, Patrick. It's your job to look scared and helpless."

They quickly penetrated further through Whitehall, successfully intimidating groups of staff and Horned Edge guards. Fred's arms were occupied with holding Patrick, and his face scowled. Hermann led them grimly, sword ready, his prominent teeth snarling. Lewis did his best to project an eerie spirit of deep power, like Lord Charon striding to a secret Horned Edge meeting or a meditation with Saoma.

However, compared to Charon's persona, a very different spirit filled Lewis's mind. Self-destruction, fear, doubt, and murder were no longer necessary parts of his personality. He was out – spiritually out – of the dreadful place where his soul's choices had led. But he wasn't yet full of perfect peace. Now he saw himself on a dusty, level, cliff edge with God. There was little to see yet besides a beaten desert path following the edge – not even a cactus! Plus, God seemed to say, *My path is not a path to safety and fun, but trust me; you are on the way to a good place.*

"Will you help us get out of Whitehall? Will you get Patrick to safety?" Lewis murmured.

"Did you say something, Lewis?" Fred asked.

"Uh, nothing, Fred, I was just mumbling." *Hope hurts. Dragon, why did you have to make me feel again?*

CHAPTER 53
THE PATRIOTS' REBELLION

Just after Fred and his companions slipped through the double doors into the kitchens, Fred saw a small army of cooking staff. About a hundred men and women shed aprons and hats, put on green smocks to mark themselves as Patriot soldiers, and armed themselves. Apparently, they had gathered the very best weapons available. Fred saw the bluish gleam of diamond-blade swords from the forges in northern Tor, and some people carried crossbows, throwing blades, trip-nets, and even exotic weapons that he didn't recognize. However, all the Patriots' weapons were within the parameters of The One Law, and Fred felt queasy, noting that their opponents would be cheating with Earth weapons.

From among the Patriots, Curly Tuttle saw Fred's group and shouted, "Praise Radyah, you're all right!" He ran to Patrick, grabbed him from Fred's aching arms, and kissed him.

"Bleh!" Patrick exclaimed. "I'm not a girl, Uncle Curly, remember?" But he grabbed him around the neck and began to cry.

Curly hugged him harder. "When you were lost, my heart tore —"

"Where is the way out?" interrupted Hermann.

"*Ditleh!*" Curly passed Patrick back to Fred. He led them to an innocuous door. "This leads to the loading dock area." Fred and the others approached the door, while Curly ran to join the other Patriots to prepare for war.

Hermann carefully rotated the door's bronze handle. "No keys necessary, I hope," Fred breathed.

"It opens."

The way to the loading dock had Whitehall's carved marble beauty. It was dimly lit and quiet. It seemed safe. "Maybe Tom will join us," Fred said hopefully, "and we'll all get out together. By the way, Hermann, what did Curly tell you that we should do?"

"To follow my leadership!" Hermann snapped. "Now wait a minute." He stepped forward, tense, his cloak very black in the dim corridor.

"Now what?" asked Fred, hoping to learn more.

"We wait here a while," Hermann answered.

"Sounds fun."

Arms aching and trembling, Fred set Patrick down. His stomach rumbled, and he kept thinking, even in this crisis time, *Kitchens: Food.* Right now he wanted a hamburger, a really big one. *Kitchens: warmth.* Would he ever be warm and safe again? He disliked Whitehall intensely. The walls, the floor, were cold! Nor was the place safe. He'd rather be back in his Earth kitchen with his crazy mom after she'd had a big snort of cocaine. *Kitchens: love.* No love at home, Earth home. *Supposed I stayed here on Lanthra?* Fred imagined warm food in the Tuttle's kitchen, and the pretty oval face and dark hair of his favorite Patriot lady, Jane. *Kitchens: food ... warmth ... love. I want to marry Jane Tuttle. Yes, kids and all, because I always wanted to be a daddy. I wonder what it will be like to be stepfather to three little girls? Assuming that Jane ever likes me. Assuming that she would even marry me. Assuming that we all live through this.*

CHAPTER 54
A WELCOME INVASION

From Charon's office, Daniel could tell that daylight was broadening, but the sky brooded, and thunder growled. Meanwhile, like an automaton without an "off" switch, Barth talked endlessly, describing the battles in Whitehall blow by blow, his voice rising like an excited sports commentator at a particularly gruesome gladiator tournament, until, reluctantly, Daniel began listening again. *Now I understand what Hell is like. Satan has his captives reliving and retelling their most sickening experiences over and over and over.*

He remembered his own most awful experience: The day Ielen died.

* * *

When Hermann stepped back to where the escapees waited, he was not alone.

"Mark!" Patrick shouted, his insides jumping for joy.

Fred bellowed, "Tom!"

In the service corridor, Patrick smelled heat and sweat, with a strange mix of blood, copper, steel, sharp fear, and cooking food. Fred let Patrick down and helped him stand, introducing him to a young aristocrat in fine clothes who carried a lute: "This is Sir Thomas." Patrick nodded, but then turned to his Lanthran brother.

"Mark," observed Patrick, his voice a little quavery, "You look like a Horned Edge poster-boy." And he did: The Horned Edge uniform and ring were very prominent; Mark's cheeks had sunken gray areas under the eyes, and he looked hard, like a man with few scruples, like a soul-less Hitler Youth.

Mark removed the Horned Edge ring. "Feel my hand, Patrick.

I'm still Mark Gregory inside, your brother." Mark's hand felt warm as well as strong. He hugged Patrick and when they drew apart, Mark's eyes seemed to have extra moisture, which he wiped away. "But I have to pretend –"

"No! Please!" Patrick begged. Mark threw the ring away. Patrick heard it ring on the marble floor and felt glad.

Meanwhile, Tom described his escape, "The concert was great, Fred; the audience was so responsive! They called for an encore, and I played until I was ready to drop, so Mr. Swa ordered a special intermission where I was able to slip away. Mark got me out of Rose Hall – before the fighting started, thank goodness. We climbed the catwalk over the stage, exited by a door on a higher level, and –"

"That's enough!" Hermann said. "Let's go now!" The Bardian spy's big front teeth shone in a manic grin and his sweat-soaked hair hung limp on his forehead. He pointed to the loading doors. "This way: down to the river!"

Once again, Fred's arms swooped Patrick off the floor; however, before they moved far, someone banged into them. Patrick screamed, and Fred shouted, "Watch it, you –"

"Get out of our way," snarled a large soldier. In an olive black uniform with a helmet and tall boots, he touched his sword pommel as a warning.

Patrick's heart pounded; his ankle was on fire. His stomach ached with a flu-like nausea when he comprehended that their escape route was blocked. Even worse, some frightened civilians straggled toward them from the other direction and they were all squished together.

"Get out of our way!" snarled the soldier again. Fred and the others had no choice but to carry Patrick back the way they had come. Like an avalanche of black gravel, more soldiers crowded after the first. "Keep moving forward!" rang out a militant voice from outside the loading doors, the direction of escape.

Patrick and the others were forced through Patriots in the kitchen area and on into the large front chambers of Whitehall. Patrick guessed that Fred's muscles were about to give out, because he kept shifting his weight. "At least they're not trying to kill us," Patrick said with some of his old humor, hoping to distract Fred. "Yet."

"Yeah, we're just getting slowly squeezed into dough balls." Fred held his arms around Patrick tighter.

"Let me down, Fred. I'll walk!"

"Nope."

Patrick saw that, besides soldiers in sleek olive black uniforms, some soldiers wore loose tunics the color of rosy peaches, and yet others wore brown with silver trim. "Fred, what do those colors mean?" he asked in confusion.

"Who are these people?" Fred yelled to Hermann, shifting Patrick's weight yet again as they inched through the great hall.

"Didn't you learn anything in the College of the Magi, you blockhead?"

Fred growled, "Apparently not, so tell me!"

"All have come to help the Patriots and us. Those in olive black are King Norhe's Raiders; they can pierce through the worst of any enemy resistance. The fuzzy fellows are from Polunking; that's the distinctive style of the cotton they grow. They're, well, … they're trained. The brown and silver ones, as you should know, are –"

"Bardians!" Mark threw a saluting gesture toward someone in the crowd and called out, "Dad!"

"Captain Gregory!" Patrick felt elation rocket high as he saw the mature crinkly-haired Bardian captain in the crowd respond with a raised hand. "Captain Gregory!" he shouted. "Help us! We're over here!"

However, trying to get special attention was useless. They were caught in the middle of a clash. The friendly military invaders and Patriots began to pile up against a dam of hostile Whitehall and Horned Edge defenders. Mark had just yelled, "I have an idea …" when a group of the Polunking soldiers knocked him behind a large marble pillar. In that minimal shelter, the others joined him. "Well, forget my idea," Mark said.

A roar like the end of the world hit all of them. Whitehall shook from the sun-lit top of its marble dome to the never-lit depths of its unexplored caves. Gunfire from Earth's attack rifles exploded somewhere inside the citadel. Patrick covered his ears. Curling up into a little ball, he saw little but heard too much: Painfully loud blasts, splintering marble, *ratta-ratta-ratta-ratta, boom!* Cordite stunk like sneezes from the devil's nose. Bellows, shouts, shrieks, screams, hysterical laughter, moans …

He peeked. A great gash had broken through a wall, opening into another chamber. There, too, soldiers piled in and fought.

Fred, good old Fred, kept his solid body between Patrick and anything that might get around that pillar to hurt him. A chip of marble had sliced Fred's cheek and a short line of bright red blood flowed down his chin. However, although it was probably only a shallow cut, Patrick knew that it was only a matter of time before one of those bullets found deeper and more vulnerable flesh to eat.

Dear God, don't let us die, he prayed with fingers in his ears.

However, pandemonium continued. God wasn't doing anything.

God! What do I have to do to get your attention? Patrick clenched his fists with fury and pain. He squirmed out of Fred's arms, but his ankle hurt like white fire and tears blurred his vision. His hand swung up; Lewis's robe brushed against his fingers, and Patrick made the fine silky cloth his security blanket, pulling it hard down toward his cheek. He wished Lewis's warm hand would come down and rest on his head, too, but it didn't.

"Our Father, Who art in heaven …" *Maybe it doesn't count if I don't use the praying position.* Trying to endure the din of battle, Patrick folded his hands and bowed his head. "Hallowed be Thy name …" *What does 'hallowed' mean? Heck, I don't know! Maybe it won't count if I don't understand!* He swallowed to pray some more, but his throat was so dry that his tongue stuck in his craw.

An accusing voice inside said, *Patrick, stupid boy, you're not doing anything helpful!*

While fear, explosions, and bursts of gunfire flared like giant sunspots, Patrick tried another way to make God listen and stop the fighting. For each of his companions, one by one, he felt a deep, awful feeling in his chest. The feeling intensified. Soon his middle felt compressed and hurt like multiple G's in a spaceship at escape velocity. He concentrated on the sensation, made it stronger while he felt sicker and sicker. If only he could feel hard enough, God would understand how hard he cared.

* * *

After several hours, the assault lessened. Fred, Mark, and Hermann stood together with their swords shining silver. Patrick felt they were guardian elves or angels. Lewis and Sir Thomas stood beside Patrick, who sat on the floor.

During their breathing space, Patrick wondered about Sir Thomas, the Bard of Bardia. The guy was a real puzzle. Although he was only about nineteen years old, Mark and Hermann reverenced him like he was the Ancient of Days. And it was obvious that the lute was a treasure, the way Sir Thomas held it close to his body.

Although pain smote his foot again, Patrick fought with to learn about Sir Thomas. *Understand, understand, understand ... There is something very important to remember ...*

Oh yeah.

He remembered waiting in the Forschwynn building a long, long, time ago to meet Viceroy Daniel Higgins. There was a carving of the Bard of Bardia who had defeated all the bezubs way, way back in Lanthran history. Sir Thomas with the lute looked like the Bard in the carving.

Some tumblers clicked and clunked away in the back of his head. At that moment, the bard's head swung around, and their eyes met. There was a connection, an instant friendship. As if he knew exactly what Patrick needed – and Patrick knew that he did – Sir Thomas signed, in the Blue People's language, a wiggle of fingers that would have made Patrick howl with laughter and roll on the floor in a less terrible situation. He'd been given a fuzzy Blue Mamma's command to her babies at bedtime, and it meant, "Settle down kid, or you'll turn into a bald Person!"

The message made no sense, but somehow it made all the sense in the world. Patrick felt stronger. He prayed. He forgot to "do it right" and just sent up a desperate prayer. "Hey God, I want to live," he whispered. "I want everybody with me to live. Also, I want to go back home – Earth home. And I want Lewis and Gracie to come home with me!"

* * *

Before long, the gunfire eased completely. The Patriots and their allies seemed to have vanished. Patrick heard deep-throated voices as Horned Edge magi chanted a victory chant to Saoma. Their receding footsteps echoed against the marble walls, leaving behind wreckage – and bodies.

"Stay behind this pillar until all is clear," Mark said, pushing back Lewis who had started out into the hallway.

"*Dittiean ta fean dit!*" Hermann hissed. "Using weapons from Earth! Thank *Tabaon* that they haven't gathered the ancient weapons of Lanthra!"

Mark's face twisted. "Oh, the Horned Edge has some of those, too."

Hermann rolled his eyes.

Fred noted practically, "Whatever weapons they have, they're going away. Can we still get out of the palace?" The drips of blood on his cheek had clotted blackish red.

Mark answered, "Maybe, but —"

"Where would we go after that?" Patrick asked. "We can't go back to Mama Jane's. The whole city will be —"

However, before he could finish, a pellet of hard-thrown debris hit his shoulder. "Ow!" he yelled.

"Ye seemed so distracted, and I only want to get your attention," an airy voice called. Everyone's faces snapped around. Patrick saw a handsome bearded man in rich clothes approach them, limping. He was well surrounded by plum-uniformed swordsmen. They stopped a few yards away, swords bristling.

"Hello, Uncle Trager," Tom said with a carefully impassive face, bowing slightly. However, Patrick could see the tension around his eyes and guessed that "Uncle Trager" was not a safe person.

"Who is this?" Patrick whispered. "What's going on?"

"I don't … know," Lewis said, and coughed again.

"This slime ball is Tom's evil uncle," Fred told them in a low voice. "He's one of Lord Charon's marked cards in the cheater's pack."

"Stay back, Sir Thomas," Hermann commanded softly. "And ye also, Fean Lewis, with your brother. We who are armed will go forward." Mark, Hermann, and Fred stepped out into the battle-scarred hall to face the baron's men.

Baron Trager turned his head back and forth to examine each person in Patrick's group. His blue eyes passed over Patrick and dismissed him; Patrick felt much relieved.

For a long time, Trager studied Lewis. "Let's see," Trager said appraisingly, "you're familiar, even though I haven't seen you before. Who are you, laddie?"

Lewis cleared his throat but did not speak.

"Oh, I think I know who you are, but your last name is hard to pronounce. Oh yes, Lewis Brah-min-dura, that's it. Lord Tahei Charon's favorite assistant, formerly loyal to the bone, but no longer? I may be able to use you, though; reward you, too if you like."

Lewis raised his head, his jaw set. "No thank you," he replied calmly.

Patrick saw a spasm contort the baron's features as if any form of "No" was unacceptable. "You may yet change your mind," Trager said shortly, nodding toward Lewis's sling.

Continuing his assessment, Baron Trager glanced at Hermann. Apparently amused, he spread out his feet, leaned back, and smiled broadly. "And who's this flapping black bat in a cape? Do you have rabies?"

Hermann scowled.

When he noted, Baron Trager raised an eyebrow and commented, "What, one of the Horned Edge brethren defending the enemy? You look nice in a Horned Edge uniform – are you a double agent? A triple agent? Or are you so confused that nobody knows what you're doing, including yourself?"

Mark did not answer.

Next, the baron stared at Fred, a light of recognition growing in his eyes. He said contemptuously, "Oh, you're Sir Thomas's *subua,* wagging his tail among the big boys. You look as big and stupid as ever."

Fred smiled with teeth showing. "I can bark, chase a ball, and fetch. I bite, too."

Baron Trager only laughed.

Patrick scowled, feeling black anger growing in him. He shifted his weight and got to his knees, planning to stand up and throw himself at Baron Trager, even though his anklebones screamed inside that left leg.

Lewis pushed him firmly back down with one hand.

Without any signal, the baron's men attacked. Fred's sword flew away, twirling in the air, bouncing with a metallic clatter onto the marble floor, leaving him unarmed. Charging, he managed to knock down several of the attackers.

Hermann deliberately left himself open for a hacking blow

from one of Trager's men, which he dodged so skillfully that the man's sword made a *whoosh* through empty air. He then stabbed the attacker's throat and the man collapsed with a spurt of bright red blood.

Patrick turned his face away. *I hope I never see blood again.* Yet, he had the strong feeling that he wasn't done with the terrors of violence yet. He heard Mark's voice yell and then Mark's booted foot slid into him, shoving Patrick's injured ankle hard. "Ooow!" Patrick screamed, the agony spiking up his whole body. He suppressed a second scream by inserting his fist into his mouth.

"Hermann, surrender before you get dead!" Fred shouted.

Another *clunk* and *clatter* on the floor – Whose sword was that?

Baron Trager laughed, making Patrick shudder. He peeked around. Near the pillar, Hermann knelt with his head drooping. Mark lay against the pillar, very, very still.

Fred stood protectively in front of Patrick and Lewis, but he had no weapon except his fists against swords.

"It's over," the baron said, his voice smooth and flat. "Give it up."

Patrick saw Fred's muscles sag.

"Bind them all."

Two of the baron's men held Fred's arms behind his back while a third secured his wrists with a cord. They bound injured Mark and Hermann.

Patrick didn't let himself think. Everything was totally awful. He wished he could turn white as a light bulb and then burn out with a loud *blink.* He wanted to get up, interfere, stop the baron, but his ankle screamed with red, raw pain, and he collapsed against the wall.

Two soldiers grabbed Sir Thomas's arms. "My dear nephew," Baron Trager crooned, "by now I assume that my army has invaded your daddy's rich little province and taken everything. By now, your father and brothers will be dead. You, of course, the rightful heir of his property, gave your share away to buy your stupid subua. And you, heir of my property through your mother, my younger sister whom he stole from me … well, I'll take care of that. Ah, how I loved her! I love her still! If your father had not come and outshone me, we might have –"

"You pervert!" Sir Thomas cried.

Baron Trager stepped closer until he was directly in front of the young man. "Well, no time to sing a ballad of unrequited love. I'll get what is mine. But for now … just as insurance for my future and a foretaste of good things to come …" Two of the baron's retinue took hold of him and fastened his hands behind his back. They were not gentle, and Tom winced.

Several others approached Patrick and Lewis. One of them, an older bearded fellow with a kinder face than the others asked the baron, "Must you bind these also? They are both injured, and one is but a boy."

"Are you deaf?" Baron Trager snapped at him. "Take them to the meeting. You know the place. Quickly now – go! I'll meet you there!"

CHAPTER 55
NEW PASSWORD

My Lord, the fighting's done at Whitehall," a battle-bruised, cloak-torn, and exhausted Horned Edge magus reported, bowing low before Lord Charon in the palace study. When the man saw Barth's ravaged face, he flattened himself on the floor and kissed the toe of Barth's boot. "O Master Saoma, beautiful ointment in your earthly vessel, blessed art Thou for bringing us the victory."

Barth gave the man a sharp kick on the nose, enough to make it bleed. "Get up, you idiot. Gather a score of nice big security guards, well-armed with guns, to escort us to the cave chamber."

Daniel saw the magus cringe.

Apparently, Barth saw it, too. "Yes, downstairs – the cave chamber – where we connected with the Forbidden Planet, the devil's hometown. Hurry! We're not done with winning yet."

Soon, twenty Horned Edge guards arrived at Charon's study. Daniel noted, flinching, that they carried machine guns slung over their robes. They walked to either side of him and Lord Charon, who smiled as if he had achieved nirvana. *He's full of drugs. Years of bitterness and slow deterioration have worn down his soul to a diseased bone.*

Robed in gold, his head high and his manner grave, Daniel knew that he looked very much the High Magus. And, yes, the scared and troubled eyes of the Moorway staff who were back in the hallways cleaning up after the battle, did follow him with respect, and even fear.

Although many of the light globes in Whitehall's main level had been smashed and the light was dim, his gold robe glimmered and shone like the promise of sunrise through dark clouds. The Horned Edge magi bowed to the ground as he and Charon processed toward the laboratory.

No, I haven't come to bring you peace and joy, Daniel mentally told them, his heart sagging with sadness. *Charon has determined to make me his figurehead.* The idea made him sick to his stomach, which roiled and clenched until he was swallowing back the urge to vomit. *I don't want this! How can I show the world that I still serve you, Baonea Radyah?*

He felt no answer.

Bizeor. He could sense them all around, like happy flies who had all the rotten meat they could eat, worming busily into the fears and shames of the working crewmen and soldiers and Horned Edge magi. Besides bizeor and visible to all, the hallway was filled with corpses and war debris – swords, hats, shoes, bits of clothes, torn hunks of hair, sliced-off human limbs … Daniel set his face like a rock. Inside his thoughts, demons taunted: *Your plan, your plan, your plan … haha, Ielen was right. It's all gone wrong and now you lost everything. Or worse! You won! You're going to be one of us now!*

Daniel doubted his Radyah-given power. Could he clear the spiritual area with a word?

There was no answer. His stomach sank. The Master, at least temporarily, had denied his power. He walked on, in the column of Horned Edge magi, trying to hold his head up in spite of the awful hollow in his soul.

They came to the laboratory. When they entered, Daniel saw that all of Charon's scientists and technicians who had not escaped the palace were lined up for inspection. Upon seeing Lord Charon, they simultaneously knelt. Their faces were gray with fatigue. *Probably like mine,* he thought.

"Has the destruction sequence been purged from the system?" Barth asked.

"Aye," said one of the scientists. "'Tis clear."

Charon walked up to Labeth, who dropped her eyes. He lifted her chin with his finger and asked, "Labeth, my dear, have you had the cave chamber cleaned up for us?"

Labeth's dark almond eyes, glistening with fear, looked up at Charon's. Her lips trembled and although she opened her mouth several times, she could not answer.

Barth sneered with his hideous swollen, purple lips. "What's the matter, darling? Has someone removed your tongue? Or perhaps that's on this evening's menu?" He looked over the rest of the staff, his blood-streaked eyes resting at last on a big woman kneeling next to a small man.

Daniel recognized her. *Mildred!* He also saw her bland, deliberately innocuous husband, Jeffrey not far away, kneeling with the rest of the laboratory experts. *What happened to you? You were two of my finest students!*

Mildred broke in roughly, "The cave chamber is not cleaned up, because none of us can get in there." Her broad, thick face glowered, and she radiated intimidation and resentment. Ignoring Barth, she said to Charon, "My Lord, I was your lab manager for fifteen years. Yet, you did not give me the authority to go through the door. In fact, no one but you had sovereign authority – until you gave it to Fean Lewis." She made the word *fean* sound like an expectoration and Daniel read jealousy in every syllable.

Curious, Daniel broke in, "Tahei, where is Lewis now?"

Charon began to speak, but Barth broke in, "Probably right where we left him. He's indisposed. Therefore, we'll put you, Millie, in charge long enough to clean up the cave chamber. Here's your password: Say it: 'I am a fat wash bucket.' Say it!"

Charon nodded. "Say it."

A few feet away, Daniel saw Mildred's husband Jeffrey hold back a snigger. Her face turning scarlet, she mumbled, "I am a fat wash bucket."

"Get up. Go get to work. But don't take the mess up here – trash and bodies exit by way of the dungeon door. I don't want to see you again for a long time." Barth gave a fierce, ugly jerk of his chin, Mildred rose. The scientists and staff followed. Grinning, drooling bloody saliva, Barth pointed to cleaning supplies; and down she went.

During the laboratory cleanup, Daniel and Charon stood by the beautiful noretha in their cases. Tahei continued his earlier conversation, "To succeed in our larger plan, we must control all of Lanthra's magi. You and I have to capture either their allegiance or their lives."

I'm getting really tired of this, Daniel thought. He let his eyes roam over the noretha, reading their labels, remembering them like old friends. "And what do you imagine my part is in that task?" he asked tonelessly.

"As the High Magus, you control them, at least symbolically, and I will control you," Charon said.

Tahei talked on, expounding in intricate detail, but Daniel tuned him out. For some reason the jewel-like light from the noretha seemed too bright. Why? Then his vision fractured into a lattice pattern. *Oh groan. Another migraine coming on.*

The headache grew worse as, standing for hours, he and Charon waited for the cave chamber to be cleaned. Daniel pictured the laboratory below, the compelled labor of hauling out bodies and weapons through the dungeons, sanitizing it for the next connection to Earth.

Eventually Mildred returned. She came up from the cave chamber, and her robe could not conceal the filth of battle that she had removed. "The chamber is ready, my Lord. I ask if I may be dismissed."

Lord Charon nodded graciously. He began to speak, but Barth stuck out his chewed, ravaged tongue, which was now covered with pustular warts. "Did you think you were done? Stay up here in the lab. Keep track of our activity on the thoyo-on, because we're going to put quite a load on it! Vehicles full of Earth weapons are going to roll into the rendezvous. Carts full of our ancient weapons will be delivered to our allies."

Mildred gave him a vicious stab with her narrowed eyes, but she did not dare to retort. Behind her, Labeth sagged against a wall, her eyes closed.

"It's time, Master, for the next step," Barth said. He was commanding Lord Charon, Daniel knew as he rubbed his throbbing temples. *The bizeor are ruling Barth, and he is ruling Tahei.* Finally, they processed down the spiral stairs into the cave chamber.

CHAPTER 56
SORROW

It was almost noon, but the sky was so dark that it looked like evening. Rain hurled down incessantly; thunder rolled as ominously as war drums in Mordor. Gracie and her "sisters" sat in the Tuttles' kitchen. The morning's joy had completely worn off. Lunch was skimpy – leftover fish sausage, mostly, which wasn't much to look forward to. It was market day, but nobody would venture out into the combat.

"At least there's plenty of coffee," Jane Tuttle said, trying to sound bright and totally failing. She helped herself to another cup – her fourth, Gracie observed – and her hand was trembling so that some coffee splashed into the saucer.

Little June got the last of the sweet milk, but it wasn't very much, and she whined, "I wanna mo' milk!"

"There's no more, June," Gracie said, tilting the bottle so that the toddler could see it was empty.

June cried.

Bessie, Gracie's "older" sister, tried to comfort her. "Here, sweetie, have some of my sausage."

Katie complained, "I didn't get any milk; why did June get some and I didn't?"

"Because she's the littlest, Katie," Bessie explained, but Katie pouted.

June threw fish sausage on the floor, slid off her chair, and ran around the kitchen, pulling tools and objects off shelves and the table. "She's tired of being cooped up," Mama Jane said, but Gracie was thinking, *We're all scared, and she's scared, too.* The toddler's groping hand snatched Jane's napkin, which fell off the table and brought down Jane's cup of coffee with it. The cup smashed, some of the hot coffee splashed on the baby's hands and she screamed.

"Oh, June bug, let me cool your hands down before they blister," Mama Jane said. She snatched the little girl up and poured a gentle stream of cold water over her fingers from the kitchen pump. After a while, June's sobs lost their terrified tone, and Mama Jane told the other girls, "I'm going to rock her awhile." She left the kitchen cuddling the child, but Gracie wasn't sure whose face looked more scared, Jane's or June's.

Now Gracie, Bessie, and Katie had the kitchen to themselves. Nobody said much. Katie kicked the table leg. Bessie intentionally spilled a lot of salt on a plate and began drawing squiggles in it with a toothpick, like a tiny Zen garden.

A nail of sorrow pierced Gracie's heart. *I wish and wish and wish that I could make everything all right again for them. I wish that the Patriots would win the war. I wish that Uncle Curly would come back and tell us that all is safe and that everybody is okay.*

A loud knock sounded at the door, and Gracie jumped up. *Wow, God! That was quick!*

Nate, their Patriot friend, stood at the door. Rain streamed over his jacket and puddled onto the kitchen floor.

"Gracie, don't just stand there with the door and your mouth open – let him in!" Bessie shouted.

Gracie stepped back and let Nate come in. He took off his coat, which dripped worse than a soggy towel, and Gracie hung it on a hook on the wall without saying a word. Inside she chanted, *I hope, I hope, I hope ...*

"Would you like some coffee?" Bessie asked, getting a clean cup and saucer from the shelf over the stove.

Nate hardly seemed to hear her. He sat heavily down at the table and slumped forward, his face in his hands.

CHAPTER 57
THE MASTER'S PLAN

When Daniel and the Horned Edge retinue reached the cave chamber, he could see that the Mildred had cleaned only half-heartedly. Their feet stepped onto a filthy floor. Debris still lay in corners. The chamber's amethyst walls were chipped, pocked, scratched, splattered, and stained.

Daniel felt a small joy because the chains that dangled from the walls were all empty. "Where is Fean Lewis?" Lord Charon asked the guards. His voice was curt. "I want him here to help us!"

The Horned Edge magi looked down at their feet, afraid to answer, but one mumbled, "He was not here when we entered, my Lord."

That Lewis might have escaped seemed possible, as Daniel could see an odd pile of keys on the floor near one of the sets of chains. "Never mind," Barth growled. "We'll find him later."

The Horned Edge group in the cave chamber moved into place for a ceremony, gathering in a rehearsed hexagon around the obsidian table. It looked black and smooth, inviting them to complete the nexus to Earth.

"Tahei," Daniel said, feeling that his head might explode, "Do you really believe your rituals will cause Saoma to bless your great plan?"

"Aye," Charon replied confidently in his deep, rich voice. "Ours is a great plan; it is the work of God."

"Ours?"

Barth sneered, "Your Excellency Daniel, you contributed quite a lot to make all this happen.

Cold chills crept down Daniel's spine. *What does he mean?*

"You mismanaged your defenses and let your province Rockeerie be taken. You thought that you could control us even as our prisoner." Barth tipped back his throat and laughed with a sickening gurgle. His face looked as if it had been beaten with a bag of oranges, but his big body grew until his presence seemed to fill the entire chamber. "One minute your dear Patriots were winning, pressing us back, and suddenly they found themselves overpowered. All your plotting, all your daring schemes are undone, and ..." he laughed once more, "everyone thinks you are behind what we did! There's absolutely nothing you can do to change your reputation. You cannot even pretend to be innocent. Whether you knew it or not, *your* plan turned out to be *our* plan!"

Daniel could not control the trembling that seized his knees. They buckled and he found himself kneeling. *Oh, Ielen, what have I done! Baon, I am no longer your child; what I've done is unforgivable.*

Barth went on, "You fool, do you want to know how you can atone for the ruin you've caused?"

Daniel's head hurt so much that he could not see. "Atone?" There was something wrong with the question, but he could not think, either.

"Why, you can rule the way you've always wanted, that's how, Hegofean, High Magus!" Barth said. "It's that simple."

Lord Tahei Charon began to elaborate: "Daniel, you can persuade those who will to join us, and you can let those who will not join us to endure destruction." Even through his migraine, Daniel saw that Charon's dark eyes sparkled with the old excitement that they had enjoyed when they had been friends. Charon smiled and extended his hand to Daniel. "Did you think we were going to kill you? To make you suffer and be ashamed? Nay, friend! Together we'll restore this age to its former glory!"

Dumb, Daniel accepted Charon's hand.

"Let your soul admit this victory, Daniel. You've done much to deserve it. Now, Barth, let us begin."

"Yes, Master." Barth turned to the obsidian table and fingered some controls. Daniel's universe sparkled with the awful migraine pattern, but he saw the images on the tabletop.

It was an ordinary scene – a parking lot on Earth behind a remote and apparently abandoned big box store. The store's outside walls showed rusty colored streaks from water damage and the parking lot was weedy. The facility was busy, however. Semi-tractor trailers, trucks, vans, and loaders had parked at bays all around. A touch of the controls, and Barth moved the view to inside the huge building. Men – yes, all men; there was not a woman to be seen – in bland gray service uniforms moved crates to a central area and – as if through a glittering screen – those crates disappeared. They could even hear the supervisors talking with mobile devices to their counterparts at Lanthra's pick-up sites.

"Magic!" Barth said with fruity satisfaction. "Actually, not really – It's good science. Lewis showed us this trick … a multiple connection on the system. Did he learn it from you and your Bardian magi? I suppose so. Danny boy, aren't you the talented one? Aren't we happy to serve the benevolent new dictator and representative of Saoma?"

Around him, Daniel smelled coppery blood, heavily exercised bodies, strong cologne, and a certain stench of fear. Tahei Charon and the reverent Horned Edge magi crowded forward to see the view of Earth while the weapons transfer continued, which left Daniel on the outside of their formation and blocked his view.

Suddenly Daniel felt a sharp rap on his skull. "Ouch!" he yelped. No around him appeared to notice.

How long do I have to put up with your stupidity, Daniel, son of the goat farmer!

He recognized the Master's voice.

All this anxiety about your plan, your plan indeed! Don't you understand that I have a plan, too?

Instantly there was a feeling like an earthquake in Daniel's head. All of the patterns of his neural synapses shifted violently, and he saw … he saw … He saw the magi, the people, and the worlds and stars praising, not the Master, but him! "Worthy art you, Daniel, of glory and honor!"

The Master told him, without mincing words, *You played God. You took on the entire responsibility for the trouble in your world. Yes, because you are a clever man, you made intelligent plans to achieve a very intricate and favorable outcome. However, in your pride, you opened up your domain to the enemy, thinking that you could be the devil's punching bag and save the people*

*behind your omnipresent covering. You treated me as if I were
only a magic wand in your hand.*

Daniel hid his eyes. His skull pounded, and even shut, his eyes
saw a horrible haze of red. Trusting his own strength and magic,
he had completely underestimated the enemy. He had not asked
for help. He had just made plans. There had been many deaths.
Homes destroyed. People suffering – the people under his care.

"I don't deserve to live!" he whispered. "I deserve
punishment! Yes, even the torture of crucifixion …"

An echo of his own words ricocheted through his thoughts. It
was very, very clear. He didn't like it.

Yes, even the torture of crucifixion …

But –

A tremendous aftershock nearly collapsed his mind. Someone
had already been tortured, crucified. On Earth. On that skull-
shaped hill in a Roman-occupied country, circa 33 A.D. The
Lanthran magi had watched it; they had recorded it; he had seen it
for himself and had read it in the history books; he had taught it to
his students; as the High Magus he presented it, via the magi, to
all the people of Lanthra …

"Jesus!" Daniel breathed softly. He quoted the common
saying: "Jesus Christ died on the cross to save me from my sins
…"

His heart felt suddenly light and his headache disappeared.
Though power-hungry Horned Edge and POG representatives
pressed around him from every side, with him as their prisoner
and chosen representative of demonic power, he now understood
that he was completely free from them. He'd seen danger coming
and he'd made a plan. His brilliant plan had failed. Now, whatever
happened was out of his control – he had to rest and let the Master
work.

Daniel laughed out loud, the merry sound ringing in the
locating chamber. Lanthran Horned Edge magi and the Earth
counterparts turned to stare at him. Barth wrinkled his spider-
veined nose; Charon's eyebrows raised; even the shadows of
demons that filled the chamber froze.

Daniel laughed until he bent over and roared. Finally, finally,
finally, he saw how limited he was. "Master, I'm only Daniel
Higgins!" he cried aloud joyfully. "Thank God!"

One of the Horned Edge magi whispered to another, "He's gone mad."

The other sneered, "Good."

Making no attempt to conceal this conversation with God from the people in the cave chamber, Daniel continued, "Master, I'm not fit to be the High Magus. O *Baon,* dear One, please remove me from my office and replace me with another."

The Master said, *No. I gave you that office. You remain under my authority.*

Charon, Barth, and the others thought that he was talking to them. Drawing away from the table, Tahei said gently, "Daniel, you must retain your position. We will not let you leave."

Barth's battered face wrinkled with ironic amusement. "You can't get out of this one, Hegofean."

Daniel ignored them. He continued his prayer, "I am your Hegofean, your High Magus. However, save your people, my Master, because I cannot."

Yes, the Master said. Daniel felt a chuckle in the unheard voice. *I already have.*

Barth interjected, "You fool, the Patriots in Tor have been destroyed. Your province belongs to us now. All of Bardia is next on the agenda. Every nation on Lanthra will come under our control. All of Lanthra is … yours," he sneered, "my Lord High Magus."

One man, so thin that his cheeks looked like caverns and his hands looked like the gnarled gray hands that crawl by themselves on the floor during Earth's Halloween, turned blazing fanatic eyes on Daniel. He held up one hand that showed his large gold ring with the onyx stone on the bony finger, and then swept low in a formal bow. "The Shields on Earth, who are servants of Saoma also, will be under your power, my Lord. Saoma will rule Earth as well as Lanthra."

They might as well have been bleating in goat language. Daniel listened to only one voice, which said, *And now, High Magus Daniel, Viceroy of Rockeerie, and son of a goat farmer named Higgins, watch what will happen according to* my *plan …*

Yes, the nexus to Earth was still open. Weapons continued to be exchanged from the warehouse on Earth to various places on Lanthra – and vice versa. In the cave chamber, men chanted, touching each other's ringed fingers, until, heightened by the slight hum created by the locating system's connection through space, the entire cave chamber resonated.

When the last few loads of weapons were transported, the Horned Edge magi and the Shields who worshipped Saoma cheered. Lord Charon stepped away from the table. He raised his hands high.

At first, Daniel thought Tahei was merely praising Saoma. However, when he saw an umbra about him, a dangerous, dark presence that he knew were *bizeor,* his heart jumped. The umbra palpitated against the amethyst crystals and made them seem oily.

The Horned Edge magi gloried, and even Barth drooled like a happy dog, Lord Charon cried, "We have won! This task is finished! We are powerful, and we are many, and we are going to rule!" His smile broadened, showing all his beautiful white teeth, as he stretched out his long arms in victory.

He's drowning; the bizeor are removing his soul, the Master said.

In quick understanding, Daniel pleaded, "Don't, Tahei! Don't lose yourself! You – and I also – have tried to be God, but we are only ourselves. You know who the Master is! At least you can remember that he knows who *you* are, Tahei! Come back, friend!"

Tahei Charon looked him right in the eye and kept smiling. Daniel perceived the man's spirit being pulled like a turkey wishbone by the supernatural world, and then it snapped.

Daniel yelled, "Tahei!"

But it was too late. Tahei Charon's began a hideous thin screaming. Everyone in the chamber gaped. The magus's whole body stiffened, spiralling around and around until he sprang toward Daniel, hands clawed, teeth gaping.

Daniel headed toward the stairs that led up out of the cave chamber. Charon's hands snatched at him, trying to catch at his gold robe, but the robe tore. Charon again attacked, this time with deadly, masterful coordination. Daniel slipped free from throttling fingers. Using his magus training, he brushed against Charon, only a small brush, but it sent the man into a crazy swirl. Charon tripped, fell backwards, and instantly disappeared into the nexus.

Everyone, including Daniel, froze in a hush of suspense. The table's glow held steady, showing a dirty cement floor nearly empty of crates, loaders, and people, but they did not see Lord Tahei Charon.

Barth advanced toward Daniel, his huge hands opening and closing. His blistered lips said sweetly, like poisonous saccharine, "No matter, Hegofean. We lost one madman, but we still have you."

"Oh, no you don't!" a new shrill voice shrieked, and Daniel's heart shot with alarm. All whirled toward the dungeon door. In the shadows at the back of the cave chamber crouched a wraith-like figure: An old woman in a filthy dress, a knife gleaming in her hand.

'Tis Crazy Lady!" one of the Horned Edge magi shouted.

Barth pointed at her. He – or rather the bizeor in him – ordered, "Die."

One by one, the old woman's fingers loosened their grip on the knife. Jerking, convulsing, she fell to the floor and writhed like a poisoned spider.

Barth turned away from her. A juicy laugh made him heave, and he lunged for Daniel, his huge fist catching his robe at the neck. "You will be sorry, our dear High Magus and representative of Saoma's new order, so sorry that you were ever born … we'll let you live a long, long time while you die inside, screaming silently while you watch friend after friend fall under our power …"

He laughed and shook Daniel, pushing his face into Daniel's own. Barth's breath blew on him with putrid fumes, stinking of infection …

But the whole man began to collapse. Daniel jumped back yet tripped; Barth fell sideways on top of him and onto the obsidian table, a knife blade sticking up from his back.

Daniel yelled, "Master, help!" He heard a loud *crack!* The table split into two slabs. Its light went out; the view vanished … And there he lay, trapped under Barth and wedged between two great hunks of polished obsidian rock.

"Get her!" a magus called out angrily.

Horned Edge magi seized Mary's arms while Shields tried to pull the knife from Barth's back, but the withered old woman laughed. "Think you can call your magician lord and his parasite Barth Layhew back from hell? Ha!"

The officer snarled, drew his sword, and started to say something very ugly, but apparently realized what Mary had just said, because the color drained from his face. "Put a chain on her. Leave her here, with the Hegofean, but make sure the doors are sealed. We must go report to the authorities – if we have any left!"

CHAPTER 58
FOLLOW SPIRIT

Gracie laid her head down on the table in the Tuttle's dark kitchen. Everyone was so smushed and sad and scared after this awful day that they were exhausted, including her, but she couldn't sleep.

The surface of the table felt cool on her cheek, which was good, because the city was guaranteed to heat up again after the wild stream of thunderstorms. Gracie's stomach growled and pinched itself, but she didn't bother to look for a snack; the Jane Tuttle's pantry was empty except for salt. *Heaven help us when the baby wakes up and wants her breakfast.*

Gracie got up. Softly she padded to the hallway, to the mirror where Jesus once had stood beside her. "Hey, Jesus," she whispered, "are you there?"

However, the house was too quiet; the absence of sound lay on her ears like a heavy blanket. Ordinarily, by now, she'd hear rumbles through the house's brick walls of carters bringing fresh cow and goat milk, swamp fish and leeches (yech!), meat, veggies, and fruits, and the tenor vendor singing, "Boiled eggs, fresh for breakfast!" and the loud, deep call of a local baker with his basket of yummy warm bread. But not today. The people in Moorway were cowering in their houses and apartments, hoping that they would survive the upcoming house-to-house searches, arrests, and probable executions, tortures, and horrible so on.

"Jesus," she called again, "where are you?"

Nothing happened.

Feeling worn out as the heel of an old sock, Gracie retreated back into the kitchen. Once again, her head drooped onto the table.

Sometime during this adventure, she had turned nine years old, but she couldn't remember celebrating it, inside or out.

Good grief – what is that stink! Sniffing here and there, she came to the awful conclusion: *It's me! I haven't bathed for so long ... Glag.*

She remembered that, when she was just a little girl back home, she smelled good. Before all the hot marble business began, she wore her favorite pink gingham dress and never had to worry about how she smelled. Her favorite activity – besides climbing and running – was to sit under her favorite tree in her pretty dress and write stories in her notebook.

I was just a silly little girl. The discouraging thought made her heart sag.

You weren't silly, an answer contradicted her.

Gracie sat up. She did want to write stories in her notebook! And she had a notebook that she'd bought when they still went to the shops. *Ha, ha – Maybe this time I can finish my story with a happy ending!*

Immediately, Gracie lit a small candle lamp, found a pencil and the notebook, and returned to the kitchen. Elbow on the table and head resting on her hand, she sat, waiting for a story to come out. *Martians? Nope. Intelligent dinosaurs in flying saucers? Absolutely not! That's Patrick and Lewis stuff! What do I have in my Gracie head that's a good story?* Images drifted through her mind: flowers, rainbows, castles, horses – but they didn't fit the situation. *I have to write, even if what I say is stupid!* Of all the pictures that had crossed her mind, one wouldn't go away.

"What does that have to do with my story?" she asked God.

Deep inside, she felt an answer. *Everything. Just do it.*

Gracie began, her pen digging into the paper.

*   *   *

In hasty words, she described a big old, male hound dog. Its name was Spirit. No, she'd never owned a real dog, but in this story, Spirit was her "BFF – Best Friend Forever." It went with her everywhere.

You are so silly, a thought pricked her mind. She almost threw the story in the trash. But she struggled and kept going.

The hound stood in the courtyard in back of the Tuttle's tall, narrow house. Sniffing at the enormous tree, Spirit lifted a leg, showing its speckled tummy that would be so soft to rub, and peed profusely.

Lifting her pencil, Gracie didn't know whether to laugh or scream. *Where is this story going? Honestly – a hound dog? Peeing?* The sarcastic thought put her down, but she shook it off. Her pen flowed again.

Spirit wanted Gracie to follow him, because it bowed its big head on his front paws, big intelligent brown eyes staring intently at her. His eyes reminded her of Lewis, and the real Gracie said softly, "I miss you, bro'!"

"*Aaoooooo!*" hound dog howled suddenly. Spirit stood stiff all over, the fur bristled along its spine, and its lips curled back in a snarl that showed enormous sharp teeth.

Gracie jumped, almost tipping the kitchen chair over backward. "Wow!"

In her story, the hound pointed Gracie to look toward a white mountain. It looked like death, like bones … *That's Lord Charon's palace.* However, the story inside her insisted that she had to go there.

Her stomach shrank into a fluttering sour ball. "No! I won't go back there!"

You have to go back there. All you have to do is follow Spirit. Keep writing!

Gracie bit her lip, but she wrote without stopping to correct mistakes or to consider the best words. Her body was in the kitchen, but her mind followed as the hound dog left the big tree and trotted through Moorway. Attached to the hound dog like a captive balloon, Gracie allowed Spirit to pull her down streets, over canal bridges, finally to the great river gorge that separated the palace from the city. There, Gracie balked. *Lord Charon's marble mountain … Daniel and I were prisoners …*

"Stop, Spirit! I don't wanna' go there!"

You have to.

Never mind doors or barriers or guards – Spirit snuffled its way inside Whitehall and Gracie floated with it into the awesome white marble entranceway. "Where are you going, dog?" she asked.

Just follow the Spirit, said a calm inner voice.

CHAPTER 59
BACK IN THE CAVE CHAMBER

Lewis and his friends sat on the floor in the much-too-familiar cave chamber. His chest felt like a bag filled almost to bursting with hot glue, his wrists bound together behind his back so tightly that his injured shoulder had nearly popped out of its socket again. *It hurts like* ... Well, the pain was indescribable. He looked around at the heart-breaking scene.

At first, Lewis didn't recognize the filthy old woman who was chained to the wall, with one wrist, as he had been, but then – *Mary!* Looking around, Lewis saw that on the cold floor lay Mark Gregory, his skin gray and his body limp. He and even unconscious Hermann were tied up like the rest of them. *What did you do that for, you stupid Baron, tying up severely injured men!* Tom's lips moved, and Lewis knew he was praying.

All of Lewis's company lived – so far, but Barth Layhew's body lay very dead with a knife in its back. The obsidian table with its marvelous controls, the door to other worlds, stood in two huge pieces like a toppled, broken Stonehenge. The hot marble was stuck in its control panel, inactive without the system to give it meaning.

Meanwhile, Baron Trager berated Lewis. "Yes, you opened the door. However, when I need to use the monitor and its controls, I find they are destroyed! I will make sure that you see each of your friends disemboweled unless you repair it for me!"

Lewis had no doubt that the crazy baron would do as he threatened. Hot tears welled in his eyes. They ran down his cheeks, and he replied, "I ... I will do ... whatever you want."

Baron Trager stretched to his full height with cold authority,

"You, Fean, will be in charge of my thoyo-on and you will be my magus. I will keep your friends – most of them – alive to make sure that you comply." He tapped each of the prisoners on the stomach with his cane. When he got back around to Lewis, the baron hit his injured shoulder hard. "Say it again! 'I will do what you want!'"

Lewis screamed. "I will … do … what you want."

Baron stumped back and forth, ranting grandiose plans. "Saoma will make me ruler of Tor, and eventually Bardia, and after that, Lanthra and Earth!"

In a little space in his head, Lewis fought back. Despite all the fear, or maybe because of it, he thought: *Baron, O Baron, if you only knew* … He pictured the little piece of clear plastic in his pocket, almost insubstantially thin. In it was Lord Charon's entire hoard of the ancient technology, including all the information to navigate and travel to other worlds. *But I'm not telling, and after I die, you, foolish man, will probably bury it with me.*

*   *   *

The baron's men were building a scaffold. Fred shivered. *Who will die on that?*

Baron Trager, his handsome face swollen and red with anger, had decided that all his problems were Tom's fault. He raged, "I'm going to hang you, stinking would-be ruler of my domain!" He aimed a kick at Tom but hit the wall instead, and a crystal flew off, striking his own cheek. Putting a hand to his face and seeing some red blood on it, Baron Trager's mouth streamed forth Lanthran curses so vulgar that even Fred's drug-addicted mother could not have rivalled them. Trager struck Tom with a fist to his mouth, yelling, "I'll make sure you never sing again!"

Fred strained forward. "Do not hit him again, or I will –"

"Do what, you stupid slave?" Baron Trager sneered. He turned to his guards. "Bring Sir Thomas to the scaffold."

The guards dragged Tom to the scaffold and forced him to climb up onto the broken table. His face resolute, the bard seemed to relax as the guards' hands held him. He did not cry for mercy. Tom only looked at Fred. There was love in his eyes. "Radyah bless and keep you, my friend."

The guards slipped the noose over Tom's head and around his throat. Tom took one great breath.

"No!" Fred screamed. Horror raged in his heart; he strained to throw his big body forward … anything to stop this abomination …

But Trager's guards kicked him back into his place at the chamber wall. Fred's heart nearly burst with the need to rescue his friend. "Take me! Hang me! Don't kill Sir Thomas; don't murder the Bard of Bardia! He is just a boy, and he is your own family!"

A guard punched Fred on the temple. He fell over sideways but kept shouting anyway, "No! No! Nooo …"

Baron Trager himself pushed Tom off the edge of the table. The young bard struggled to breathe; his feet kicked but could not find purchase; his face turned red. As Fred watched, his master's face purpled …

CHAPTER 60
GIFTS DESPITE SHAME

As he watched the awful scene, Daniel remembered the Master's prophetic words so long ago, *You will be overrun, Daniel.* And the words had come to pass. He felt ashamed, ready to die.

He thought, *I was proud. I had a plan, but it failed. Now I shall see young Tom strangle!*

However, deep inside, he felt rather than heard: *Open your hands and receive gifts.*

Those words repeated again, immediately, urgently: *Open your hands, Daniel!*

What are you talking about, Master? My hands are tied! In fact, his hands, tied tightly behind him, were so swollen and painful and numb that he could hardly move his fingers.

Open your hands! Literally, do it!

He struggled and managed to assume a semi-lotus position. A few yards away, Baron Trager threw him a dirty look but left him alone. Trager turned, entranced, watching Tom hang. Daniel watched, too. The boy still kicked.

What shall I do? What can I do?

Nothing. Open your hands!

As well as he could, Daniel cupped his hands like a wee child receiving a surprise from someone who stood behind him. One by one, he felt small round weights drop into his hands. They felt smooth and warm. "What are they?" he whispered. Closing his eyes, he imagined each one as a child's marble. Then he imagined them as jewels, polished round gemstones like rubies, diamonds, topaz, sapphires ... *Noretha!*

One of the marble-jewels felt very familiar.

"Dear Master," he whispered softly, "What are you giving me? I sense that one of these noretha is the 'hot marble' that led the Brahmindura children and Fred from the Forbidden Planet to my world."

I'm giving you worlds. Earth. Lanthra. Amim. Hegethlua. And eight more worlds.

Daniel began to sob. Hot tears rolled down his cheeks into his mouth, but he could not wipe them away. He tasted salt, the salt in a wound. *I don't deserve your gifts! Look at what's happening! Instead of blessing me, save Tom!*

Take them, High Magus Daniel. They are mine, and I give them to you. I trust you to advise their future.

Unable to control his weeping, Daniel bowed his head over his knees.

CHAPTER 61
GRACIE GOES TO WAR

Writing had gotten hard because Gracie was hungry. Her poor stomach cramped, and she ached all over. Once the Tuttles came downstairs, baby June would start screaming, and Gracie knew she'd never finish the story if she stayed in the kitchen with all its distractions and deprivations. *All right – I'll get out. Then I can finish my story in peace upstairs in my room.*

Gracie grabbed her pen and the notebook and headed upstairs.

*   *   *

Maybe because Gracie was extremely hungry, her story led her into Whitehall's kitchen. Cooks and helpers scattered everywhere, there was a smell of burning bread.

Gracie wrinkled her nose. "Okay, Spirit, what's next?"

Time to save the universe! Spirit howled, and Gracie about had a heart attack. She saw Curly and some other cooks together pull open the loading door. They welcomed a great river of brown-and-white-uniformed soldiers.

Cheers resounded from the marble walls. The soldiers shouted. Under bronze helmets, their faces looked set and purposeful, and their swords glared with reflected light. *Bardians!*

Nor did they carry only swords; they also carried what looked like small flashlights. They headed straight for her. When some Whitehall guards, Horned Edge military magi, came forward in opposition, the forces clashed. Gracie withdrew to one side; Spirit stayed with her. Some Horned Edge soldiers aimed Earth-style guns, ready to annihilate them, but all the Bardians fired their silent hand weapons and those Horned Edge magi vanished: *Poof!*

Gone! It was as if they'd stepped into one of Patrick's video games or, worse, Lewis's deadly black holes. Gracie's heart squeezed tight, and she put a hand to her chest. For the first time ever, her knees turned to jelly.

"Help me!" she squealed.

A quiet voice inside her soul assured her, *Calm down, Gracie. Their weapons cannot touch you. Get going; I have something for you to do.*

She raced after Spirit, who bounded after a company of Bardians. She recognized one of them. Immediately, Gracie felt her heart expand and glow with joy. "Captain Gregory!" she shouted with all her might, running up for a big hug, but she was only an imagination inside this story, invisible to everyone.

With extreme haste, Captain Gregory, his men, and Gracie with the hound raced until they reached a grand white gallery with pillars. Various doors and hallways led off from it; the gallery was obviously an important central area in the palace.

However, what seemed what like hundreds of Horned Edge magi entered and clashed against them from many sides. Gracie screamed; she backed against a wall. There was much fighting, screaming, and blood. There were swords hacking and stabbing, Earth guns shattered some of the Bardians to bits, but the Lanthran weapons that the Bardians used were so powerful that most of the enemy were killed quickly. Gracie saw a piggy Horned Edge officer – Commander Gort – throw down his gun and run away, leaving his company to surrender. Finally, the fighting was over. Captain Gregory's men secured the surviving Horned Edge magi and marched them away.

All the action happened in such a fast time that Gracie had to stop to catch her breath. The gallery was now clear. Beside her, the hound dog panted, lowered its head, and licked a red puddle on the floor.

"Yuck! Dog, that is so nasty!"

However, Spirit raised its face. Jowls dripping with bright red blood, he looked at Gracie as if to say, *This is part of war. War is ugly, and there's nothing that you can do about that.*

CHAPTER 62
PATRICK BARGAINS WITH GOD

Eyes shut tight, Patrick felt as if he were buried alive inside the crystal-lined geode, surrounded by the spirits of dusty mummies. When he breathed, he smelled sour rot; he sensed malice creeping toward him. A hate-creature worse than a pedophile touched his injured ankle. It reminded him of the presence in the field way back when he and Gracie had found the hot marble. Once again, he was the terrified bunny facing a big snake.

He cuddled against Lewis for comfort, but his brother's body was scalding hot against Patrick's cheek and his chest sucked desperately for air. Even through Lewis's clothes Patrick could hear the fluttering of his brother's heart.

Shuddering, Patrick inwardly cried, *Pain, pain, pain, pain – how can I stop everybody's pain?* Yes, with the ghost squeezing it, his ankle hurt worse than a skull bashed against a rock, but the agony that he perceived around him hurt like hellfire inside his soul. The bard was strangling; Fred struggled and raged; Mark and the spy lay silent as dead men. Viceroy Daniel seemed frozen as a stone.

While Tom was dying, Baron Trager intoned a formal sentence upon his other prisoners. His voice resounded in words of hate and death. "Whereas these members and affiliates of the Bardian nation have conspired to overthrow the rulers of our nation Tor and our Horned Edge order …"

A giant splinter of fear pierced Patrick's heart. The Baron condemned the kicking bard. "…Whereas Sir Thomas Forschwynn has deliberately incited war in Moorway … Whereas he has threatened my own province ..."

The world around Patrick went dark. He had trouble breathing. Every emotion from every person broke through the boundary of himself. Patrick felt Lewis's submission to death, Fred's fury, the High Magus's grief. He felt Baron Trager's crackling hate and fury. Even Mark's and Hermann's dim, gray emotions penetrated Patrick's heart.

God, save Sir Thomas! Save him! Let me help! I will help! When I grow up, I'm going to become a doctor. If you save him, I'll go to medical school. I'll go to the very best university and I'll be the very best doctor there ever was, and I'll heal everyone I can get my hands on.

CHAPTER 63
LABETH

Panting, her heart pounding, almost ready to vomit, Gracie huddled in a shadowy corner of the palace gallery. Spirit came up to her, tail wagging and friendly, and she backed off because of the blood on his face and paws. Some of it got on her hands and clothes, anyway.

Suddenly, Spirit howled very, very loudly, making her jump. Her story had magically transported her to a new room. This was a great laboratory – it smelled metallic and technical, definitely a Lewis-type of room. The space contained incomprehensible scientific stuff ... and a beautiful oriental woman with black hair like a waterfall. *Labeth.*

Huh? How did I know her name? Gracie's heart pounded so hard she thought it might break out of her chest. *She knows Lewis!*

Labeth sat on the floor slumped against a wall, crying her eyes out. However, she heard something, because her face turned.

Jowls swinging, mouth dripping and drooling, tail wagging fast, the old hound dog trotted up to Labeth. It nudged her with its nose, hard, over and over again. Gracie could almost feel that cold, wet nose against her own skin.

Fists pounded on the laboratory door; voices shouted, "Let us in!"

Wiping her swollen eyes, Labeth slowly got up. Walking as if each step brought her closer to a precipice, she approached the door. She spoke, "*Golanoya*" softly with lips that were soft like flower blossoms; the door opened ... and Bardians rushed into the laboratory.

CHAPTER 64
GRACIE KEEPS WRITING

Tom took a long time dying. Fred quit shouting and looked away; he looked at anything else but the murder. In the middle of the horror, he heard a mournful howl, like a coyote that had found a carcass. "What was that?" he whispered, and trembled.

Lewis didn't answer. Nor did he look good. His skin was gray. He coughed uncontrollably. Fred felt sick just listening to him.

Patrick, who leaned against Fred, did not look good, either. His face muscles jerked with pain. The boy whispered, "Huh? What'd you say, Fred?"

Fred heard the howl again. "It sounds like Old Yeller," he muttered. *Right now I could care less about Old Yeller.* Shifting, he tested the ropes on his wrists. He strained and strained until his wrists were bloody, but he could not free himself.

"What's that?" Patrick asked. The boy turned his head to one side. His eyes reddened and dripped tears.

Fred knew that the boy, too, could care less about some stupid dog. Here was the dreadful circle; here Macbeth's witches chanted and cackled. He wished he could kick Baron Trager hard on his funky kneecap.

*   *   *

Labeth led Captain Gregory to a special door in the back of the laboratory. But that door stopped them, one and all.

"Can you open it?" Captain Gregory asked. War had deepened the lines in his face, and Gracie could see that his hair was dripping wet with sweat. "We must get down there."

Labeth shook her head. "No one but Lord Charon and Fean

Lewis can open this door. I cannot help you."

* * *

Back in the Tuttle's house, back in reality, Gracie looked up from her writing. Downstairs she heard voices, and baby June howled from hunger and fear, no doubt, but nothing immediate disturbed Gracie except uncertainty and the oppressive Moorway heat. "How is Captain Gregory going to get into the dungeon? What's happening in there? I'm stuck! What's next?"

She waggled her pen. "I don't know, so I'll just keep writing whatever's in my head."

* * *

The cave chamber's ancient entry would not open for Labeth or the Bardians, but Gracie suddenly knew what to do. "I'm both the author and the character inside this story, and I can get through this door!"

* * *

She did; Gracie slid right through it like a ghost. However, on the other side of the door where spiral stairs descended, she found that she was alone without her dog companion. "Hey, Spirit," she called, feeling her stomach lurch, "aren't you coming with me?" But there was no answer. She was just Gracie with a little girl's strength.

* * *

Gracie looked down. "I guess I'm going to the cave chamber," she said, and took a tentative step forward, putting her hand on a brass stair rail.

At that second, a weight smashed down on her shoulders, and Gracie clutched the stair rail with all her might. This presence hated her; Gracie could feel its hate in every molecule of her body.

Go on down, an order came, but it felt wholesome, not sick and stinky like the ghost. Quivering, Gracie started down.

The stairs ended in a large cave chamber, the inside of a huge geode, and the walls were made of violet amethyst crystals. But the place looked, not pretty, but horrible. Chains hung on the walls. The floor was bloody. There were tied up prisoners and cheering purple-clad soldiers. The atmosphere – not the physical one, but the spiritual one – smelled like acrid burning plastic.

The hair rose on Gracie's scalp, her forearms and neck prickled, and she suddenly felt cold all over because …

When she reached the cave floor, she saw –

and screamed –

and her knees buckled –

"No! Oh my God, they're hanging someone! And he's just a teenager!"

The young man, hands tied behind him, gasped for air, got none, and his face purpled. His tongue stuck out and swelled. His legs kicked.

Gracie shrieked.

CHAPTER 65
GRACIE FIGHTS A DEMON

This was real! Gracie knew – it was really happening! Magically, she was in both the cave chamber and Jane Tuttle's house!

While the bard was dying, an awful invisible thing pressed against her. It wanted to touch her in inappropriate places, both in body and soul.

"Help!" Gracie gasped. For some reason, her cry came out muffled, as if she were gagged. "Hhh …"

This is a demon, not a man, and you are going to fight it, came a thought from inside.

Her spirit grew cold and firm; her voice came back. "I'll kill you," she hissed at the thing. "You're just a bezub."

Strategy? None. Her first attack was pitifully inept. She swatted it open-handed with the same force as she might use on a fly, and the bezub's deep voice laughed. Gracie trembled. The bezub was stronger than she was.

You are writing this story, not the bezub, a different voice told her.

Gracie's mind grew strong again. The demon was only a big, stupid bully. She imagined that she weighed three-hundred muscular pounds, a lady sumo wrestler. Her super-strong legs wrapped against the now visible demon's waist and twisted while her massive right arm leveraged against its neck. With a startled cry, the demon toppled, and Gracie rolled onto it. Pinning the thing, she squeezed her huge hands around its neck.

However, even as strong as she was, the demon surged and flipped her over. It now had a snout, flapping ears, and red, flaming eyes. Its piggy arms grasped her tightly, burning like an iron on high setting. *Hey, stupid little girl, I'm not limited like you are! I'm a demon!*

But you *are in unlimited control of this story,* a helping voice reminded Gracie, and she steadied. In her mind, she made herself, body and soul, into an ocean – the Gracie Brahmindura Sea – until the demon's fire went out.

The bezub tried to vaporize, but Gracie prevented it. She began to drown it. Now it squealed, just like the mouse at home that had been caught in the trap but not quite killed. So horrible!

The thing writhed and cried. For a tiny moment she felt sorry for it. How could she destroy a living creature?

That demon is living death. Gracie, you know the difference between life and death.

As if it heard the voice in her mind, the bezub morphed, turning into a monstrous nightmare lizard. It reared over her, Tyrannosaurus teeth grinning. *I will eat you,* it said. *I will eat your living flesh.*

Gracie knew that was true. If it attacked, and if Jane came up into the bedroom, she would find Gracie's bloody, mangled, half-eaten corpse. The monster towered over her, and she trembled, but she replied, "You can only do bezub things. But I can do anything – even become the thing I'm most afraid of!"

A long time ago, she had seen a movie poster of the Blob. It had terrified her for days. Now Gracie made herself that huge monster, a gummy red mass that ate people – and dinosaurs! "You are jelly," she growled, breathing meaty, putrid breath into the bezub's fanged face. Gracie oozed hard, dissolving the demon …

Stop the hanging! A voice shouted in her head, and Gracie remembered, *Oh my God, that young man can't breathe!*

But if she let go of the demon, she and her loved ones would all die. Gracie squeezed harder and pressed the demon until its blood spread onto the floor and became a large hideous pool. *I am destroying you!* she mentally screamed at it.

But the demon somehow twisted free, blood streaming in great pulses. Dissolving like smoke in a fog, it reappeared in the form of a red-eyed snake, rippling with muscle. It breathed out its insolent forked tongue, and it sneered in a real voice that Gracie heard with her real ears. "You stupid little child, can you really defeat the person that owns your soul? Now ... experience a little hell, dear Gracie!" Flames roared out of its mouth; the snake began to swallow her.

Gracie felt searing pain, smelled roasting flesh and hair – her skin blackened, exposing the muscles beneath and even the bone. She shrieked and struggled. The snake promised more torture to come – eternal tortures. "I will enjoy you, Gracie. It will be so very much fun to teach you despair."

You cannot physically destroy a spirit, her soul's mentor told her. *Demons live in relationships. However, you can force it out of yours.*

But the snake is eating me!

Rest! Trust me!

Gracie quit screaming and fighting, and she suddenly realized, *It's so easy. I can do this!*

First, with her story power, she mentally cut the rope that choked Sir Thomas. He fell hard onto the floor, but Gracie had the demon to deal with, so he would have to help himself from this point on.

Next, Gracie Brahmindura, the girl with curly auburn hair, hazel eyes, long athletic legs, and a young body with stinky armpits, faced the demon, hands clenched into fists.

The bezub snake reared up and opened its fanged mouth to strike her, but Gracie surprised herself and relaxed. She was herself, just herself. And she had a special relationship where demons could not live: Jesus, sweet Jesus, God of God, Light of Light.

"You are dead," she whispered calmly to the demon. "Go back to Hell."

And it did.

CHAPTER 66
VICTORY

Scared and chilling to the roots of his hair, Patrick screamed, "I saw an angel! And a bezub! They were fighting!"

He heard a tremendous *crack!* and a *boom!* worse than lightning, so he screamed again and threw himself onto Lewis. However, when he dared to look again, he saw that Tom's noose had broken. The young man lay gasping on the floor beside the gallows; the air smelled like ozone; Baron Trager's jaw had dropped and his covered his ears.

Drawing close together, all the baron's people clinked their weapons nervously and Patrick heard multiple drawn breaths. "*Sisappa!*" one of them whispered. "Black blood. Saoma has lost a warrior." The guard pointed at the ground; the others drew back.

Patrick's skin crawled because he, too, saw the blood that pooled on the cave chamber floor. It was as black as the inside of a sewer pipe and smelled worse – and a slow trickle was headed straight for him. He gulped and squirmed away from it as well as he could, but his hands were tied behind him, his ankle agonized, and there was only so far to go before his back met a sharp crystal. "Help!" he shouted, "Anybody – Help!"

He turned to Lewis, but his brother slumped, his skin pale as a zombie's. Fred was the only "good-guy" in the chamber that looked half-normal, but even his face was flabby and blotchy with terror. "Help!" Patrick screamed.

Fred gasped, "Patrick, I'm going insane. I see a dog, a goofy speckled drooling dog coming the stairs! And behind it – a whole lot of Bardians!"

*   *   *

The disgusting black blood had not yet soiled Patrick when brown-clad soldiers, a stream of human military, pounded through a door and filled up the cave chamber. In an instant, as it seemed to Patrick, they rescued everybody. He couldn't understand how things could go so quickly from absolute horror to victory. He heard Captain Gregory, his Lanthran dad, cracking out orders. The Captain himself helped up Tom and turned him over to a military doctor. Bardian soldiers freed Patrick's hands; they laid him aside on a cot, safe from blood or mess, with his ankle wrapped properly by a medic and elevated. They gave him something to drink; it tasted like fruit juice.

Not far from Patrick, Mark lay limp on a cot, covered with blankets. The strange old lady … she had been taken out already. So had Hermann. His arms freed, Fred got up and staggered over to help Lewis.

"Is this one dead?" a soldier who bent over Lewis asked Fred in a low tone. His eyes widened. "Could he be Lord Charon himself?" The man stepped back.

"*Dit,*" Fred answered. "Feel him; he has a fever. Don't be afraid; this is my friend Lewis! But watch that left arm – the shoulder's out of joint."

When the medic began to treat Lewis's arm, he awoke with a groan and a sick, stuffy cough. From his cot, Patrick cheered.

"Hey, Lewis," Fred told him, "the cavalry has arrived."

Now alert, Lewis looked around.

"Hi!" Patrick called, no longer afraid. This turn-around was amazing – totally amazing!

Seeing Patrick, Lewis sent him the special "love ya, bro'" look and smiled a wide goofy smile. He mouthed the words, "See you soon, Sport," but coughed and gasped so much that Fred and the Bardian medics wouldn't let him stand up. Like Mark, Hermann, and Patrick, he too was placed on a stretcher.

Meanwhile, a new arrival, a hawk-faced magus in an autumn-gold lined robe, spoke a few words and the horrid black blood disappeared. Instead of sewer plus ozone, the place smelled like crystal, leather, and steel.

There was no more fighting. Baron Trager and his plum-colored guards surrendered, dropping their swords, knives, maces, and other weapons onto the floor with a great metallic crash. Now they stood in a line, hands tied, secured to one another from neck to neck, like knots on a kite string tail. "I'll have my revenge, ye Bardian filth," Baron Trager stated in a calm, sure tone that chilled Patrick's spine.

"If you attempt revenge, Arthur Trager – and I'm sure you will, sometime in your worthless life – you will fall with your own knife in your stomach," Daniel prophesied. "And your death will be neither quick nor easy."

The baron spat a nasty thick luggie at Daniel.

* * *

Patrick was enveloped in a warm, soft blanket. His ankle hardly even hurt when some brown-uniformed rescuers picked up his stretcher. Patrick said, "Thank you!" He closed his eyes with a great sigh.

Suddenly a poisonous waspy thought attacked him. *This mess was your entire fault, you know. It all started with that hot marble. Sneaky little liar, you took it to the picnic without permission. You've been very, very stupid.*

Comfort vanished. His heart broke. Over and over to anybody and everybody in the world, he cried, "I did it! This is all my fault! And, after people got hurt, I tried, but I couldn't help them, not one person! I just made things worse and worse!" Hot tears streamed down his face.

One of the soldiers who carried his stretcher said, "Hush. The Bard himself could not have been a greater hero."

CHAPTER 67
AFTERMATH

Gracie felt like they crawled along back to Bardia. Summer had ended, and it kept raining. At the Gapstand Inn, about halfway back toward Bardia, she sat on her narrow bed in the little room she shared with Patrick. She wanted to cry, but no tears would come. Outside the window, a dim, yellow courtyard light wavered through pouring rain and mist.

She crept to where Patrick slept, his bandaged foot propped up. "Patrick!" she whispered. "How are you?" Patrick only moaned and turned his face away. "All right, I know you're not feeling good."

Trotting downstairs, Gracie pulled open the door that led to the parlor, which was off the main serving area. In here, the air smelled of clean soap, a fragrant wood fire, and something like rosemary. There was a cozy sofa and several recliners. Near a glowing fireplace, Lewis lay on a hospital-type bed.

Gracie stood by Lewis's bed. She looked at Lewis's haggard face, and then she stroked his cheek. He stirred, opened his eyes, and smiled at her. His long, too lean body, dressed in a soft cotton nightshirt, tried to move with some kind of purpose, but after a few seconds he fell back into oblivion.

Gracie combed his long, wavy dark hair with her fingers. Then she took his hand in hers. "Lewis, you've gotten so thin. You were always skinny, but you look ..." She was going to say, "like a skeleton," but she winced and changed the cliché to ... "like a stick." Laying her head on Lewis's chest, Gracie could hear the faint *squish, squish* of his heart. "I love you, bro'," she whispered. "Keep living. Please."

*　*　*

Morning. Too wet, too mucky out there to move on.

In the middle of the night, during one of his violent chills, Lewis could not breathe at all. He couldn't suck air in nor expel it. Drowning in his own fluid, he struggled, but it was no use. The world slowly shrank – *Oh, God, dying is painful!* Someone nearby was sobbing – it sounded like Deirdre.

Something hairy touched him, and Lewis wondered if it was his teddy bear. He smiled. *Bobby, it's good to see you!* He cuddled the dear stuffed animal that Gracie had given him.

"My name's Fred," the teddy bear declared, and Lewis blinked. Bobby had Fred's face, blond hair, blue eyes, and big, square hands. Fred's voice ordered, "Don't die yet, Lewis."

Can't help it. He felt his body burn from the inside out. A great pressure of carbon dioxide tormented him; he had no more breath; soon his brain would die …

Sharply, Bobby ordered in Fred's voice, "By Radyah, you are going to stay alive!"

With his last flitting imagination, Lewis squeezed the bear. *Goodbye.*

Fred slapped him. Hard.

CHAPTER 68
DR. ZADOK AND THE ONE LAW

After what had seemed like an eon, the Bardian caravan approached Nutman. *Finally, bright sunshine and decent roads! Finally, back home!* From his bumping and lurching coach, Daniel looked out of the dust-spattered window. A forested peak or two showed itself through the dirty coach window when the road hugged a mountainside, but most of the time the view was blocked under a canyon of lush-foliaged trees. Finally …

Look! I can see the city! Daniel's heart leaped up with wings. Through dust speckles, he could see that the meadows in the valley were filled with autumn glories such as the gold plumes of king's scepter and purple clusters of queen's collar, lavender phlox and sassy yellow daisies. The Loudmouth River sparkled in the afternoon sunlight. Mid-day sun whitened Nutman on its hill. The city looked intact – ready to begin a new era.

Mentally, Daniel addressed the Master about the rebuilding of his province Rockeerie and the College of the Magi. As the coach descended the final curve, he told the Master, *The Brahmindura family should be reunited. One Law or not, I'm going to send the young people go back to their parents on Earth.*

You decide what you are going to do.

Daniel retorted, *Master, sometimes you make me choose between two wrong actions! It's not right to make them stay, so they must return home. However, that means that we must connect to Earth so that they may pass through. And I know that breaks the One Law. The connection can bring more demons than have already come!*

Who is the Lord of the One Law? I am.

Daniel sat back, thinking. He decided, *After our system has been repaired, Lewis, Patrick, and Gracie are going home!* However, then he asked, *What about Fred?*

The Master said, *Do not send him back. He is subua to the Bard. Also, I have plans for him here.*

* * *

Fred pitied Dr. Zadok. He was still the College's lead scientist, but to Fred he looked terrible. The man's left eye twitched and his iron-gray hair sported a brush-bristle cowlick. The black robe hung loosely on his body, and his limp was worse. The scientist led the team of magi to rebuild the College's Toy – the *thoyo-on,* assembling parts imported from Moorway.

Fred helped. In fact, he helped a lot, but often he felt ready to burst into messy confetti. At last, he insisted, "Let's do it! Observation tests are all done; it's time to connect."

Dr. Zadok stood behind the chair, one hand on it for support. His heavy shoe tapped the floor. "You are too hasty, as always. Listen: Do you want us to connect to deep space? Or next to a solar flare?"

The idea made Fred's skin crawl, but he waved away Zadok's excuses. "No, you listen! We've done enough tinkering. Our Toy locates as accurately as ever – maybe even better – and we will not have any accident! The whole schmear is done! It's done, Dr. Zadok; get that into your thick skull: It's done! Now, let's test the system! I have the hot marble, the Toy is repaired, and we can connect to Earth! And then we can send Lewis and the kids home!"

Dr. Zadok's thick eyebrows drew together as if Fred had uttered a horrible curse. "Your Earth! Yes, Earth – the home of the bizeor … We must be very, very careful. I want to scour the computer once more."

Restraining the urge to punch Dr. Zadok's face or at least the wall, Fred exploded, "Just how stubborn can you be? Are you going to wait until Lewis is dead before you send him back to his parents?"

* * *

From his office, Daniel heard Dr. Zadok's clumping footsteps even before his secretary James announced the scientist's presence. "Come in," he called, looking up from a projection of Earth between his hands.

Dr. Zadok entered. He bowed low.

"Sit down," Daniel said, waving toward a small sofa. "Have a snack."

Zadok sat – almost collapsed – on the sofa. James brought a pitcher of cool lanzone juice from Eleaemana – it was the height of the season – and a plate of pastries. Zadok politely ate a pastry, his moustache gathering crumbs. He ate another and devoured another; Daniel guessed that he had not eaten for at least a day. He let the scientist eat and drink until he slowed down.

Finally, while Dr. Zadok wiped his moustache with a napkin, Daniel began. "The bizeor are massing there." Daniel said, circling a finger around Earth's sphere and focussed on a certain country, which darkened to show the invisible realm. "Also the *foroya,* Radyah's angels, are gathering." With another movement of his finger, dazzlingly bright patterns appeared on the hologram in various spots. "They are preparing for a great battle."

Dr. Zadok scowled. "Such is always the case on that planet." Pain and heaviness lined his face. "I know that you want the Brahmindura family reunited, but must we risk so much for a few Earth people?"

"You know that creating a nexus to Earth is reckless," Daniel stated. "This concerns you very much; in fact, it almost eats your stomach up because you are sure it will invite another invasion." *And it* will *invite another invasion,* he thought privately. "You know that the resurgence of technology in Lanthra will make it easier for the Horned Edge at other locating stations to connect to Earth and get weapons again. Plus, you know that through those connections the bizeor can swarm through. In other words, you desire to keep that can of worms closed."

Dr. Zadok nodded. A pastry crumb clung to his right eyebrow; a drop of juice fell from his chin.

Daniel added, "You want me, the High Magus, to use my influence to go back to the way we were: Observing the Earth, but not crossing, worshipping Radyah by obeying the One Law completely"

Dr. Zadok nodded emphatically. He wiped his mouth with a napkin and hid a small belch.

"However, *Radyah* is Lord of the One Law." Daniel leaned forward. "He gives me freedom to make choices. Therefore, not only will I return the Brahmindhuras to their home, I will also send some of our own people to Earth. Later."

Zadok's eyes popped, he gasped, and flakes of pastry spattered the air. "But it is the Planet of the Curse!"

The Earth's hologram hovered between the two men, rotating gracefully. Daniel's heart filled with peace. "Yes, but it also brings us a Treasure."

CHAPTER 69
DEIRDRE

Lewis forced open gummy eyes and saw the woman he loved. *Deirdre!* He felt his heart beating, leaping with joy. He took in a breath, which felt so sweet and clean that he nearly cried.

Deirdre, a fragrant golden rose, sat next to him. He felt cool dew upon his forehead and tasted cold water. When he tried to speak, no words would come out, but he raised his right hand and felt her soft cheek.

She cried, kissing his forehead with her soft lips, "Thank you, Radyah! Thank you for returning my love to me!"

Lewis felt her hot tears drop onto his face, salty against his lips as she kissed him. There was just enough strength for him to squeeze her hand.

*   *   *

Later, Lewis's body trembled violently. His body was so cold that he couldn't quit shaking. *Why am I so uncomfortable?*

"Lewis, my love, your fever has broken." said Deirdre's voice. "We're here at my father's mansion, safe in Nutman."

He felt something soft. Deirdre had put a blanket on him. He almost relaxed. However, then Lewis remembered something very, very important. Somewhere he had a scrap of plastic that recorded the locating Lanthran technology, the path to Earth – all of it! He had become responsible for worlds! If that information got into the wrong hands …

When he opened his eyes, he saw no Lord Charon, no Barth, no sinister Shields from Earth. He saw a lovely woman, with long honey-warm hair and cool gray eyes, wearing autumn brown.

"Deirdre!" His heart leaped with joy.

She kissed him. She grinned like a little kid. "You're back! We're together again!"

Lewis smiled but, to his dismay, Deirdre's beautiful face faded out of his vision. *Hey God, I've got Lanthran technology – in fact, you told me to copy it! What am I going to do?*

You, Lewis, Lanthran magus and Earth scientist, will have a tremendous responsibility when you return to Earth. You will have authority, character, and wisdom. And you also have to clean out your basement.

Huh?

* * *

Later, maybe it was a dream, but Lewis was sure that he saw Tom Forschwynn, the super-talented kid who had played his lute at the Red Oak Tavern. The last time he'd seen Tom, the young man was dying, strangling by the hand of his own uncle, nasty Baron Trager. "Are you really here? You didn't die?"

"I'm alive and well," Tom replied. And the Bard did look well. His level brows and brown eyes focussed on Lewis with affection. Tom's dark hair was tied back, and he wore a fringed leather jacket. Also, the famous lute hung from his shoulder.

"You look like Daniel Boone," Lewis commented.

Tom raised one eyebrow. "Who is ... well, you look much, much better." Tom sat in a chair by Lewis's bed, holding his lute.

"I'm sorry that I didn't get to hear your concert when we were in Whitehall," Lewis said. "During your concert, I was ... otherwise occupied."

Then Lewis felt a draft on his lower parts. He quickly tried to cover up, but he lay on his side, supported by pillows, and his arms had tangled in the blanket. Lewis started to panic. "What the –! Who tied me up?"

"Don't worry," Tom said. He covered Lewis with the blanket. "Just before I came in, you had a grand mal seizure, very violent. Deirdre told me you thrashed, kicking and screaming. She felt terrified. But the doctor came right away."

Lewis tried to sit up and failed. Anxious, he asked, "When will I have another? Will I ever be normal?"

"I don't know," Tom admitted. "But for now you are okay. Relax. Let me play you a song."

Lewis choked and coughed, did it again, and then settled back to listen.

Tom warmed up his fingers on the lute strings, playing a light, easy melody that brought a fresh sea breeze into Lewis's heart. After that, Tom played in earnest. Lewis was carried away to beautiful, forested hills, and he stood on a peak overlooking a calm ocean. It was cool there, with piles of stars overhead.

"Am I actually seeing you?" Lewis asked after the music. "You are alive?"

"Yes!" Tom smiled. He played more music, perhaps for hours, until Lewis felt completely at peace and fell asleep.

*　*　*

Lewis woke up. He could breathe! His body lay comfortably on a bed in a light-blue room, and morning sunlight beamed through the windows. Outside he could see a wonderful view of the Rockeerie mountains. Trees exploded with autumn red, yellow, and orange. At his side, he saw ... "Deirdre!"

"I'm here," said Deirdre. Her hand stroked his hair.

He reached up to touch her cheek. "I love you," he whispered.

"And I love you," Deirdre answered. Her eyes shone with delight.

Lewis gathered all his strength. "I want to marry you, Deirdre. I want to have children with you and live together a long time. I want it so much!" Then he was out of breath and the light went gray for a while. Struggling, he came back to consciousness.

"Yes. I want it, too." Deirdre kissed him on the mouth. He had enough energy to touch her smooth face and feel her soft lips.

"How can I say goodbye?" he cried with all the breath he had. "I'm going back to Earth soon with Patrick and Gracie." Taking another breath, he added, "And I have no idea how you and I are going to have a life together unless you come with me."

"Don't lose hope. The Master has assured me that we do have a future." She added with a twinkle in her eyes, "And so has Dad."

Deirdre's hair, coiled up elegantly, shone like golden amber in sunlight. Her cheeks were soft as peach skins, and her gray eyes glowed beautiful and large. Even in a casual blue walking suit, she looked royal. Lewis could hardly believe how blessed he was that, among all the knights and heroes in the universe, she should love him. "How can you remain with me, faetha of Smythe? You have lands on Lanthra to manage. I live on the Planet of the Curse."

"I love you. I choose you. My father is at peace with my decision and so is the matriarch of Smythe. Trust me. I cannot go to Earth with you just yet, but I will. I will." She kissed him again on the lips, and he fell into a deep, relaxed sleep.

*　*　*

Slipping into a dream – or maybe it was real – Lewis felt himself flying. His dragon clutched him in its claws, and they were flying over deep water. "Where are we going?" Lewis asked.

I will show you what kind of Master we serve, fean.

Lewis asked, "What is this? How can you still call me a magus?"

Even now, the Master calls you his fean, answered the dragon.

Lewis tried to speak, but nearly choked. Coughing, he managed to ask, "Tell me truly, how can I escape torment after what I chose to do? I served Saoma!"

We know, the dragon replied, its scales glowing brightly as the moon rose.

"How can my soul be with the Master? I believe he is real. But I also know that I served the devil; I helped the invaders destroy people. All Lanthra and Earth were almost wrecked because of me!"

The dragon said, *All because of you, Fean Lewis?*

Lewis started crying. He felt hot tears roll out of his eyes.

The dragon answered, *If you want to be clean, let me immerse you in the sea.*

"Will I survive it?"

You will drown, but I, your soul-dragon, will never leave you. I – and you – belong to Radyah, and Radyah will lift you.

Lewis's heart thumped as he felt himself pushed under the ocean. His skin crawled and, when he breathed water, it reeked with the smell of old demons.

CHAPTER 70
BREATHING AGAIN

Once more Gracie sat at dinner at the Gregory's house. She and Patrick and Lewis were going back to Earth soon. However, instead of excited, she felt scared. *What will happen to us? Will we make it home, or will we end up dead in space somewhere? What if the Shields catch us when we get to Earth?*

As she looked around the table, eating Sadie's great cooking, she took in her Lanthran family: Captain Gregory, Sadie, their son Allen, and … she refused to spoil the evening by thinking about Mark, who was so wounded that he might … *I won't think that!* Her Lanthran "dad" Daniel had come to dinner, and her "sister" Myra smiled next to her. Deirdra had stayed at Daniel's mansion, taking care of Lewis. *What a mixed-up group! What a mixed-up life!*

Fred sat next to Patrick, and Gracie felt like he was like her honorary brother. The bezub claws that had made him so ugly were gone. These days, he hummed all the time. He hugged her and joked like he did in the old days.

However, Patrick, her real brother, looked unhappy. That really bothered her, but she guessed why, since she, too, was afraid of Shields and bezubs. For now, though, she decided to be happy.

* * *

Time for Patrick seemed to be measured from meal to meal. Tonight, he had eaten, not stinky fish sausage from Moorway swamps, but excellent rainbow trout from shivering cold mountain streams and a late-season salad. Sadie had baked amazing cracked-grain crusty rolls served with butter and raspberry preserves. He ate and ate; his stomach seemed to be a bottomless pit these days. Sadie had told him that he had grown taller.

Dinner was not as pleasant to Patrick as he would like because there was an issue even more important than food. He wiped butter off his mouth – politely with a napkin, not his sleeve. *Will bezubs hurt us when we go back to Earth? Or the Shields?* He finished chewing and asked, "When are we leaving?"

"I don't know," Daniel told him. "Lewis is too unwell to travel yet. Be sure, Patrick, we'll tell you."

Patrick nodded. He looked for another roll, but they were all eaten.

CHAPTER 71
GOODBYES

Patrick breathed a deep, long sigh. It was time to go back to Earth. He stood next to Fred, who put a comforting hand on his shoulder. Gracie held Daniel's hand. Lying nearby on a cot and looking reasonably alive, Lewis met Deirdre's eyes and smiled. They all waited in the College of the Magi's locating chamber, with its brilliant white walls, gold trim, and obsidian black monitor. Although on Lanthra it was now late fall and chilly, the kids and Lewis wore Earth-style summer clothes, home sewn by Sadie.

"It's late spring at your home on Earth," Daniel explained while a young magus set the controls. "The temperature is 76 degrees Fahrenheit. You will arrive on May 22, a little more than two years from the time you left, at 10:00 a.m., local time."

"Two years?" Patrick yelped. "That's crazy!"

Daniel smiled. "Remember, time is relative. You may have read that the astronauts who travelled to Earth's moon came back slightly younger than the people who had stayed on Earth. The time gap between Lanthra and Earth is much greater."

"Really? Does that mean I'll be younger than I am now?"

"No, not physically," Daniel replied. "Just in comparison to Earth's people."

Fred stated, "You will be starting the eighth grade, Patrick."

"Oh, wow." Patrick's stomach turned over. *I'll probably look really stupid when school starts.*

Patrick asked Fred, "Are you sure you can't come back with us?"

"I'm sure, Patrick. The way things have played out, I'm meant to stay." Fred continued, "In fact, I *have* to stay. I'm *subua*; I belong to Sir Thomas."

With one foot, Patrick rubbed a circle on the laboratory floor. He fought with his emotions and imagined the worst. On Earth he'd get teased and even bullied. He'd feel down and depressed. Worse, he would have to use a cane, at least for a while. *I'm stupid.*

An invisible presence brushed aside Patrick's self-pity. *No shame. No shame. Have no shame.*

However, guilt rolled within Patrick's being. His heart swayed with it. He grabbed Fred's waist, and they both nearly toppled over. "Fred, I was so mean to you when we were at the Tuttle's house in Moorway!" He tried to speak again, but his voice got incoherent, and he stifled his tears.

"You know that I deserved it," Fred replied. "I betrayed you and your brother. Please forgive me. I want to be a better man from now on. Sir Thomas gave me everything he had to rescue me, and I intend to honor that. I love you, buddy."

Fred ruffled Patrick's hair. For once, Patrick didn't complain.

Once Patrick let him go, Fred turned to Lewis. "I'm really going to miss you. I wish I could have been a better friend."

Lewis's smile was like the bright sun. "I'm really going to miss you, too, Fred." He extended his hand, which Fred shook. "You *are* a great friend. Come and see me, when you can!" His brown eyes glistened as he looked at Deirdre. "My love, come soon!"

As the minutes ticked on, Patrick could feel his face getting redder and thicker, and his eyes and nose tickled and swelled. Somehow, he choked the emotion back. *I can't bawl like a baby.*

The student magus called, "Get ready!"

Daniel hugged each of them. The group lined up before the large obsidian table. On its slightly glowing surface, Patrick saw a meadow. The view showed daytime, a bright morning. There were pretty wildflowers in the meadow, and he heard a cow lowing. Not far away was a small but dense cluster of hardwood trees. It was an out-of-the-way spot, and Patrick knew it wouldn't be a shock to people when their group arrived from thin air.

Daniel told him, "Patrick, you are in charge."

Patrick nearly fell over. "Me? In charge?"

"Yes. You are able. Your brother is very ill, and I want him to rest."

Patrick felt his back straighten. *He trusts me!* "I'll do the best I can!"

Lewis threw Daniel a questioning look, and the High Magus said, "It is probable that you will faint in the connection process. I want Patrick to lead the return to Earth." Lewis nodded.

"Listen, Patrick." Daniel reviewed the procedure: "You will arrive near a two-land highway. Leave the others in the secluded spot and go to the highway. Wave and beg urgently for help. When a motorist stops, ask him or her to call 911. Do *not* get into anyone's car. Stay exactly where you are until the police arrive. That's important!"

Patrick understood Daniel's line of reasoning, "Oh, I get it. Don't go away with strangers."

Daniel added, "*Bizeor* may send some Saoma worshippers. However, the *foroya* are also with you. Follow my instructions, Patrick, and you'll be all right. Lewis is still very sick; he may have a seizure when you come to Earth. If he does, leave him alone; it will pass. When help arrives, have the emergency medical technicians take Lewis to the hospital as soon as possible. Also, the police will see that you are reunited with your parents."

"Yes, sir," Patrick replied.

Next, Daniel emphasized, "Don't forget the story we've rehearsed about what happened to you. Tell that to everyone. You can tell the true one to your parents, but no one else."

They all nodded. Patrick lifted his cane and straightened; Gracie looked somewhere between dancing and sobbing. Lewis and Deirdre kissed so long that Patrick wanted to joke, *Get a room!*

"Now it's time to go."

Patrick, Gracie, and Lewis held hands. Then, they limped, leaped, and dropped through the portal.

CHAPTER 72
HOME, BUT …

Patrick banged open the back door at home and sat down outside on the back steps. The June air felt dry and warm, and the sky was darkening as the sun set, but it was nice and clear. It had been a long, long week. He and Gracie were back home; Lewis was in the hospital. *It's so incredibly good to see Mom and Dad again!*

Venus shone brightly in the southwest. Just a few stars were out. *Here is where I was when it all started, when the hot marble streaked down from the sky.* Tonight, there were no falling marbles or UFOs … just ordinary Earth stuff. And he was glad.

He had two big worries (except for the ankle, but that infection was clearing up): First, in the fall he'd be starting … "Middle school," Patrick said softly, shaking his hair, which had gotten long. "I've skipped two entire Earth years." He thought about the challenges ahead: studying, getting grades, avoiding bullies… Drooping his head onto his knees, which were higher than they used to be, and letting his hair tickle his hands. he told the birds and fireflies in the dark backyard, "I wanted an adventure, but I got a big mess. When I stole that hot marble, I hurt Lewis, I hurt Gracie, I hurt Fred, and I hurt my parents. The bad things that happened were all my fault!"

While he berated himself, Patrick played a memory-movie in his head.

* * *

Patrick had felt his transition back home from Lanthra to Earth as a soft *plop*. There was just a little bump, a small ripple of light, a stumble, and then Gracie, he, and Lewis were in a nice meadow by some woods.

But, he thought, shaking his head, *The next thing that had happened was awful.*

Lewis had arrived screaming. Maybe the screaming was a neurological thing (*How did I guess that?*); Gracie ran to him, but Lewis started convulsing and she backed away, terrified. Patrick hopped around like a one-legged chicken, yelling, "Help! Help!" Finally, when he got control of himself, he hobbled to the country highway.

At Patrick's waving and shouting, a motorist stopped. The driver phoned for help. An emergency squad and some police cars arrived. The EMTs hauled Lewis away in an ambulance, and the police took Gracie and him to the police station in town. Within the hour, Mom and Dad arrived. *Everything happened so fast!* Patrick and Gracie got into Dad's car, which felt very familiar, very strange, and very good, because he could just take a deep breath and let Dad drive off.

Gracie and he were now home with Mom and Dad! *But it's still all my fault.*

*   *   *

Behind him, as he sat at home on the back steps, Patrick heard cheerful female conversation. Gracie and Mom chatted about upcoming tasks, like getting Lewis's room ready for when he came home from the hospital. They talked about what back-to-school items Gracie needed, and how Gracie had already signed up for sports. Gracie's voice sounded older, calmer, not nearly so silly. That was good; he was older and less silly, too. At least he hoped so.

He heard Mom call, "Are you okay out there, Patrick?"

Patrick turned halfway around. "I'm alright!."

He wasn't done thinking yet.

Yes, he was happy to be home, but it felt weird. At first, nobody knew exactly what to say. Everybody smiled and touched each other all the time as if to see that this reunion was real. Mom cooked delicious meals for the family. She made Southern or Indian cuisine, and he ate everything he could get. "You love food!" Gracie teased him, but now he didn't get mad at her like he used to.

However …

As Patrick sat, crickets creaking, less happy images came to mind. Patrick pictured the pain in Mom and Dad's faces when he first saw them again. It made him wince when he remembered the shocked look on their faces when he'd told them the "official" story: "We were kidnapped by terrorists."

Mom looked sad, and there were dark violet shadows under her eyes. Dad looked thinner, graying, and his posture was not as straight. He imagined how they must have felt for *two years*.

Immediately, Patrick got up. He didn't think; he fled into the house, past Gracie and Mom, into the living room.

Dad sat on the recliner, reading the news on his tablet and watching the television news at the same time. When he saw Patrick, he smiled and put down the tablet.

"I'm sorry, I'm sorry," Patrick bawled, "I'm so sorry I did this to you!"

Dad crushed him in a hug and stroked his head.

"If I hadn't been so stupid," Patrick said, weeping so hard that his shoulders racked, "then this awful thing might have not happened!"

Dad said, "Patrick, some evil is much greater than you are. I don't know what really happened to you yet, but I do know this: You are my kid, a great kid, and I love you."

While Dad held him, Patrick cried his heart out. Much later, Mom and Gracie joined them in the living room. In soft lamplight, TV off, parents listening carefully, he and Gracie told them the whole story, the real story.

Meanwhile, outside, the night followed its course. The moon rose and set. The stars wheeled according to their season. Right before dawn, every draft of wind stopped, and the Earth held its breath.

CHAPTER 73
NOT THE END

*C*ough, spit, burp, breathe, fart. Body opera – but it meant that Lewis was healing. The ventilator was gone; he had just an IV now, and a heart monitor. *Thank God I'm back and I can see my parents again! But ... What am I going to do with myself when I get out of here? I want to go back to Dr. Zhartha's energy project! Tapping into a singularity is the step to the Lanthran locating technology.*

He remembered the copy of the Lanthran entire system that he'd brought back with him. *What am I going to do with that?*

An extrapolation that followed the theory behind the Lanthran technology suggested – no, shouted – that controlled time travel was just as possible as connecting apparently far removed points in space-time. He'd desired to explore time travel since he could remember, as much as Scott Amundsen and his team had travelled to the South Pole, as much as Edmund Hillary and Tenzing Norgay had been the first to stand on Mt. Everest.

*   *   *

The following day, two men in dark suits came to visit. "We just want to ask you a few questions," one of them said. They were about the same height and the same weight; they stood with military postures. "My name is Mr. Namib, and my partner's name is Mr. Gonzalez."

Lewis felt a bit dreamy from his anti-seizure medication, but he was awake enough to talk. "What kind of questions?"

"You, your siblings, and your coworker disappeared. You were gone for two years. Mr. Jontz still hasn't returned. Can you tell us what happened?"

"Uh," Lewis tried to remember his concocted story. He asked

warily, "Can you show me your badges?" *They could be Shields.*

The two men looked at each other. Both said in easy tones, "Sure." Both held out their badges: FBI.

Oh, Great.

"Now, what can you tell us, Mr. Brahmindura?" said Mr. Namib, who seemed to be leading the conversation.

"It … it's complicated."

"Just try," Mr. Namib said gently, but his voice was firm.

Lewis told them, in brief, his story, leaving out "another world," and "magi" and "kidnapped by aliens." He even chose to omit "the hot marble."

"When we went to the park for a picnic, some men with guns – I thought they were with the Shields – captured us. I was tied up, and they took me away somewhere. They took the kids and my friend, Fred Jontz, too." That was mostly true, if you skipped a lot of scenes and characters. "I ended up in a place – I remember it was a laboratory – and they forced me to work for them …" he swallowed, "on a technical project. I cooperated." *Absolutely true.*

"What kind of project?" Mr. Namib asked. There was a change in his expression, a suspicion, a hardening. Mr. Gonzalez's face was completely neutral, observing. Lewis knew that they were recording the interview.

"Uh, a new way to spy. They were developing very, very accurate long-distance visual and sound monitoring. I think they were planning an invasion." *Oh, yes, they were. And, to some extent, they succeeded.*

"Who were 'they?'"

"Uh, I don't know. I guess the Shields, the weapons makers, had a part in it."

"The Shields?" asked Mr. Gonzalez.

"Well, I'm not sure …"

"But you just said that they might be Shields. You believe they kidnapped you and so on. Yes or no?"

"Yes."

"Tell us again; why did you work for them?"

This was very hard to talk about. Lewis didn't want to remember it.

Mr. Namib waited so long for his answer that the silence and the steady eye contact stretched out painfully, and Lewis finally looked away and lost the competition. "They threatened to hurt Patrick and Gracie." His stomach lurched and he closed his eyes. He knew that they watched every tiny move to evaluate his truthfulness. One more question and he would start weeping, no doubt.

A little switch in his head clicked on and off, and Lewis felt his body tremble. Fear? Or another seizure?

Bright red fireworks exploded behind his eyes. *Another seizure,* he realized, just before he blacked out.

*　*　*

When he hadn't had a grand mal seizure for several days, Lewis could wander around the hospital corridors, tethered to his IV. A super-antibiotic was clearing up the pneumonia. They'd stuffed him full of anticonvulsants, and he felt very weird, sort of like having a head cold in his brain's attention center. He rode up the elevator; he rode down the elevator, he got tea in the cafeteria, he walked in the corridors, trying to get stronger.

For a time, he was immune from reporters and media. Mr. Namib had ordered him to avoid personal interviews and to refer any calls to the FBI. *Good.* Mr. Namib had also said he would be calling Lewis again, in several weeks, to make appointments for a series of in-depth interviews. *Hmmm. I'll worry about that when I get there.*

Later, to Lewis's great pleasure, Dr. Abel Zhartha, the energy project leader and his boss, came to visit. He met Lewis at his room, and they went down to the hospital cafeteria. "You look like a poster boy for famine relief," Dr. Zhartha commented with concern. "You've gotten so skinny! How do you feel?"

"Good!" Lewis said, trying to sound bright and soon-to-be employable. "I get to go home day after tomorrow; then the doctors will just monitor whether the medications will control the seizures. Also, I have to gain some more weight and exercise. Soon, I'll be right back to normal!"

To his surprise, Dr. Zhartha sighed and shook his head. The older man took a sip of his ice water, Lewis munched a few chips, and the silence drew on and on until Lewis couldn't stand it anymore. "How are things going on the energy project?" he asked.

Dr. Zhartha smiled. "They're going all right. Funding is always a problem, of course, but Congress has appropriated 3 billion dollars for the project – we just need the president to sign the bill. We have to operate with a very tight budget, but I think that will carry us through."

"Are you still pursuing the singularity idea?"

"Ah, no."

"Why not?"

"Political pressures, environmental fears, etc."

"But that would work!"

Dr. Zhartha's eyes seemed to agree with Lewis, but the scientist said nothing.

"Tell me, then, what's been happening? What aspects of the project have you pursued?" Lewis asked.

"Hmmm."

His stomach clenching with frustration, Lewis pushed back from the table. "Dr. Zhartha, you are just brushing me off!"

However, the physicist held up one finger, telling Lewis to hold. A year seemed to pass. Dr. Zhartha finished a bite of a sandwich then said, very directly, "Lewis, I know that you would like to come back and work for me. I would like that, too! However, I cannot and will not take you back. Why? Not because you aren't worthy, but because you aren't ready, and you've also been compromised as a security risk."

The direct answer was a hard punch in the stomach. Although Dr. Zhartha's face radiated respect, Lewis wanted to snarl that maybe the politicians held Dr. Zhartha by the –

However … it was no use arguing. Lewis felt light-headed; he felt that his stomach was full of lead. It was extremely to swallow while he picked at his food.

When Dr. Zhartha prepared to go, he hugged Lewis. "Please don't be a stranger, son. Call my house. Come to visit Aimee and me sometime. You cannot work on my project right now – but perhaps I can work on yours, when the time comes."

With a lump in his throat, Lewis watched the old physicist leave with his energetic gait that made him look thirty, not seventy. *What now?* What project could he ever take on again? He felt Dr. Zhartha had both cursed and blessed him at the same time.

After he went back up to his hospital room, Lewis lay on the bed, bored, fuzzy headed, and furious. *No job! No future!* And, now it was finally sinking in – *No Deirdre!*

*   *   *

Immediately, Lewis heard a knock on his door. "It's us!" Patrick bellowed, and the whole Brahmindura family came inside.

"Technically, 'it is we,'" muttered Mom the librarian.

Everybody grouped around Lewis's bed while Dad and Mom discussed the future. "Your previous apartment is unavailable, of course," said Mom, "and so you'll be living with us for as long as you need to."

"Wait 'til you see your room!" Patrick exclaimed. "And your computer system!"

They all chatted excitedly. During a moment when the others were involved with each other, Dad said to Lewis, eyes not meeting his, "We weren't able to keep up the payments and insurance on your car. It was repossessed, Lewis."

Lewis tried not to be gloomy, but he failed. "Well, nobody knows how long it will be before I can drive. And I don't have a job – Dr. Zhartha won't take me back; at least, not yet. Also …" he hesitated, "I don't have any way to pay the medical bills. I'm broke, and I'm so sorry that I've put such a burden on you folks."

Dad said, "It is *not* a burden. We are so glad to have you back!"

"Me, too," said Lewis fervently.

Dad cleared his throat and said, "I have an idea. I thought you might work with me in the shoe store for a while. I mean – it's a very far cry from physics – but it would give you something to do and some income until you're ready to …"

Lewis felt an awful hollow in his stomach. Working in a shoe store instead of with Dr. Zhartha? *I hate retail work!* However, he also thought, *It's easier to find a job if you already have a job.* And, so he said, swallowing down an indigestible lump of anxiety, "Thank you, Dad. I'd like to take you up on your offer."

"Good!" Dad said. "Not having a car won't be a problem. We can ride together to work."

The family hung around and talked with him for a while longer. Then, Lewis breathed a deep sigh. He felt exhausted. Apparently, the family could read the signs, because they made time-to-leave conversation. "I will be back tomorrow morning when they check you out," Mom said.

"Check out," echoed Lewis. "Yeah. That sounds good." His

eyes felt heavy.

"Yes, I'll bring you some fresh clothes, too."

"Fresh clothes." He was almost asleep. Suddenly, he remembered the little plastic recording he had made of the Lanthran locating technology, from the design of the sonic computer to the rings for resonance tuning to the *noretha,* the hot marble. Pushing himself up with his elbows, he cried, "Do I still have the clothes that I was wearing when I came back? There was something in one of the pockets …"

"I took those home to wash," Mom assured him. "They're all nice and clean."

Lewis felt desperate. "But was there anything in any of the pockets?"

She looked a little puzzled. "Yes, a flimsy piece of plastic. It looked like a candy wrapper, and I thought that I'd throw it away …"

"Tell me that you didn't throw it away!"

Mom answered, understanding dawning in her eyes. "The plastic piece is in your room at home, top drawer of your dresser, with your new socks."

"Thank God!" Lewis breathed. "Thank you, Mom!"

"And it will stay there until you get home."

"Please," said Lewis, looking around carefully in case there were nurses or other people around. "Please don't tell anyone about it."

Just as they gave him the last hugs and kisses, Gracie leaned close to him and whispered, "Patrick and I told them the real story, Lewis. They know the whole thing."

Lewis sighed and he relaxed like a down quilt. "Thank you, Gracie."

POSTLUDE
A NEW DANGER BEGINS

Before Lewis was discharged from the hospital, a pharmacy representative named Peggy Gnudst walked down the hallway. Glancing into room 326, she saw a patient in a faded green hospital gown, a man about her age, maybe twenty-five. He was very thin, but also dark and handsome, with the large, brown puppy-dog eyes that made her heart melt. Something inside told her, *This one is important. We want you to snare him. So, take off your ring.*

Obeying the inner voice, she took off the gold Horned Edge ring from her right hand and stored it in her purse. Then she approached Lewis's door.

*   *   *

"Hello," said a dulcet female voice out in the hall. Lewis looked up and saw a gorgeous, tall, elegant woman with long honey-colored hair and a name badge on her classy midday blue suit. "Mind if I come in?" she asked. "My name is Peggy. I'm a pharmaceutical rep."

"Uh, sure." He felt awkward and arranged his gown.

She came in. Lewis sat up on his bed, and she sat on the visitor's chair. "It's really good to meet people who aren't just … medical," Lewis said. "I can't wait to get out of here."

"When are you leaving?" Peggy asked.

"Today, I hope."

Lewis couldn't help being impressed with her. She radiated Deirdre's confidence. She had Deirdre's honey-colored hair and her fair skin. Her voice was calm and well-articulated. *Oh, how I miss you, Deirdre my love.*

Just as he opened his mouth to say something, a nurse came in. She said, "Perhaps you'd like to watch television, Dr. Brahmindura? The news is showing your story right now."

"No thank —"

But the nurse turned it on anyway and left.

On television, two newscasters talked into the camera and traded turns commenting. "Dr. Lewis Brahmindura is still in the hospital, recovering from his long ordeal in the hands of terrorists after apparently being kidnapped two years ago," said the female announcer.

"I don't have my Ph.D. yet," Lewis confessed to Peggy. "They're giving me status that I don't really have."

In answer, Peggy smiled radiantly. Her eyes measured him and suggested, *You're definitely worth all the honors, though.*

Lewis felt the compliment warm him, even though he tried to dismiss it. Meanwhile, the announcer began to talk, and Lewis leaned forward. "Although Dr. Brahmindura's brother and sister returned with him, his coworker, Fred Jontz, is still missing. Official sources refuse to comment on where he might be."

"What do you think will happen to Dr. Brahmindura now that he is safely back?" said the other newscaster. Do you think he can resume his previous position as a research team-leader with the famous scientist, Dr. Abel Zhartha?"

"I don't know. His credibility was compromised. For one thing, a source suggests that he possibly cooperated with his kidnappers!"

"Why would he do such a thing?" the other asked with rehearsed surprise.

"Well, one source indicated that he may have been recruited by an anti-American extremist group during his college years. After all, his father's side of the family is from northwestern India, from an area near Pakistan —"

"Wait a minute!" Lewis broke in indignantly. "My family immigrated seventy years ago! My Dad's as American as they come! And so am I!"

Meanwhile, on the television, the first announcer said, "One anonymous source suggested that he was kidnapped but fell under the Stockholm syndrome and identified with his captors so much that he was willing to work for them."

"That's one of the possibilities …" The news announcers went on, with many variations of the same words, with little detail but much rich speculation.

Lewis felt nauseous. "They're destroying my reputation –"

Peggy leaned forward, touching his leg. "No. All they want is something to keep the audience glued to their sponsors." Changing the subject, she pointed to the television. A commercial break had interrupted the news, and some middle-aged people spoke highly of a new pharmaceutical product that relieved their sexual difficulties. Peggy smiled mischievously. "The company that I represent makes that one."

Lewis turned back to his television dissection when the announcer said, "Not only is there a government investigation of Dr. Brahmindura for possibly passing top-secret research to unfriendly powers, but he faces a lawsuit by the weapons manufacturer called 'The Shields.'"

"What?" cried Lewis.

"What does that have to do with these other events?" asked the other newscaster in their practiced duet.

"Well, Dr. Brahmindura claimed that the Shields organization is responsible for his disappearance. Apparently," (small laugh) "according to the source, he said they allied with other organizations for possible world domination. The Shields company insists that is ridiculous. They are suing him for defamation and slander."

Peggy took up the remote control and switched off the TV. Putting it down, she rested her slim, cool hand on his arm. She crossed her legs so that he could see a long way up her skirt. Lewis couldn't help himself … she was really, really pretty … and then he felt guilty and miserable. *I miss Deirdre so very much!*

"Well, I have to go now. Here's my card." Peggy handed it to him, touching his fingers. She gave him a warm look with sparkling eyes, shook her honey hair, and stood up. Those legs were marvelous. "Call me. And don't wait too long."

*   *   *

Soon after Peggy left, Mom came to pick up Lewis. "Want to have second breakfast on the way home?"

To his surprise, Lewis felt very hungry. "Yes, Mom, yes! That would be great." He dressed in the fresh clothes that she'd brought him. Then, after the nurses forced him to sit in a wheelchair down the elevator and out to the curb, he walked over her car, and they took off.

Adventure over, Lewis decided. *Everything from here is just cleanup.*

However, a very clear inner prompting told him, *Wrong.*

ACKNOWLEDGEMENTS

First, thank you dear family. Throughout the writing of this *Soul's Warfare* series, despite all my groaning, floundering, and despair, my husband Skip has remained level-headed and encouraging. Our amazing offspring, Peter, Amy, and Mary, cheer me on always.

Thank you, dear friends who can smell the difference between a sinner and a Pharisee, to help keep me from becoming the latter. I am grateful for those in Decatur, Alabama, who kept me sane when I quit believing in God at all. Because two University of Kentucky college friends prayed for me and with me, I crossed the abyss to the side where Jesus lives.

During my undergraduate studies, Kentucky poet laureate, Wendell Berry, taught me to be a writer. He taught me to write from my heart. (He also made me cut out extraneous, pompous verbiage.)

Drs. Richard Perloff, Leo Jeffres, Gary Petty, and other professors at Cleveland State University taught me to be a scientist. However, in order to crack open my shell enough to reach my emotions, I thank counselors. Along with that, I am exceedingly grateful for the opening to teach interpersonal communication (which I desperately needed to learn) at Lakeland Community College. Thank you, Ileen Linden, for becoming my friend while I was there.

Authors Dianne Haynes Miley (see www.diannemiley.com) and Michael Dobson (see www.dobsonbooks.com) helped me with words and beyond words. Linda Porcello, my prayer partner and author of *Little Letters from Linda at the Lake House*, has been with me all the long, long way.

There are many other beloved Folks who have helped me. Thank you!

ABOUT THE AUTHOR

Rosemary Althoff has been fascinated by science fiction from a very young age, pretending that aliens with flying saucers would invade Earth. When she was a student at Decatur High School in Alabama, Rosemary began writing science fiction stories.

She graduated from the University of Kentucky with a bachelor's degree in English. Then, between jobs and having children, Rosemary kept writing. From Cleveland State University, she achieved her Masters in Communication Theory and Research Methodology. Over the years, Rosemary has worked for professional book publishers and taught at various community colleges and universities. She now lives in New Orleans and enjoys reading, painting, walking, and writing.

Appendix 1
LANTHRAN VOCABULARY

Note: Words in italics are in the Lanthran language. Words in regular font are English versions of Lanthran terms.

***

-a = suffix to make a word an adjective or adverb

Abag = Keep, enclosure for protection

Aine = winter, cold, white, also a moon

-al = long

alla = street or way

alor = yes, I agree, or I will ("no" is *dit* or *dee*)

amibib = warm, not very hot

amim = hot (also the name of a terraformed world)

-an = old in years

appa = water

as = behind (*asde* means move backward. *Asbo* means climb down.)

at(h) = body (Prefixes or suffixes are added to indicate what kind of body. *Ath* with no prefix or suffix is a human body.)

aya = person, human being, sentient being

Ba = father

Ba-rad-yah = the Bard (the 'father' of Bardia who sings about God)

Bao = grandfather

Baoan = great-grandfather

Baon = God the Father

bat = male

bath = female

Bardia = (From *Baradyah*, the country that houses the College of the Magi)

be = tea

bi- (or *-ib*, in certain word constructions) = small, little

bibat = boy (*e bibat* means "son")

Bibo = name of a small, azure moon; also, Summer.

Note: Aine, Noreth, Bibo, and Wega are the four seasons of the year on the northeastern side of the Lanthran continent, each beginning on a new moon. There are six moons of Lanthra, so the southeastern continent and the continents over the sea have different names for the moons which they can see in their quadrants. The other two moons are *Get*, a bright moon, and *Rel*, a large blue moon. The area of Swetha sees Bibo, Wega, Noreth, and Get. However, Raphe over the sea sees Get, Rel, Aine, and Wega. The southwestern continent sees Get, Rel, Wega, and Noreth.

bilan = (generic) for noretha (marble), meaning "ancient plucked sound."

bilit = pluck, pick, play a stringed instrument

biliterad = lute or mandolin (big bellied stringed instrument, without the bent neck)

bimibath = girl (*e bimibath* means "daughter")

bionin = penny, or one-sixtieth of a Lanthran brot, also a minute in a time context, or the number or amount one (1)

birela = bushes (small trees), used with adjectives

bleth = leaves, also their rustling sound

bizeor (pronounced bee-zay-or, or bee-zor, for short). Fred names them "bezubs. = demons, e.g., small, dark, openings (such as insects's maws)

bo (*-ob*) = deep; (also, down)

boon = very deep, also friendship love (*taboon* means friend)

boonappua sia = beer

boonua = sweet love, as a romance; the emotion of love

bonob = deeply depressed; reversed into *nobbo* is an insult in which someone is a chronic discourager of others

brot = Tiopatath dollar; also refers to a financial, pecuniary, money context

cena = ten (10) or one sixth of a *harbath*

cil = hair

cilat(h) = mammal (hairy body. To call a human this

is an insult.)

cilathanx = cat

cilathanxon = big cat

cilatboz = dog

cilavitboz = wolf

da- = suffix meaning front (*dadde* means moving toward the front); also used in front of words to indicate dependent sentence structures such as "this," "the," "that," and "which" – depends on context.

Da farad = The Bible; the Scriptures, Old & New Testament

de = movement (toward, away, up, down, in any direction)

de nob metlanath = flabby, weak, going "downhill,"

de-an = time

dileh = here, close by

din = like, as, similar to

dit = not, no; but the more polite version uses, *Dee* to avoid any reference to death

ditfama = be quiet, shut up, hush

dittiean = an insult for stupid, fool, idiot; literally: dead brain

ditla = death

ditlabath = any human or animal which is no longer living; a dead body

ditrela (or *ditra*, a short term) = firewood, coal, fuel

dola = there, farther away

Don = building

Doon Abag = Great Castle

Doon = big building

e, es, et = of, for, at, to (with a direction syllable for prepositions)

ea = (pronounced e-ah), added to nouns to indicate possessive

ean = mind, think, thought

eaya = I have (possess), for instance, *gela eaya* means "my ear." [*ea oya* is "we have," *eaye* is "you have" (singular), and *ea oye* means "you have" (plural);

el = be, exist

Eleaemena = Bardia's nearest neighbor to the south
eplaithon = invade, enter by force, penetrate
f- = strong, durable (added to other words)
fa- = peace, Shalom. As prefix, means quiet
faetha = squire/property owner
falu = peaceful, quiet emotion
fama = breath (and *hefama*, Holy Spirit); also to speak, say, produce words
famaradyah = the Word of God, Jesus
famor = throat
Fao = Master, the Lord of Rest (*Ta Fao* = the Triune God)
fath = air, wind. Sometimes used as *famath.*
farad = any book
faradean = textbook (*da farad* = *Bible*)
farel = sleep (quiet eyes)
farel abag = inn, hotel
fean = wise, mage, intelligent (strong minded), magus
fetuh = cotton, cloth, clothes, all kinds of smooth fibers
fit = skin
fo = strength
fomath-on = storm, tempest, strong wind and weather; *fomath-oon* = very big, dangerous storm
for = to push, to go on a long journey (*f* + *or*)
fora = work, labor
forde = search, look for
fore = (verb) send; (noun) messenger *(f* + *or* + *e)*
foreya = angels (messengers of God)
fortil = future or past, depending on direction.
fortilasde = the past, some time ago, etc.
fortilda = the future, some time from now, etc.
fup = a sliding noise, squelch, also *setefup* is the word for poop, feces, shit
Forschwynn = to push one's way ; also a famous family name in Bardia
gan = name (*unsa eaye gan?* What is your name?)
gela = ear

gemen = grain

get = very bright, dazzling (contrasted to *reth*, which is shimmering bright); also the name of a moon.

getlue = joy, exuberance, happy emotions, blessing. *Hegetlua* means very great gladness.

gola = open

golanoya! = Open up for us!

golanoye = Come in.

golanor = door

go = heavy, also a word for glory

get go = gold

gn- = prefix: foods made from grain

gnim = a salty multi-grain stick

gnum = a sweet granola bar.

har = far, a great distance

harbath = carbon 60, or any unit of 60

hareth = far lights, = or stars

he = very or intense

hefama = Holy Spirit

he fup = very strong stink, as of feces

hega = suffering, deep mourning

hegetlua = very great gladness; the opposite of suffering.

hego = glory (as of God)

hegoyah = title for a magus (see *Radhegoyah,* title of the High Magus)

hesa = ugly, disgusting

heseplaitha = angry

heseditla = murderous

heth = silence

im- = salty, mineral; added to other words as a suffix

-in = small (suffix added to words. Also see, *bi-*)

-iin or *-niin* (pronounced "-een" or "neen") = very small

ion = piece of metal, money, a coin equivalent to a silver dollar (*brot*), or also metal salts

la = alive, living

labath = carbon compounds, or a living body

lantern = one third of the distance from a sea-level

measurement to an arc of lanthra, or about 12 miles

lanthra = one complete circle of horizon from a fixed observer (about 125 miles), everything is measured in units of lanthra, which are degrees of horizon of the planet

Lanthra = Horizon, also refers to the whole world

linath = a foot of the human body, also: *wisto:* about a meter; the measurement of the diameter of a special stone's shadow at noon in the spring solstice at the equator. A more advanced technological measurement used in the laboratory at Nutman is the *nolin,* which is the gravitational resonance of Lanthra's orbit around its sun at the same hour.

lip = horn or projection or outcropping. *Ta Lipplaitha* are the Horned Edge sect of the Reach

lu- = good character or work or art produced by a skilled person; good, anything praiseworthy;. With a suffix, means positive emotions.

lua = beautiful, lovely

luean = noble person or mind or thought, one who is honored

lurad = thanks, praises

lutaya = praiseworthy person, good man or woman, good ruler, title for a ruler.

Ma = mother

mara = help, aid, assist

marador = save, rescue (*maradoyra!* means "save me!")

Mao = grandmother

Maoan = great-grandmother

me- = soft (prefix)

metlinath = weak, as in flabby feet; helpless

mibath = female

mima = three (3)

nexus = English for a corridor to other worlds

nin = six (6)

no- = hard, durable (prefix)

nob = down as in depressed, apathetic

nobbo is an insult in which someone is a chronic

discourager of others; a MGR (Much Grace Required) person

noditlabath = diamond, also the name of a moon.

nolin = exact technological measurement of a *wisto* or *linath*

noreth = shimmering jewel, e.g., an opal, also the name of a moon; also, Spring

noretha = hot marble, of place (locating coordinates storage crystal)

Norhe = A king of Bardia and father of current king, Edward. He was of a prominent Bardian family with Torish connections, who had married Catharine Forschwynn. His son Edward was actually his second son, but the first, Norhatha, had renounced all legal claim to the throne and had settled with a Polunking wife by name of Marme on the south coast of Bardia, where he and she ran a huge plantation, and were active anti-slavery proponents.

ola = hello (to one person)

oloma = hello to you all

oma = all

omalanthra = round, spherical, a planet or a ball or anything round

-on = big, *-oon* [doubled vowel between two consonants] = very big indeed

-or = passageway, through, into

-osa = him, her, himself, herself

-oye = you, yourselves

-oya = we, ourselves, us (see *ya*) for "I"

pasa = rise, arise, get up, stand; resolve to do something

pat = oncoming breakers, high tide, or the noise made by slapping waves

pi, pim = no, not

Pigolanor = Earth ("Don't go there.")

plaitha = reach out, extend, rope, rod, any type of extension (*eplaithon* means "invade")

pli-, plit = do, achieve, or accomplish; also, walk; *he plit* means walk fast *poie* = sheep (*cil poie* = wool; also *poiecil,* depending on preferred sound and emphasis on the animal)

Poiemana = a country across the sea and between Siphe and Raphe. The word means "shepherds."

poth = sit down

ra = come, approach, proceed forward

rad = sing

radath = body of believers (church)

radyah = a term for Jesus: singing Lord, God the Son

Radhegoyah = title of the High Magus

rad te tosa = song book ("see and sing") (*farad* = any book) (*faradean* = textbook) ((*da farad* = *Bible*)

radyo = (verb) fly

Raphe = a country next to Poiemana and across the bay from Siphe. The word means "sea people."

The Reach [English translation of *plaitha*] = a sect of the magi who worked with the kyrioi to extend the nexi to other, untouched worlds for occupation/domination. The northern district of the reach is called "The Horned Edge."

reb = soft

rebleth = tobacco, big leaves, later used as a metaphor for smoke

Rel = the big Blue Moon of Lanthra

rela = plants in general; *cil rela* = cloth made from plants

relaon = trees in general

relabaon = very big tree, such as an oak

rel, or *reth* = blue or green light, or color; or eyes or sight, depending on context

rethappa = sky or ocean

rida = one-twelfth of a *brot*, in the money or coin sense.

ris = pain, also noise

risi = bugs that make noise, such as crickets and cicadas or buzzing flies or mosquitos

ro = it

sa = he (or she)

Saoma = It Is All: the Horned Edge name for God. Also, "total control."

se- = dark, or black

sebizorath = anus, dark hole, ass (*sebizor* is the term for a chamber pot or a city honeywagon, the carts that transport sewage to the treatment plant). To call a person a *sebizor* is a great insult, because it means "you're full of shit." Also, another name for the devil, or Satan. The term may also be used to combine all of the demonic forces into one entity.

sebiztha = a dung heap or any place where shit or feces may be seen or smelled

seris = black, deep festering anger

setefup = shit, dung, feces

sewega = also the name of a moon; also, Winter

sia = red (also a common nickname for red-haired people)

siappa = red wine

siappla = blood, platelets, alive, life, always a good thing; used as a verb means fix, repair, improve

siarela = witch hazel, a potion for fever

siphe = hemp or other fibers used for rope

Siphe, Raphe, and Poiemena = a trio of countries about the Bay of Siphe across the sea. Siphe means "laborers" or "rope pullers"

sipit = anything such as a rope used to bind, or the bound object contained by the rope; also the emotion of resentment.

siplaitha = rope used for a pulley, or the pulley itself

sisappa = bloody (unhappy, scary, alarming as in a wound)

sisasa = clothing of any kind (*sesasa* = dark clothes)

subua = property, anything claimed to be a possession

szttit = judge, damn, curse, prosecute;

swa = fast, speedy, run, race, quick

Swetha = a country far south of Bardia

tarelabaon = immense forest

tarelaon = forest

ta- = prefix or particle making words plural. Also means "many." For instance, *ta-relaon* is a collection of many trees.

Ta = people, race, species

Ta Fao = the triune God, Elohim

Ta tomima Yah = the Three in One, the Holy Trinity

Ta rethappath = the Blue People (who are covered with blue hair and usually live near water)

Ta rethacilappath = a derogatory name for the Blue People, insinuating that they are no more than hairy animals

taboon = friend or friendship, depending on the context

tac = coffee

tasa = they, themselves

te = and (a joining word)

tern = distance, how far

tess = receding waves, low tide, or the noise made by receding waves

tessappa = the sea

tha = place

tharadyah = place of worship (church or chapel)

Thamaon = matriarch of theland, a term usually used only for the ruler of Smythe

thoyo-on = locating system (*e.g.,* "journey to other places")

til = time, also means now, depending on context

tio- = tall, high

Tiorpatath = Tor (tall waves of land), sometimes misprounced on purpose as *Tiopatta,* or "tall noisy people."

to = one (number)

tod = stop, surrender, rest, depending on context

Tor = Bardia's nearest neighbor to the north (tor is an English word for a mountain)

tosa = see, watch out

tot = head

tot-Ba (head of the fathers) = king or ruler

Tot-Baon = high king, a title sometimes used for God

um- = sweet; usually presented as a suffix

-uh = suffix meaning, a bar shape

un- = suffix signifying a question.

unsa = what

untha = where

until = when

unulu = how

unya = who

vam = two (2)

vina = why, in order to

vit = cut, slice

vitath = wound, cut on the body; emotional cut on the soul

vittil = now

vituh = sword

wega = bright copper, also the name of a moon; also, Fall or Autumn

welth = holy, set apart for special use, pure

wisbath = carbon-12 or any kind of sugar (also refers to the number twelve (12)

wisena = a twelveth part of a *harbath* (60), or five (5)

wisto = measurement, equals roughly a meter, based on a function of the nuclear resonance of pure carbon at the Lanthran equivalent of 0 degrees Centigrade temperature in a certain place in the College of the Magi

wo- = a prefix meaning deep, a gorge, cleft place, cave, female vagina; depends on the context

ya = I, me, myself

Yah = God (also called *Tot-Baon*)

ye = you, yourself (singular)

yo- = go, proceed. Additional sounds are added to indicate prepositions. For instance, *yo-or*, "go through"

yo-hegetlua = goodbye, farewell, blessing

yo-on = journey

yo-or = go through, pass through, also refers to childbirth

yovinavit = oppose, go against